Holly thought how very handsome Clayborne was as he stood before her. He was in shirt sleeves, and his shoulders seemed particularly broad, his grin particularly engaging. He came close to her, and put his hands on her waist, and she did not mind. "I've seen the way the men look at you, Holly. They'd tell you anything you wanted to know, if you'd just ask them."

Holly averted her gaze. "You exaggerate, Randy."

His grin evaporated, and his face was suddenly serious. "I would, too, Holly," he said. "Tell you anything, I mean."

She turned partially away from him, her face flushed.

He turned her back, and pulled her to him and kissed her on the mouth. She was surprised by the kiss, and its sudden passion, but she did not try to break free. Something inside her responded quickly to it, almost against her volition. In a moment she was finally breaking away, breathing shallowly. She moved away from him, unwittingly toward the bed—and he followed her. . . .

ENTRANCING ROMANCES BY SYLVIE F. SOMMERFIELD

DEANNA'S DESIRE (906, $3.50)
Amidst the storm of the American Revolution, Matt and Deanna meet—and fall in love. In the name of freedom, they discover war's intrigues and horrors. Bound by passion, they risk everything to keep their love alive!

ERIN'S ECSTASY (861, $2.95)
Erin was a beautiful child-woman who needed Gregg's protection. And Gregg desired her more than anything he'd ever wanted before. But when a dangerous voyage calls Gregg away, their love must be put to the test. . . .

TAZIA'S TORMENT (882, $2.95)
When tempestuous Fantasio de Montega danced, men were hypnotized. And this was part of her secret revenge—until cruel fate tricked her into loving the man she'd vowed to kill!

RAPTURE'S ANGEL (750, $2.75)
When Angelique boarded the *Wayfarer*, she felt like a frightened child. Then Devon—with his gentle voice and captivating touch—reminded her that she was a woman, with a heart that longed to be won!

REBEL PRIDE (691, $2.75)
For the good of the plantation, Holly must marry the man chosen by her family. But when she sees the handsome but disreputable Adam Gilcrest, her heart cries out that it's Adam she loves—enough to defy her family!

Available wherever paperbacks are sold, or order direct from the Publisher. Send cover price plus 50¢ per copy for mailing and handling to Zebra Books, 475 Park Avenue South, New York, N.Y. 10016. DO NOT SEND CASH.

Charleston

BY
RALPH HAYES

ZEBRA BOOKS
KENSINGTON PUBLISHING CORP.

ZEBRA BOOKS

are published by

KENSINGTON PUBLISHING CORP.
475 Park Avenue South
New York, N.Y. 10016

Printed in the United States of America

adventure. The whole world and her entire future lay before her, and she wanted somehow to experience their mysteries before settling down to act out the role of wife of a southern gentleman. Actually, Holly was more interested in the recent secession of South Carolina from the States, and its political ramifications, than she was in courting. The trouble between the North and South, which had blossomed like a poisonous flower since Abraham Lincoln's election to the presidency just a few months previously, had changed the emotional climate throughout the South during the winter, and spring had come warily to Charleston that year, like a Virginia deer emerging onto an unknown feeding ground, scenting the air for danger. There was no exhilaration in annual renewal among most southerners that spring, but only a tense waiting. From the piny woods to the bustling cities, from the back-country plantations to the great seaports, a repressed and unpleasant excitement permeated the magnolia-redolent air, tinged with uncertainty and anxiety.

Holly was very aware of these negative ripplings through the ether on that balmy spring day in April when the new Confederacy took a further step toward separation from Washington, and in Charleston. But Charlotte Ransom Quinn wanted to talk about Holly's love life on that sunny vernal day, and had been bringing it up, off and on, all through the morning. By noontime, when mother and daughter had lunch together in Charlotte's large kitchen—Uriah Quinn did not come home for lunch, from his import business down at the water-front—Holly was already impatient with Charlotte's persistence on the subject of Stuart Blaisdell.

"I realize that Stuart isn't the most handsome young

man that's ever come courting," Charlotte was saying as they finished some barley soup and homemade bread from pewter bowls. They sat across a kitchen table from each other, and not far from a very large dry sink and cupboard. When they ate with Quinn, they always set the table in the adjacent dining room, but Charlotte and Holly often had light meals together at midday in the kitchen. Across the wide room, a middle-aged black woman puttered with some silverware, paying no attention to their conversation. "In fact, I suppose you would have to describe him as plain. But he's a wealthy, robust young fellow, Holly, and as nice a boy as you'd ever want to meet."

"More importantly," Holly said in a voice much like her mother's, only with a more melodic lilt, "Stuart's family has money." Her manner was sardonic, and Charlotte caught it immediately. "Why is it that parents always think of money and position first, and compatibility much later?"

"Compatibility?" Charlotte said quizzically. She was dark-haired, like Holly, but her hair had lost much of its richness and luster. She kept it back in a roll or bun at the back of her head now, so that she had a more severe look than she had had at a younger age. There were fine lines around her eyes and mouth, but she was still a pretty woman, and had kept a good figure. She and Holly were both dressed in pretty but rather plain calico dresses, floor-length, long-sleeved, with frills at the bodice and wrists. "What do you mean by compatibility?"

"I mean I'm not in love, Mother," Holly said firmly. "I have affection for Stuart, of course; I've known him from our early days at school. But he's always seemed more like a brother to me than—well, like a potential lover."

8

Charlotte was shaking her head. "You mean you'd rather have some flashy young colt running after you, like that Randy Clayborne that Jennifer is so crazy about? Is that the kind of fellow you'll settle for, Holly? I know he comes from good stock, but he has bad manners, and he thinks too highly of himself."

Holly sighed. "I don't want either Stuart or Randolph Clayborne, Mother. I don't know what kind of man I want, yet, and that's just the whole point. I don't know what I want from my life."

"What's the matter with marriage, and babies, and the beautiful home that Stuart can eventually give you?" Charlotte wondered. They were finished with the soup now, and Charlotte turned to the black cook. "Cleo, come and take these dishes away, will you? And then go heat some water for my bath."

Cleo, very dark with close-cropped, wiry hair, wore a big apron and a yellow kerchief on her head. She came over expressionlessly, and picked up the pewter bowls. "Yas'm, I gots to scrub some other things up, anyway. Ah's got some water on for you-all; I knowed you was fixing to bathe."

Cleo moved off and Holly looked after her. Cleo was the only slave that Quinn and Charlotte owned, and she had been owned by Holly's father, Col. Ashby Ransom. She had always been treated like a member of the family by the colonel, and now less so by Charlotte, who did not understand black people. Uriah Quinn, a displaced northerner whom Holly disliked on first sight, treated Cleo as he would a trained horse or dog. He was not really unkind to her, but he made no effort to reach her as a human being.

Holly now directed a reply to Charlotte's question to

9

her. "All of that will be fine someday, Mother. With the right man, under the right circumstances."

"Someday?" Charlotte said sourly. "Holly, you can't just go along like this, living here with Uriah and me, year after year. Not that I don't appreciate your being here, you understand. But you need a home of your own, a life of your own. You need it now. Please, at least consider Stuart's interest seriously. Go places with him when he asks you. Sometimes love has to develop slowly, Holly, and be nurtured carefully. I feel that Stuart could make you a wonderful husband."

"Like Uriah has made you a wonderful husband?" Holly said with acid in her young voice.

Charlotte frowned at her daughter. "Uriah came to us when we needed someone to take care of us," she said deliberately. "I know he's not like your father, Holly. But he's given us security."

"He came to live in our house, and to sleep in your bed," Holly said, her face clouding over. "The bed that you and Father shared, at one time. He's crude, Mother, and he's not a southerner. He has no feeling for Charleston, or the South. He looks at women; I've seen him. He—looks at me." She had never said the last to her mother before. She looked quickly to her now, to see her reaction.

Charlotte's face colored slightly, and she glanced toward Cleo, who was washing up some dishes busily across the room, humming a little tune under her breath. "Looks at you?" Charlotte said darkly. "You're saying Uriah looks at you in a—desirous way?"

"I'm saying that I feel uncomfortable around him," Holly said, now hugging her arms across her full breasts. "I have from the moment he moved in here, usurping

Father's place with us. Maybe it's me, Mother, but I don't like him and never will. That's another reason, I suppose, why I can't stay on here indefinitely. Until this secession thing started, I thought I'd like to go to Baltimore or Washington and try to find a job. Now, I don't know. I suppose I could try to get one here."

"A job?" Charlotte said incredulously. "You're not trained for any kind of *work*, child! Ladies do not go out and find employment outside the family. God, I hope you don't talk that way around Stuart Blaisdell. I just don't know what's gotten into you. Ashby and I didn't raise you to have such thoughts and feelings."

"Father raised me to think for myself," Holly said firmly. "That's what I'm trying to do, Mother. That's all I'm trying to—"

They both heard the street door open, at the other end of the house, and Quinn's buggy horse whinnied on the drive. Charlotte glanced at a Seth Thomas wall clock across the room, and frowned, wondering why Quinn would be arriving home at midday. She and Holly had just turned toward the doorway to the dining room, when Quinn burst through it, looking flushed in his square face. He was fairly tall, with a meaty, lined face and side whiskers, and there was graying in his brown hair. His eyes were rather deep-set, giving him a serious, sometimes fierce look. He was dressed neatly in a high-vested suit, and carried a bowler-type hat and a walking stick in his right hand. He came over to the table and took in a deep breath.

"What is it, Uriah?" Charlotte asked him, seeing the emotion in his face.

"Well, those hotheads finally did it," he exclaimed in a deep, hard voice. "They bombarded the federal troops at

11

Fort Sumter, and forced them to evacuate. The Confederate flag is flying over the bulwarks even as I stand here. It's the same at Fort Moultrie. They were obviously encouraged by those rascals at Savannah and Pensacola. Somebody ought to tell General de Beauregard that he's playing with fire, by God."

Holly was suddenly excited. "The forts in the harbor are in our hands now?" she said wonderingly. "Confederate soldiers occupy both of them?"

Quinn gave her a long look, and his eyes softened as his gaze traveled down briefly over her tight bodice. "That's right, Miss Ransom," he said evenly to her. Holly had insisted on keeping her father's name, and the matter had become a parrying ground for them in the two years Quinn had been Charlotte's new husband. "Does that please you? That irresponsible forces in this state are heading us inexorably into a shooting war with the North? That all we've worked to build may come down around our ears soon, that this city could end up a battleground?"

Holly stuck her chin out defiantly. Her long, thick hair was in curls behind her head, and in ringlets beside her face. Quinn could not admit it to Charlotte or even to Holly, but just being near her stirred some animal thing inside him, made him hungry for her flesh.

"Of course, I don't want war, any more than you do," she said to him. "But if taking charge of our own destinies will bring the tyrannical guns of Washington to our city gates, then let the shells fall where they may!" She had raised her voice on that pronouncement, saying things she had only felt before, but had never verbalized.

"Amen, Miss Holly," Cleo said, from across the kitchen.

12

Quinn turned and scowled toward the black woman, in the way that he might have if he had been interrupted by the antic behavior of a pet. He then turned back to Holly. "So, the daughter of the colonel takes a militant stand. Maybe you wouldn't be so hasty in your decision to involve yourself in a war, little miss, if you yourself were obligated to go off and fight in it. Or maintain a business in the face of a possible naval blockade of this port, in order to feed a family. It may all seem glamorous to you, as a young woman, but there is no glamour in war, believe me."

"I didn't know that you had had any experience in war," Holly said coolly to him.

"Holly," Charlotte said to her in a heavy voice. She had had to listen to these verbal exchanges many times before, between Holly and Quinn, and it all made her nervous. "Uriah supplied the federal army with equipment in the Mexican War, even though he didn't wear a uniform. You know that."

"Oh, yes, excuse me," Holly said. "I keep forgetting that Uriah had close ties with the army. Of course, that isn't the same as fighting the Mexicans in the mountains at Buena Vista, as Father did, is it?"

Quinn scowled at her. "I'm sorry I can't be just like your father, Holly. But there always have to be those on the home front who keep the army supplied so it can fight. The reckless and carefree go off to the battle grounds, but the steady heads often have to stay at home to keep the world running while the military adventurers are out covering themselves with so-called glory."

Holly was angry so quickly that she had no time to think of controlling it. "My father was not a military adventurer! He was a brave man, who went to war so that

13

people like you could stay at home and go on making your profits from your businesses without inconvenience or interruption! There are many like him in Charleston now, who will gladly defend our new Confederacy with their lives if need be, so that we may run our lives the way we know is best! I imagine some of them were out there at Fort Sumter today, and I applaud them, Uriah!"

"Holly, that's enough," Charlotte told her. "You don't know all the possible consequences of what's happening, honey. Uriah is right, we should be trying to solve all of this peaceably."

Holly rose from her chair, and Uriah's gaze fell on her rather spectacular nineteen-year-old figure. Holly saw the hint of lechery behind his irritation with her, and despised him doubly for it.

"If nobody minds," she said in a bitter voice, "I'm going down to the waterfront in the second buggy. There will be people celebrating what happened today, down there. I would like to be a part of it."

Before either of them could say anything further to her, she quickly left the room, with Quinn and Charlotte staring after her.

"That daughter of yours is going to have to learn it all the hard way," Quinn said in his cold voice. "Mark my word. The hard way."

There were celebrations in the streets that afternoon, as Holly had guessed there might be. Charleston's shady boulevards with their elm and live oak trees were hung with bunting in places, and there was a spontaneous parade along the waterfront area, where the two forts could be seen across the harbor, with the Confederate flags flying bravely from their walls.

14

Holly did not join in the festivities, though. She drove the buggy across town to see her close friend Jennifer Armistead, who lived with an aging grandmother in a rather modest house on the outskirts of town. Jennifer, who was a year younger than Holly, had lost both of her parents to an influenza epidemic when she was quite young, and that loss gave her something in common with Holly, and had made them closer. Coming from a poorer home environment than Holly, and not having Holly's exceptional beauty, Jennifer placed more importance on finding a husband than Holly did. She was being courted by a friend of Stuart Blaisdell named Randolph Clayborne, whom Charlotte had mentioned when talking with Holly. Clayborne was a handsome son of a merchant seaman. His money was comparable to that of Blaisdell's family, and the boys had grown up as close friends. It was Jennifer who had asked Clayborne to glamorize Blaisdell to Holly, because Jennifer thought it would be nice to go out double-dating on outings. The four of them had done so on occasion, too, and Jennifer had particularly enjoyed those get-togethers. But people seeing the couples together often thought Holly was with Clayborne, the better looking fellow of the two, and that Jennifer must be with Blaisdell, who was rather plain-looking like Jennifer. Clayborne was quite a flirtatious young man, and he played up to Holly quite a lot when they first met, much to Jennifer's irritation. But when the little attentions were not returned by Holly, he quickly gave it up.

Jennifer was out in the small garden behind her house when Holly arrived there, and Holly was ushered out there by Jennifer's gray-haired grandmother, whose name was Amanda. Amanda was a pleasant woman who

15

always wanted Holly to have tea in the parlor, with iced cakes and silver trays.

"Holly!" Jennifer greeted her exuberantly when Holly stepped out into the garden. "Did you hear what happened?"

Holly walked over to where Jennifer had been pruning some oleander bushes according to Amanda's exact instructions, a job she did not particularly like. She was wearing a gardening apron and a wide-brimmed hat that was very becoming to her. She looked pretty in it, with her sparkling eyes and light-glinting blondish hair. Jennifer's hair was not quite blond, her eyes were not quite green, her face was not quite distinguishable from other young faces. But she had a verve about her that was disarming and enchanting, and it gave her the appearance, often, of being prettier than she was.

Holly nodded to her, smiling at Jennifer's exuberance. Because of their slight age difference, Holly had always had to be the steady hand at their ship's helm, the quieting influence, the one who maintained reason despite juvenile excitement. But now that they were nineteen and over eighteen, the differences between them were no longer really attributable to maturation.

"Yes, I know," Holly said. Now that she was with Jennifer, she felt exuberant, too. "Isn't it great? Federal troops are gone. We own our own city now."

"Throw all the Yankees out!" Jennifer said happily. In a tight-fitting blouse, she was slightly more full-blown than Holly, and more earthy-looking than elegant. She had always been very open about sex, and had allowed intimacy with Clayborne despite her seriousness about him. Holly had experimented with intimacy too, but before she met Stuart Blaisdoll. The experience had been

16

unsatisfactory, and she had decided to be very careful with men from that moment on, and physical involvements with them.

"Uriah and Mother are scared," Holly said more soberly now. "And I guess I am, too, when I analyze my feelings. The northern states are very powerful, Jennifer. They could do us great harm, if there's a war."

"Our boys will show them," Jennifer replied blithely. She had little understanding of or interest in politics or the military. "You'll see. Randy said we could beat the Yanks in a week, with the kind of soldiers the South would field."

When both of them realized she was referring to a real war, with men shooting at each other, and killing, a silence suddenly settled between them, like a dark fog in the spring sun. Holly imagined she could hear her own heart pounding inside her.

Jennifer changed the subject. "Listen, there's going to be a big celebration tonight, with a ball at the armory. Randy has already asked me to go, and I know that Stuart wants to invite you, Holly. It's just that you've turned him down a couple of times recently, and he's become gun-shy. Why don't you stop by the bank and show yourself there? Stuart will ask you to the Confederation Ball, and we can all go together. You do want to celebrate Charleston's new independence from the Washington politicians, don't you?"

Holly hesitated for a moment, then her face broke into a lovely smile. "Yes, of course, Jennifer. I'll make some excuse to stop at the bank, and speak to Stuart. He may not ask me, of course, and I'm not going to ask him."

"Don't be silly, dear girl. Stuart is infatuated with you; he has been from the moment Randy introduced you to

17

him. He told Randy recently that you're the most beautiful girl in Charleston."

"Oh, God," Holly murmured, embarrassed.

Jennifer smiled. "He may be right. If I had your looks, I'd have had Randy's ring on my finger long ago, I suspect. But I'll noose him yet, you just wait and see."

Actually, Jennifer had been intimate with a couple of young men other than Clayborne, before she had met him, and having been little interested in marriage, had been headed toward promiscuity. But then, when she had met the handsome and well-to-do Clayborne, who managed his father's ships' chandlery business, Jennifer had fallen in love as much with Clayborne's position and money as she had with his good looks, and she had also become enamored of the notion of marriage to Clayborne as a kind of personal accomplishment; the winning of a gold cup or blue ribbon that she could show off to her friends and to girls who had never thought much of Jennifer, in school. The trouble was, Jennifer was not quite pretty enough to be matched with Clayborne, who could have gone with prettier girls from better families. But she had kept him interested with physical teasings and then intimacy, playing him carefully, as a salt-water fisherman would play a game fish, drawing him in closer and closer to her net.

Holly had watched this campaign of Jennifer's with amusement and some concern, wondering if Jennifer had not gotten caught up in some kind of game she ought not to be playing. First of all, Clayborne was not that great a catch, despite his looks and money. He had always seemed a rather shallow boy to Holly, and she wondered how he would be as a life mate, even if Jennifer got him to the church for a wedding. Also, Jennifer herself had

18

demonstrated a strong interest in playing the field, so to speak, and Holly was not certain she would be content to play wife, after the first six months.

"I think," Holly said after a long moment, "that Randy Clayborne would be a very lucky fellow to get you for his wife." She came and kissed Jennifer on the cheek, feeling a deep fondness for her. Jennifer was just like a sister to her. Holly had been going to seek commiseration from Jennifer about Uriah Quinn, but she did not want to spoil Jennifer's bright mood, now. "I'll see you later and tell you what happened at the bank."

Jennifer smiled widely. "Can there be any doubt?" she said.

Stuart Blaisdell did invite Holly to the grand ball planned by the city fathers to celebrate the taking of Forts Sumter and Moultrie, but the ball was delayed for several days because of uncertainty about what the reaction of Washington would be toward the move. The answer was not long in coming. The new president proclaimed that the South had declared war on its brethren states of the North by ousting its military at the various southern forts, and that a state of war did in fact exist between the seceded states—others were now joining in the Confederacy: South Carolina, Mississippi, Florida, Alabama, Georgia, Louisiana, and Texas—and the now-lesser United States. Lincoln called for the procurement of an army of seventy-five thousand men, and Jefferson Davis retaliated, in Richmond, with an even greater demand from the South. Lincoln ordered the Federal Navy out in force, and everyone knew they would soon be headed for the great southern ports of Charleston, Pensacola, Savannah, and New Orleans.

19

An even deeper sobriety settled over Charleston, with war in the offing. Some went so far as to proclaim that De Beauregard had acted hastily. But most of the populace stood firmly behind the military, and the Confederation Ball was held, to raise funds for the war effort.

Holly, Jennifer and their young men attended the ball in their finest. It was a gala affair, the hall hung with bunting and cutout decorations. A military band played, and they already wore the new gray uniform of the Confederate States Army. City officials attended the celebration, and even P.G.T. de Beauregard made a brief appearance. Holly was very impressed with him, in his brass buttons and gold braid. It was De Beauregard's action against Fort Sumter that had precipitated present hostilities, and he was already a Confederate hero.

Holly wore a lovely pale-green gown, cut low in front, and her long dark hair, swept up at the sides and back, was worn up on her head; she looked like a Hungarian princess. Jennifer wore a yellow gown and matching yellow ribbon in her hair, and was very pretty. Both Blaisdell and Clayborne were in cutaway coats and cravats, and looked very important. Clayborne was dark and handsome, with a square jaw and sparkling brown eyes, and Blaisdell was slightly bigger than Clayborne, but quite plain-looking with brown hair and pale-blue eyes. He looked more like a farmer's son than a banker's, except for his clothing. But he was a serious, substantial young man who took much more interest in political happenings than Clayborne, and now he was very fired up about the coming struggle with the North.

The two couples danced for over an hour to the waltzes and minuets the band played. The floor was full of dancers, old and young alike. Holly saw the mayor at one juncture, and at the end of a waltz somebody yelled out, "God save the Confederacy!" and the band struck up "Dixie," with all joining in to sing the adopted tune. At midevening, the two couples walked to a corner where mint juleps were being served, and Clayborne treated them all to a drink. They took the drinks out through a rear door then, to a porch out in back, where there were two other couples. There they stood at a railing and looked out into the night, as if they might find their future out there in the blackness. During an intermission from the music, they could hear crickets out in the yard beyond the armory porch.

"Gosh, this is a beautiful night!" Jennifer said, leaning on the railing. "I'll always remember it!"

Clayborne put an arm around her waist, looking out into the darkness beside her. Beside him stood Blaisdell, facing the open doorway to the building, and beyond him was Holly.

"I can make it even more memorable for you, honey," Clayborne said quietly to Jennifer.

She turned and grinned at him, and Blaisdell, having heard the remark, turned quickly away from them. "Are you comfortable out here, Holly?" He was always very solicitous toward her; too solicitous, she often thought. It did not make him more attractive to her, but less so.

"Yes, I'm fine, Stuart."

"I hope I wasn't too awkward in there. I'm not much at dancing."

"You were very good," Holly told him.

"Did you see De Beauregard in there?" Clayborne said, turning to Blaisdell and Holly. "Strutting around like Napoleon in that gray suit? Isn't he great?"

Holly gave him a look. "He wasn't strutting, Randy.

21

Military men hold themselves like that."

"We're damned lucky to have a man like De Beauregard defending the honor of the South, Randy," Blaisdell said seriously. "Him and Lee."

"Hey, I'm not criticizing him," Clayborne said lightly, grinning a handsome grin. "Frankly, I'd like to get one of those uniforms on myself. The girls are crazy about them." He turned to note Jennifer's sour look. "Oh, sorry, honey. I wouldn't pay them any mind, of course."

"Of course," Jennifer said.

"My father won't let me think of joining up with our army, though. He calculates all of this will be over in a couple of weeks, and he can't spare me at the supply house."

"I get the same from my parents," Blaisdell admitted. "But I don't think this is going to blow over, Randy, and we're sure not going to whip the North in a couple of weeks. Not with our ports blockaded."

Holly looked into Blaisdell's somber eyes, and realized that this sober, rather dull young banker's son was just the type who would go off to save the southern cause, if a shooting war blossomed into something portentous in the following weeks. That gave her a feeling for him that she had not had previously, and made her realize that she preferred Blaisdell to Clayborne, despite his plainness and his awkwardness.

"Well, when McDowell sees that long gray line and understands we're serious about defending ourselves from tyranny," Clayborne said pompously, quoting liberally from recent news comments, "I think a truce will be called and a treaty signed. Nobody really wants to fight over this."

Blaisdell glanced toward him gravely, but said nothing.

22

"Gosh, I wish they would just leave us alone, and let us get on with our lives," Jennifer offered, always putting everything on a personal level. "I mean, we have families to raise and homes to make." She gave Clayborne a sidewise look, and he grinned slightly at her.

Holly turned to Jennifer. "The North will fight," she said simply.

They all looked toward her. Inside the building, the band was warming up again, and there were buzzing conversations and suppressed laughter.

"Lincoln can't allow a dozen or more states to just unilaterally separate themselves from the nation," Holly went on slowly, as if telling herself rather than them. "We're all bound together by the Constitution. Secession is an insult to the sovereignty of the United States, and a dangerous precedent. Not only here, but around the world."

Clayborne and Blaisdell were frowning slightly at her. "Do we have a northern sympathizer in our midst?" Clayborne said curiously.

"Oh, really, Randy!" Jennifer said.

Holly's face went straight-lined, and her mild anger made her even more beautiful to Blaisdell. "I believe deeply in the southern cause, Randy," she said. "I'm just pointing out realities. Lincoln doesn't understand what the South has been through, at the hands of a North-dominated Congress. It may be that he never will. That doesn't make him an evil man, as some suggest. But it also doesn't lessen the righteousness of our cause."

Blaisdell was studying her closely. "I didn't know you thought so deeply on these subjects, Holly. You have an admirable grasp of the issues."

"She's always been a thinker," Jennifer said breezily.

23

"As if looks wasn't enough!"

"Humph," Clayborne grunted.

Holly smiled at Jennifer, ignoring Clayborne. "I just read a newspaper once in a while, Jennifer, and try to make my own judgments based on what they tell me. There's nothing exceptional in that."

"I think pretty girls should keep their heads clear of such things," Clayborne commented. "It can give you worry lines." He grinned at Holly, and she found the grin irrepressible. She returned it with a reproving look. "You are incorrigible, Randy."

"Well, I think pretty girls can do just what they want to," Blaisdell said in his slow drawl. "No matter what it is. What do you want to do at this moment, Holly? The band is preparing for another waltz. Or we could take a walk out in back here."

"I think I'd prefer the walk," Holly said. "Will you excuse us for a while, you two?"

Jennifer gave her a knowing look. "Of course. Just don't get into any trouble out there in the dark." She suppressed a small giggle.

Blaisdell appeared flustered, and Holly sighed inwardly. "Thanks for the advice, Jennifer," she said in mock irritation.

Blaisdell and Holly went down a short flight of steps leading into a walled yard, while Clayborne and Jennifer went back inside the building. The band was playing again now, and Holly liked the sound of it, coming to them from the small distance. They walked along a wall, past a cannon, to the dark shade of a young tree. Holly paused underneath it and looked up through its new greenery. It was a lacy elm, with buds and young leaves all over it.

24

"Spring is a wonderful time of year," she said quietly.

Blaisdell came around to face her, standing several inches taller than she and looking broad-shouldered in his formal suit. "Holly. You're so beautiful tonight—you make my blood race." He blushed slightly.

Holly averted her gaze toward the ground. "Thank you for that, Stuart. But I think we shouldn't talk of racing blood."

"I—care for you, Holly. I think—I'm in love with you."

Holly looked up into his serious, young farmer's face. "Please, Stuart. Don't say that. We haven't known each other long enough or well enough. You're attracted to me physically, and that's a different thing."

"Yes, I am attracted to you physically," he said. "Like a moth to a beautiful flame, I guess. But it's more than that. I like the way you use your head, the way you think things out, and speak your mind. I—well, I—"

Suddenly Blaisdell reached to Holly and pulled her to him. He had kissed her twice before, but the kisses had been short, perfunctory ones, the only kind Holly and his bravery would allow. Now, though, he was suddenly kissing her hungrily on the mouth, and before she knew what was happening, his hands had found her breasts under the tight-stretched cloth of her low-cut gown.

Holly pulled away, breaking loose from his strong grasp, surprised by his iron strength and his quick passion. She was breathless, her breasts rising and falling in the gown, making her striking cleavage more prominent to him.

"Don't, Stuart. I don't think we should."

"Why not?" he said huskily.

"I don't think . . . this should go beyond what it is

25

now," she said, trying to get her breath back.

"Didn't you hear me, Holly? I love you. Don't you feel anything for me? Please, Holly. Don't hold me away!"

He drew her to him again, and she tried to pull back, but then he was kissing her again, this time more physically, using his strength to hold her. She was inflamed sensually by his physical assault, but angered slightly by his awkward insistence. She broke away again, and fell up against the tree trunk behind her.

"God, Stuart!"

His expression changed, and a worried look came into his square, bucolic face. "I'm sorry, Holly! I can't seem to keep myself under control when I'm with you, honest to God!"

"You can't use your masculine strength to . . . force a girl," she said darkly. "You have to employ some . . . finesse, Stuart."

"I didn't hurt you, did I?"

Holly sighed deeply, and came away from the tree. "No, you didn't hurt me, Stuart. If you had, you'd know about it. Now, I think you ought to take me back inside."

"You're not angry with me, are you?"

"No," she said easily.

"I mean it, Holly. I love you."

"Let's discuss it some other time."

"All right, Holly," he said to her.

Just a little later that evening, the two couples left the ball and the girls were escorted home separately. Holly said good night peremptorily to Stuart Blaisdell, not wanting to rehash what had happened earlier in back of the armory. But across town, at Jennifer's place, dark and handsome Randy Clayborne had taken Jennifer out to a

26

woodshed behind the house, beyond the garden. There was no privacy in either of their homes, so that was where they had met previously for intimate moments. On two different occasions in the past few months, Jennifer had been seduced there by Clayborne, and as he led her into the shadows back there again this dark evening, she felt that he had the same idea in mind.

They stepped inside the shed, leaving its door open. There was a stack of cordwood on one wall of the old place, and a low cot at the other wall, where a slave had once slept, before he died of old age. Jennifer's grandmother could not afford to buy another slave nowadays, so Jennifer and she got all the work done about the place. The cot, though, had served a very intimate purpose on those other occasions when Jennifer had calculated it was the right moment to show Randy Clayborne what he was missing as a bachelor.

"Look!" she said as she turned back to him just inside the shed doorway, looking past him to the black sky. "Fireworks down at the waterfront! Aren't they beautiful?"

Clayborne turned and watched the explosions of color in the sky for a couple of moments, then grabbed Jennifer and kissed her hotly on the mouth.

Jennifer was taken by surprise, but she responded with readiness. Now was one of those times when she might have to use her body to whet Clayborne's interest. The kiss was a long, breathless one, and she felt his hand move onto her full-blown breasts as his mouth explored hers avariciously.

"Oh, God—Randy!"

"You know what I want, honey. We can have our own little celebration, make our own fireworks. You know how good it is between us."

Jennifer pulled back from him slightly. "You seem to keep forgetting I'm a single girl, Randy. We're not married, you know."

"Married?" he said distractedly, moving his hand up onto her rather voluptuous curves again.

"We could do all of this we wanted," she said. "If we were husband and wife."

He was fondling her persistently. "Sure," he muttered.

"You . . . ought to think about that, Randy."

"I will." Impatiently.

Clayborne was pulling the gown off her shoulders, and she did not stop him. Bare flesh was exposed, and then he was kissing and caressing.

"Oh—Randy!" In a soft sibilance.

Somehow they were on the cot after a couple of moments, without either of them consciously planning that move. Then there was the hot seeking, the baring of more flesh, and finally the cries of pleasure that issued from the very depths of Jennifer's arched throat.

Out over the walls of Fort Sumter, the fireworks exploded wildly, and a new moon rode high overhead.

Chapter Two

Charleston was rather quiet, that morning after the big celebration. There had been a light rain through the night, and the bunting along Broad and Meeting Streets now hung in limp tatters and broken strands, like memories of unredeemed sins. The armory was being scoured clean by slave caretakers, quietly and methodically; there was a cleaning crew to sweep the streets clear of fireworks debris, down around the Exchange Building, and at the Slave Market. The mood of anxious expectation had returned even more strongly, it seemed, than before the taking of the harbor's forts by De Beauregard's troops. But the new Confederate flag flew above those battlements now.

Out in the harbor, ships and smaller craft were departing every day, their captains afraid to be caught in the blockade they knew was coming, so the harbor was rather empty-looking now, in the aftermath of the temporary excitement. Out at the Citadel, which was considered the West Point of the South, cadets drilled grimly on their parade ground that gray morning, and fired out-of-date muskets on their firing range—getting ready.

At the Ransom-Quinn residence, Holly felt a letdown after the glamour and excitement of the ball, and the small confrontation with Stuart Blaisdell. More than ever before, she felt that her life had no direction or purpose at that moment in time; her feeling was particularly frustrating in view of events that were developing around her. She wished there were some way she could participate in those events, share in their movement in whatever directions they took. But it seemed that women were excluded from participation, and were expected to be largely spectators in the world's turning—even now, in this explosive period. That was upsetting to Holly, because she was not the kind of girl to just sit back and monitor events from a safe distance.

Charlotte was very pleased that Holly had gone to the ball with Blaisdell, thinking that that was an indication that Holly was taking him more seriously. She did not understand Holly's deep longings to make something of herself, to be something apart from a southern gentleman's wife and the mother of his children. In Charlotte's mind, Holly was lucky to have the beauty to attract young men like Blaisdell—other girls had exhibited an interest in him, but without any reciprocation on his part—and she could not believe that her daughter was vacillating about making something permanent with him. He could give Holly everything that Charlotte felt was important in her world, and she thought Holly should marry him at the soonest opportunity.

"You may not have as much time as you think, young lady," Charlotte had told her that day after Fort Sumter. "Stuart keeps talking about going off to a war, if there is one."

Some days, Holly wished she were a man. If she were,

30

she herself would be joining the ranks of De Beauregard's army, to defend her city and the South. There would be nurses needed, she knew, when the big shooting began. But nursing, too, was a passive role. It was not something that appealed to Holly's nature.

On that day after the ball, Charlotte asked Holly to take a letter downtown to Uriah Quinn. It had come to him at the house, and pertained to his import business. Holly was going shopping for Charlotte, anyway, and the extra errand would not take her much out of her way. Holly agreed reluctantly. She kept away from her stepfather as much as possible, these days. When he was not being ornery and overbearing with Charlotte, he was maligning the Confederacy. Or, more and more frequently, he was staring at Holly lecherously, or grinning at her in that special way he had, that made her flesh bump up slightly. Quinn had made it all too obvious that he had noticed Holly's growing up, and considered her an appealing morsel, as he would appreciate the cut of a T-bone steak. He had no respect for her as a person, but she had unwittingly captured a base interest in him that was unnerving and sometimes frightening to her. Long glances into her bedroom, unwanted glimpses at off-guard moments, studied appraisals of her contours, especially when Charlotte was not present.

Charlotte was not unaware of Holly's attractiveness to Quinn, and that was one reason she wanted Holly married and gone. A grown, beautiful daughter in a household with a new stepfather was a bad situation, and Charlotte recognized it as such. But she had no knowledge yet of Quinn's little clandestine attentions to Holly, except for small hints Holly had given her, and she wanted to believe in her second husband, despite his

31

apparent deficiencies, so she attributed Holly's remarks to dislike of the man.

Holly took a buggy down to the central area that noontime, a dun mare under her reins. She drove down Church Street, with its double row of tall, lacy trees, and there were some women out strolling under parasols, as if everything were just the same as it had been last fall. But their somber faces revealed that things were not the same. Holly drove past open carriages, a wagon carrying peat moss, a couple of men on horseback. One of the men tipped his hat to her, as he was an acquaintance of Charlotte. Down on Broad Street there were massive baroque buildings, including the Episcopal Church. Building canopies and awnings hung over the walks at the street line, and gave the city an attractive look.

Holly had been born and raised in Charleston, and loved the old city. She loved Charles Towne Landing, where the first settlers had landed in 1670; and Catfish Row, the open market; and she particularly loved the view past Forts Sumter and Moultrie, looking out through the harbor to the open sea, where ships came and went from all around the world.

The building Quinn's business was situated in was down near the old waterfront, in a small enclave of ornamented façades. Holly parked her buggy on the street, picketing the mare to an iron post with a black slave's head sculpted on its top. Then she went inside the building and to the second floor, where Quinn's business was located.

Quinn was alone when she arrived, filing some invoices from a recent shipment of fruit from the Caribbean. When he turned and saw her come in, a brittle grin crept onto his square, lined face.

"Well, well. The colonel's daughter. Have you come to pay your loving stepfather a visit, Holly?" He was in his shirt sleeves and a vest, and he was trim for his age, and very physical-looking to Holly.

"Mother asked me to bring you this letter, Uriah," she said without smiling. "It was just delivered this morning. It's from the Mason Company in Norfolk, and she thought it might be important."

Quinn came over and closed the office door behind her, and Holly immediately felt uncomfortable with his proximity. Quinn took the letter, and glanced at the envelope. "It's undoubtedly just a billing," he said. "Why don't you sit down for a moment, my dear? You always seem to be in such a hurry."

"I can't stay," she said quickly. "I'm on some errands. Is there anything I can do for you, while I'm down here?"

Quinn stood quite close to her, smiling into her face. "You could try being friendly to your stepfather for just once," he told her.

Holly glanced at him suspiciously, then averted her gaze. "I wasn't aware that I was unfriendly toward you," she said only half-truthfully. "I don't mean to be, Uriah."

He reached and took her chin in his hand, and she had an almost irresistible impulse to pull free. But she controlled herself. "You know what I'm talking about," he said. "There's this ongoing war between us. There has been, ever since I came into the household. You made up your mind not to like me, didn't you, girl?"

He released his light grip on her, and she began breathing a little shallowly. "Of course not, Uriah."

"I think you got it into that pretty head of yours that I've been trying to take your father's place in your life,"

33

he went on. He grinned. "Nothing could be further from the truth, Holly. I have no desire to be another father to you. You're a grown woman; you no longer need a father. I'd prefer you think of me as a—well, let's say, an uncle. Or better yet, as a friend."

Holly suddenly met his gaze openly. "I'm not sure what you would expect of a friendship with me," she said deliberately and slowly.

Quinn grunted out a small laugh. "What do men usually expect of young women in your world? I would want nothing more, nothing less. I could make your life more—comfortable, Holly. If you'd let me. I'd like to buy you something now and then—clothing, jewelry."

Holly frowned. "Jewelry?"

"Don't all young ladies enjoy the feel of gold and silver against their cameo skin?" he said in a rather different voice. "Lace and silk to caress their milky flesh?"

Holly blushed slightly, and turned away from him. "Those are things you should be buying for Mother," she said darkly. "Not me."

"But your needs are no less, are they?" Quinn persisted, coming up close behind her. He had not touched her, but she had the feeling that he was mauling her physically, that she was enclosed in his iron grip. "Perhaps," he added significantly, "they're more. Youth always has more demands to be met—emotionally, physically."

Holly turned back to him, anger and shock in her lovely face. "How dare you speak to me in that manner! Charlotte would be outraged!"

"Really?" he said innocently. "I have no idea why!"

"Do you think I'd let you buy me presents?" Holly said a little emotionally. "Don't you think I know what

34

that would imply, so far as you were concerned?"

He shrugged. "It would imply only what you wanted it to."

"I don't like you, Uriah," she said now. "I don't want to be your friend, or anything else you might have in mind. What I want is for you to keep your distance from me—now, and always. If that isn't clear enough for you, I'll have Charlotte explain it to you."

His face darkened with his own anger, suddenly, and his eyes narrowed on her. "The self-righteous colonel's daughter. Always looking for evil where it isn't. Always ready to judge others, to place herself above them on some pedestal or other. Well, I'll wager you weren't so virtuous last evening, my dear daughter, when that Blaisdell was under the influence of your charms."

Holly glowered at him. "What are you saying?"

"Your mother was asleep, but I know when you got home. I heard you come in. You weren't dancing all that time; I'd bet good money on it. You have no interest in marrying the banker's son, but you're not above a little behind-the-armory diversion with him, are you now, Miss Ransom? Let the truth out, your Uncle Uriah won't gossip about it."

Holly's face was flushed crimson, and her blue eyes flashed hatred at Uriah. "Damn you, you wicked man! There is nothing between Stuart and me! We danced and talked last night, and he brought me home!"

Quinn grinned. "Just as you say, Holly. Just as you say."

"It *is* just as I say!" Holly insisted, gasping with anger. She moved quickly past him to the door, then turned back to him for a brief moment. "Keep out of my business, and out of my life, Uriah!" Then she opened the

35

door and hurried out.

Over the next weeks, events seemed to spin out of control. The Confederate Army made an attack on the arsenal at Harper's Ferry, but were driven off. Southern forces attempted to take Fort Pickens in Pensacola Harbor and failed. The Navy Yard at Norfolk was assaulted but not captured.

It was not going to be as easy as some had thought.

Lincoln sent a fleet of warships to Charleston and other southern ports to blockade the harbors, and now Charleston residents could look out over the water past the harbor mouth and see ironclads and brigantines sitting out there beyond Fort Sumter. There was an exchange of gunfire when the ships first arrived, but from then on firing, between the fleet and the forts, was only intermittent, with occasional bombardment of the city itself. When the first shells exploded in town, some residents panicked and evacuated. Most stayed. De Beauregard assured locals that personal danger was minimal, and that the city could not be deserted if it was to be defended. Some fine old buildings were hit, though, and that made locals angry, rather than afraid. As usual in war, hatreds began developing that had not really existed at the outbreak of hostilities. Jennifer was scared at first when some shells landed in town, then she relaxed when she saw that her edge-of-the-city area was probably not going to be hit. Holly felt little fear, not even in the beginning. She reacted as most men did, with raw anger. But unlike the men, who were now volunteering to go off to fight in large numbers, Holly had to sit and do nothing and allow her frustration to build.

As summer neared, the armies were building on both

sides, and both Jefferson Davis and Abraham Lincoln were calling for unconditional victory, no compromises. Then unexpectedly, it seemed, the opposing forces met at Phillipi, West Virginia, and young General McClellan of the Union Army carried the day. Not long thereafter, at Big Bethel Church on the Peninsula of Virginia, the Confederate Army won a rather limited confrontation.

In mid-June, on a warm afternoon when Holly was driving a buggy across town, the federals began bombardment of the southern section of the city, and Holly was caught right in the middle of it. Shells burst all around her for a short while, and her mare reared and bolted, and she was almost thrown from the buggy.

Holly was shaken by that real taste of war. But when it was over, and Jennifer and her mother had expressed their amazement that she had not been hurt and congratulated her on her bravery through it (Stuart Blaisdell was very angry with her for having gone across town by herself when an attack by the gunboats was expected), Holly had changed inside. She finally knew what she had always guessed, that she was a person who was not afraid of any challenges the world might offer her. The fear of injury, even of death, was so tenuous in her as to be unnoticeable.

Now that the shooting war was really on, both Blaisdell and Clayborne talked of joining the rebel forces, although Clayborne, unlike Blaisdell, was not really eager to go to war. Clayborne was more interested in his own personal, private life than in going off to fight for a cause. Blaisdell, on the other hand, was more like Holly in his feelings about what was happening. He was all afire inside about the war and what it meant to the South to win it, and he was already preparing his father for his

37

eventual enlistment. On Blaisdell's insistence, his father hired an assistant for him, to train in his work in the fiduciary business, a middle-aged man who was too debilitated to be sent off to fight on the battlefield.

Then in July came the development that cinched it in Blaisdell's mind. There was a sizable Confederate Army now at Manassas Junction, in Virginia, guarding the only rail line through to Richmond, the new Confederate capital. McDowell, under Lincoln's urging, moved his Union Army south to Manassas to defeat the rebel force there commanded by Stonewall Jackson, and to make a quick strike at Richmond. But after a bloody battle that looked at first like a Union victory, the rebels drove the Yanks back into the District of Columbia.

The Battle of Bull Run, as it was called later, was a Confederate victory technically. But the losses on both sides were sobering, and it became clear in that one confrontation that the war was going to be a long one. Blaisdell was at once fired emotionally by the success of the Confederates, and sobered by the losses. It was clear that his Confederacy needed him, and the sooner the better. Maybe he and some others like him could shorten the war for the South.

One afternoon only three days after the Manassas confrontation, he appeared at the Ransom-Quinn house with a rather flushed appearance. Charlotte met him at the door, and was surprised at his presence there.

"Oh, my goodness, Stuart! What a very pleasant surprise!" She pushed at a wisp of dark hair at her face, feeling a little self-conscious. Knowing she was still attractive to men, even young ones, Charlotte did not like being caught off guard socially, so that she did not look her best.

"Is Holly in?" Blaisdell asked her. He wore his usual formal suit and stiff collar and cravat, despite the July heat, and there was a dew of perspiration on his brow and upper lip.

"Why, yes, she is," Charlotte replied. "Please do come in, Stuart. Let me offer you an iced lemonade while I get her."

Blaisdell came into the large living room of the old house. Out on its porch were high columns and ivy, and inside there were hardwood floors, potted palms, and some antique furniture that had come down to them from Charlotte's family.

"Don't bother with the cold drink, Charlotte," Blaisdell told her. "I had one just before I left the bank."

"Are you absolutely sure?" Charlotte asked coyly. She had the same facial structure as Holly, though not quite so dramatic in shape. If the lines of age could have been removed, and the slight flaccidity of skin around the chin and jaw, she would have been almost as pretty as Holly. But Holly had gotten some of her looks from her military father, too, and there was a strength in her face that added to its beauty, and that Charlotte did not have.

"Yes, quite, Charlotte," Blaisdell said a little impatiently. He fingered his hat awkwardly, looking uncomfortable.

"Very well. Please sit down, Stuart. I just wish Uriah were here, he enjoys so much speaking with you." Charlotte did not mind telling little lies to accomplish her purposes.

Upstairs, Holly had heard Charlotte's voice and was just coming to the head of the broad staircase to see who was visiting, when Charlotte called up to her, from the doorway to the foyer.

"Holly! Stuart Blaisdell is here!"

Holly was curious about the visit. It was not like Blaisdell to come calling in the middle of the day. He had been more persistent in his attention lately, but his contacts had always been in the evening. Charlotte was sure that these visits portended marriage, and was excited about it.

"Oh, Stuart," Holly said, coming down the stairs in a smooth, gliding motion. She had been trying on clothes up in her room, and was wearing a white gingham dress with fluff and lace on it. Her long, loose, shoulder-length hair looked particularly striking against the white of the dress, and Holly seemed especially lovely to Blaisdell as she came down to receive him.

He rose as she came into the parlor from the foyer, and she noticed the excitement in his face immediately. "Good afternoon, Stuart. Is anything wrong?"

"Oh, no," he said. "I just wanted a few private words with you, Holly, if you have a few minutes."

Charlotte smiled knowingly. "I'll just leave you two alone. If you want anything, Stuart, I'll be right in the kitchen."

"Thanks, Charlotte," Blaisdell said to her.

A moment later, Holly and Blaisdell were alone in the spacious parlor with its bay windows, heavy furniture, and Persian rug. Holly asked Blaisdell to sit down again, and then she joined him, on a long felt sofa.

"Now, Stuart. What brings you here visiting in the middle of this hot day?" Holly asked curiously.

Blaisdell fingered his hat, and looked down for a moment. Then he met her quizzical gaze. "I've joined the army, Holly."

Holly raised a hand slowly to her lips, and rested it

there. "Oh, God," she murmured.

"All the young men are going," Blaisdell said. "Bull Run isn't the end of the war, Holly. It's the beginning of it. We drove the Yanks back there, but they showed us they have an army that's willing to fight. This may last quite some time. We're going to need as many men in uniform as will put one on, I'd guess, before it's all over. Already there's a conscription law. I'd be drafted sooner or later, anyway."

"I guess I should have expected it," she said. She felt a sudden rush of affection for Blaisdell. Not as a potential lover or husband, but as the friend he was. She did not want to see him go. She did not like to think of him out there, exposing himself to danger—to violent death.

"My father is angry, but he'll get over it," Blaisdell went on. "Randy joined up with me. He didn't really want to, I think, but he saw the handwriting on the wall."

"God," Holly exclaimed. She had not had much of a world or much of a future in the past months, it had seemed to her, but Blaisdell and Clayborne had been a big part of it. She suddenly did not know what to say to him. His enlistment had raised an even greater wall between them than had existed before, somehow. He was a soldier now. He was the same Stuart Blaisdell sitting there looking neat and awkward, but an aura of mystery arose around him now. She could almost hear the distant thumping of cannon and musket fire, smell the acrid odor of gunsmoke in the air; she visualized flags fluttering in the breeze, and brass-buttoned uniforms. Holly envied him that aura; it was both fearful and glamorous.

"Does Jennifer know?" she added.

"Randy is going to surprise her with the news," he said. "At some opportune time in the next day or two,

41

he says."

Holly felt very hollow inside, suddenly. "Can I get Cleo to bring you a cold drink, Stuart?"

"No, your mother asked," he said. He averted his gaze to the floor, fingering the hat between his hands. "Holly, I won't have long here. A week, maybe a little more, they say. Things are different for me now. Different for us."

Holly looked into his wide-set eyes, and had a glimpse of what he was thinking. Something grabbed at her, deep down inside her. "Yes, of course, Stuart," she said quietly.

He cast a scared look at her. "Holly, you know how I feel about you. Maybe someday you could have the same kind of feelings for me, if you'd just give yourself the chance." Holly started to object to the line of conversation, but he would not let her. "Just hear me out," he said more forcefully than was like him. Already he had changed. "If this war wasn't on, I could just let things develop more naturally. But I feel now that every day is precious, Holly."

"I understand that," she said tightly.

He took a deep breath. "Holly, I want you to be my wife."

Her heart sank in her chest.

"Marry me, Holly, before I go off to war," he said, his eyes pleading with her. "Give us some time together. I mean really together." He blushed slightly. "Before I'm taken off to the fields of battle."

Holly's ears were ringing, and her breath was short. She turned her face away from him, so he could not see the dismay in her eyes. "Stuart, I thought I'd made it clear to you," she said almost inaudibly. "I'm not ready for marriage. I don't know why, but I'm not."

42

An impatience crowded into his square face. "Maybe it's time you got ready, Holly. I don't think the war will wait for you to make up your mind."

"I know, Stuart," she said, turning back to him. "But I don't know that you and I are—suited. We don't really know each other all that well." She was trying to be kind to him. She still did not see Blaisdell as the kind of husband she would want to spend her life with.

"Marry me," he said urgently to her, "and we'll get to know each other in a hurry."

She shook her head. "Not in a week or two," she told him. "I just couldn't rush into something so big, Stuart—so permanent."

He rose from the sofa, anger flushing his face now. "You're a beautiful girl, Holly. But you have to get your head straight inside. You don't want marriage, but you don't know what you want! Damn it, don't you see that you're spoiling it for both of us? Withholding our chance for the only kind of happiness that counts?"

Holly rose, too, and her face had gone somber. "I don't see it that way, Stuart."

Charlotte's head poked through an archway to a dining room off the kitchen. "Is everything all right in there?" Nervously. "Can I get you something, Stuart?"

"No, ma'am, I'm about ready to go."

"Please leave us alone for a few moments longer, Mother," Holly said somberly.

Charlotte disappeared again, and Holly moved closer to Blaisdell. "Please, Stuart. Don't be angry with me. I feel very close to you, you know that. I'm very fond of you. This is all just too fast, too unexpected."

"Sure," he said tautly, disappointment etched onto his face. "Well, I'll get back to the bank. Maybe I'll get to see

43

you before I leave."

"Anytime, Stuart," Holly told him.

A moment later he was gone, and Holly stood staring at the door he had closed behind him, feeling terrible inside. While she was still standing there, Charlotte came into the foyer behind her.

"What happened?" Charlotte said darkly.

Holly turned to her. "Stuart asked me to marry him," she said. "He's going off to the war soon. I said, no."

Charlotte looked at Holly for a moment as if she thought her daughter must have lost her mind, then she turned away and leaned heavily against the wall behind her; lilies of the valley grew in profusion on its patterned surface. Holly was regarding her gravely, but Charlotte did not meet her gaze. She stared at the wall across the foyer as if it might be constricting her, narrowing the room and her world.

"My God," she said bleakly, so that Holly could hardly hear her. "Oh, my God."

Chapter Three

Charlotte was greatly upset by Holly's rejection of Blaisdell's proposal of marriage, perhaps even more than Blaisdell himself. She had not really believed her daughter could act so foolishly and irresponsibly, despite Holly's repeated negative comments about Blaisdell. In the world that Charlotte came from, proposals of marriage were rejected occasionally, but there was always good reason. Usually it was because the young man came from a lesser social station than the courted girl, or because he possessed some terrible physical infirmity. To reject an eligible young suitor like Stuart Blaisdell simply because Holly did not feel deeply enough for him seemed an unforgivable outrage to Charlotte. Girls on Charlotte's side of the family had been sent off to nunneries for lesser offenses of social grace. If Holly had had anywhere to go but the street, Charlotte would have thrown her out of the house, so disturbed was she by her daughter's behavior.

Uriah Quinn was very pleased with the sudden rift between mother and daughter, although he did not show it openly. He liked the idea that Holly had become more of an outsider in the household, and less an object of maternal protection. The situation was pregnant with possibilities.

It would have been a difficult enough time for Holly if her mother had understood her. But with new hostility lying heavily in the house like a river-bottom fog, Holly was very low. She did not even go over to visit Jennifer in the next couple of days, because she knew about Clayborne's surprise for Jennifer and did not want to spoil it. Anyway, she and Jennifer were heading off in very different directions now, it seemed. It would not be the same, commiserating with her. Jennifer would not understand much better than Charlotte did.

The girls in Charlotte's family had always been marriage-oriented, Holly recalled, even more so than other southern belles. Charlotte's sister Eugenia, who lived now in Baltimore, had married at fifteen. Another sister had traveled five hundred miles to marry at sixteen. It had been like a competition with them, Holly realized, without regard for the kind of relationship they were getting into.

Stuart Blaisdell was very angry and disappointed for about twenty-four hours. But he could not stay angry with Holly. He loved her too much. Nothing she did could seem completely unreasonable to him.

Both Blaisdell and Clayborne had received commissions in General de Beauregard's South Carolina divisions, as lieutenants. Blaisdell's banker father knew De Beauregard personally, and made sure that the young men were not overlooked when the officers' ranks were being considered. They were also to serve with the same command, and leave together; and that made it all seem much more exciting and glamorous to them. On the afternoon after Holly's refusal of his proposal, Blaisdell and Clayborne were issued new gray uniforms with boots and wide-brimmed hats and sabers. They were told they would receive orders for deployment within just a few days, when their brigade was expected to move out.

Along with several other young officers, they cast off their civilian clothing at the armory, and quite suddenly they were soldiers. Clayborne finished the transformation sooner than Blaisdell, and came and sought Blaisdell out where he was changing. Blaisdell was just buttoning the brass buttons on his tunic when he saw Clayborne round a corner, in his new uniform. Clayborne stopped and stared at Blaisdell, and Blaisdell stared back.

"My God, Stuart. You look so damned—different!"

Blaisdell grinned. "You, too, Randy. Your uniform fits a little better than mine, I think."

"There's a nigger tailor around here somewhere," Clayborne said. "He'll make it fit like a glove if you want him to. By damn, Stuart! I'm beginning to believe it!"

"You'd better believe it," Blaisdell said. "There's talk of our being shipped out to Tennessee to bolster General Bragg's army there. Not all of this war will be fought in Virginia and South Carolina. Opposing armies are even squaring off in Missouri. We'll get a few days of training here, and then the rest of it out there somewhere. Maybe on the field of battle."

Clayborne adjusted his tunic carefully, holding his light-gray hat in his hand. He was a handsome fellow in the uniform, and he knew it. He wished he could just stay around in Charleston, showing it off to the girls. "Well, I just hope they don't want me to dirty up this uniform too much out there." He grinned. "Maybe we can get assignments behind the lines somewhere."

Blaisdell's face went serious slowly. "Randy, maybe you should have thought this over more. I hope I didn't talk you into anything. You could have waited for them to come and get you."

Clayborne shrugged. "They might have had all the officers they wanted, if I had. Who wants to roll around in the mud with the enlisted men, for God's sake? Anyway, I feel—important in this uniform. Maybe for the first time ever. How about you, don't you feel a little less like a banker, now?"

Blaisdell allowed his expression to soften. He had never seen much wrong with being a banker. "A little, I guess," he said.

"The most important thing is, we can go off together this way," Clayborne added as an afterthought. "We can stand together against the world!" He came and threw his arm over Blaisdell's shoulder. "Isn't that right, old chum?"

Blaisdell grinned awkwardly. "That's right, Randy. I'm very glad we're going together."

Clayborne had already turned and was admiring himself in a mirror on the nearby wall of the supply room. "Another little bonus for me," he was now saying, "is Jennifer. We'll have a quick marriage in the next couple of days, and then I'll spend twenty-four hours a day in bed with her until I'm gone. This uniform will make her little tongue hang out, Blais. She's a damned firecracker, you know, when you get her all heated up. I'm going to have a real send-off, believe me."

Blaisdell was embarrassed. He could not imagine talking to another man about Holly in that manner. He wished that Clayborne had not shared such thoughts about Jennifer with him

48

"I'm damned sorry that you couldn't be in the same situation, old buddy, I really am. It will be nice to go off with those hot memories still in my head. White thighs, soft breasts. What the hell, maybe she'll hand me a son when I come back. It could happen. It gives a man something to think about."

"Yeah," Blaisdell mumbled.

Clayborne clapped him on the arm. "Well, soldier. Shall we go to the commission house and the bank and show off a little? I think we have it coming."

Blaisdell smiled uncertainly. "I'm with you," he said.

That evening, Jennifer met Clayborne at her front door with anxious anticipation. She knew that he and Blaisdell had enlisted and were commissioned. She also had heard from Clayborne that Blaisdell's proposal had been refused by Holly. She had almost gone to Holly, but had thought it better to wait a couple of days. Now, she was worried that she was going to lose Clayborne, that he would go off to the war without proposing marriage to her. If that happened, she figured it might be over with them. Distance and time changed things. They would both be different people when he came back.

When she saw him at her door in the handsome uniform, her mouth dropped slightly open, and she made a small gasp in her throat.

"Randy! What a shock to see you in that costume! You're absolutely—beautiful!"

Clayborne grinned. "Lieut. Randolph Clayborne, at your service, ma'am."

Jennifer's grandmother was impressed, too. She insisted that Clayborne have a cup of tea, which she served with silver, and Clayborne was obliged to tell the older woman all about his enlistment. She expected him to know De Beauregard personally, and all about how the war was going. Jennifer suppressed a couple of smiles. After about an hour, Jennifer excused them and they went out in back of the house into the garden. Jennifer was tense inside, not knowing Clayborne's intentions. She thought it might be one of the last times she'd ever see him. They stopped finally at a path juncture, under a persimmon tree, not far from where Holly and Jennifer had talked, before the celebration ball.

"How long do you have now?" Jennifer asked him.

Clayborne shrugged dramatically. "Maybe a few days, maybe a week or more. We'll be heading out to Tennessee by rail, I expect. Stuart and I will go together."

"That's good luck, Randy," she said.

"Stuart isn't very in tune with the real world sometimes," he said in an offhand way. "Maybe I'll be able to smooth some things out for him. I hope so."

"I wish—"

"What, Jennifer?"

"I wish you could have waited. It all seems so sudden."

Clayborne smiled his handsome smile. Actually, he had been as influenced by Blaisdell's decision to propose to Holly as he had by his friend's insistence on enlistment. Clayborne would not have thought of proposing to Jennifer before leaving, if Blaisdell had not gotten him excited about his proposal to Holly. When he learned that Holly had rejected Blaisdell, he had almost pulled back from this thing tonight. But he had worked himself up about those few days—or more—in Jennifer's bed. It was just that simple.

"It would be hard for us, whenever I left," he said in his man-of-the-world manner, keeping his secret well—

50

enjoying Jennifer's anxiety.

"I want to see you every day," she said. "Until you leave."

"Well, of course," he said, teasing her now, "there are other matters that will demand my attention: training, issuance of equipment. I'm a soldier now, you know."

"I guess after you're gone," she said, "you won't think about me anymore." She was very low. "You could even get . . . hurt."

Clayborne was grinning a playful grin. "What if I told you we're going to see each other for certain when I get back?"

She looked at him. "Really?"

"In fact, I rather like the idea of our being together day and night, before I leave. In some private place with a nice, soft bed."

She regarded him sidewise. "Oh, Randy. I couldn't do that. My grandmother would know. No, I couldn't do that."

His grin widened. "Not even if we were married?"

Jennifer's face changed, and became prettier in its sudden wonderment, softer and more innocent. "Married?" she said hollowly.

"Yes, married. Will you marry me, Jennifer? Tomorrow would be best, but I'll wait until the next day if you feel it's necessary. That ought to give us a little time."

Jennifer swallowed hard, then a wide smile erupted onto her youthful face. "Do you mean it? Do you really mean it, Randy?"

"Hell, yes, I mean it! Well, what's your answer, Miss Armistead? Yes, or no?"

Jennifer was overwhelmed with her sudden success, giddy with the victory for which she had fought so hard.

51

She had won one of the major prizes of the bachelor world in Charleston, and she had done it without looks, or money. Her eyes moistened slightly as she understood the magnitude of her accomplishment.

"Oh, yes, Randy!" she exclaimed breathlessly. "Yes, yes, yes!"

Clayborne pulled her to him and kissed her hard on her mouth, and she responded quickly, openly, without restraint. When it was over, he looked into her almost-green eyes. "Shall we go tell Amanda?"

"God, I can hardly wait to see the look on her face!" Jennifer said in hushed excitement.

Holly was very exuberant about Jennifer's quick engagement. She and Jennifer had a nice talk that next day, and Jennifer said they were planning the wedding for the following day. It would be small and brief, because there was no time for anything fancy. But Jennifer did not care. She had a lovely gown handed down to her from her mother, and she knew that she and Clayborne were going to make an attractive couple, standing before the altar at the First Baptist Church. Holly helped her try on the wedding gown, and pinned it in a couple of places where alterations had to be made. Amanda promised to do the sewing that very evening, and there was a lot of excitement flooding through the small house.

When Holly got back home that afternoon, she found a very different atmosphere there. Uriah Quinn had been home for lunch, and he had fed Charlotte's anger and frustration with regard to Holly and Blaisdell. Holly found Charlotte sitting alone in the kitchen—Cleo was upstairs doing some cleaning—ruminating about recent events over a cold cup of coffee. She was sitting there hunched over her cup, looking hostile.

"Jennifer wanted to know if she can expect you and Uriah at the wedding tomorrow," Holly said to her, as she came and sat down across from her mother at the kitchen table.

Charlotte looked up at her. "The wedding. Jennifer's wedding. That should be you going down that aisle tomorrow, Holly. You. You're ten times the woman that Jennifer will ever be. Except for that craziness in your head."

"Mother," Holly said heavily, "don't talk about Jennifer that way. She wants to get married, and I don't. It's not difficult to understand. We're very different persons."

"That's the damned truth!"

"Mother, I don't know what you expect of me. To do what *you* want me to do, to live my life the way *you'd* like to live it? What would be the point? The world already has one Charlotte Ransom. There's no reason to give it a duplicate now, do you think? I have to live my own life, Mother, wherever it leads me, follow the voices inside *me*."

"You can be a wife and mother and still be an individual," Charlotte said wearily. "I think we've been through this before, Holly."

"Yes, we have," Holly said. "And it always seems to end up the same way. Each of us keeps making her own proclamations about the way things must be, without ever establishing any common ground of understanding. I don't seem to be ready to marry, Mother. When I do get ready, I probably will not marry a man like Stuart Blaisdell. If you try to make sense of those two facts, you'll see what I've been trying to tell you."

"Stuart is as fine a suitor as any girl ever dared expect," Charlotte insisted, looking stony-faced. "Now it appears you've lost any chance with him. Unless you go to him before he leaves the city, of course, and tell him you've reconsidered."

Holly shook her head slowly. "Mother, you don't listen to me."

Charlotte rose, and went over to the nearby dry sink, leaning heavily onto it, faced away from Holly. "Well, if you're not ready for marriage, young lady, I just have to wonder what you *are* ready for. I won't have you going out and seeking employment in this town. I would be disgraced if others thought my daughter had to go out and work for a living."

"Disgraced?" Holly said wonderingly. "I don't understand that, Mother. It isn't a disgrace for a man to get a job, to go into business. Why should it be so shameful for a woman?"

"I don't know why!" Charlotte said irritably. "I just know that that's the way it it! You can't make the world over to your liking, Holly."

Holly sat there thinking about that. *Why not?* she thought. *Why can't I influence the world just a little, attempt to change it so it more closely fits my expectations?*

"It's just that so many things are happening right now," Holly told her. "Things I would like to be a part of. Maybe women can play some part in this war, besides tending to men."

"What do you want to do, put on a uniform and go to the battlefield with men?" Charlotte said sardonically. "They have a word for women like that, Holly, in case you haven't heard."

Holly was dismayed by her mother's lack of understanding. She rose, too, from the table. "You never answered my question, Mother. Will you and Uriah be at Jennifer's wedding tomorrow?"

Charlotte turned to her. "Oh, we'll be there, Holly. It will break my heart to see Jennifer being wed, with you standing off to one side, but we'll be there."

Holly nodded. "Jennifer will be happy to hear that, Mother."

As it turned out, there were a number of weddings taking place at the local churches in those weeks, with young men binding themselves more closely to their girls before they went off to the war. It gave them something more to come back to, something to carry along with them in their insides that made them feel less afraid. It was a tie to back home that was strong and important, and gave the soldier a strong and important reason for survival.

The Baptist Church had a wedding preceding Jennifer and Clayborne's, that next morning, and then one was scheduled later in the afternoon after theirs. Theirs was set for two-thirty P.M., and by one-thirty people were beginning to arrive. Jennifer herself arrived at about that time, in a hired carriage, already dressed in her wedding gown. She was all white satin and lace and rosy cheeks, and she looked very pretty. Her grandmother, Amanda, was everywhere at once, it seemed, arranging flowers, receiving gifts. There was to be a small reception afterward, in the churchyard under its magnolia trees. Jennifer secluded herself in an anteroom in the church, making last-minute preparations and hiding from Clayborne. She allowed only Amanda and Holly into the room with her, except for a brief visit by the minister. Out in the church, friends from school days arrived, and Clayborne's parents and relatives—his retired-seaman father looking very nautical with a pipe stuck in his bearded face. Blaisdell arrived at about two, but did not seek Holly out. He took a seat with his parents as the church filled up. Both he and Clayborne wore their uniforms now, and he looked very military sitting there somber-faced. In the anteroom, Holly was with Jennifer at the last minute, while Amanda was out greeting some guests.

"My God, I think I'm going to faint!" Jennifer said, standing there before a mirror in her wedding finery. "I feel very dizzy!"

Holly went and hugged Jennifer to her. This was a big day for her, too. Things would never be the same between them again, she knew. A married woman had different interests from a single one, made different friends, planned her life differently. "You're going to be all right, Jennifer. You look beautiful, and this is your big day! Keep calm, and think happy thoughts."

"Is Randy here? Have you seen him?"

"I haven't seen him, but he may be here by now. If not, he's on his way."

"What if he gets cold feet? What if he doesn't show up? God, wouldn't that be awful? What would I do, Holly? How could I face all those people?"

Holly sighed, went and opened the door, and looked out into the auditorium of the church. A smile broke onto her beautiful face. She was Jennifer's maid of honor, Blaisdell was Clayborne's best man. A distant uncle had come into town to give Jennifer away.

"He just came in," Holly announced. "My God, he's handsome!"

Jennifer came and peeked out, and swallowed hard.

"Yes, he is, isn't he?"

"You're a very lucky girl, Jennifer Armistead." Holly smiled. "There, that's the last time I'll address you by your maiden name."

"God!" Jennifer said.

Blaisdell was getting up to walk over to Clayborne, and so were a couple of other people. Clayborne looked stiff and uncomfortable. Holly closed the door again. "Well. It's only minutes now."

Jennifer looked over at her. "I wish it were a double wedding, Holly. I wish we were both doing it today."

Holly sighed slightly. "You know what?" she said. "I do, too. Right at this moment, I wonder if I made the right decision in turning Stuart down. He looked very impressive out there, too."

Jennifer put her hands on Holly's shoulders. Holly was wearing a wispy yellow dress and a yellow hat, her thick dark hair hung down. There would be more men looking at her when they came out, than at the bride. "It's not too late, Holly! I'll postpone this until this evening! We can still do it together!"

Holly hesitated. It was tempting. There was a lot of excitement and glamour attached to weddings, and there would be a double portion at a double wedding. It would be something she would remember always, standing up and taking her vows with her best friend—their men in their impressive military uniforms, on their way to a war. It was the stuff that dreams were made of.

"No, Jennifer," she said at last. "I can't."

There was a knock on the door, and then it opened on the smiling, bespectacled minister. "We're all set, Miss Armistead." Holly saw Jennifer's grinning uncle just behind him. Over at the altar, Clayborne stood stiffly,

57

with Blaisdell standing beside him. They already looked rather formidable, together, in their spit-and-polish uniforms. At the rear of the church, she could see a couple of other uniforms: Clayborne's commanding officer who had had to give permission for Clayborne to marry, and possibly, Holly thought, an aide. She turned to Jennifer.

"Well. Let's go," she said.

A moment later the organ began, and the minister was in place. At a nod from him, Jennifer and her uncle, with Holly in attendance, started around the outside of the church to its front door. Then Jennifer was marching down the aisle with her uncle. Holly came up a few steps behind.

It was all quite grand, despite the hurried preparations. Heads turned to see the bride. The organ played beautifully. In a moment, Jennifer stood beside Clayborne and they faced the minister. They exchanged a smile. Blaisdell glanced at Holly, and gave her a weak grin. The feeling came back even more strongly that she had made a mistake in rejecting his offer of marriage.

"Dearly beloved," the minister began, *"we're gathered here in the sight of God and man to join these two people in holy matrimony."*

It was a somber moment. Back at the rear of the church, Holly had seen Charlotte and Quinn, both looking grim. She wished they were not there. She wished she were not there. She wished it were she getting married. At least she would be doing something to move her life off dead-center.

"Do you take this woman, Jennifer Armistead, to be your lawfully wedded wife, to have and to hold, in sickness and in health, for richer or for poorer, so long as you both shall live?"

"I do," Clayborne replied. A bit uncertainly, Holly thought.

Jennifer was asked and replied to the same question, and a ring was produced, one that had been in Clayborne's family for a couple of generations. Suddenly it was on Jennifer's finger, and Holly saw a look of awe on her pretty face.

"By the authority vested in me by God and the state of South Carolina, the great mother of the Confederacy," the minister said, adding a few words to the traditional proclamation, *"I now pronounce you man and wife."*

There was a kiss, and in that special moment, Holly believed in Jennifer's marriage. It was a sacred thing blessed by God, and it would make them both happy, she was sure of it.

There was a hug by the uncle and Blaisdell, and then by Holly; and then Jennifer and Clayborne were headed back along the aisle, Jennifer looking buoyant behind her veil. The organ played loudly, and the spectators beamed happily; some rice was thrown as the couple stepped outside. They were followed by the spectators, who began shaking Clayborne's hand and kissing Jennifer. Holly was suddenly so envious she wanted to run and get away from it all.

Jennifer was busy now with friends and relatives. She told them all to meet behind the church, where there would be a cake and drinks and dancing. Clayborne kept his arm around Jennifer most of the time. Jennifer threw a bouquet of lovely flowers toward Holly, but some young girl from Jennifer's family caught it, reaching out in front of Holly. Holly was disconcerted for a moment, and when she caught Charlotte's eye, Charlotte was glowering toward her darkly.

When Jennifer and Clayborne headed toward the churchyard for a couple of ambrotype photographs, most of the guests went, too. Charlotte and Quinn did not stay. Holly looked and they were just gone. She went inside the church to say a few words to the minister, before going out into the churchyard behind the building, and suddenly she was face-to-face with Blaisdell. He had just left the minister, and they were quite alone at the entranceway there.

"Oh, Holly. Gosh, you sure look beautiful today."

Holly averted her eyes awkwardly. "Thanks, Stuart." She looked back up at him. "You look very nice yourself. You're handsome in your uniform. You really are."

He hung his head. "This was hard for me today, Holly."

"For me, too," she said. "Jennifer and Randy sure seem happy, don't they?"

He nodded. "Randy has taken a room at the Ladson Hotel. He can't wait to get Jennifer there." He blushed slightly.

Holly smiled. "I believe she feels the same way," she said.

Blaisdell looked into her deep-blue eyes. "We got our orders early today, Holly. We're leaving for Tennessee in four days."

"Oh, gosh," Holly said.

"Our Sixth Brigade of the Second South Carolina Volunteer Regiment will be assigned to General Bragg, in all likelihood. Randy and I will be in different companies, but will go everywhere together."

"At least that part is nice," Holly said. "I think it would be more frightening if you were going alone, each of you."

"We're scared, anyway." Blaisdell grinned. "Randy won't admit it, but I know he is, too. We've never done anything like this. It's all for the first time. That's what scares you. You wonder how you'll behave under all that stress. You hope you'll be a credit to your outfit, and your people back home."

"There isn't any doubt about that, Stuart," Holly said. "Not as far as you're concerned. Everybody knows you'll make a fine soldier."

He looked down again. "The other day, Holly, when I asked you—about us. You said that this was all too fast. That it was unexpected."

Holly held his gaze soberly. "That's right, Stuart."

"Well, it occurred to me. Maybe when this is over—in six months, or a year, or whenever—you'd be willing to reconsider. I mean, giving us a chance to know each other better. Maybe you wouldn't mind keeping your mind open until then. Things might seem different to you then; I might seem different."

Holly felt taut suddenly inside. "Why, I don't know, Stuart. I can't make any promises."

"Just say you won't close your mind to the possibility," he said rather urgently. "I mean, unless you meet someone else, of course. Just say you'll consider the question all fresh again, when it's over, or when I'm back. It would mean a lot to me, Holly, when I'm out there—an awful lot."

Holly sighed inwardly. "All right, Stuart. I'll do that."

He was suddenly grinning from ear to ear. "I sure appreciate that, Holly. I sure do appreciate that."

Holly felt very bad for him. "You don't have to be appreciative, Stuart. It's a good idea."

"Do you have an ambrotype or ferrotype I might carry

with me?" he said boyishly. "In my tunic?"

"Why, yes," she said, feeling a heaviness inside her, of responsibility. "I believe I have a picture somewhere. It might be a year or more old."

"That would be wonderful!" he grinned. He seemed like a different person from the one who had come to the wedding. He stuck his arm out for her to take. "Shall we go back to the reception?"

She took his arm uncertainly. She hoped she had not unduly encouraged him. It could only be worse later, if she had. She looked up at him with a warm smile. "Lead on, Lieutenant!" she told him.

Chapter Four

In a few days, Blaisdell and Clayborne were gone.

To Jennifer, who had spent those days in Clayborne's arms, it seemed as if half the city had been emptied, when Clayborne left.

For Holly, the war suddenly seemed like a real one. Even when she had gotten caught in the shelling from the blockade ships, she had not felt like this. Now all the young men were leaving, and some of them might not come back. In fact, reality dictated that some would not come back. One of those might be Blaisdell, or Clayborne. Or both could be killed.

Those were sobering thoughts.

The hospitals were beginning to overcrowd slightly, with the few injuries from the shelling, and a fall virus. Holly volunteered to help out at the main hospital, just to get out of the house, and this sort of thing seemed acceptable to Charlotte. Holly tried to get Jennifer to do the same—Jennifer was suddenly very lonely—but Jennifer preferred to sit at home and write letters to Clayborne, and read accounts of the war, hoping to find mention of the Second Volunteers.

Holly's duties at the hospital were administrative but menial, and they palled on her quickly. She disliked the white frock that she was required to wear, the smell of drugs and antiseptics in every corner of the building, the atmosphere of quiet that prevailed, tomblike in its pervading ubiquity.

Charlotte and Uriah Quinn went through a rather somber period. Quinn's business was going bad because of the blockade of the harbor, and their only other income was from a small house across town that Quinn rented out. Things became tight for them, and Charlotte was very aware that there were three mouths to feed. Holly offered to try to get a paying job at the hospital, but Charlotte forbade her. Quinn began drinking regularly, and Charlotte joined him.

Jennifer visited Holly with regularity, and invariably when she had a letter from Clayborne. Actually, Holly received more letters from Blaisdell than Jennifer did from her husband, but she did not let Jennifer know that. Jennifer told Holly that she missed Clayborne in her bed, and she told Holly details of their honeymoon intimacy that Holly would rather not have known. Holly thought that Jennifer thought too much about that aspect of her marriage.

In October there was a naval battle at Hilton Head, about halfway between Charleston and Savannah, and the federal men-of-war prevailed. Now Charleston knew that the blockade was not going to be lifted unless they somehow managed to win the war on the land. There was a resurgence of the bombardment of the city, and a few people were killed. A mood of gloom suddenly settled in, like a virus, eating at the heart of the proud city.

But there was more to come, and it came in the winter.

The letters from Blaisdell and Clayborne had tapered down, and then about the first of the new year they stopped coming entirely. Holly and Jennifer realized that their fellows were probably close to contact with Union troops in Tennessee. It was on a chilly winter afternoon not long after the letters stopped that Holly went over to visit Jennifer directly from her duties at the hospital. Jennifer had dropped into a deep gloom when the letters had stopped coming, and acted like a different person, moody and withdrawn. Holly felt it was her duty to try to cheer her friend, so she stopped by with a bouquet of flowers from the hospital, and some gossip about patients there. But halfway through her visit, the girls heard fire bells clanging in the distance, more than they had ever heard before. They both went outside to take a look, and a red engine went rumbling past, four horses galloping before it, firemen hanging on to its sides.

"My God, look!" Holly suddenly exclaimed.

They were both staring toward the center of town, where black smoke rolled skyward in several places, and they could even see some flames licking above the building tops. There was an enormous fire centrally, and it looked as if it were out of control.

"Oh, dear!" Jennifer muttered. "It looks—awful!"

"It's heading toward our house!" Holly said hollowly. "I have to get back!"

Just moments later she was driving her buggy home. When she came near downtown, she found the streets blocked off, and firemen waving traffic around. She could see now that there were store buildings burning, and a couple of public buildings, and a church. There were a number of private residences involved.

Her mother's house was just down the street where

many houses were burning. A fireman stopped her at the intersection.

"You can't go down there, miss! It's too dangerous! Some Yankee saboteur set fire to the whole damned town!"

"I have to go down there," Holly said fiercely. "I live down there! I'm Holly Ransom!"

He looked her over. "Well, it's your pretty neck. Go on in, but there's nothing down there we can save, now."

Holly whipped the dun mare, and the buggy jolted forward past the fireman. There was smoke thick in the street now, and charred pieces of wood and other debris. Sparks flew through the air. To her left as she drove past, a burned branch from a tall elm tree fell heavily to the ground, still blazing. It came close to the buggy, and the mare reared and whinnied loudly. Holly whipped it again, fear mounting in her. The horse responded, moving along at a nervous trot. Houses on either side were burning, and now she could see her mother's place loom through the smoke, on her right.

"Oh, no!" she murmured.

It had caught fire from the house nearby, and was already flaming. She drove the buggy right up to the curb there, and jumped off and ran toward the house. *"Mother!"* she yelled out. *"Mother, where are you?"*

She could not get inside. There were flames at the front door. She ran to the back, and as soon as she came around the house, she saw Charlotte, her hair bedraggled, her face smeared with char. She had just carried some silverware outside and placed it on the kitchen table out there, along with some other things salvaged from the house. Not far away, Quinn and a couple of neighbor men were carrying pails of water from a well to the house, and throwing it onto the siding.

"Mother!" Holly said loudly. She went over to her and embraced her, and Charlotte sighed heavily. "There's no saving it, Holly. It's gone. It's been in the family for three generations, and now it's gone." She was staring toward the house.

"Are you all right?" Holly asked her, observing the smears of black on Charlotte's face and arms.

"Yes, I'm all right," Charlotte said. "Fortunately, Uriah heard what was happening and hurried home. He helped me save some things."

Holly touched her mouth with her hand. "Oh, my jewelry! My books!" She started away toward the house, but Charlotte stopped her.

"It's too late now," she said. "You can't go back in. There's fire throughout the house."

Holly sank inside herself as she saw the flames appear at an upstairs window. It had been such a beautiful house. She had never thought much about it until that moment, but she had loved it. She had been born in it, and her father had bounced her on his knee in it. She had had birthdays in it, and sparkling, snowy Christmases in it. Seeing it burning now, it was like watching the entire first portion of her life being destroyed. Tears filled her eyes. "Oh, damn," she said.

"I know," Charlotte said wearily.

Down the street they could hear fire-engine bells, but they were not coming to their house. There were too many others, too many important buildings.

The men had stopped bringing water to the house. There was obviously no point in it. The ones who had been helping Quinn now walked to the next house down the line, to throw water on its siding. It had not yet

67

caught fire, and probably would not. Quinn came over to Charlotte and Holly, looking dirty and tired. Holly had never seen him looking like that.

"They might as well not have been here," he said angrily. "The crazy bastards were throwing the water just anywhere. Now it's gone. I don't even know where we'll stay tonight."

The flames were coming through the roof now, and the house was being fiercely consumed before their eyes. Quinn looked toward Holly, as if seeing her there for the first time. "Where have you been?" he said sharply. "You could have helped."

Holly narrowed her blue eyes on him. "I came as soon as I knew about the fire," she said darkly. "Don't you suppose I have an interest?"

"Sometimes I don't know where your interests lie," he said. "You could have been here saving some of our things, if you hadn't been socializing down at that hospital."

Holly was incredulous. "Socializing? Is that what you think I've been doing there?"

"All right, please, you two," Charlotte said. "Not now. For God's sake, not now."

The fire crackled and roared not far away. Holly was in mild shock; everything she owned had been destroyed in the house. Quinn's attack on her only served to deepen the shock. She turned to her mother.

"There seems to be nothing I can do here. If you need me to help move these few things somewhere, I'll be at Jennifer's place. I'll be staying there tonight. You two probably can, too, if you don't mind the lack of privacy."

"No, thanks," Quinn said sourly, staring toward the fire.

Holly gave him a sober look, then regarded her mother with suppressed emotion. "When you want me, Mother, you'll know where to find me."

She returned to the street then, making a big detour around the flaming house, trying not to look toward it. As she passed, the roof caved in at the front, making a fiery crash that echoed darkly in her head, and caused her to quicken her pace in fear.

The fire finally was gotten under control in Charleston, but not before its fury had wiped out a portion of the central city. The rumor persisted that northern spies and saboteurs had set the blaze, but there was never any evidence to support the theory. Regardless of its cause, though, the fire could not have come at a worse time. The blockade and intermittent shelling of the port had already lowered morale considerably, and the fire had dropped it to even lower levels. Over those succeeding winter weeks, debris was hauled away and a general cleanup took place. But nobody's heart was in it. The ruins of Charlotte's house were razed, and she sold the lot, not having the money to rebuild, with Quinn's business so bad. The tenants in Quinn's smaller house across town were given notice, and in March Charlotte, Quinn, and Holly moved into the place. Amanda had asked Holly to stay with her and Jennifer, but Holly realized that the house was too small for the three of them, and she did not want to wear her welcome out. Anyway, Charlotte insisted that Holly come to Quinn's house. She had the notion in her head that it was a slur on her somehow if her unmarried daughter went to live with someone outside the family.

The house was a two-story one, but about half the size

of the one Charlotte had owned, and no more comfortable for three adults than Jennifer and Amanda's place. There was no privacy. Holly could even hear Charlotte and Quinn in their bed, and that was very embarrassing to her. Even more, too, than at the other place, it seemed that Quinn was everywhere. Holly could not seem to get away from him, and she sensed that Quinn liked it. He liked being able to catch her partially clothed, or putting on make-up, or fixing herself before a mirror. He liked the extra familiarity.

Holly hated it.

General de Beauregard had gone off to Tennessee, too, taking the rest of a division with him, and leaving the defense of Charleston to subordinates. An upstart Union general named Grant had attacked Confederate garrisons at Fort Henry and Fort Donelson in Tennessee, and had won the day each time, earning the nickname of Unconditional Surrender Grant. So De Beauregard, considered one of the South's finest generals, took a sizable force to the area to halt the momentum of the Yankees under Grant. Blaisdell and Clayborne were shifted back under De Beauregard's command, and their companies saw some skirmish action in the first part of April, as the southern army squared off with Grant's gathering hordes.

The large opposing forces finally confronted each other on a sunny April morning near Shiloh Church, in a wooded section of Tennessee. Blaisdell's and Clayborne's companies were wakened before dawn with the blast of bugles, and then ammunition was being disbursed and orders shouted. The two knew this was going to be the big day.

70

There was some sparring between opposing cavalry for a while, and then the big guns opened up to soften resistance on each side. Despite explosions all around them, Blaisdell's and Clayborne's companies waited side by side under the shelling. A few men were hit. Then the commanders were out before them, brandishing sabers, their flags and banners waving. Blaisdell, crouched with his company under a large, spreading oak tree, glanced off thirty yards and could see Clayborne kneeling with his men, waiting. Blaisdell's company moved off first.

He could not see the enemy for a few minutes, then they became visible through some trees. Muskets were cracking now, and the new rifles that some units had, and men were moving forward slowly at first, then more quickly. Blaisdell was up and moving, firing his musket and reloading, his blood coursing through his veins. Men began falling all around him. There was a hand-to-hand confrontation in a gully, and he became involved in it. A blue-suited Yank tried to run him through with a bayonet. Blaisdell jerked back and missed being skewered, the blade ripping shallowly along his side. He clubbed the soldier in the head with the butt of his gun, then fired a shot into his chest. He saw his first enemy die by his own hand.

His stomach was upset for a while.

The Union forces fell back, and he and Clayborne followed up, bringing their companies forward. The cacophony was ear-dinning, with the rattle of small fire and the thunder of cannon. Blaisdell stepped on a soft thing; it was a Yankee corpse. He kept moving forward.

But then, finally, the Yanks held and began pushing back. There were so many of them that every time one was killed, two more sprang up to take his place. The

71

woods and fields were full of them. Hot lead sang around Blaisdell's head, and he thought surely he would be killed. He felt it deeply inside him. The call came to fall back, and there were more bugles piercing the other noise. Blaisdell reluctantly ordered his people to withdraw, and he saw that Clayborne was doing the same, over on Blaisdell's left flank. A cavalry rider went thundering past on a gray stallion, badly wounded, and a shell exploded right under him. When the smoke cleared, there was almost nothing left to bury.

Blaisdell tried not to look.

Finally, five hours from the start of the battle, it was finished. De Beauregard's rebels had fought valiantly, but had been overwhelmed by Grant's superior numbers. The southerners had retreated from the field, and Shiloh belonged to Grant.

None of them would know it that grim spring afternoon, but the total casualties on both sides that day would amount to twenty-three thousand, and both armies would refer to the battle as Bloody Shiloh.

De Beauregard encamped that evening miles from where the battle took place, and his army licked its wounds. De Beauregard regarded Grant now as a crazy man, to throw troops so wantonly into battle. But Grant had again won the day.

At the encampment of the Sixth Brigade, Blaisdell was tended and bandaged in early evening, but then forgotten. There were too many wounded and dead to give much attention even to the seriously wounded. Blaisdell's wound was shallow and unimportant, so long as he did not allow it to become infected. There was a mess call at dark, for those who were ambulatory, and shortly afterward, Randy Clayborne walked over from his K

Company. He had not been wounded, but he was dirty-looking and fatigued. He came and sought Blaisdell out where Blaisdell sat under a young tree, his canteen and eating implements beside him on the ground.

"Oh, there you are. Hey, did you catch one?" Clayborne said, as he knelt beside Blaisdell, studying the bandage.

"No, it was a bayonet," Blaisdell told him. "It's just a light wound, Randy. You look as if you got through it all right."

Clayborne sat down beside him at the base of the tree. Out in the growing darkness were the fires of the encampment, glowing like fireflies in the night. "You bet I did, old buddy. I spent half of the battle crouching under a mulberry bush, hoping the fight would pass me by."

Blaisdell squinted curiously at his friend. "Really?"

"Why not? Are you surprised, after what you saw out there today? That was a living hell if I've ever seen one. Rebs were running away from the fire all around me. At least I stayed to fight, if anybody wanted to look for me. I kept some of our people with me, and they thanked me for it, later."

Blaisdell found himself a little angry with Clayborne. If he and a few others had not been intimidated by Yankee numbers, they might have held. Fortunately, most rebels fought like tigers on that bloody field, and put up a fight to be proud of.

"Well," he said, "I guess each of us gets through it in his own way."

Clayborne gave him a look. Randy's gray uniform was torn along its right sleeve, and his face was smudged with dirt; his dark hair hung onto his forehead. It was very

73

unlike him to be anything but neat and tidy, and his present appearance gave him a rakish look he had never had at home. Blaisdell, however, looked more physical, more masculine—possibly more handsome.

"Look, Stuart, I think it's time I clued you in before you get yourself killed. You don't play hero out there. Nobody does that has any sense. You get crafty, you sneak around a lot, and if somebody gets in your way, you kill him before he gets the chance to kill you. That's the way real wars are fought. I saw you out there today, at the head of your company, waving your gun. This isn't some dime novel, Stuart. None of these people will thank you after you're dead. Try to survive, so we can go home together. That's what the Yanks are trying to do."

"Is that why I saw thousands of them lying on the field out there today?" Blaisdell asked acidly.

Clayborne shook his head. "It's getting hard to talk to you. Maybe you'd feel differently, if you had a wife back home. It would kill Jennifer if I didn't make it back. I have others to think about, Stuart."

Blaisdell thought that he had never known Clayborne, not really. Maybe it took something like a war to bring out what was really inside a man, he thought, sitting there in the darkness.

"I have Holly back there," he finally said.

Clayborne looked over at him with a small grin. "Maybe. But I doubt that she's exactly holding her breath until your triumphant return from battle," he said lightly.

Blaisdell turned and stared darkly into Clayborne's face. Suddenly he had had quite enough of Clayborne for one evening. "Maybe Jennifer isn't either," he said evenly.

74

Clayborne gave him a dark, hostile look. "That's a damnable thing to say to a married man! I'd be back there with Jennifer now, making us a family, if it weren't for you, by God!"

"Me?" Blaisdell frowned. "What the hell are you talking about, Randy?"

"I only joined up to keep you company. I could have held off in Charleston for another six months, maybe a year, with my father pulling some strings. I could be at home with my loving wife."

"You wouldn't even have married Jennifer if you weren't leaving," Blaisdell said in a level voice, being tough on Clayborne. "You as much as told me so."

"I never said that!" Clayborne said rather angrily. "And you never spoke to me this way, back home. What's gotten into you out here? Do you think you've become a hero, suddenly?"

"Maybe I've become a man," Blaisdell said.

"And I haven't?"

"Oh, hell, Randy. Let's cut it out. I didn't mean any of that; I just had to get some bile out of me. It must be the wound."

Clayborne eyed him sideways. "Well, you are different."

"Just lay it to the battle," Blaisdell said. "Oh, I meant to ask you how you fared at the camp girls' tent a few nights ago. Did you get what you went looking for?"

Clayborne turned to him and gave him a handsome smile, and he seemed, for a moment, like the friend Blaisdell had known back in school. "Does a nigger like watermelon?" he replied conspiratorially.

In Charleston, summer neared again and there was no

75

evidence that the war was winding down. Holly resumed her work at the hospital, and kept out of the house as much as possible. She and Charlotte were required to do all the housework now. The woman, Cleo, who had been off on errands when the fire had taken their house, had been just too expensive to keep on, and too difficult to maintain in a small place. Quinn sold her to a lawyer for five hundred dollars, and a month later she had run off, heading north, it was thought, via the underground railway. She had not liked her new master. The lawyer threatened to sue Quinn for return of the sale price of Cleo, but he was not on solid legal grounds and knew it. A man was not responsible for the antic behavior of a sold horse or mule; nor was he for the recalcitrance of a slave.

Of course, Charlotte considered it a step down to sell Cleo. Her family had always owned at least one slave; all the good families of Charleston did. It was like being without a good buggy, or proper silverware for the table, not to have a slave about. The loss of the house and Cleo had been quite a blow for Charlotte.

The war continued to seesaw back and forth in the East. In March, McClellan had taken Yorktown for the federal forces, but then lost at Williamsburg. Now, in June, he made an attempt to take Richmond, and that, too, was a dismal failure. Lee began taking a more active part in the field, and the war took a turn for the South.

Jennifer was changing with every week that passed. She had hoped to become pregnant with Clayborne's child, but now was glad she had not. By some twist of logic, she blamed Clayborne for going off and leaving her, after marrying her.

"Maybe you did the right thing after all," she told Holly one late afternoon, when Holly had stopped by to

76

see how Jennifer was doing.

"What do you mean?" Holly asked her. They were upstairs in Jennifer's bedroom. Jennifer was propped on her bed, against the headboard, with just her under-pantaloons on, and a laced-up vest covering her full torso. Holly, her white hospital frock on, her dark hair caught up on top of her head, was sitting in an armchair near the bed.

"I mean, in rejecting Stuart's proposal," Jennifer said. "I mean, maybe I was hasty in marrying Randy just before he left for the war. I'm beginning to wonder what I get out of it. Even the letters have stopped, now."

"They're probably prohibited from sending letters," Holly told her. "It's all part of the war, Jennifer. It's something we have to live with."

"We?" Jennifer said. "I didn't think you were in the same situation."

Holly gave her a look. "I didn't mean that I was. Jennifer, you're going to have to accept the war and Randy's involvement in it. It will all be over one of these days, and with a little luck, we can all take up where we left off."

Jennifer eyed her narrowly. "What if I told you that Randy never left off?" she said slowly.

"What?" Holly said.

Jennifer sighed. "One of Randy and Stuart's old school chums came back on furlough a couple of weeks ago. He's gone again now. But while he was here, he told this girl I know that Randy has been having a fine time. He thinks Randy has been visiting the camp girls. When this girl from school saw me at market the other day, she could hardly wait to repeat the story to me."

"Oh God, Jennifer!"

"So now you can see why I'm a little bitter. Sitting here on my thumbs, bored to tears. While Randy lives it up in Tennessee."

"Did this soldier say he had actually seen Randy with a camp follower?" Holly said.

Jennifer shrugged. "I don't think so."

"Then there isn't any real proof, is there?" Holly said. "This guy might be just a malicious gossiper, or maybe he has some grudge against Randy."

"Sure, maybe," Jennifer said with bitterness. "It's easy to assume things like that, when you're in your position."

Holly made a face. "You mean, like losing my home, and all my belongings, and living under the same roof with a man married to my mother but who looks at me as if I were a South Battery Street whore?"

Jennifer looked chagrined. "I'm sorry, Holly. I really am."

"It's all right," Holly told her.

"Does Uriah really act like that toward you?"

"I'm a little afraid of him, Jennifer."

"You could come back here," Jennifer said.

"No, I can't impose on you and Amanda, Jennifer. I'll be all right. I'm sure Uriah's leer is worse than his intentions." She smiled. "Don't forget what I told you, now. Randy is off fighting a war for us. Give him the benefit of the doubt; he deserves it."

Jennifer grimaced. "I'll try, Holly," she said.

It was about an hour later when Holly arrived back home at the small house on a small lane just off King Street. The neighborhood was quite different there from the one at Charlotte's house. The yards were rather small, the houses closer together. Some of the houses were run-down, with flaking paint or busted windows. A shell from an early federal bombardment had cratered an empty lot, and nobody had done anything about it.

Holly was unhappy there.

She drove the buggy around the small barn behind the house, and stabled the mare, noting that the other buggy was there, too. She figured that meant that Quinn and Charlotte were both home. But when she let herself in at the rear door, into the kitchen, there was no odor of cooking about the place, and Charlotte was not visible anywhere.

"Mother, I'm home!" Holly called out.

There was no reply. She walked through the house, and saw no one. Sometimes Charlotte insisted Quinn take a walk with her before supper. They were probably out on foot together, Holly thought.

She went upstairs to her room, and began undressing. She would change and start supper, to surprise Charlotte. She was glad nobody was there; she enjoyed the privacy. She took off her white frock, and her shoes and stockings. Then off came her underclothing. She would run a hot cloth over her body and wash away the fatigue of the day. She went to a pitcher and bowl at the side wall across from her bed, took a cloth, and poured some water into the bowl. She was stark naked, and she liked being able to stand there so without having to lock and bolt her door, as usual. But then she felt a presence with her, eyes on her. She whirled back toward the corridor door, which she had left partially ajar.

Uriah Quinn stood there.

She gasped loudly. His gaze traveled over her breasts, her hips, her thighs. She reached for a big towel on a rack beside her, and held the cloth up to her nakedness. *"Uriah!"*

He was in his shirt sleeves. He had obviously been in the other bedroom, and had chosen to keep his presence secret from her, until that moment. He was looking at her hungrily from the corridor. With an easy movement, he pushed the door further open, and stepped into the room.

"Well. My darling stepdaughter. How beautiful you look this way, Holly dear." His voice was low and purring.

"What are you doing?" she said loudly. "Get out of here at once!"

"Now, that isn't friendly. I'm sure you don't really mean it, not after parading yourself for me like you just did. Like you do often, dear Daughter."

"What?" Holly said incredulously, trying to cover her nakedness with the towel. She saw a breast exposed, and covered it, but the towel came up on her thighs higher. "I'm telling you, Uriah! Get out of here at once! *Mother!*"

Quinn grinned. He closed the door behind him, and then walked on over to her. Holly moved away from him, backing up toward her bed. The towel fell away and exposed her hip to him. She was frantic.

"Charlotte has gone shopping," he said in a level voice. "She asked me to tell you that she won't be back for a while."

"Oh, God," Holly muttered.

He came up very close to her. "Don't you think I know what's going on here? You want something to happen between us, don't you? Flaunting your young flesh around this house, tempting me."

Holly was outraged and terrified at the same moment. "That's a lie, damn you! Get out of here now! Have you

80

gone mad?''

But it was not madness that had taken hold of Quinn. She could smell the liquor on his breath now, and see the dull look in his eyes. It was alcohol that had hold of Quinn, together with his lust. He reached out to her with a grin. She backed up to avoid his touch, and fell onto the edge of the bed. The towel fell away where her thighs met, and Quinn stared hungrily.

''Yes,'' he growled.

In the next moment he had dropped down beside her on the bed, and was grabbing her flesh into his arms. ''You know you want this, don't put on an act for me, honey!'' He pressed his mouth to hers, and she smelled the reek of alcohol about him.

She broke away from the kiss, in a panic. The towel had fallen to the floor, and he had her nakedness in his grip. His rough hands were on her breasts, mauling and hurting. She screamed loudly, but the windows and the door were closed. He did not mind. He got her under him on the bed, and was preparing to mount her. He intended to rape her, and it was all happening very quickly.

''Come on, don't play games with me,'' he growled. ''Let it happen, nobody will know but you and me.''

''*Stop!*'' she cried out, as he fumbled with himself. ''*Stop it, damn you!*'' She found his whiskered face with her hand, and dug her nails into it and raked them across his flesh.

There was a guttural cry from his mouth, and his hand went to his face, where blood popped out in three long, deep scratches. Fury darkened his eyes, and then his hand came and slapped her hard across her face. She was dazed by the blow, and lay gasping and weak under him.

''Is that the way you want it?'' he spat out. ''Well, I

can oblige!"

But in that next moment, there was a sound outside at the front of the house. Charlotte was back, and was opening the door down there. Quinn rose off Holly quickly, looking toward the sound. Then a crafty look came on his face as he straightened his clothing.

"Of course not, you terrible girl!" he said loudly. "You ought to be ashamed of yourself!" Then he turned and hurried to the door, flung it open, and retreated down the hall to the other bedroom.

Holly was too much in shock to be bewildered by his behavior. She shuddered all over when she realized that he was really gone; then she took in a deep breath and called out to her mother.

"Charlotte!" she cried out in anguish, lying there bruised and trembling. *"Oh God, Mother! Please help me!"*

Chapter Five

Charlotte stood staring down at her daughter, eyes wide, mouth slightly agape. Holly sat on the edge of the bed, the towel back over her, trembling visibly. Her long hair was unkempt-looking, and there were tears on her cheeks; her face was red where Quinn had slapped her.

"Good Lord, what's going on here!" Charlotte whispered.

Before Holly could reply, Quinn came to the door for a brief moment, neatly attired again. But there were the three scratches along his face. "Whatever she tells you, it's a damned lie!" he said loudly. Then he pounded down the stairs, and slammed the door as he left the house.

Charlotte turned back to Holly, bewildered. "Holly, what happened here?"

Holly looked up at her. "He—tried to rape me. He was going to—rape me." She held back small sobs.

"What?" Charlotte said in disbelief.

"I told you about that man! How he's been looking at me! I thought I was alone in the house. But he came in here, and—" She broke off, trying to control her shaking.

Charlotte came and sat down beside her. "Why are you undressed, Holly? Why would you be undressed with Uriah in the house?"

Holly looked over at her, a hardness gathering inside her now. "I was undressed to wash, Mother! I thought I was alone in the house! He was here somewhere—hiding from me, damn it!"

"That doesn't sound like Uriah," Charlotte said levelly.

Holly stared at her. "Didn't you hear what I said, Mother? Don't you understand what he did?"

"Are you saying that Uriah came in here and tried to . . . have sex with you?" Her voice was hollow-sounding and faint.

"I'm saying that he tried to force me!" Holly insisted, getting herself under control finally. "I'm saying that he would have raped me, if you hadn't come back when you did! Don't you see the mark on my face? Didn't you see the scratches on his, where I defended myself from his grasping hands? Do you think I'm making all this up, Mother?"

Charlotte looked down at a partially exposed breast of Holly, and found Holly's young, ripe flesh angered her, for the first time ever. She stood back up, and clasped and unclasped her hands. Her face was very pale. "I'll go find Uriah and discuss this . . . thing with him. Get your clothes on, Holly. I'll be back."

Holly stared blankly after her mother as she left the room. She could not believe the reaction she had gotten. She thought Charlotte would be as outraged as she was, maybe more. She went and dressed quickly, trying to quiet herself inside. She heard Charlotte's voice outside the house, and then Quinn's. It sounded like a surprisingly reasonable dialogue, from that distance. Holly went and combed her hair out, and then sat numbly on the bed, just beside where he had pinned her down with his strong arms. She wondered if she could sleep in that bed again. She wondered if she would ever feel the same in this Quinn house. She heard Charlotte coming back up the stairs. She tensed inside as Charlotte appeared at the door, and came into the room. Charlotte closed the door behind her, her face sober.

She crossed her arms defensively across her breasts, and walked to a window that looked out over their small yard. "I spoke to Uriah," she said.

Holly turned to regard her soberly.

"He says you lured him in here."

Holly rose slowly from the bed. "What?"

"He says you've found ways to show yourself to him before, Holly. He admits he lost control, seeing your young flesh. But that it was you who tried to seduce him. He admits it might have happened, too, if I hadn't returned. He seemed very honest about it."

Holly could not believe her ears. "Honest! My God, Mother, he's lying to you!"

Charlotte turned and met her gaze, but said nothing.

"What about my bruises? His scratches? Does that sound like I seduced him, for God's sake?"

"He says you did that to him when you heard me outside, and that his natural reaction was to slap out at you. He says you did it to make me believe he was the aggressor. He says he's sorry if he hurt you."

Holly turned away, staring blankly. "My God," she said.

"I knew it was bad, having two women in one small house with a healthy, virile man," Charlotte said, rather

85

to herself. "I knew it was bad to move in here. But we had no choice."

Holly came and looked into Charlotte's eyes. "Mother, do you believe that I tried to seduce your husband?"

Charlotte held her gaze for a moment, then looked away. "I don't know what the truth is, Holly," she said quietly. "I know that something happened in here that wasn't good. But how can I place blame, with Uriah telling me one thing, and you something else?"

"That man is a bastard!" Holly said angrily. "If he'll do this to me—and to you—what else is he capable of? You can't stay with him, Mother! Don't you see that?"

Charlotte cast a weary look at her daughter. She looked ten years older than before the blaze that destroyed her family home. "Uriah is all I have, Holly—besides you. I'm sorry, but I have to place some credence in his version of this. I won't blame him, and I won't blame you. But I don't want to see anything like this again in my house. This isn't a brothel here."

Holly found herself short of breath, so angry was she at the moment. She hesitated for a long moment, then walked to a nearby closet, opened it, and began taking her clothes out of it.

"What are you doing?" Charlotte asked her.

"I'm not living in this house with that man," Holly said hoarsely. "If you won't tell him to leave, then I'll go. You won't have to concern yourself about this sort of thing happening again, because I won't be here to expose myself to his damned lechery!" She was throwing clothing onto the bed, blindly.

Charlotte could not bring herself to go touch Holly, to deter her physically, not at that moment. "Don't be foolish now, child. You have no place to go."

"I'm going over to Jennifer's house," Holly told her in the thick voice. She threw some more things onto the bed. "She and Amanda will take me in temporarily. I'll find something while I'm there. Maybe they'll put me on the staff at the hospital. I could pay for a private room in a boarding house, with a small income."

"Holly, please," Charlotte said. "This isn't necessary. I think you and Uriah and I should sit down and talk this out like three mature adults. You are obviously an adult now, even though underage. We can come to an understanding about this."

Holly turned to her with a deep scowl. "Talk, you say? You want me to talk reasonably with the man who tried to rape me? Maybe encourage him to try again, later? I'm your daughter, Mother! Don't you care what's happened to me?"

Charlotte did finally come over and place her arms around Holly, her own eyes moist now. "Holly, Holly! Don't go off like this!"

But less than a half-hour later, Holly was gone.

Amanda and Jennifer accepted Holly into their house graciously. Amanda allowed Holly to help with chores, when she was not at the hospital, and Holly realized that that was a sign of warm acceptance. Jennifer and Holly were like schoolgirls for a couple of weeks, staying up late at night together and rehashing old times. But even with Holly there, it was apparent that Jennifer was getting more and more bored with her life. For months a girl cousin in Savannah had been asking Jennifer to visit and tell her all about her marriage, and Jennifer now decided that with Holly there temporarily to keep Amanda company, this summer might be a good time to go away for a short time. There was no war around Charleston and Savannah, except from the sea, so it was still safe to travel that distance. One bright July morning, not long after news of a rebel failure at Mechanicsville, near Richmond, Virginia, Jennifer left by coach for Savannah.

Jennifer's brief absence made Holly realize even more acutely how crowded it was in the small house when all three of them were there, and she accelerated her efforts to secure a job at the hospital that paid a salary. But none was forthcoming at that time. Charleston was suffering from the blockade, and there was little money around. Even food was becoming scarce in some quarters.

After Jennifer had been gone three days, Charlotte stopped past, had tea with Amanda and Holly, then got Holly alone and asked her to return home. She was more embarrassed at having Holly living with Amanda than she was afraid of what might happen between Holly and Quinn at her own home. But Holly would not go, anyway. She would not return to the same household with Uriah Quinn.

Jennifer was gone less than two weeks. When she returned, she looked more alive, and prettier, than she had since the wedding. She was anxious to tell Holly about Savannah, and when they were alone in their shared room that first night, she began confiding to Holly about her good times there.

"Beth has all these beaus," she said to Holly as they lay and sat on Holly's bed in their long nightgowns. Holly lay on her side, her long hair flowing down over her shoulders; Jennifer sat cross-legged beside her, her gown hiked up to bare her thighs. "She's like you; she likes being single. And does she have a great time, Holly! She goes out two or three times a week, and with different fellows

88

There are still a lot of young men around in Savannah."

Holly did not even enjoy talking about men nowadays, since the incident with Quinn. She had made that clear to Jennifer, but Jennifer was becoming insensitive to Holly's feelings, it seemed. She even seemed to take the Quinn incident rather lightly, after the first day.

"It sounds as if she must have shown you a nice time, Jennifer," Holly said with forced enthusiasm.

Jennifer rolled her green-gray-hazel eyes. She was using more make-up now to enhance her looks, and it made her prettier from a short distance, but up close she looked a little harder than before. "Did she ever," she replied. "I wish you had been there, Holly. She has enough men hanging around for all of us."

Holly frowned slightly. "Why so many, Jennifer?"

Jennifer glanced at her coyly. "She keeps them happy, Holly. Do you know what I mean?"

Holly's frown deepened.

"She—well, she's nice to them."

Holly narrowed her blue eyes on Jennifer. "Are you saying that she sleeps with them?"

Jennifer grinned conspiratorially. "When it pleases her to."

Holly did not return the grin. "That must have been . . . interesting for you, Jennifer."

Jennifer laughed in her throat, a laugh that was new to her. "It was more than interesting," she said.

"Yes?" Holly said slowly.

Jennifer glanced over her shoulder, as if Amanda might have sneaked up to the door in the corridor to listen to their conversation. When she turned back to Holly, she lowered her voice so that it was almost inaudible. "Beth introduced me to this very masculine

89

fellow," she said. "He's off to the war in another week, with a captain's commission. God, he was fun!"

"In what way?" Holly pursued carefully.

Jennifer took in a deep breath. "I hope you can keep a secret, old friend of mine."

"Of course, Jennifer."

"Well. He took me to this park, and we kissed under a tall elm, in the dark. Then he spread out his jacket on the grass behind this lilac bush."

Holly studied Jennifer's young, made-up face.

"We were—lovers, Holly."

"Oh God, Jennifer," Holly whispered.

When Jennifer saw the look of shock on Holly's face, she was suddenly defensive. "Do you see anything wrong with that?"

"Jennifer. You're a married woman."

"So is Randy married. Isn't he? Why should it be so much nicer for him? I have physical needs to be satisfied, just as Randy does. The war has changed all the rules, Holly. I shouldn't have to tell you that. It's bringing women into the modern world."

Holly got up off the bed and walked to a dark window. "I suppose so," she said.

"Come on, Holly. It isn't as if I just lost my virginity, you know. It isn't as if either one of us did."

Holly turned to her. "It's just that you made promises to Randy, Jennifer."

"Just as he did to me," Jennifer said, defiantly.

"Well, of course, there's more than that, too. This thing in Savannah was so—casual. You can't take it all so lightly, Jennifer. You can't give yourself to a man as if you were kissing him on the cheek. It can all become too—easy."

Jennifer was regarding Holly darkly now. "I think your experience with Quinn has changed you, Holly."

"Why, do you think I was promiscuous before that?" Holly said.

Jennifer's face flushed. "No, I don't! And I'm not promiscuous, either, damn it!"

Holly went over to the bed, across the small room from the window, where Jennifer still sat cross-legged, thighs bared. She glanced at Jennifer's nicely turned thighs, and at the fullness of her breasts under the nightgown, and realized why a man would be attracted to Jennifer, if he thought he could get her into bed without difficulty.

"I didn't say that," Holly said heavily. "I think we'd better drop it, Jennifer, it's all over and past. It's none of my business, anyway."

Jennifer held her gaze. "Agreed," she said soberly.

A year ago, Jennifer would never have spoken to Holly like that. She would have deferred to her, listened to her. But she was emerging into the world as her own person now, and it was apparent that Holly was going to have a few surprises along the way. It was also apparent that the Armistead house was becoming too small for Holly's accommodation as a guest.

Holly came around the bed as Jennifer got off it to go to her own, and kissed Jennifer on the cheek. "I hope I haven't said anything to hurt you. I want us to be friends always."

Jennifer returned the kiss, her dark mood gone as quickly as it had come. "I can't imagine why not," she said in her new, worldly way.

The war was gaining even more momentum. There was another big battle at Antietam Creek in September, near

91

Sharpsburg, Virginia, McClellan against Lee. McClellan carried the day, but failed to press the advantage of his success.

In Tennessee, the Second South Carolina Volunteers were defending the Chattanooga area from Union harassments, and there were some skirmishes and limited offensives on both sides, but nothing like Shiloh. Blaisdell and Clayborne's companies, J and K of the Sixth Brigade, were encamped in the Cumberland Valley not far from Chattanooga. They had both been involved in small engagements, but nothing serious. Blaisdell's wound had healed, and neither of them had been hurt again.

Randy Clayborne had terminated his visits to the camp girls when they became less accessible. He had not become more loyal to the memory of Jennifer; it was just that the girls available were not worth the extra bother, now. Clayborne was becoming more and more disenchanted with the army, and in particular the infantry. He felt he was not that much above the gun-toting soldier in the forefront of all the fighting, and he figured he was better than that. He began complaining about everything—supplies, the food, the guns they had to fight with. Blaisdell did not much like being around him anymore. He did not seem like the same fellow he had befriended in school those several years ago.

One warm October afternoon just after Blaisdell had gotten off picket duty at the perimeter of the encampment, he went and had something to eat at the outside mess area, where trestle tables were set up near the canopied company kitchen. All around Blaisdell were tents, rows of them that stretched out along the riverbank in both directions. Rifles and muskets were stacked before the tents. Down by the river were wagons with and without canopies, and picketed horses and mules. A couple of the wagon canopies had red crosses painted on their cloth. In an artillery company down the line, cannons could be seen lined up facing the river, and a couple of big-mouthed mortars rested on platforms with wheels.

Blaisdell had a plate of stew and a chunk of hardtack bread, and it tasted good to him. When he first arrived at the front lines, the food had seemed terrible. Now he relished it. It was all a matter of adapting, he decided.

He had just about finished the stew when he saw Clayborne walk up to the long table where he sat. The only other man at that officers' mess was a first lieutenant down at the far end of the table. He wore a heavy beard and spectacles and made no sign that he knew Blaisdell was there. Clayborne came up and heaved himself onto the bench across the table from Blaisdell.

"Just come off guard, eh?" Clayborne asked him.

"Yes, I had to place some pickets along the rear of the encampment," Blaisdell told him. "One fellow had a musket that wouldn't fire. He didn't seem to see anything wrong with that. I had to get him a good one."

Clayborne made a face. "Such are the responsibilities of leadership." In a sour tone, "I've just been checking out the number of tent stakes in our company supply. Can you imagine? Counting tent stakes? God, I thought we'd have some authority here, Stuart. A couple of brigade people have been promoted to first, but not you or me."

Blaisdell grinned slightly. He looked older than he had when he'd arrived in Tennessee, and the new character in his face made him better looking. "I guess our fathers'

93

influence doesn't reach clear into Tennessee," he said lightly.

Clayborne did not smile. "You don't mind this a whole hell of a lot, do you?"

Blaisdell shrugged. "I'd rather be in Charleston, if that's what you mean."

Clayborne sat staring out past Blaisdell, toward a row of canvas tents that sat on muddy ground. "Well, I'm tired of the dirt and the mud, my boy. I'm tired of menial work and bad food. I don't particularly like the prospect of being shot at regularly, either."

"Hell, none of us do, Randy," Blaisdell said. His uniform was torn and dirt-smeared now. He washed it every few days, but could not seem to keep it clean. Some of their enlisted men had only half-uniforms, or none at all. A few had only the guns they had brought from home.

"Don't you think we ought to do something about it?" Clayborne suggested to him. "Instead of just sitting on our butts talking about it? Day after day, night after night?"

"Do something?" Blaisdell said. "What can we do?"

"Transfer, that's what we can do," Clayborne told him.

"Transfer?" Blaisdell said curiously. "Out of the front lines, you mean?"

"I mean, out of the infantry," Clayborne said, lowering his voice. "Listen, there are other units in this army that aren't getting shot at every other day: the engineers, transport, communications—even intelligence."

"Intelligence?" Blaisdell said. "What's that?"

Clayborne made a face. "Honest to God, Stuart. Didn't you ever hear of information-gathering? Spying on the enemy? Both sides have people that do that. It's exciting, and adventuresome. Civilized, in comparison with this."

"Spying," Blaisdell said, rolling the word around in his head. "I don't think that would be for me, Randy. I'm more for an open, straightforward confrontation."

"Where you get your head blown off if you move the wrong way?" Clayborne said.

"I hear they shoot spies when they catch them," Blaisdell countered.

"So which is better? To have the off chance of being caught as an enemy agent, or go out and risk your neck every day with bullets flying around you? That's what it will be like, you know, before this is over."

Blaisdell sighed. "Randy, that's a fun idea. But war isn't supposed to be fun, is it? I think we're needed right here where we are. I think we can serve better here than almost anywhere else. I couldn't ask for a transfer under those conditions."

Clayborne was dark-visaged. "My God, I'm not suggesting we desert! We'd still be serving the Confederacy, doing something else. Something more suited to our standing in the world."

Blaisdell shook his head. "If you want to look into it, Randy, go ahead."

"You wouldn't care if we separated?"

Blaisdell looked at him. "I think each of us has to follow his own feelings in this. If that takes us down separate paths, I guess that's the way it will have to be."

Clayborne nodded. "All right. I see I can't talk any sense into that hard head of yours. I'm going to look into getting the hell out of here. If you want to stay, that's your business."

"Yes," Blaisdell said to him. "I guess it is, Randy."

*　　　*　　　*

Just a couple of days after that exchange between Blaisdell and Clayborne, Holly applied for a job in a millinery shop in Charleston, one located on Broad Street. Holly knew a woman who had quit there, owing to ill health, and she thought perhaps there would be a place for a newcomer. But the job did not materialize. With business so slow, the owner of the shop could not afford to replace the lost clerk. He had to say no to Holly.

Holly was at a dead end, it seemed. She could not stay on at Jennifer's place indefinitely, particularly since she and Jennifer had had the disagreement. But she could not move out into the street, without some means of support.

She was mulling that situation in her head, on that cool October afternoon at the hospital just before time to leave her tour of duty, when Charlotte stopped by to see her. Holly had just finished some assigned work— cleaning up a couple of rooms vacated by discharged patients—and Charlotte found her in an employees' lounge, having a cup of tea before going back to Jennifer's house. There was nobody else in the room. When Holly looked up and saw her mother enter, she was quite surprised. Charlotte had never come to see her at the hospital.

"Mother! What are you doing here? Is something wrong?"

Charlotte came over and sat at a table with Holly. There was a teapot on the table, with a cloth caddy covering it to keep its contents warm. "Will you have some tea with me?" Holly offered.

"No, nothing is wrong, and yes, I'll have some tea." Charlotte smiled at her.

Holly went and got her a cup and saucer from a sideboard and poured for Charlotte. The tea steamed in the coolness of the room.

"Is everything all right at home?" Holly asked her, finally.

"Oh, yes," Charlotte said, looking wearily at Holly. She was a handsome woman, Holly thought, despite what she had gone through recently. She had not looked nearly her age, before the house fire. Now, she pretty much did. "How is everything at Jennifer's house?"

Holly shrugged. "How can it be, with three women in that small place? I don't feel that I can keep on there, Mother. But I can't find a position to earn any money, and I won't return to your place." She figured she might as well close off that possibility immediately, so that Charlotte did not bring it up again.

"Are you and Jennifer still getting along?"

Holly narrowed her lovely eyes slightly. "Has anybody told you we aren't?"

Charlotte smiled. "Oh, oh. I smell trouble."

Holly sighed. "No, there isn't any real trouble. Jennifer and I are just becoming different people from the ones who were so close in school, Mother."

"You two were never alike," Charlotte said. Her eyes were a lighter, more washed-out blue than Holly's, and her hair was not so dark. Her eyes had lines around them now, and Holly hated to see them there.

"Maybe not," Holly said. "Maybe we just thought we were."

Charlotte looked down at her teacup. She had not tasted its contents yet. "I wrote to your Aunt Eugenia in Baltimore not long after you moved out," she said. "To tell her our bad news, and to ask how things were there."

"How is Baltimore?" Holly asked.

"It's a divided city, Holly. Some wanted secession,

some didn't. Of course, the Union Army settled the question by moving in and taking control of Baltimore and Maryland. A lot of citizens moved south while they could. There is still some movement back and forth, among relatives. There's kind of a truce on the matter, between the armies."

"What about Aunt Eugenia and Uncle Preston?" Holly wondered. "What are their sentiments?"

"My sister is nonpolitical," Charlotte said. "I believe Preston favors the North in this great dispute."

"That makes sense," Holly said sourly. "Preston always backed the side that seemed most likely to win. He backed the Mexicans in Texas, until the United States came into the struggle. Father told me that."

"Ashby never liked Preston very much, I guess. But he's a greatly respected lawyer in Baltimore, Holly. He and your father were very different men."

"I always liked Aunt Eugenia," Holly said.

There was a momentary silence between them, then Charlotte spoke again. "Holly, when I wrote to Eugenia, I told her that we have an—uncomfortable situation at home, between you and Uriah."

Holly frowned at her. "Why would you mention that?"

Charlotte sighed. "I asked her, Holly, if she and Preston would mind taking you in for a while. I said you wanted to work, and that you could probably pay your way after you were settled in there."

Holly was speechless. She looked past Charlotte, as if trying to see her future somewhere there in that white, glistening room.

"I just got a letter back," Charlotte went on. "Eugenia said that she and Preston would be glad to have you."

Holly looked back at her mother. "It really does bother you, doesn't it? My being here across town with Jennifer?"

"It isn't right, Holly. I think you know that, now. Eugenia is my sister, and she has a large, roomy house and no children. She says there are job opportunities in Baltimore for young women. Since that seems to be what you want, you could look into that. There are also some very eligible young men available there, despite the war. She would like to introduce you to some, and put you in a position to meet others. She says she would enjoy having you in the house." She studied Holly's face. "What do you think, Holly?"

"Well, first of all, I don't know how I would like being in the same household with a Yankee lawyer, somebody who might try to convince me that the South is wrong in its struggle for freedom."

"Preston isn't like that, Holly. He wouldn't press you to change your views."

"How would I get to Baltimore?" Holly wondered. She had visited Eugenia and Preston Fayette once there, when she was only fourteen, and had liked Baltimore quite a lot. There were theaters and concert halls and big libraries, and the stores and shops were crammed with interesting merchandise. "I'd have to cross Union lines."

"That's no problem," Charlotte told her. "I've already asked an adjutant of General de Beauregard. You would be given papers for safe passage, and the federal troops would honor them. It's done quite often."

"I wouldn't want the Yanks doing me any favors," Holly said grimly.

Charlotte smiled. "They wouldn't be. Southerners and

99

Yanks cross the lines from both directions, in situations like this. There's a kind of treaty situation agreed to by both sides. Eugenia says Preston would meet you at the picket line, in case there would be any difficulty there."

Holly's head was buzzing with the ideas Charlotte was thrusting at her. "Well," she finally said, "maybe I do need a change of scenery."

Charlotte smiled again. "If you didn't like it there," she said, "you could always come back to Charleston."

Holly looked into her mother's face, and saw the extra lines there that the world had drawn on it, and felt a great rush of affection for her, despite what had happened in the Uriah Quinn incident. "I couldn't stay there permanently, Mother. Charleston is my home."

"You wouldn't have to—not unless you wanted to. It would all be up to you, Holly."

There was another silence between them; then Holly's face broke into a slow smile. "All right. I'll go."

Charlotte felt tears in her eyes. "Oh, I'm so glad, honey!" She came around the table and leaned over and embraced Holly warmly, and Holly felt close to her again.

"You won't forget you have a daughter in the hands of the enemy?" she joked lightly.

Charlotte shook her head vigorously. "Never, Holly," she said tearfully. "Never."

Chapter Six

There was a stagecoach line that was still making runs between southern cities and Baltimore, at the sufferance of the Union and Confederate Armies. Private vehicles were being allowed through, too, with proper papers. But the crossing was a bit easier on the public carrier. So Holly and Charlotte arranged to purchase a fare for Holly on the coach, and she left Charleston just before Christmas.

It was all very difficult for her. She had traveled some before, but never with the idea of living somewhere other than Charleston. It was very frightening. Even the idea of the trip was unsettling in this time of war.

Holly left on a cold December morning. There was frost on the grass and a threat of snow flurries in the air. Charlotte was at the depot, and Jennifer and Amanda. Quinn would have come, but Holly requested that he not be there. Quinn was going to work only about half a day now, and was drinking more and more heavily. Holly imagined none of it was easy for Charlotte.

There was a teary good-by, and then Holly was off, riding through the streets of her beloved Charleston with a very heavy heart. She was riding with two middle-aged men: one an emissary of Jefferson Davis on his way to Washington to complain about the treatment of rebel prisoners of war, and the other a Connecticut businessman who had been allowed to visit a dying brother in Charleston. They both were formally polite to Holly, but then after the trip started they spoke between themselves only. Holly did not mind.

The trip was to include stops such as Wilmington, Norfolk, Richmond, and Washington. Military lines were to be crossed at Fredericksburg or thereabouts. The front moved every so often—Union General Burnside had attacked Fredericksburg earlier in the month, and had been repulsed in six charges against Confederate positions—but not much activity was expected during the colder weather.

Overnight stops were made at Wilmington and Norfolk, at coach inns. Holly was given warm, comfortable quarters at each stop, and had no complaints about her treatment. During the day the ride on the coach was long and tedious, with only a lot of barren, sometimes snowy terrain to look at. Holly bundled up in a blanket and kept fairly warm in the vehicle. On the afternoon of the third day, they reached the front.

They had glimpses of the military all along the route, but now it was different. There were soldiers everywhere, particularly in and around Fredericksburg. Uniforms and more uniforms were what Holly saw on all sides, and mounted officers and tents. All kinds of military wagons jammed the roads and streets; cannons and mortars were everywhere. In the south part of Fredericksburg, Holly saw a field hospital. Men in bloody bandages were limping around or lying on stretchers. It was not a pleasant sight, and she thought immediately of Blaisdell and Clayborne, and hoped they were all right.

Not far north of Fredericksburg the coach stopped at a military checkpoint, and the passengers were obliged to disembark there to have their papers looked over. They were taken into a tent one at a time, Holly first. A lieutenant and a corporal sat at two tables, and the lieutenant examined papers. He looked at Holly's for several long moments, then looked up at her. He was a sandy-haired fellow with a strong drawl, and Holly figured he was from Georgia or Alabama.

"You're going to Baltimore to live, miss?" he said to Holly.

"Yes, with an aunt," Holly told him.

"Do your sentiments lie with the South, Miss Ransom?"

Holly was indignant. "Of course they do. Do yours?"

He grinned. "They had damned well better, if you'll excuse my French. What about this aunt of yours, Miss Ransom? This Eugenia Fayette? Is she a northern sympathizer?"

"No, she isn't," Holly said. "Why, would it matter?"

"We like to keep track of these things, ma'am," he replied. "This Preston Fayette. What does he do for a living?"

Holly sighed heavily. "He's an attorney, Lieutenant. Maybe you'd like his life history?"

He grinned again, and so did the corporal, sitting nearby. "I don't have time for that, I guess. Well, I guess your papers are in order. Why would a nice southern girl like yourself want to go to live in Baltimore?"

Holly shrugged. "It's personal, Lieutenant. There are things that are still personal, you know, even in a war."

103

He nodded. "You're plain right about that, Miss Ransom. Sorry if we've inconvenienced you. I hope you spend a good time in Maryland. I hear it's a beautiful state."

Holly smiled at him, finally. "Maybe the South will own it, one of these days soon," she suggested.

"Now there's a good thought." He grinned at her.

It was only a few miles to the Union lines. There was another guard post, and another tent, and this officer was a captain. He questioned Holly at even greater length than the Confederate lieutenant had, and was less friendly. Holly did not like him. But she had to admit that there seemed to be more efficiency in this Union post than she had witnessed in the rebel one, and there was more of a military bearing about the place. Uniforms were new-looking; rifles and muskets gleamed with cleanliness. *Putting on a show for us*, Holly thought. But she knew it was more than that. The North was better organized, and better equipped. It had been from the beginning, and she guessed the disparity between it and the South would increase, rather than diminish, as the war continued. When she was finished in the tent, she waited outside near the coach while the men were questioned. She had been there only a few minutes, when two Union soldiers came up to her, from the nearby encampment. One was a sergeant, the other a private. Their uniforms were neat and clean, but their manner as they approached seemed rather arrogant to her.

"Well, look at the southern belle!" the sergeant said as they walked up to the coach. The vehicle was anchored to the ground with iron anchors, and the team was hitched to a rail there. The driver had gone off to a smaller tent for a cup of coffee, so Holly was alone there, except for the newcomers.

"Say, she is something to look at!" The private grinned.

Holly glanced darkly toward them as they came up. The sergeant leaned against a large spoked wheel on the stagecoach, and looked her over openly. She turned away from the twosome.

"Hey, don't turn away, sweetheart," the sergeant said to her. "We want to talk to you. Are you from Virginia?"

Holly turned to face them again. "I'm from Charleston. If that's any of your business."

"Charleston!" the sergeant said. "That hotbed of rebellion! My, you must have a lot of ginger in you, honey."

"If you don't mind, I'd like to be alone here until my coach leaves," she said in a firm voice. She looked away again.

She heard them laughing softly between them. "Hey, honey. You own any slaves down there in Charleston?" the private said to her. He was slightly shorter than the sergeant, but thicker through the chest and shoulders. They looked like drinkers, to Holly.

She did not bother to reply.

"How are them southern gentlemen in bed?" she heard the sergeant say, with another throaty laugh. "Do they make your blood run hot, Charleston belle?"

Holly turned red-faced. "Please leave me alone or I'll call the captain!" she said loudly.

They did not concern themselves with that warning. "I'll bet you make them southern gentlemen's tongues hang out all the way down to their belts, honey," the private said. "Hey, maybe you'd like to come over to our

105

camp and meet a few fellows. They all like southern belles, you can bet. We could show you a real good time. You could get a later coach on into Washington."

Holly was furious inside. "You damned—Yankees!" she said harshly to them. She was trying to decide whether to get into the coach, or return to the post tent, when the emissary emerged from the tent and walked over to them. He became dark-visaged when he saw the soldiers grinning at her.

"Excuse me, ma'am," he said in a level tone. The soldiers turned to look at him. "Are you all right?"

Holly took a deep breath in. "Yes. I believe so," she said.

He looked at the sergeant balefully. "If you boys will excuse us, we have private business here," he said in a low voice.

The two held his gaze for a moment; then the sergeant shrugged. "Hell, let's go get us some coffee, Tad. I can't stand the smell of perfume on a man."

The private grunted. "It does kind of clog up the sinuses," he said. He looked at Holly. "Have yourself a good time up north, ma'am. I'm sure you will."

A moment later they were gone. The emissary turned to Holly with a grim look. "All Union soldiers are not like that, Miss Ransom. I've seen some rather pleasant ones."

"Don't make excuses for them, sir. They are just exactly as I thought they might be. Don't attempt to rehabilitate their image in my mind. It isn't possible."

He nodded. "I understand perfectly, Miss Ransom."

An hour later they arrived at a big camp, and the coach stopped again. There were several private buggies and carriages sitting about. When Holly disembarked, a tall, silver-haired man walked up to her, and removed a

106

tall hat.

"Holly!" He smiled. "I'd have recognized you anywhere, I think. How you've grown, and how lovely you are!"

It was Preston Fayette, the maritime lawyer, and he looked even more distinguished to Holly than when she had seen him several years ago. He kissed her on the cheek, and she returned it. "It was so nice for you to meet me, Uncle. I know it was a long drive for you."

"Nonsense," he told her. "We'll be back home before nightfall. Traffic in Washington ought to be light today."

They left before the coach, and very shortly were driving through the North's capital. The last time Holly had been through it, it had been her capital, too. It was all very strange, this war—brothers fighting brothers, cousins killing cousins. It was a particularly sad war, from that aspect. They drove past the capitol, and Holly had difficulty reminding herself that it was the capitol of the enemy. Troops were in evidence everywhere, with their blue uniforms and caps and their polished equipment. They seemed formidable to Holly, when she remembered that Blaisdell and Clayborne were out there somewhere, challenging their might. It was all frightening.

The drive from Washington to Baltimore was not a long one, and they did arrive there well before dark. It was a cool, rather blustery day, and Holly was glad when the trip was finished. The Fayette home was located on the south side of the big city, so they did not have to drive through the heavily trafficked downtown area. When they finally pulled up onto the drive of the rather sizable mansion with its high pillars and wide portico, Holly was very impressed. There were big trees lining the drive from the street, and an expanse of lawn. The house presented a glistening white façade. Eugenia was out on the portico to meet them as they drove up.

"Holly, dear!" Eugenia greeted her, as she climbed off the carriage with Preston's help. "How good it is to see you again!"

Eugenia looked a lot like Charlotte, although she was two years older, and there was some gray in her dark hair. Her eyes were hazel rather than blue, and she had never been as good-looking a woman as Charlotte. Her facial structure was not as interesting, her mouth not as sultry, her eyes not as pretty. If she had had a daughter, she could not have been the beauty that Holly was. Eugenia and Preston had had a son, but he had been killed in an accident involving a horse-drawn wagon, when he had not quite reached puberty. The couple had finally gotten over the tragic loss well, but had never bothered to move into a smaller house when they had had no more children.

Holly hugged herself to Eugenia. Eugenia had always treated her like a daughter, and Holly felt a special warmth toward her. "You look wonderful, Auntie! Not a day older!"

Eugenia smiled at her. She had thrown an elegant-looking shawl over her against the cold. That, in fact, was Eugenia's hallmark—her easy elegance. She was slim and delicate-looking, and she had always had the finest clothes to wear, even some things from Paris.

"Come now, Holly. I see you've come into some of that charm your father had."

They all went inside where there was a big fire going in the fireplace in the library just off the entrance foyer. Holly was given some hot tea there, and then while

108

Preston brought her things in, Eugenia took her up a wide staircase to her room on the second floor. The room was spacious, and had two large windows that looked out over a wooded lot. There was a canopied bed, a bureau, washstand, and even a short sofa. Holly liked it. She had slept in it when she was fourteen, but had not appreciated it then. Eugenia showed her the large wardrobe against the wall, an ornate oak affair where her clothes would be stored and hung. Then Holly went and sat on the big, soft bed and Eugenia joined her there.

"I'm glad I came, Aunt Eugenia," Holly said.

"Please, dear, just Eugenia. I feel old enough as it is! Preston and I have been looking forward to your coming, you know. We're glad we could help you escape from what had become a bad situation for you there in Charleston. Charlotte told us how difficult it was for you, with a new father in the house—the lack of privacy, and so forth. He was, after all, just another man to you. You can't be blamed for being an attractive young woman."

Holly met her gaze. "Is that what Mother said? That I'm not to be blamed?"

Eugenia raised her arched brows. "Well, she mentioned how Uriah lost some control because of his close proximity to you; how he was tempted by your youth and beauty." She smiled in embarrassment. "I suppose that's natural for a man."

Holly was angry inside all over again. "Eugenia, it isn't the way Uriah reported it. He would have raped me."

Eugenia stared at her curiously. "That's a strong word, Holly. Of course, I suppose anything could happen under those circumstances. We won't conjecture on it or discuss it further. Things will be different here, won't they?"

Holly regarded Eugenia with the same kind of look Eugenia had given her a moment before. "Why, I would hope so, Eugenia."

"You've always been like our own, to Preston and me. I think coming here is just what you've needed, Holly. You'll be off on a right course now, headed in a different direction, so to speak."

"I don't think I understand, Aunt Eugenia."

Eugenia touched her shoulder with a slender hand. "There will be a different environment for you in this home. We'll read the Bible regularly, Holly. I'll have little talks with you, about social amenities and womanly behavior. Hopefully, we'll find something for you to do, so that you're kept busy outside the house through the day. Preston has a couple of ideas. When you're ready, I want you to go out to some social functions, meet some of the right young men."

Holly nodded uncertainly. "All right, Eugenia."

Eugenia took a deep breath in and let it out, as if she had accomplished something very important. "Good. I know we're all going to get along just fine here. You'll be responsible for your room, and you may help me plan meals if you have an interest in that sort of thing. We have a Negro cook and maid, Holly, but they're paid servants here in Baltimore. Next month, Lincoln is expected to make it all official. He'll issue a proclamation freeing all slaves, here and in the South."

Holly stiffened slightly. "That seems a rather presumptuous thing to do. Since he no longer has any authority over the South."

Eugenia smiled again. "Charlotte told me you have strong feelings about the war and secession. A lot of local citizens here have the same feelings as you, Holly, and we

110

all live together without trouble. I suggest you do what Preston and I do: keep out of political discussions. Nothing productive can come of them."

"I'll keep that in mind, Eugenia," Holly said.

"I just know it. I just know we're going to get along fine," Eugenia said.

Holly was a bit apprehensive about her new home, after that indoctrination speech by Eugenia. Eugenia seemed to be under the impression that Holly had grown up a little wantonly, and that it was up to her to make things right—to turn Holly into a proper young woman. There had been a militant air in the briefing, a feeling that cooled Holly's previous ardor for her aunt. She had never thought of Eugenia as a prude or a martinet, but there was a little of both in her manner on that first introductory day.

She decided, however, not to concern herself too much with it. Charlotte had made it clear that Holly could return to Charleston if she did not like it here, and Charlotte would help her find a way to settle in back home. Or, once Holly found herself a job, she could just move out if she so wanted, and find accommodations elsewhere in Baltimore. There would be little Eugenia or Preston could do to stop her.

Holly had a pleasant Christmas at the Fayette house. There was a big tree and a lot of decorations, and Holly received presents not only from Eugenia and Preston, but from several of their friends. There was a gathering on Christmas Eve, and some talk of the war. Holly began hearing, for the first time, references to the Confederates as the enemy. It seemed strange.

There were no presents from Charleston, even though

111

she had sent one each to Charlotte, Jennifer, and Amanda. It was as if all of them had just written her off and forgotten about her. It was clear that she was out in the world on her own now, and had to make a new life for herself.

In January Abraham Lincoln issued an Emancipation Proclamation that supposedly freed all slaves in all states, and further angered and alienated the South. General Lee avenged that move shortly thereafter by soundly beating General Hooker at Chancellorsville. Hooker was the recipient of some bad publicity, and the camp girls he tolerated in such profusion began being referred to as "Hookers." The northern newspapers were full of lurid accounts of the war, many of which were gross exaggerations of fact.

The Emancipation Proclamation even earned the President some enemies in the North, and the press reported the unearthing of a couple of plots against his life, apparently by southern spies.

In February, with snow on the ground in Baltimore, Holly got a job in a small florist's shop down near the port's sprawling waterfront area. She had been alerted to the opening by Preston Fayette, but she secured the job through her own charm and persuasion, and that pleased her very much. The salary was modest, but it allowed her to pay the Fayettes a room-and-board allowance and made her more comfortable in staying with them. More importantly, too, Holly knew she could pay about the same amount at any of several houses and hotels for young ladies, and be completely independent. That gave her a new look at life, and a new feeling for it. She began buying her own clothing, having teas in lovely down-town parlors, patronizing the libraries on her own

She had really become a woman.

As of that moment, she quit waiting for letters from Charlotte and Jennifer. She could no longer send letters to Blaisdell, so she was cut off almost completely from her old, rather adolescent life.

That now pleased her, too.

The religious aspect of the Fayettes' home life was not as severe as Holly had imagined it might be. There were little prayers at the table, and a couple of Bible-reading sessions on week nights, and church on Sunday. It was the Episcopal Church that the Fayettes belonged to, and Holly found it all rather interesting, with its overtones of Catholicism. But she had gone, irregularly, to a Baptist church in Charleston—the one Jennifer had been married in—and the Episcopalians seemed a bit formal and stiff to her.

There were brief instruction sessions, too, with Eugenia trying to bolster Holly's knowledge of etiquette and social protocol. The sessions soon began petering out, though, when Eugenia saw Holly's natural poise, grace, and charm. Holly was not likely to do much to embarrass herself in public, and that quickly became clear to Eugenia.

Probably the worst aspect of Holly's living with Eugenia and her lawyer husband was the tendency on Eugenia's part—Preston treated Holly very objectively and very remotely—to treat Holly like a fallen woman in need of reform. Eugenia was very careful never to leave Holly alone in the house with Preston, even if servants were about. Preston was given the duty of transporting Holly across town in the carriage only infrequently, and if there was an appointment on the other end. Holly had her own bathroom, and it was made clear she was not to use Eugenia and Preston's. She was told by innuendo that she was not to move about in the house unless fully clothed.

It was apparent that Eugenia had been convinced by Charlotte that Holly had a bit of the seductress in her, and that she was not to be trusted with husbands. Holly ignored the implications of Eugenia's tactful rules because she saw nothing wrong with them, and she figured Eugenia would eventually come to see her for what she was.

Holly kept to herself as much as possible, and learned her work at the shop, and met people at work and at tea rooms who were also sympathetic to the Confederate cause. All in all, she was glad she had come to Baltimore.

By April of that year of 1863, the snow was gone for good and Baltimore began to warm up. Holly knew that in Charleston there would already be trees and shrubs in greenery, and flowers would be out. But there were also reports of an increase in the bombardment of the city, and she found herself worrying some about Charlotte and Jennifer. Apparently, the federals had established shore batteries adjacent to their warships, and were now able to shell Charleston from land and sea.

Holly would go down to the harbor at lunchtime on some days. It was full of federal warships: brigantines and ironclads. Looking out at them, Holly thought they represented a physical superiority of the North that the South might find it difficult to overcome. She resented it that these citizens of Baltimore and the eastern shore of Chesapeake Bay were safe from the guns of those ships, and that the people of Charleston were made to suffer under them.

In the middle of April, Eugenia came to Holly one early

evening in Holly's room with an invitation in her hand.

"There's to be a state reception at the Maryland Hotel," Eugenia said quite excitedly. "The ambassador of France is here from Washington, and will be honored at a banquet and ball. There will be young government officers there, and the military, and some very prominent young businessmen. Preston's invitation includes you and me, Holly, and I'd like you to go."

Holly was standing near her bed, and had been putting away some clothes. She frowned slightly. "I don't think that sounds like my kind of thing, Eugenia."

Eugenia made a long face. "Please, Holly. Preston thought this would be so good for you. There's a rumor that the President might show up. He's coming to Baltimore to talk with a couple of business leaders about the war effort."

"Lincoln is *your* President," Holly said. "Not mine, Eugenia."

Eugenia sighed. "All right, forget Lincoln. There will be excellent food, good wine, dancing, and fun. We'll bring you home early if you're not enjoying yourself."

Holly hesitated, then smiled at her aunt. "All right, Eugenia. I'll go. But I'll hold you to that promise."

It was only three days to the reception, and Eugenia spent most of the time finding just the right gown for Holly. The one they ended up with was a little conservative, Holly thought, cut high in front and back. Holly accepted Eugenia's choice, though, and soon the evening of the reception was there.

They drove to the hotel in the carriage, and a black valet parked the rig for them on a parking area behind the building. Many other local dignitaries were arriving, and Preston Fayette knew most of them. Holly was intro-

115

duced to some people in the lobby of the hotel, which was all glass chandeliers and potted palms. Then they all went to the banquet and ballrooms.

The dinner was excellent, featuring Baltimore seafood. Lincoln was nowhere in evidence, so Holly figured the story about him was pure rumor. After the meal, they all moved slowly into the ballroom adjacent, and a couple of young businessmen danced with Holly. She was polite to them, but they did not appeal to her. There were also military officers present, and they looked smart in their uniforms. Holly was introduced to the French ambassador, a small, elderly fellow who did a lot of smiling and spoke poor English. Holly heard a lot of talk about the war, as she moved about.

A lot of men looked at Holly, younger and older, and she found that she did not mind the attention. Despite Uriah Quinn and the aftermath of her encounter with him, Holly liked being attractive to men now. In Charleston, it might have been different. But here she could treat the episode with Quinn like a bad dream.

Holly turned down a couple more offers to dance, and she and Eugenia walked among the onlookers. Men were standing together, carrying on discussions in earnest tones.

"Oh, yes, it's definite. Hooker will be replaced. Probably by Meade. The President is disgusted with him."

"There's going to be a big confrontation in Mississippi." By a colonel in the Union Army: "Grant is massing a large force there."

"The rumor is that Pemberton will defend in the Vicksburg area. Jefferson Davis has a lot of confidence in him."

Holly passed among them, awed by the real information that could be overheard about the war, at a gathering like that one. Information that could help win a battle, possibly—or a war.

She and Eugenia stopped at a punch bowl and a black servant poured them each a cupful into cut-glass cups. While they were still standing there sipping at it— Preston Fayette was off discussing politics with a couple of other prominent lawyers—the band suddenly struck up "Hail to the Chief," and all eyes turned toward the doorway. Holly's jaw dropped slightly when she saw the tall, bearded, black-suited man standing there, surrounded by his itinerary. It was Lincoln.

"My God, the President!" Eugenia said in a hushed voice.

Lincoln was smiling and waving to the crowd now, but the smile was a weak one. Holly was impressed with the fatigue written on his face, and the intelligence and melancholy in his dark eyes. She had not dreamed she would be favorably taken by the looks of the man whom the South hated and ridiculed, but she was. He was passing among the crowd now, speaking here and there to a general or an official. The band continued its playing, and some dancers went on with their dancing. Lincoln stopped and spoke to several women as he passed through the hall.

"Oh, my! He's coming right past us!" Eugenia whispered.

In the next moment, Lincoln was there at the punch table, with three of his aides beside him. One of them offered him a drink, and he declined. He came past Eugenia and Holly. He nodded to Eugenia. "Madam. I hope the punch has a little punch this evening."

117

Eugenia smiled at the joke. "It's very good, Mr. President."

Lincoln turned those melancholy eyes on Holly, and she felt the great charisma of the man. "My, what a lovely young lady. Shouldn't you be out dancing, miss? In such a pretty gown?"

"I will be, Mr. President," Holly said. "I'm just taking a short rest."

An aide came up to Lincoln. "This is Mrs. Eugenia Fayette, Mr. President, the wife of Preston Fayette, the maritime attorney. And their niece Holly Ransom." He had already been briefed by an official host also walking along behind the group.

Lincoln nodded. "Mrs. Fayette. Miss Ransom. You both grace this hall with your charm and elegance."

Eugenia murmured a reply, but Holly was tongue-tied. Then the President was gone, moving on to speak with a couple of generals.

Lincoln left the ballroom with the French ambassador not long thereafter, and then Preston came up very upset because he had not been with Eugenia and Holly when they met the President. He had never been introduced to him. Holly danced one more dance, with a young Union officer—she was becoming more objective about the people she socialized with—and then the three of them returned home.

Holly had enjoyed her introduction to Lincoln more than she ever would have thought, and her opinion of him changed abruptly. Nobody with eyes like that could be a villain. He might be wrong in some of his views, but you could not doubt his sincerity, his devotion to the cause of right as he saw it.

The next time Eugenia asked Holly to go to a gala affair, she would not hesitate. There was, after all, nothing wrong with rubbing elbows with Union elite, so long as her own convictions were not compromised.

The summer came again. Grant and Pemberton squared off at Vicksburg, Mississippi, and Grant whipped the rebels again. Then, at Gettysburg, Pennsylvania, General Meade, who had replaced Hooker, beat the almost unbeatable Robert E. Lee.

The South was very low in morale.

At their camp in Tennessee, Blaisdell and Clayborne had seen some more action, but on a limited scale. De Beauregard was off to other sectors of fighting now, but the Second Volunteers had been left in place under General Bragg's command, which occupied Chattanooga and most of the Cumberland Valley. A fellow named Rosecrans had been put in charge of the Union's army of the Cumberland, and it was rumored that Rosecrans was planning a big attack on Chattanooga in the near future.

It was hot that summer in Tennessee, and Blaisdell was not accustomed to such heat untempered by the winds off the Atlantic. He tried to keep cool, but could not. Clayborne suffered too, but not in silence like Blaisdell. Finally, though, he came to Blaisdell one evening with a broad smile on his handsome face.

"Well, Stu, old sport, I finally did it."

Blaisdell was sitting outside the tent that he shared with another lieutenant, and was trying to read a book of poetry by an oil lamp. He put the book down as Clayborne took a seat on a campstool beside him.

"Did what?" Blaisdell asked him. "What are you so damned happy about Randy?"

Clayborne's smile widened. "I got it, Stuart. I got the transfer I've been looking for all these months. I'm out of the infantry, my boy, and into intelligence!"

Blaisdell had not thought much about Clayborne's intrigue to get out of the fighting. He had hoped if he did not make anything of it, it would just dissolve into smoke. But it had not, obviously.

"You're leaving the Second Volunteers?" he asked his old friend.

"Probably. I don't know what outfit I'll be attached to, yet. I just know I won't be carrying a rifle anymore. What do you think of that, old school chum?"

Blaisdell did not know what to say. "Why, I guess congratulations are in order, Randy."

"They are, indeed, Stuart! God, I only wish I could have talked some sense into you. Now you're going to be alone out here in the mud and dust."

"Well, that's war." Blaisdell grinned.

"Listen, maybe we'll still see each other once in a while. If I can—"

Clayborne paused as a young soldier came up to them, from the direction of K Company. "They said I'd find you over here, Lieutenant. Some mail came in, and there's a letter for you." The fellow handed Clayborne an envelope, and Clayborne took it and looked at the return address.

"All right. Thanks, soldier."

The fellow left, and Clayborne tore the letter open. "I thought it might be from Jennifer. I haven't heard from her lately. But it's from my cousin in Walterboro. You've heard me mention him; he's just a kid." He began reading the letter aloud.

> *Dear Randy,*
>   *It sure seems like a long time since you went off to the war. I'll be old enough pretty soon now, and I'm going to enlist just like you did.*

120

"Oh, God," Clayborne commented.

> *Everything is pretty good here in Walterboro,
> it's not like being shelled in Charleston. Nobody
> we know has been hurt, though. I hope you're
> O.K., and that friend of yours, Blacewell, isn't
> it? I know the shot must be flying out there. Have
> you killed any Yanks yet, Randy? Gosh, I wish I
> was out there with you, sleeping in tents and
> waking up to the call of bugles.*

"Hell, isn't that just like a kid?" Clayborne said sourly.
He looked back down at the letter, and his eyes narrowed
down some.

> *There's something about Jennifer, Randy. I
> don't even know if I should mention it or not. But
> here goes. I was in the city for a week and this guy
> I know told me that Jennifer was seeing a man,
> and the way he put it, he meant more than just
> seeing him.*

Clayborne stopped, and sucked in his breath slightly.
"Jesus Christ, Randy," Blaisdell said in a hollow voice.
"Who would say something like that about Jennifer?"
Clayborne's face was suddenly straight-lined with
emotion. He went on reading aloud.

> *I told the guy he was crazy, Randy. But then I
> talked to some other people. I even did some
> snooping; I hope you aren't mad. I saw Jennifer
> come out of this man's flat, Randy. At night,
> late. I think they had both been drinking. I know
> it sounds crazy, but there it is. I don't think*

121

Clayborne stopped reading aloud, but let his eyes quickly scan the letter to its bottom. "It just goes on like that," he finally said to Blaisdell, in a low, hard voice.

"Jesus, Randy," Blaisdell said.

"Why didn't he tell me the guy's name?" Clayborne said hoarsely. "The stupid bastard should have told me his name!"

"It's probably better you don't know," Blaisdell offered.

Clayborne looked over at him. "Can you believe this? When the cat's away, Stuart. By God, I never thought I'd be cuckold!"

"God, I am sorry, Randy."

Anger crowded into Clayborne's handsome face. "I've never been so insulted in my life! I'll kill that son when I get back! I don't care who he is! He's a dead man, just as if he already had copper pennies on his damned eyes! I mean it, Stuart! He's probably some damned sissy who's afraid to come out here and fight!"

Blaisdell sighed heavily. "Don't be too hard on Jennifer, Randy. The flesh is weak, as they say. You found that, out here." Deliberately. "Didn't you?"

Clayborne looked at him quizzically. "You're comparing what I did with the debauchery of my wife? I went to a whore, Stuart. Well, a couple of them. My sweet Jennifer is having a full-blown affair! Whispering nice things into his ear, doing exactly what he asks her to do! Making pledges of love, for God's sake!"

"You don't know that," Blaisdell said quietly. "It might be little more than your experience out here."

"Goddamn it, she's a *woman!*" Clayborne said loudly. "She's my goddamned *wife!* I don't see what you're

122

talking about!"

"I didn't mean to butt in," Blaisdell said.

Clayborne stood up, and paced back and forth before Blaisdell. And as he paced, Blaisdell saw the emotion drain out of him. There was no deep wound, after all. Clayborne's ego had been bruised; that was all. Blaisdell found himself wondering if Clayborne was capable of really being hurt by someone.

"Well, at least I know," Clayborne finally commented. "I'll get an annulment as soon as I get back, of course. In the meantime, two can play Jennifer's game. I consider myself a free man, as of this moment. Actually, I feel rather good about it."

Blaisdell regarded him soberly. "Why don't you try to find out more about it, Randy?"

Clayborne turned to him. "More about it? You mean, details from the bedroom? No thanks. I know what I have to know."

Blaisdell thought of Holly. She had written to him from Baltimore, and he had been disturbed that she was uprooted. She had not mentioned the incident with Uriah, and hoped to keep it from him. Blaisdell knew only that Holly and Charlotte both thought it would be good for Holly to have a change in her life, and some time with Eugenia would give that to her. He had already written her a letter since her move, but had not sent it.

"Maybe Holly knows about it, and could tell us more," Blaisdell said. "You would get the straight truth from her."

Clayborne shook his head. "Forget it, Stuart." Darkly. "O.K."

"I don't want to talk about it anymore. Let's just drop it. I mean for good."

Blaisdell sighed heavily. "Anything you say, Randy."

123

*   *   *

It was a warm September in Baltimore. The tall trees at Federal Hill and along Fayette Street still wore full greenery, and blossoms were still very much in evidence at Spring Gardens and around private residences throughout the Hempstead section. Federal troops out at Fort McHenry sweated in their uniforms, and the men at Fort Carroll on the Patapsco River.

The city had largely succumbed to the notion of being a northern port under federal command, although perhaps a majority of its citizens regarded the port as occupied territory. Discussions regarding the merits of the North and South issues were hot and open, and prominent leaders such as John W. Garrett of the Baltimore & Ohio Railroad were torn in their sympathies, as well as the city fathers. General Butler of the Union forces recognized this situation, and tried to understand it rather than condemn it. His troops commanded the valuable rail line of the B. & O., but he developed a congenial relationship with Garrett that aided the Union cause.

Holly was finally settling into her new surroundings well. She met a number of Eugenia and Preston Fayette's friends at teas and dinners, and some influential young men were among them. They all were interested in Holly, the unmarried ones, and Holly went out with a couple of them, but they did not interest her. Near the end of September, not long after fighting had broken out around Chattanooga where Blaisdell and Clayborne had been stationed, and Holly had become worried about them, Eugenia arranged for Holly to attend a rather formal ball again, where there would be young military officers and government officials in attendance. Eugenia was determined that Holly should meet the right young men, and

124

was making a veritable campaign of the project.

It was a lovely September evening when Holly arrived at the ball at the Abell House, escorted by the Fayettes. Inside, the place was all high-ceilinged rooms set off by potted palms and rich carpeting. Outside on the portico, fancy carriages arrived one after the other, received by a uniformed doorman. It was all very elegant.

The Fayettes were soon occupied with acquaintances, and Holly was busy dancing with one young man after another. She looked radiantly beautiful that evening, with her thick black hair piled high on her head, and wearing a lovely light-blue off-the-shoulder gown. Men escorting other young women could not take their eyes off her. Her job at the florist's shop had given her a feeling of independence that showed in her face and her manner, and made her even lovelier than before. The gown she was wearing had been purchased with her own money; she was buying all of her own personal things now. Preston Fayette thought she evidenced a bit too much independence—the women in his family had never had any—and it made him somewhat uncomfortable. But Eugenia did not mind it, and it was Eugenia who managed Holly's relationship with them.

An army captain was particularly enchanted by Holly's beauty and charm, so was a junior official from the mayor's office, and these two returned and returned to dance with Holly as the evening progressed. Holly enjoyed their company for the first hour, but then was wondering how to avoid them when she received her biggest surprise since her arrival in Baltimore. She was just being asked for the next dance by the captain of artillery, and trying to think of a way to decline gracefully, when the young lieutenant walked up to her and she recognized his face.

It was Randy Clayborne.

Holly was stricken dumb. Her mouth fell slightly open as the captain turned to see who had interrupted her reply to him.

"Randy!" she said in a half-whisper.

Clayborne was smiling his wide, handsome smile. He looked very military in his blue uniform, very masculine and virile. He took her hand. "Hello, Holly. What a surprise to see you here. It's been a long time since we met in Washington, hasn't it?"

Holly's head was whirling from the sight of Clayborne in a Union uniform, his being there in Baltimore, his greeting to her.

"Washington?" she said numbly.

"Ah, you've forgotten me already," his voice came to her as if from the other end of a tunnel. "Don't you remember our little tête-à-tête at the officers' club?"

The captain was eying Clayborne sideways. "Lieutenant, we were just about to dance," he said sourly.

Holly remembered the captain's presence, and turned to him. "No, it's all right, Captain. The lieutenant and I are friends from the capital. Would you excuse us while we renew acquaintance?"

The captain was miffed. "Yes, of course, Miss Ransom. Perhaps we can dance later?"

"Yes, perhaps," Holly told him.

The captain nodded to Clayborne, and then was gone. Holly turned back to Clayborne, and looked him over slowly. "Randy. What in the world are you doing here? And wearing that uniform?"

Clayborne looked around them, and then took her arm. "May we step out onto the back porch for a moment, Miss Ransom?" he said in a very conspiratorial tone.

She went with him, looking over her shoulder to see if

either Eugenia or Preston had seen her with Clayborne. She could not see them anywhere. A moment later Clayborne had guided her through wide, open doors onto a blossom-scented porch that overlooked a lovely garden. They were alone there. Clayborne turned to her.

"Can I trust you, Holly? You haven't become a Yankee up here, have you? Living with your rich aunt?"

Holly's head was still in a whirl. "Of course not, Randy."

He looked around him again, and moved closer to her. "Don't let this blue uniform fool you, Holly. I'm just wearing it for convenience."

"Convenience? I don't think I—"

"I'm still in the Confederate Army, Holly—in military intelligence. Just recently transferred from the infantry. I was with Stuart at Chattanooga just a few weeks ago."

The more he said, the more confused she became. "How is Stuart?" she asked him.

"When I left he looked great. There wasn't any fighting then, of course. He'll be right in the middle of it, I suppose. But he's a pretty tough fellow."

"Oh, dear," Holly said.

"Listen to me, Holly. I'm here undercover. Posing as a Union officer. It's part of a military mission."

Holly stared at him, and he found himself thinking how beautiful she was. More beautiful than she had been in Charleston.

"I'm here to gather information. For the Confederacy."

Holly glanced around them, rather fearfully now. "Really?"

Clayborne smiled his handsome smile. "That's my job now. I tried to get Stuart to come into this with me. But you know how bullheaded he is. He thinks the only way

127

to serve is carrying a musket."

Holly met his gaze. "Are you—on the job now? At this minute?"

He nodded. "That's right. It's amazing how much information is available in this town. And how freely it's bandied about. At social gatherings like this one, for instance."

Holly held his gaze for a moment, then turned and looked back into the brightly lighted ballroom with its chandeliers and wall fixtures of gaslights. Clayborne was right, she realized. Many military officers spoke openly of missions and forthcoming plans of their generals. All of it was not known to the Confederacy, unless someone carried it to Confederate lines. Holly looked back at Clayborne. "My gosh. If Eugenia and Preston heard this conversation, they would be outraged. At least Preston would."

"I'm counting on you not to convey what I've said to them," Clayborne told her. "Or to anybody else, Holly. I'm trusting you to be a true daughter of the Confederacy."

Holly eyed him soberly. "There is no southerner more dedicated to the cause of secession than I am," she said firmly to him.

He smiled at her spirit. "Good, Holly. Maybe you could be of some small help to me from time to time, since I'll be here for several months, in all probability. What would you think of that?"

Holly hesitated, then shrugged. "Maybe, Randy."

He smiled again, and leaned to her, kissing her lightly on her lips. Holly was slightly surprised, then more so by her reaction to the intimacy. The touch had been unexpectedly exciting to her, had moved her somewhere deep

128

inside. She recalled Clayborne's early flirtations with her, when he had first been going with Jennifer, and then she thought of Jennifer and felt guilty that she had liked the kiss on a physical level.

"I'm glad I found you here, Holly," he was telling her. "It's like having Charleston here with me. You make it like home."

Holly looked away, flushed slightly from the kiss.

"It's over between Jennifer and me, Holly."

She looked back at him.

"Jennifer is going out with other men, back home," he said. "I'm sure you know about it."

Holly recalled Jennifer's fling in Savannah. "I'm not sure what you're referring to, Randy."

"Well, I guess maybe you haven't heard from Charleston lately," he said. "It's a married man, Holly. Maybe more than one; I don't know. My source is a good one. I'm finished with her; I've already told her so, in a letter."

"Oh God, Randy. I'm so sorry."

He made a face. "It's O.K. I don't think we were right for each other, anyway, Holly." He averted his eyes for a moment. "I guess I should have courted you instead, during those early days."

Holly blushed, turning away. "You shouldn't say that, Randy. Jennifer is still my friend."

He touched her arm. "Let's go back inside. I want you to introduce me to the Fayettes. I think it would be a wise move to win their confidence right at the beginning."

Holly eyed him curiously. "All right, Randy. But how shall we introduce you?"

"Just leave that to me," he said with a sly wink.

Chapter Seven

Charleston was now suffering from the blockade. Admirals DuPont and Dahlgren had bottled up the port tightly; their warships lay in the harbor and few blockade-runners were getting through. Hunger was widespread in the city, even among the wealthier families, and disease was taking its toll. Rats were breeding in shelled buildings, making the situation worse.

General de Beauregard advised the good citizens of Charleston to hang on, that the war was far from lost. But many were worn out with the struggle already.

Holly's mother, Charlotte, was one of them. Uriah Quinn's business was almost at a standstill, and both he and Charlotte had taken to drinking more regularly, but not together now. Quinn was gone from the house a lot, and Charlotte often had no idea where he was.

Jennifer was not seeing the married man with whom she had been caught by Clayborne's cousin. She had turned him out of her bed for a Bible drummer, and then that fellow had gone off to Atlanta. Now Jennifer was seeing a widowed businessman occasionally, a much older man, and she no longer had any illusions about real love. She was convinced, rightly, that she did not have the capacity to give or receive it, but that did not much concern Jennifer. She had had a dull and rather impoverished childhood, and what she felt she needed now was excitement and adventure in her life.

She was getting it.

Of course, Jennifer's reputation suffered. At her tender age she was already considered a fallen woman, and none of the men she dated regarded her as a marriage prospect. Her grandmother, Amanda, was saddened by Jennifer's behavior, but if she criticized Jennifer, Jennifer always threatened to move out, and Amanda did not want that. She would not have known what to do with herself, alone in her house. So she stopped mentioning Jennifer's indiscretions.

Charlotte and Uriah Quinn took note of Jennifer's promiscuity, and a couple of times when Quinn met Jennifer downtown, he gave her a knowing grin as he greeted her. Jennifer ignored him. Then, one day when she was having lunch alone at an Elliott Street café down near the waterfront, Quinn walked in and saw her eating alone. He came over past her table and stopped there, and Jennifer looked up and gave him a sour look.

"Well, well. Eating alone, Jennifer? What happened, did you run out of male friends?"

Jennifer looked back down at her salad, hoping Quinn would go away. Dressed in a pretty blue velvet dress that revealed her nice cleavage, Jennifer looked at once more elegant than a year ago, and harder. Her face was made up, but it was more than that. The change was in her eyes, her expressions, her manner. She was more worldly looking, more knowing, more mature. But in a way that

131

suggested cynicism and disillusionment.

"Good afternoon, Uriah," she said darkly.

Quinn sat down across from her without being asked, and she gave him a hostile look. "What happened to Will Harner?" he said jovially, referring to the widower. "Has he stopped squiring you about town?"

Jennifer met his gaze with a sober one. "That's my business, Uriah. Don't you think?"

He raised his hands defensively, arching his dark eyebrows. "Well, no offense, Jennifer. Your social life seems to be no secret in Charleston, so naturally I thought you wouldn't mind discussing it."

"Go to hell, Uriah," Jennifer said.

He laughed good-naturedly. "Of course, I can see what the men around town see in you. You're quite attractive in your way." His gaze dropped to her bosom, and held there for a long moment. Jennifer forked some salad up and tried to ignore him.

"I've meant to ask," Quinn went on, rubbing at his side whiskers slowly, "how is that young Clayborne doing out there in the war? Your husband, I mean?"

Jennifer looked quickly at him, and saw the glint in his eye. "I don't know," she said tightly.

"I guess you'll have a couple of surprises for him when he gets back here, won't you?" He grinned again, and it was an evil grin.

"Uriah, I'm trying to finish a meal. Do you mind?"

He leaned toward her, and when he spoke, she could smell the alcohol on his breath. "Listen, Jennifer, we don't have to play games between us, do we? I've been looking at you for a long time with a certain amount of admiration. Not unlike the widower, Harner, I'd guess. Why don't you let me buy your lunch, and we'll talk about it?"

Jennifer stared at him with hard eyes. "Maybe you'd like to ask Charlotte to join us?" she said levelly.

His face fell into straight lines. "Seeing a married man never bothered you before. You're not going to tell me you've suddenly gone and got moral on us, are you?"

When she spoke again, her voice was brittle. "I asked you once already, Uriah. Please leave me alone to finish my lunch."

There were no patrons within earshot, but a waitress at a nearby table glanced toward them at Jennifer's remark.

"What's the problem, Jennifer?" he was saying to her in an oily tone. "It can't be that you don't like older men. Don't you think my favors will be as attractive as Harner's?"

Jennifer had had enough, and her experience with men had taught her how to protect herself with the toughest of them. She, too, leaned forward over the small table. "Holly told me all about you, damn you. Do you think I'd ever let a man like you touch me? Even if Charlotte weren't my friend, and even if I didn't know how you cheat on her? You damned—rapist!"

Quinn's dark eyes narrowed down in swift anger.

"Go ahead, get angry, threaten me!" she said in the repressed voice, full of emotion. "Let's start shouting at each other, right here in the restaurant! Take the first turn, and then we'll see how it all comes out!"

Quinn rose slowly from his chair, and glared at Jennifer. Then a taut grin broke through his hard look. "I should have known better than to treat you like a mature woman. You and that stepdaughter of mine are both misguided adolescents still, in your heads." The grin that was not a grin widened. "Maybe sometime I'll catch you

133

at home alone, and we can finish this little dialogue."

Jennifer fairly spat the words out at him. "Don't threaten me, you bastard."

But Quinn merely held the grin, and then turned and left the restaurant.

Jennifer was not able to finish her light lunch there that day. That evening, she accepted an invitation by Harner to a poetry reading, and then she took him to her bed throughout a long, dark night.

Quinn did some more drinking before going home that night, and arrived there quite late. Charlotte had held supper for him for a couple of hours, and then put it all away. When he came into the house, she was waiting for him.

"Oh," he said in a rather slurred voice. "You're up."

"I expected you home for supper, Uriah," Charlotte said to him. She was dressed in a floor-length robe, with a nightgown under it, and her hair was combed out long. "Where have you been?"

Quinn removed his suit coat and threw it onto a chair in the corner of the rather small living room. The only light was from an oil lamp on a nearby table, and it cast a dull glow onto Quinn's heavy features.

"Do I have to start making accountings of my time to you now?" he growled at her. He walked past her without looking at her, through a doorway and into the kitchen.

Charlotte followed him. He took a bottle of liquor from a cabinet and poured himself a drink.

"Uriah, don't you think you've had enough of that for this evening?" she said to him.

He swigged the drink without responding to the question. He leaned against a counter then, staring darkly at the wall.

"I got a letter from Holly today. She's well, and enjoying her work at the floral shop."

Quinn grunted.

"I miss her, Uriah. I sent her away for you, you know. So there would be no more trouble in the house."

"Hell," he said.

She came up closer to him. "We don't see much of each other nowadays, Uriah. You keep blaming the war, but I don't think the war has anything to do with it."

He turned and eyed her acidly. She could smell the alcohol on him. "What the hell is all this about, Charlotte? You're still eating, aren't you? What do you want from me?"

Charlotte's eyes moistened slightly. "I want it the way it was when we were married. I want us to be close again."

"Oh, Christ," he muttered.

She came and embraced him, and he did not return it. "I'm afraid nowadays, Uriah. Afraid of the war, afraid of what's happening to us. There doesn't seem to be anything I can hold on to, now. My house is gone, my daughter is gone. And now it seems you're leaving me."

"Don't lament your situation, woman. There are many worse off than you. Go down on Unity Street and take a look at how people are living down there if you don't believe me. There are people living in bombed-out shells, by God, down by the water. Flavoring their soup with rat meat."

"I'm not talking about food or physical surroundings," Charlotte told him. "I'm talking about love, Uriah—affection."

He made a face.

"Why don't we go to bed?" Charlotte said, brushing at her eye. "I feel the need for you, Uriah. I feel it strong

135

tonight. Let's go to bed and show our affection the way we used to, and make it all right again. I'd like that, Uriah."

He pushed her away from him. "It's late, Charlotte. You don't have nearly the passion inside you that you think. I'm very tired and sleepy. I'll sleep on the sofa tonight, so we won't disturb each other.

Charlotte felt empty inside. Her eyes moistened up again, and she turned away from him. "What's gone wrong?" she murmured to herself. "Oh, God, what's gone wrong?"

Quinn made no attempt to reply to the rhetorical question. He brushed past her and moved unsteadily into the next room.

Over the next weeks there was a deadly struggle for Tennessee. Rosecrans occupied Chattanooga for the Union almost without opposition, then Bragg beat him soundly at Chickamauga Station nearby. But now, in November, General Thomas won for Grant on a wooded height called Missionary Ridge and Lookout Mountain, and all but drove General Bragg out of Tennessee.

In Baltimore, Holly had become what amounted to a Confederate agent, in her liaison with Randy Clayborne. She had been to a couple of social functions in addition to the one where she had met Clayborne, and had overheard or been directly given military information that she had passed on to Clayborne. The data was not important intelligence, but it was a start. And Holly had committed herself to playing an active and dangerous part in defending the Confederate States.

Holly saw Clayborne socially, too. Eugenia thought Clayborne was a bright young Union officer and eligible

136

to court Holly. Actually, Clayborne was a lieutenant in the Confederate Army, but could never wear the insignia of that rank, on that uniform.

Clayborne was obviously enamored of Holly, and Holly was reminded again how attractively charming Clayborne could be. One evening on a cool November night, after Clayborne had taken Holly out to a play and to give her instructions for further undercover work on her part, he invited her up to his room in a small hotel in the Jonestown section of the city, not far from Fells Point, and she accepted.

Holly had promised herself she would not get too close to Clayborne. After all, he was married to her good friend, no matter what the present situation between him and Jennifer. And then there was Blaisdell. Holly now knew that she would never marry Blaisdell, despite the small bit of encouragement she had given him before he had left for the war. But he had the right to be told of any new love of Holly's, she thought.

Clayborne's room was small but clean, with his bed in a far corner of it. There was a small desk where Clayborne laid out a map of Virginia for Holly, showing her where the opposing armies were located, the situation around Charleston—on another, hand-drawn map—and how her information could help the Confederate military. Holly felt, deep inside her, that Clayborne's motive for asking her up there might be an ulterior one, but on that November evening she did not mind. She had not found any young man that she liked in Baltimore, and she was a little lonely. Clayborne, coming out of her past like a memory of another life, gave her a feeling of belonging again; she liked being with him just because of that, and because he had been an important part of her growing-up days in Charleston.

"So you see," Clayborne was saying to her after he had pointed out a number of details on the maps, "just the small bits and pieces you've gathered so far could help our cause, Holly." He was folding the big map up as he spoke, and replacing it in an oilskin case.

"That pleases me, Randy," Holly said with a smile. "I felt like a kind of traitor, running off to the North like I did, just because Charlotte didn't want me around. Now I feel as if I'm a part of the rebellion again. I'll help you right to the very end, if I can. No matter how the war goes."

Clayborne grinned, and she thought how very handsome he was. He was in shirt sleeves, and his shoulders seemed particularly broad, his smile particularly engaging. He came close to her, and put his hands on her waist, and she did not mind. "Only a beautiful girl like you could pull this off," he told her. "I've seen the way the men look at you at these gatherings. They'd tell you anything you wanted to know, if you'd just ask them."

Holly averted her gaze. "You exaggerate, Randy."

His grin evaporated, and his face was suddenly serious. "I would, too, Holly," he said. "Tell you anything, I mean."

She turned partially away from him, her face flushed. "Oh, Randy."

He turned her back, and pulled her to him and kissed her on the mouth. She was surprised by the kiss, and its sudden passion, but she did not try to break free. Something inside her responded quickly to it, almost against her volition. In a moment she was finally breaking away, breathing shallowly. She moved away from him, unwittingly toward the bed, and he followed her.

138

"What's the matter, Holly? I know you feel something. I think you always have, just like me."

Holly turned back to him. "My God, Randy, you're married to Jennifer."

He laughed in his throat. "Do you call that a marriage? With her in one man's bed after another? I'm not laying any blame, Holly, but there's nothing left between us." He watched her face, and saw the loneliness in it, and the desire. "As for old Stu, he was never right for you, and he knows it." He paused, deciding to bolster that statement with a small lie. "He told me so, at Chattanooga."

Holly looked up at him. "He did?"

Clayborne nodded, and took her to him again. "He knows the score, all right. I can't say it bothers him much, either, frankly. You don't have to worry over old Stuart, he's a grown-up boy now. He can take care of himself, believe me."

The suggestion was apparent. He was telling her that she was just another girl to Blaisdell. That she did not have to concern herself about betraying him, in any way. While she was still mulling that, Clayborne pulled her to him and kissed her again, and this time the kiss was even more passionate than before. There was hunger in the kiss, a hunger on both sides, and Holly was mildly surprised at hers. Clayborne pressed her gently backward, and she was suddenly on the bed, lying back on it, her feet still on the floor. His hand was on her rich curves, and she put a hand on his, but made no real effort to stop what he was doing. Something inside her was taking hold of her, some passion she did not even know was hidden there. In her early intimacies in Charleston with schoolboys, she had not responded like this. Now she was a woman, and her reaction was womanly. It was

139

strong, vibrant, and almost beyond her control at that moment.

"Randy, please—" In feeble protest, her cheeks flushed, her heart pounding.

"Let it happen, honey. Just let it happen. It's all right."

Almost without her knowing how, her skirts were pushed upward and her thighs were being bared to him. All through it he was kissing her and fondling her. His hot touch was on her face, her mouth, her throat, and finally on the warm, ripe flesh of her breasts. Then he had moved her up and onto the bed, and she saw her sculpted knees on either side of his broad shoulders, and suddenly and unexpectedly there was a union that widened her eyes and made her gasp aloud. She had not even decided whether she would let it happen, and it was happening. She was full of him and his hot breath was at the side of her face and there were hot ripplings of raw pleasure pulsing through her.

Later, her soft cries filled the small room with their urgency, and then he lay on her, collapsed against her warm flesh, breathing unevenly. The bed covers were knotted up in his fists, and his damp flesh lay against hers, and she was still full of the heat of him.

She felt a last gentle kiss on her right cheek; she met his gaze for a long moment, and then turned her head away.

"Oh, damn," she said quietly. "What have I done? What in the world have I done?"

Chapter Eight

Holly pledged to herself that same night, before she ever left Clayborne's bed, that there would be no further intimacy between them. She felt a heavy weight of guilt pressing inside her after she left him that night, and the weight would not seem to go away. She had betrayed Jennifer with her husband. She had betrayed Blaisdell's trust in a way.

About two weeks after that passionate episode at Clayborne's private room, Clayborne finally got Holly to go out with him again, though, by insisting that he had another Confederate agent to introduce her to, a young actor who had gathered information for Clayborne in past weeks much as Holly had. The other agent might be used in the near future in conjunction with Holly, and Clayborne wanted them to be acquainted with each other.

"Maybe afterward we might stop at a waterfront café and have a late meal," Clayborne suggested to her.

"I told you, Randy. From now on it's strictly business with us; I can't live with anything else. I'm sorry, but that's the way it is. What happened between us was a mistake, one that we must both live with but never mention back in Charleston. Jennifer would never forgive me if she knew what I'd done."

Clayborne shrugged. "If that's the way you want it, lovely lady. But we could be something, together—something special."

They went to the St. Charles Theater that evening together; there was a "sparkling new comedy" playing, and the actor Holly was to meet was one of the principal players. When he appeared on stage, Holly was immediately impressed by him. He was not quite as tall as Clayborne, but he was every bit as handsome, and he had a deep, authoritative voice and a poised manner that pleased Holly. He had a couple of funny lines in the third act, and Holly found herself laughing heartily, because of his expert delivery. When the play was over, Clayborne took Holly backstage and elbowed through some patrons to the actor's dressing room. He stood just outside it, autographing a loose-leaf book for a young woman, and when the woman was gone, Clayborne and Holly went up to him.

"Oh, Randy!" he exclaimed when he turned. His smile was flashing, his eyes sparkling. Holly felt little pricklings of excitement stab at her insides. "I'm glad you could come!"

Clayborne returned the smile. "John, this is the girl I wanted you to meet—Miss Holly Ransom, of Charleston."

The actor was already looking at Holly, and his whole demeanor had changed, his face going serious. "Incredible," he said softly. "This is one of our people? She must be the most beautiful girl in all of Baltimore."

Clayborne gave the actor a look, and smiled sardonically. "Maybe I shouldn't have introduced you two. Holly, this is John Wilkes Booth, the most promising young actor on the East Coast."

"You obviously have a way with the ladies, Mr. Booth," Holly said with a shy smile.

Booth, a southern zealot who felt Lincoln had no redeeming qualities and who had proclaimed loudly, over and over again until Clayborne recruited him, that the President intended to set up a kind of kingship that would humble and humiliate the South, had been working as an agent under Clayborne for slightly longer than Holly. "Listen to that lovely Charleston accent!" he was saying now to Clayborne. "Did you ever hear such music come from a woodwind or viola?"

"Oh, dear," Holly murmured.

"Now just a moment, John—" Clayborne grinned. "I saw her first. We even went to school together."

"Do you know that you could be a fine actress?" Booth went on to Holly, very exuberantly in his well-modulated actor's voice. "I mean it, Miss Ransom. You have looks, poise, charm, a voice like a soft southern breeze. Maybe you should allow me to tutor you in the histrionic art."

Holly was smiling, but she was blushing slightly, too. "I'm a florist, Mr. Booth. That's all I want to be, until the right man comes along."

"How modest!" Booth said. "Isn't that modest, Randy?"

"Yes," Clayborne said with a sigh, seeing Holly's reaction to this dark-haired, square-jawed newcomer. "Holly is modest. Now may we go inside your dressing room and have a private discussion?" He watched Booth staring at Holly. "John?"

"Oh. Surely, Randy. Miss Ransom, after you."

The three went into the small, ill-lighted room to discuss Clayborne's dark schemes.

After meeting John Wilkes Booth, Holly stopped seeing Clayborne at all, except for business. Booth asked her to go to a couple of plays with him, and she accepted, and she introduced Booth to Eugenia and Preston one evening. They had both heard of him as an actor. Eugenia was friendlier to him than Preston, because it was difficult for a woman not to be charmed by Booth. He was more effervescent than Clayborne, and he flirted egregiously with every woman he was introduced to. But there were times, too, when he sank into somber, serious moods, usually when the cause of the Confederacy was mentioned, or the topic of Abraham Lincoln. Holly was swept up against him as if into the tail of a comet, and they quickly became close. Holly, in fact, was afraid she was falling in love for the first time in her life, and that was very frightening to her.

In mid-December Clayborne arranged for Holly to be invited to another social gathering, this one a banquet honoring a visiting dignitary in Lincoln's cabinet. Holly spent the entire evening there, talking with generals and officials; she was becoming well-known in the social circuit of the city. Clayborne accompanied her, but the Fayettes did not go. When Holly and Clayborne were riding back to the Fayette house in a carriage after the gathering was over, they rode silently for the first part of the trip, with Holly scribbling notes onto a small pad from her purse. Finally she finished, and handed the paper over to Clayborne. He took it and began reading it, as they jogged along in the carriage, the horse's hoofs and the carriage wheels making the only sounds that came to them.

"Mmm, interesting," he said soberly, sitting there in his Union uniform. Holly wore a heavy shawl over her gown, against the coolness of the evening, and looked very lovely. "This suggestion that Grant will be elevated to three stars, and put in charge of the whole Union show. That will be very important to our people. And this item about an offensive in Georgia. You did very well, Holly. Very well, indeed."

Holly shrugged, with a smile. "I enjoy it. I want this war turned around, Randy. I feel valuable to our cause, being able to help in some way. It's exciting and challenging, and I think I'm learning some things about it. It gives me a feeling of worth that most women don't have. I'm glad you came along when you did."

He smiled at her, putting the paper down onto his lap. After he had memorized the information she had gathered, he would burn the paper. It was dangerous to be casual, in the work they were in.

"If you're glad I'm here with you, why aren't you more friendly to me lately?" he said.

Holly looked over at him. "We've been through that, Randy."

"It's John, isn't it?" he said.

"John has nothing to do with us, Randy," she told him. "But I like John very much, yes. We get along very well."

"Are you lovers?" he asked easily.

Holly turned to him quickly, her face flushed. "Damn it, Randy! That's none of your business!" She had not allowed Booth any intimacy, but she did not feel like defending herself to Clayborne. "Don't ever ask me a personal question like that again!"

145

Clayborne grinned. "Or you'll do what, old school chum?"

Holly held his look for a fierce one. "How about reporting you to your superiors as a beginning?" she suggested.

Clayborne's face clouded over darkly. "I see you have grown up," he said.

"I can take care of myself, Randy. Don't ever forget that. You caught me in a weak moment, that night at your place—a stupid moment. I didn't like you very much in Charleston, and I don't like you very much now. I don't like your familiarities, despite what happened between us. I don't like it that you don't care that I don't like them. And I won't put up with them. Does that make my position quite clear to you?"

The carriage pulled up to a stop in front of the Fayette house. Clayborne made a face, and nodded. "Oh, yes. You've made it all very clear, Holly. I thought we could mean something to each other—two old Charleston friends here alone in the northland. But I see that your interests are more like Jennifer's."

Again, Holly felt quick anger at such a preposterous comparison. "I don't know exactly what that means, Randy, but I'm sure we had better keep our meetings strictly business from now on, from beginning to end. Good night, Randy. You need not see me to the door."

When Holly got inside a few minutes later, she was surprised to find Eugenia waiting up for her. She was standing in the entrance foyer, a worried look on her face, a robe pulled tight over night clothes.

"You're in a little late, aren't you, Holly?" she greeted her niece.

Holly came up and kissed Eugenia on the cheek. "I'm

146

sorry, Aunt Eugenia. I know I told you I'd be in earlier.
But there were so many people to meet there at the
banquet."

Eugenia went to the wall nearby and turned a gas lamp
down. When she turned back to Holly, her face was still
sober. "Preston and I do feel responsible for you, Holly.
Your mother will expect that we're doing our part in
seeing that you make a place in our world here in Baltimore."

"I understand, Eugenia."

"Frankly, Preston is concerned about the men you're
seeing now," Eugenia continued. "Your Lieutenant
Clayborne seems nice enough, but he seems to have no
background, no past. He keeps you out until late hours,
and he never presents himself to Preston and me anymore. And now you've been seeing this Booth fellow.
Preston and I enjoy a good play as much as anyone,
Holly. But actors are different from us. They live differently, have different expectations from life. I have to
wonder what Mr. Booth's intentions are toward you."

Holly sighed lightly. "Eugenia, I've grown up since I
came here to you. I'm earning my livelihood now, paying
you for my keep. I feel I've earned the right to choose my
own friends, male or female."

"Of course you have, dear. But please don't make
Preston and me worry over you. Not all men are what
they seem; you'll find that out with a little experience.
Go carefully with these new acquaintances. And remember that Preston and I must have rules in our own household. Having a young, eligible woman in the house is a
tremendous responsibility, Holly. I hope you understand
that."

Holly thought of the consternation that would be

147

aroused in Eugenia and Preston if they knew she was a Confederate agent, a rebel soldier without a uniform. And in that moment, she realized that she owed it to Eugenia to find her own lodgings at the earliest opportunity. If she got into any trouble with the authorities, she did not want the scandal to fall onto her aunt and uncle.

"I do, Eugenia. I really do."

Eugenia returned the kiss Holly gave her, and smiled. "Good. Shall we have a cup of hot tea before you turn in?"

"That would be very nice, Eugenia," Holly told her.

The week before Christmas, Booth took Holly out to a concert, and they enjoyed themselves very much. The orchestra played Tschaikovsky, and later on the way to a restaurant, there was a light snow. They were to meet Clayborne at the restaurant, but got there ahead of him. Over a cup of tea, Booth exuded his pleasure in the concert.

"I love the Nutcracker Suite," Booth was telling her. "It's so modern and light. The Russians always seem to come up with the artistic genius, don't they?"

"I don't know much about Russia, John—or music either, for that matter—but it was all beautiful tonight."

"The czars make it difficult for artists over there," Booth said seriously to her now, his chiseled features suddenly straight-lined. He was wearing a dark suit and ascot, and Holly wore a lovely green gown with a light wrap over her bare shoulders. They made a striking couple, the two of them. "If the North wins this war, that's what it will be like over here, with Lincoln in power."

Holly recalled meeting the President at the ball at the Maryland Hotel, not long after she arrived in Baltimore, and how he had made a favorable impression on her. "You don't like Lincoln much, do you, John?" she said to him.

He made a face, drawing the corners of his mouth down as if he had just tasted a sour fruit. "The man is a bombastic moron with a hunger for power," he said. "He wants to be a dictator, not a representative of the people. He sees nothing wrong with depriving citizens of their property rights without due process of law, or murdering them because they want their independence from tyranny."

Holly said nothing. She had not gotten that impression of Lincoln at all, either from her personal meeting or from what she had heard about him from knowledgeable people.

"Lincoln is the enemy," Booth went on. "Congress is divided on this secession issue. But our President isn't interested in what they want, or what the people want. If Lincoln had not been elected, we'd have had a peaceful secession—or no secession at all. Yes, it's Lincoln." He was staring past her, looking pensive.

"Well, I suppose nobody is going to throw him out of office during this war," Holly suggested. "So we'll have to go on doing what we can in our small way to force at least an honorable peace on the North, John."

He was still staring across the room, to where a waiter was serving another couple at a corner table. "Bring Lincoln down, you bring down the North," he said quietly. "Our people should be thinking of Dishonest Abe as a king on a chessboard. Capture the king and you have the whole game."

149

"Capture?" Holly said to him.

He focused on her again. "Yes, why not? If a private in the army can fall prisoner of war, why can't a President?"

"That's a very bold idea, John," she said.

"Boldness is required, if the South is to survive this conflict," he insisted. He had made a promise to someone who had been dear to him, he had told her one day, not to go off to the war. But Clayborne had hinted to her that it was because Booth did not want his perfect profile scarred. "Why couldn't Lincoln be captured and made a Confederate prisoner? That would bring the North to its knees, you can wager. I rather like the notion, myself."

Holly thought there was something inherently wrong in the suggestion, even if Lincoln were an evil man. But she did not think he was. "Well, I suppose those strategic possibilities will have to be left to those with more inside knowledge than ours," she said lightly. She started to go on, but saw Clayborne enter the restaurant and walk over to them.

"Ah, Randy," Booth greeted him, rising momentarily. Both Booth and Clayborne recognized all of the social amenities. "Holly and I have been looking forward to seeing you."

Clayborne pulled up a chair after greeting them formally. He smiled at Holly warmly, and she responded less warmly. A waiter came over, and after Clayborne ordered an apéritif, he went away. Clayborne engaged them in small talk until the waiter returned with the drink, and only when the fellow was gone for the second time did he mention the purpose of their meeting, in quiet tones.

"I'm glad I could get you two here together this

150

evening. I have a very important mission for you, and you'll work together."

Booth flashed his theatrical smile. "I like the sound of it already."

Clayborne, though, was all business. "There's a play troupe here now that travels around quite a lot, called the Capital Players."

Booth nodded. "I know them well. I've acted with a couple of them, here in the city."

"Well, they're on their way to the front lines," Clayborne told them, "to entertain our officers in camp—one-act plays, readings."

"I heard about that," Booth said.

Holly was puzzled. "I don't see what that has to do with us," she said. "In particular, me."

Clayborne looked over at her. "We're going to send an agent into the front lines, to try to get a letter across. From our intelligence officer here to General Lee. A woman will carry that letter. We want that woman to be you, Holly."

Holly felt her cheeks warming slightly, and her pulse racing. "Me?" she said softly.

"All civilian personnel are searched, of course, before they are allowed into the front lines, no matter what their background. But women are let off lightly. That's our ace in the hole."

"But how would the woman cross lines?" Booth wondered, glancing at Holly. "Isn't that impossible?"

"It's not as difficult as you might think," Clayborne replied. "We'll give specific instructions, of course. The agent will have to get over and back, if she's to be of any use to us again." He, too, looked over at Holly.

"But I'm not an actress," Holly said. "What do you

151

have in mind, Randy?"

He took a deep breath. "That's where John comes in. We want John to give you some quick tutoring in voice projection and so forth: elocution, stage directions, little intricacies of stage performance. Then we want him to introduce you to the Capital Players as a Richmond actress whose loyalties are with the Union. It would be foolish to try to hide your Charleston accent. You would request, upon hiring into the troupe, to go to Virginia with them."

Holly looked past him, thinking. "It sounds so—complex."

"It could be. But I'm convinced that if anybody can pull it off, you can. My superiors are very impressed with you, Holly."

Booth was frowning. "But, Randy, Holly is just a child, really. I think this would be much too dangerous for her. After all, she's very dear to both of us. Why not just let her go on gathering information here in the city? There are others who could take on this kind of thing. Maybe an experienced actress."

"There is nobody available who would fill the bill quite like Holly," Clayborne said. "I think she'd be perfect for the job. Naturally, there would be some risk, and I'm as concerned for Holly's safety as you, John. But all of us have to take some chances for the cause." He looked over at Holly. "I think Holly should decide whether it's the kind of thing she would like to involve herself in."

Holly was sober-faced and thoughtful. "I would be entertaining Union troops?" she said.

"Primarily officers," Clayborne told her. "You would only be going to two encampments, and would be back here within a week."

"How would I carry the letter?" Holly wondered.

"It would be in the lining of your purse," Clayborne told her. "Believe me, there's little danger in that part. They're very casual about women. Your difficulty will be getting past camp guards and out into no-man's-land in the middle of the night, and then back, later. But we'll give you detailed instruction."

Booth was shaking his head. "I don't like it, Randy."

Both Holly and Clayborne looked over at him, but said nothing.

"Will I know the contents of this letter?" Holly asked.

Clayborne shook his head. "No, you won't. Not even I will know what's in it. That's the way all this works, Holly. The less of us know, the better."

Booth sighed heavily, resigning himself to Holly's obvious interest. Holly looked down at her half-empty teacup. "I'll do it, Randy," she finally said.

Clayborne smiled. "I knew you would."

"When will this happen?" Holly said.

"The troupe is scheduled to go over the Christmas holidays. That means John will have to get you ready in a hurry. Of course, the whole mission will be aborted if John can't persuade a fellow named Matthews to hire you."

Booth made a sour face. "He'll hire her, all right. Wouldn't you?"

Clayborne smiled nicely. "Who could refuse?" he said.

Holly could not sleep that night. Her role as adventuress seemed to be taking on a new, frightening shape. It had been one thing to steal small secrets at banquets and pass them on to Clayborne. But this was real intelligence work, the kind men usually carried out. It was possible she could get killed.

That was a sobering thought. It made her think of Stuart Blaisdell, out there in the thick of the recent fighting in Tennessee, and wonder if he was all right. No one had heard from him for a while, and she knew he could be dead.

The very next evening after the meeting with Clayborne, Holly decided to broach the subject of the actors' troupe to Eugenia and Preston Fayette.

They were at their long dinner table when she brought it up. They all sat at one end of it, while a maid served them their several courses. It was getting close to Christmas, and Eugenia talked about some get-togethers her friends were planning.

"Maybe you'd like to attend a couple of the parties, Holly," she said while they waited for the dessert course. She and Preston always dressed for dinner, and so Holly was obligated to do so, also. Eugenia and Holly wore dark dresses; Preston wore a brocaded jacket with a loose tie at the neck. "There will be exchanges of gifts, and eggnog, and singing."

"That sounds very nice, Eugenia," Holly told her. "But it's possible I'll be occupied at Christmas time."

Preston gave her a quizzical look, appearing very lawyerlike and judicial at the end of the table. "Occupied?" he said.

Holly placed her fork carefully down. "John Booth says there may be an opening in the Capital Players troupe," she said slowly, "for their Christmas junket to the front lines. He thinks I would qualify as one of their performers—a reader of Shakespeare, perhaps."

"A performer?" Eugenia said in surprise. "The front lines? Whatever are you thinking of, Holly?"

154

"The Capital Players?" Preston said.

Holly looked from Eugenia, who was already quite upset, to Preston, who was more composed. "Yes, Uncle. They are here for a short time, on their way from Washington to Virginia. John says they have a high reputation in the theater. They're a small group, and very professional."

Eugenia was very excited. "But, Holly! You're not an actress! Why would you want to be? Oh, God, I worried about this Booth fellow and you. Look at the ideas he's put into your head!"

Holly felt for her aunt. She did not like hurting her, and she did not like lying to her. But she was going to have to, now. "Eugenia, I don't aspire to be an actress. I have no talent for it. What I want to do is not really acting, and it's a temporary job. I'd be back here in a week. It has nothing to do with acting or John Booth. I want to do something to help out in the war effort. This is the small thing I can accomplish with the abilities I have. The soldiers at the front need relaxation, Eugenia. They're entitled to any effort we can make in their behalf, you surely understand that."

"Of course they are," Eugenia said. "But I thought you had little feeling for the Union cause, Holly."

Holly averted her gaze, wondering if either of them would believe her. "I feel for the men on both sides of this struggle, some brothers and cousins, fighting against each other. If I were in Charleston, I would be attracted to the idea of doing the same thing for the Confederate troops."

Preston leaned forward onto the table. He moved his bone-china plate slightly away from him, closer to his sterling-silver knife and fork, lying beside his Irish linen

155

napkin. "I think I understand how you feel, Holly. But people in our station in the world don't go running off to such adventures, my dear. If you were my daughter, I would not want you taking yourself off to entertain soldiers in the war. I feel no less strongly because you're my niece. There are acceptable ways of helping in the war effort, and unacceptable ways. Neither the Fayettes nor the Ransoms have ever entertained others, Holly, war or no war, and if we had, it would not be our women who would have done so."

Holly had expected this from him. "Things have changed, Uncle Preston, and are still changing. Women are taking a more active role in the world, and are engaging in occupations that were forbidden to them fifty years ago. This has been especially true since this war began. But it will never be the same again, after this conflict is over. Acting and singing and even dancing professionally will be acceptable eventually, Preston, as occupations for respectable women. Women will be lawyers, doctors, business people. It's all coming. It's no longer necessary or desirable to protect us like children. We want to take part in the world."

Preston regarded her darkly, but Eugenia was surprised at her own reaction to the short speech. She found that there was little of it with which she was in disagreement.

"There will never come a time when it will be out of vogue to treat a woman like a lady," Preston said in his courtroom voice, "or to distinguish between women of breeding and—others."

"My breeding comes from my father, Col. Ashby Ransom," Holly said tightly. "Nothing I do with the Capital Players can demean that, Preston. At any rate, I

156

am not proposing going off to become a Hooker prostitute or a Major Annie. I want to lighten the Christmas holiday for a small part of our fighting force, and then return here to continue arranging and selling floral bouquets. I don't think that can possibly hurt my reputation here. But if you feel otherwise, I'll move out and find a room. I'll be doing so one of these days, anyway."

"Oh, Holly!" Eugenia said.

"It seems that your mind is made up," Preston said. "It was made up when you broached the subject to us." He rose from his chair, just as a black maid brought desserts in on a silver tray. "I won't be having anything else, Flossie," he said to her. Then, to Eugenia and Holly, "If you'll excuse me, please." He turned and left the dining room, dark-visaged.

Eugenia sighed heavily. "It's all right, Holly. Preston is very set in his ideas. But he loves you very much."

"I know, Eugenia, but I must do this. There are reasons that I can't discuss with anyone. Since Preston seems resolute in his opposition, I think I ought to look for a room for myself outside the house. I'll begin tomorrow."

Eugenia's eyes teared up. "Oh, God, Holly! Please don't leave! We'll work something out; we always have. What would your mother say if you went out on your own!"

"I don't think Charlotte cares all that much," Holly said. "So long as I'm not there in Charleston to cause her any embarrassment. It's time I was on my own, Eugenia; I'm not a little girl anymore." She sighed, and her blue eyes were moist, too. "I'll let you know as soon as I find something."

*　　　*　　　*

Within three days, Holly had a nice room in a large old rooming house just off Philadelphia Road, and had gotten two weeks' leave from her job at the florist shop. She was forced to see Booth every day and night, because it was only a few days until Christmas, and the players were leaving for the front shortly. Booth taught her some elocution and some mannerisms used by readers, and thought she was a natural. They practiced in his room most of the time. Holly was aware that if Eugenia knew, she would be shocked. Holly had allowed Booth to kiss her a couple of times, but there had been no intimacy. They were becoming very close, and despite his extreme views and occasional dark moods, Holly decided, in those close few days, that she was finally in love.

Holly had never met a man who was so utterly charming, who had such a fine sense of humor, who made her react on such a physical level. The latter, too, was greatly emphasized in these few days when they were together most of the time; Holly just returned to her new quarters occasionally through the day, and in the evening to sleep. Booth drilled her in readings hour after hour with great seriousness, but in the teaching there were little touchings and looks that kept Holly tingling inside at his masculine proximity, aware of his desire for her and hers for him. Finally, on a cold late-December afternoon after she had finished a reading of a scene from *As You Like It*, Booth sat her down on a sofa that became his bed at night, and offered her a cup of tea.

"No, thanks, John," she told him. "I really ought to get back to my place. Did you make the appointment to see Mr. Matthews?"

Booth nodded, sitting beside her in his shirt sleeves. "We'll see him tomorrow. The troupe leaves the next day, and I'm hoping you'll be with them. They'll reach the front just in time for Christmas. General Grant himself is encamped near the Rapidan River there. It will be his officers you'll be entertaining, if you get the job."

"I'm getting a little nervous about it," she admitted.

Booth put an arm around her, and she looked up into his dark eyes. "Me, too," he said. "I'd rather be going myself, honest to God. I'm going to pace the floor while you're gone. I don't know what I'd do if something happened to you."

"Do you really mean that, John?"

Booth reached over and kissed her. It was a surprisingly passionate kiss, as Clayborne's had been on that one night. But this one was different for Holly. It touched a quick fire inside her that made raw emotions tumble through her, allowing her to respond to him without inhibition or restraint.

"Oh—God," she said, when she could speak.

"I love you, Holly Ransom," he said in a harsh whisper.

She hesitated only a moment. "I love you, John."

"That makes me the luckiest man in the world," he said.

"Oh, John." He was nuzzling her throat, her ear.

"Let us be together before you leave, Holly. That will make it a little easier for me. Please, darling. Just this time, this moment. Give us both something to remember until you return to me."

Holly recalled her mistake with Clayborne, and hesitated. But this was different. Clayborne had been a ghost from the past she missed too much, and taking him close to her had been repossession of that past, for a brief moment in time. She had known it was wrong even as she

159

had allowed it to happen. This was a relationship based on affection and trust, and Booth was the only man she had ever felt that way about.

"All right, John."

Booth went and closed the shutters to the outside; the room was darkened. Outside there was the sound of horses' hoofs on paving bricks, and in the corridor outside the room, someone was humming "My Old Kentucky Home." Holly undressed with him, not trying to hide her body from him, having no shame about what she was doing. Then they were on the sofa together, his hot flesh entwined with hers; the outside noises were gone and there was only the sound of her own labored breathing in her ear, the cries of pleasure that were torn from her throat.

Across the room, a copy of Shakespeare was open to a play that Booth had intended to drill her with, but had not gotten to. It was *Love's Labor Lost*, a reading that audiences always found amusing.

Chapter Nine

Booth asked Holly to stay with him that night at his room, but she would not do it. She did not intend to be promiscuous with him, even though she was in love. He had not spoken of marriage or permanence, and that was natural, in view of the circumstances that surrounded them. But she wanted to go a little carefully, even with Booth.

The next day they went to the temporary headquarters of the play troupe, located at a small theater near Federal Hill. The director of the troupe, one Thaddeus Matthews, received them in a small office at the rear of the building. The room was papered with playbills and flyers, and photographs of past actors who had played at the theater. Matthews was a robust, loud-speaking fellow who was stunned by Holly's beauty as soon as she walked in, and everything went quite smoothly from that point on.

"Miss Ransom is an actress with some experience," Booth lied to Matthews when they were all seated in the office around an oak desk. "She has taken small parts in Washington and Philadelphia, after some readings in Richmond."

Matthews was staring at Holly openly. "It's not often we see a young actress so lovely," he said in a deep voice.

"That's very kind, Mr. Matthews," Holly told him.

"Miss Ransom wants to accompany you on your brief tour of the battle lines," Booth said, "as a patriotic gesture. She would expect a recompense, of course. She would have no interest in staying with the company after your return here."

"I see," Matthews said. He regarded Holly seriously. "Would you want a part in one of our short dramas?"

"Oh, no," Holly told him. "I thought I'd read some poetry, or perhaps from one of the classics. I'd be much too rusty with my acting to step right in and learn a part in this brief time."

Matthews eyed her narrowly. "You'd be perfect for a small role I have in mind in a short comedy."

"No, thanks," Holly said. "Really, I'd want my participation to be limited."

"Would you mind reading for me?" Matthews asked her.

"No, of course not." But she was taut inside.

Matthews gave her a small book, opened to a page of light verse. Holly read it slowly and clearly, and she stressed her Charleston accent because she thought Matthews would like it. He did.

"That was very good, Miss Ransom. I'm sure you would do beautifully in one of our plays."

"No, really, Mr. Matthews."

He nodded. "All right, you have yourself a job for the Christmas week. You'll receive the same pay as our other two readers, and your transportation and meals. Your lodgings will be on military bases, of course. Does that sound good to you?"

"I'm very pleased, Mr. Matthews." Holly smiled.

"You won't be sorry," Booth said. "They'll love her down there in the wilds of Virginia."

"I'm sure of it," Matthews agreed. "You understand that we leave here tomorrow at noontime?"

"Yes, I know," Holly said. "I'll be joining you early in the morning, if that's all right."

"I'll get your papers ready," Matthews said. "And we'll be expecting to see you here at the theater tomorrow morning."

"Thank you very much, Mr. Matthews," Holly told him. "I'm thrilled to have this opportunity to serve the Union cause in some small way."

"The pleasure is mine, young lady," Matthews said.

The next day, after a very long good-by with Booth, in which he pledged his love anew to her and made her promise to be extremely careful and take as few chances as possible, Holly left Baltimore with the play troupe. They traveled in two horse-drawn coaches; their equipment had been sent ahead of them in wagons. The ride was a rather rough one, and very cold. There were a couple of actresses, both older than she, who befriended Holly, and there was a young man who flirted with her all the way to their destination—the Union encampment at the front lines, not far from the Rapidan River.

Although seen in the evening light, the camp seemed surprisingly large to Holly. There were rows upon rows of small tents, even more than Blaisdell had seen on his arrival in Tennessee. There were corrals and wagons, and carts and more wagons. Two rather large officers' tents had been set aside for the troupe's accommodations. She and her party were passed in by two somber guards, and then at another checkpoint they were all searched.

That was the one tense moment for Holly that day. Clayborne, in his last instructions to her on that evening before she left, had given her a gray purse with a silk lining, and the letter Holly was to smuggle across lines had been sewn into the lining of that purse. She had also been given specific instructions on how to accomplish the crossing, by Clayborne, and a password for the Confederate sentry she would run into on the other side of the battle line. Now, on this cold evening in that camp in Virginia, Holly stood before a checkpoint tent and watched the Union sergeant search the men of the troupe, including Matthews. Then one of the women was taken forward; Holly would be next. The sergeant asked the woman what she was carrying on her person, and got a reply. He opened her purse and looked into it for a long moment. Then he passed the woman through and Holly stepped up to him. Out of the corner of her eye, she could see a corporal going through the luggage of the troupe, and another soldier looking through the two coaches that stood close by.

"You're an actress too, ma'am?" the sergeant asked Holly now.

Holly nodded, and hoped her fear did not show in her face. "Yes, Sergeant. I do readings for the company."

He eyed her sideways. "That's a southern accent you got there. Where'd you pick that up, ma'am?"

"I'm originally from Richmond," she told him. "When Virginia sided with the secessionists, I could not in good conscience remain there. I moved to Baltimore, where I could support the Union."

He nodded. "A wise decision, ma'am. May I see your purse for just a minute?"

She gave it over to him. He opened it, and looked through her personal things carefully. She was certain he would hear a crinkling of paper in the silk lining, or feel it. But after a long moment, he gave the purse back to her.

"Very well, Miss Ransom. It's nice to see a southerner with some sense. I'll try to catch your reading."

"Thank you, Sergeant." Holly smiled nicely at him, feeling a small prickling of relief run through her.

Not long thereafter, Holly was quartered in one of the two large tents, the one the women were to occupy. There were four of them in all, and two were married to male actors. There were six of the latter, plus Matthews and a male assistant who directed the group. Their tents were situated in an enclave of larger tents, where staff officers were billeted, and one of them belonged to Ulysses S. Grant himself, who had become Lincoln's favorite general. Holly hoped for a glimpse of the great Union general, but was told later in the evening that he had left the encampment for a few days over the Christmas holiday.

A troupe performance was given that very evening, despite the long trip they had made to get there. It was given out in the open, with many young officers and noncoms present, and Holly read from an Emerson essay. The troupe was well received, with much applause. Holly was obligated to leave her purse in her billet tent, and worried about it all through the troupe's performance. Afterward, when the troupe was fed and met some high-ranking officers; Holly had to admit that she was impressed with their courtesy and gentlemanly manners, despite the conditions under which they were living. She could have expected no more from Confederate officers, she realized. A colonel and a major flirted heavily with

165

her, but she managed to turn them both away gracefully. When the women returned to their tent, Holly was obligated to talk with one of them about Richmond for a while, and she hoped the actress did not catch her up on her shallow knowledge of that city. Then Holly excused herself to take a walk.

There was a picket outside the tent, but not to restrict the movement of the women. He had been placed there to keep curious soldiers away. Holly explained to him that she intended to walk to the perimeter of the camp, and he had no objection.

"Yes, ma'am. Just be careful of the latrines in that direction, ma'am, if you'll excuse my mentioning it."

Holly's purpose was not to make the crossing that evening. She merely was to acquaint herself with the perimeter on that initial outing, in accord with Clayborne's instructions.

It was quite cold, but the moon rode high and bright and it was a lovely winter evening. There was no snow on the ground and Holly was grateful for that. Snow left tracks.

There were pickets on the camp's perimeter, and they were thicker on the south side, which faced the rebel lines. Seeing a picket walking his post, Holly watched him for a few minutes, from the shadow of a small tree, and saw how far he traveled along his route. Then she came forward and spoke to him.

"It's a brisk evening, soldier."

The blue-uniformed picket in the billed cap came over, and nodded to her. He carried a long Kentucky-type rifle under his arm. "Evening, ma'am. Yep, it is a little chilly. But not like where I come from."

Holly moved closer to him. "And where would that be?"

"Michigan, ma'am. The wind blows so hard with that snow in it up there that a man has to run backward to spit, ma'am."

Holly's tension was broken, and she laughed. It was difficult to think of men like this as the enemy, and more difficult to play deceitful games with them.

"That sounds very wintry." She smiled.

"Are you one of them actress ladies?" the soldier asked her.

Holly nodded. "Yes, I'm just getting a little air before turning in." She looked out across the open fields beyond the camp, and thought she could see a couple of twinkling fires off in the blackness. "Are those fires over in that direction, soldier?"

He followed her gaze. "Yes, ma'am. Them's the Confederates, over there. You don't want to wander over that way, ma'am, or you're liable to wind up shot."

A little chill passed along Holly's back. "Oh, I have no intention, soldier. Guns scare me."

"They scare most of us, ma'am," he admitted easily. Holly felt a twinge of sympathy for him.

"I can't believe the rebels are so close," Holly said. "Just how far is it to the Confederate lines, do you think?"

"Oh, the closest points are only about a half-mile off, ma'am," he replied. "None of us can shoot that far, except with cannon."

Holly noticed that about fifty yards away was a stand of young trees, with undergrowth. If she could get to that area without being seen by this picket or other ones, she would be all right. There was additional cover on the way to the other lines. The difficulty then would be in trying to keep from being shot on arrival there.

"Well, I hope that you don't have to use that rifle,"

Holly said.

"Oh, it ain't likely we'll avoid a fight, ma'am. Unless General Lee just turns tail and runs off, and that ain't like him at all."

Holly was glad to hear that judgment of Lee from a Union soldier. "Well. We'll all pray for peace," she said. She was ready to go back. She had left her purse at the tent, because she felt it was safer there than out here on the picket line. But now she wanted to get back to her belongings.

"We'll all appreciate that, ma'am," the soldier said to her. "All of us on both sides."

Holly looked into his young face for a long moment, and swallowed hard. "Good night, soldier."

"Good night, ma'am. It was good talking with you."

Holly walked back past a corral full of horses and mules, and the strong odor of manure filled her nostrils. Off in another part of the camp, a couple of the troupe men had formed a singing group, and there was a chorus of "Just Before the Battle, Mother."

"Did you have a nice walk, ma'am?" the tent picket said when she arrived back.

"Oh, yes," Holly said, a light fog of breath issuing as she spoke. "But it's too cool to stay out there long."

"It won't be much better inside, ma'am. But at least you have a camp stove in there."

"We appreciate that, soldier," she told him.

Inside, only one of the older women was there, the one who had befriended Holly first on the way there. Her name was Anne, and she had been with the troupe for a couple of years. She was married to one of the men, but there was no arrangement at the camp to put husbands and wives of the troupe together. She was sitting on her cot when Holly came in, studying a paper on which she had printed a poetry excerpt.

"Oh, it's you, Holly. I'm just trying to learn this reading. Did you have your look around?" She was a woman of about thirty, with long blondish hair and brown eyes.

"Yes, I had a nice walk," Holly told her. "I'm surprised at the size of the camp, there must be twenty thousand men here."

"I suspect more than that, even," Anne said. "Doesn't it give you a sense of patriotism, to see all these fine young men out here ready to defend the Union, Holly?"

Holly turned to her from her own cot. "Why, yes," she lied. "It's all very inspiring."

"George would have enlisted," Anne went on, "but he has a weak stomach, dear fellow. A slight case of dysentery would kill him, poor thing." Anne was a talker, but Holly did not mind. She just listened with one ear.

"I'm sure he's very patriotic," Holly said. She walked over to the head of her cot, and felt under her pillow for her purse. It was not there.

She got down onto one knee, and felt around again, then pulled the pillow aside. The purse was gone. "My purse is gone!" she said in abject dismay.

Anne turned to her. "Oh, no, honey. I saw the edge of it protruding from the pillow, and took it over here for you, until you returned." She reached under a thrown shawl and held Holly's purse out to her.

Holly was very upset. She came and grabbed the purse away from the other woman quickly, breathing hard, her eyes flashing. "You had no right to move my personal things!" she said loudly.

Anne was taken aback.

"I expect a certain respect for my privacy!"

Anne stood up, surprised by the small outburst. "Look, I was only trying to be helpful. There was a soldier in here arranging things for us, and I wanted to be sure nothing of yours was stolen."

Holly was clutching the purse tightly. She finally calmed down, and looked away for a moment. She had already felt the letter in the lining. So she knew it was undiscovered. She just hoped Anne had not also felt it in there.

"Oh, gosh. I'm sorry, Anne. It's just that this purse is a family heirloom. It was given to me by my dying mother, on her deathbed."

"Oh, dear, I am sorry," Anne said.

"It's all right, I overreacted. I never let it out of my sight, Anne, because of its importance to me. But I didn't want to carry it out around the camp with me." She was more composed, now, and sorry she had reacted in fear. "Please accept my apology for saying those things to you. They were unwarranted."

Anne grinned. "God, it's all right. I understand now."

Holly could not fall asleep that night, though. She worried that Anne had found the letter, maybe even read it and resewed the purse. She had a compelling urge, as she lay awake with the other women asleep around her, the night sounds of the encampment outside, to get the purse out again and feel the stitching in the lining, to assure herself it had not been disturbed. But she fought off the compulsion. If Anne had found the letter, she would have confronted Holly with it, or turned her in to the officers all around them in camp—or maybe even tried to blackmail her. But she would not have kept silent about it, surely. Holly lay there and imagined soldiers marching into the tent to arrest her, accuse her of treason. She wondered if they shot women for such activities, as they did men. She thought of Charlotte, and Jennifer, and Eugenia. She wished John Booth were beside her on the cot, to hold her and comfort her. She wondered if she would ever see him again. He had been so worried about her, so solicitous before she left. She was certain of his love for her, and hers for him. It was a wonderful feeling to be in love and it was ironic that it had come at such a bad time.

In the small hours of morning, Holly finally fell asleep.

The next day was overcast, but warmer. It was Christmas Eve, and there were dispensations from duty. The troupe put on a performance at midday, and some enlisted men were allowed to attend. Grant's immediate subordinates were there, and his close aides, and Holly met some of them. One was a one-star general, and he was very impressed with Holly's readings. Holly found that she liked most of the men they were performing for, and that gave her qualms about what she was doing. But the principles she was defending for the Confederacy were the same; they had not changed. So it never crossed her mind to abort the mission. She knew where her duty lay, and it was with the South.

There was a big meal in a mess tent; high-ranking officers were present and for a battlefield encampment there was much gaiety. Holly saw clearly how important it was for men in battle to have some diversion from reality, from the grimness of what they were about. She hoped that Blaisdell was the recipient of the same kind of diversion, assuming he was alive and well.

171

In early evening there were some big cannons that rumbled past on their way to new positions, but there was no rumor of action on the front. At mid-evening, Holly returned to her tent and tried to calm herself, but found it very difficult. It was this night that she was to carry out her mission to the Confederate lines.

All the women were asleep by eleven. Holly waited for an hour more, lying with all her clothing on under the bed covers. Then she took her purse, bundled up in a dark cape, and went outside.

The picket was there, as usual. She could probably have gotten past him without his notice, but she did not want to take the chance. She confronted him by calling out to him, in accord with her instructions from Clayborne.

"Soldier!"

The picket came over to her. He was the same one she had spoken with on the previous evening. "Yes, ma'am."

"I couldn't get to sleep, and I think a short walk would be beneficial. Do you think it's safe to take a short stroll through the headquarters area here?"

"Oh, yes, ma'am, it's safe," the picket replied. "But maybe you would like for an officer to escort you?"

"No, thanks," Holly told him. "I just want to be alone with my thoughts on this Christmas Eve, soldier."

"Very well, ma'am. Just stay within the encampment."

"Oh, yes," Holly said quickly.

She walked off, then, in a direction away from the south perimeter of the encampment. But in a few minutes, when she was out of sight of her tent, she made a wide circle around, past other tents and equipment, toward the same picket position she had gone to on the previous evening. At the corner of a large officers' tent, she came very suddenly upon a blue uniform in the darkness. She jumped, startled.

"Oh!"

The soldier was a young lieutenant, an officer of the guard. He tipped his wide-brimmed hat to her. "Ma'am. I guess you'd be one of the play-actors?"

"Yes, I am," Holly said, recovering from her fright.

"Are you lost, ma'am?"

"Oh, no." Quickly. "I just couldn't sleep. I'm taking a little air, then going right back to my tent."

"Would you like me to see you around on your walk?"

She forced a smile. "Why, that's very generous of you, Lieutenant. But I think I know my way around, and I believe I'm too tired for conversation. Perhaps some other time."

"All right, ma'am."

She went on past him, imagining that he would be watching her. But when she got out near the picket line, and looked back, he was gone. She walked to the shadow of a small tree, and stared out toward the picket line. Yes, there was the same fellow she had spoken with last night. He was on his way away from her, walking his post. The next picket was too far distant to see her, she figured. She watched the closer one move away from her, and glanced to the stand of trees she had noted before. There would never be a better time than the present, while the picket was moving away from her. There was no moon, and she would have cover of darkness.

She moved quickly out to the picket line, and beyond it toward the trees. She was now in no-man's-land, and she felt a queasiness in her stomach as she moved along, expecting at any moment to hear the picket challenge her. But no call came. In just moments she had reached

173

the cover of the trees.

She leaned against a young elm and looked back toward the Union encampment, where yellow lights dotted the darkness. She could just barely make out the picket, turning around to head back toward the place where she had left the camp. But she was beyond his field of vision now, and hidden from view.

She waited for a few minutes, to catch her breath. She did not feel the cold anymore; she was warm under the cape. She turned and looked into the trees, and could see beyond them, where scattered trees and undergrowth would hopefully hide her from both lines for a distance. She started out through the trees.

In a short time she was out in the open and heading for more cover, stumbling over uneven open ground. Then she was in trees again, and it went that way for three or four hundred yards. Then there was only one last open stretch between her and Confederate lines.

The twinkling fires there were now easily visible, even the outlines of rows of tents. The encampment looked almost as large as the Union one. She realized that this part was probably the most dangerous, even though she was heading toward her own people. She took a deep breath and headed across the last open field, seeing no sentry in sight.

She was almost in the Confederate camp when the soldier jumped out from behind a low tree and aimed the musket at her heart, looking very scared. She was so close she could see his finger tight against the gun's trigger.

"Halt!" he said nervously. But then he raised the musket to his shoulder to fire.

"No, wait!" she cried out. *"I'm a friend!"*

He lowered the musket slowly. He wore gray trousers

174

of the Confederate Army, but his shirt and jacket were nonregulation. That was the way it was with many of Lee's men.

Holly stood very still. "I have a password," she called quickly to him. "Suwanee River."

He lowered the musket all the way. "O.K. Come on in."

She walked up to him, and now could see his lean face clearly. He had a Tennessee accent. "So you're the one," he said, studying her face, "that we were supposed to look for."

"I guess so," Holly said, shaking slightly inside. "I have a letter for General Lee."

The picket had not been told that. "You're to be taken to Colonel Robertson," he said. "Maybe I'd better take the letter until we get there."

Holly shook her head sideways. "I can't deliver the letter to anyone but General Lee or Colonel Robertson."

He hesitated a moment. "O.K., ma'am. Come with me."

The picket gave Holly over to another soldier at a nearby tent, a corporal. The corporal seemed very awed by the fact that Holly was a woman. He led her into the encampment, past rows of tents where men were sleeping. They came to a grouping of larger tents, as in the Union camp, and the corporal took her to one in which all the oil lamps were lighted, giving the tent a warm yellow glow all over. He went in alone for a moment, as Holly waited nervously at the entrance flap. Then he re-emerged with an officer.

The colonel was thickset and partially bald, and he wore a yellow sash on the waist of his gray uniform. He looked Holly over with piercing eyes, then extended his hand to take hers.

"Colonel Robertson, Miss Ransom. It's my extreme pleasure to meet you."

"Thank you, Colonel."

"I gather you just crossed from the enemy encampment."

"Yes, I did."

"You have a lot of courage, Miss Ransom. Please step inside."

The corporal went off to another of the large tents, and Holly followed Robertson inside. There were a table, three straight chairs, and a couple of cots. Robertson offered Holly a chair, and she sat down. He took a seat behind the table, which was littered with papers.

"We've been expecting you, Miss Ransom. We knew that our Baltimore unit was using a woman, but I guess I expected her to be more—mature."

"I'm mature enough to know where my duty lies, Colonel," Holly told him.

"That's apparent, Miss Ransom. And beautiful enough to charm a sentry out of his rifle too, I suspect. Do you have the letter?"

Holly nodded, and put her purse on the table. Robertson examined it, found the letter in the lining. He cut it open with a very sharp pocket knife, and drew the folded letter out. It was the first time Holly had seen it.

"Yes, it's in good condition," he told her. He opened the letter and perused it quickly, and his face was serious. "Humph. Yes."

"I hope the information is important to you, Colonel," she said.

"It is indeed," Robertson said. "It gives details on a Union offensive here in the early part of next year. Miss

Ransom, I—"

But at that moment, another man entered, an older man wearing an almost white beard and with gold on his epaulets. Holly recognized him immediately as Robert E. Lee. He was followed in by two aides, and all of them focused on Holly immediately.

Robertson came to his feet quickly and stiffly. "Ah, General Lee. General, our letter has arrived. This is Miss Ransom, who delivered it to us."

Lee had a worn, tired look on his handsome face. He turned to Holly and assessed her for a long moment. "Such bravery in so young and lovely a lady," he said to her.

"I'm very proud to meet you, General Lee," Holly said humbly.

"You sound like a Charleston girl," Lee said.

Holly's face radiated pride. "I am, sir."

Lee took the letter from Robertson. He glanced at it quickly, and his face, too, become sober. He looked back at Holly. "You've done the Confederacy a great service, Miss Ransom. If you get back to Charleston before this war is over, please convey my regards to General de Beauregard."

"I will, sir."

A couple of moments later, after Lee and his aides made a rather formal farewell, they all left and Holly was alone with Robertson again. He seated himself across from her, and laced his hands together on the table. "Well, Miss Ransom. I believe your plan of operation calls for your immediate return to the Union encampment."

"That's right, Colonel."

He sighed heavily. "I wish there were some way to

make your crossing absolutely safe, ma'am. But I think you know that's an impossibility."

"I understood that when I accepted the assignment, Colonel."

"May I offer you anything before you leave? Something to eat or drink?"

"I don't think so," Holly told him with a smile. "I don't think my stomach could handle anything tonight, if you'll excuse my frankness."

"I understand perfectly," he said. He rose again. "Then let's get you back out to the sentry post, Miss Ransom. The sooner you get back, the safer it may be for you."

Holly was led back to the picket line then, and a couple of the colonel's aides joined them. One man wanted to take her partway across, to show her how to keep in deep cover, but the colonel would not allow him to. He thought Holly was safer on her own.

With quick good-bys, she left the encampment. She kept to the trees as much as possible again, and finally, without incident, she had arrived at the thick stand of trees not far from the Union picket lines.

She moved quickly through the trees and underbrush and came out to the far perimeter of them. Squinting, she could see a lonely figure walking along in the darkness before the fires of the spread-out camp. That would be the man she had spoken to the night before.

She stood there for a long moment, while the figure retreated along the picket line, away from her. Then she started out, hurrying across the open field.

She got two-thirds of the way there, before a rifle shot rang out from her right—the sentry she had been watching was on her left—and she felt a hot tugging at the collar of her cape.

178

She jumped and cried out, realizing she had been shot at, and narrowly missed. She turned and saw the scared-looking sentry not thirty yards away, reloading his gun. He had been hidden by a tree, and she had not seen him. As he reloaded, Holly called out to him. The far picket had turned toward them, and not far away, a couple of soldiers appeared from a guard tent.

"Don't shoot!" she yelled.

The sentry, hearing a woman's voice, lowered the rifle and began approaching her warily. The other fellow came up from behind her, and the two at the tent also started over toward the disturbance.

"I'm one of the play troupe," Holly now said breathlessly. "Out for a walk."

"A walk?" the sentry said. "At this time of night, ma'am?" He was still very excited.

But now the other sentry had come up and focused on her. "For God's sake, Graves! You almost killed this woman! I know her, she's with the players!"

"What's going on here?" an officer of the guard said as he came up. He was one of the men from the tent.

"I couldn't sleep again tonight," Holly said to them, trying to keep control of herself. "So I took a walk, as I did last evening. I guess I wandered out past the picket line by mistake."

The sentry who had spoken to her on the previous evening spoke up. "She was out here walking last night, Lieutenant. She likes the night air."

The half-dressed lieutenant studied her soberly. "May I see your purse a moment, ma'am?"

"Yes, of course," Holly told him. At the last moment before she had left the Confederate encampment, the colonel there had given her a purse exactly like the one she had carried there, and which now had its lining ripped out, and she had transfered her belongings to it. She now handed the new purse over to the young officer, and he glanced through it.

"All right, Miss—"

"Ransom," Holly said.

"Miss Ransom. You may have this back." He returned the purse to her. "You were very careless tonight, Miss Ransom. Wandering out into and beyond the picket line is not very wise. We're in a war here, you know; this isn't the Washington stage. Please confine your walks to the area around your tent, for the rest of your stay here."

His reaction was a bit officious, but Holly did not mind. "I'll do that, Lieutenant," she said. "I was very foolish."

His face softened. "It's just that we wouldn't want to harm such a lovely lady," he said more gently.

She smiled weakly, and glanced at the fellow who had shot at her, and he grinned slightly. "Thank you, Lieutenant," she said humbly. "I'll just get back to my tent, now."

"I hope you don't mind if I have one of the men escort you."

"Not at all," Holly said, relief seeping slowly into her now.

She returned in the custody of the other man from the guard tent, a corporal of the guard, her mission behind her.

When she arrived at the tent, only Anne woke upon her entering. She did not ask any questions. Holly knew, of course, that, in the morning, everybody would know about the shooting incident, and there would be a small flurry about it. But Holly did not mind any of that.

She felt quite lucky just to be alive.

Chapter Ten

Off in the distance there were the booming sounds of big guns on the warships, and from the shore batteries of the Fifty-fourth Massachusetts Infantry; these were followed by dull thuds as exploding shells hit the waterfront area of the city.

Charleston was really under siege now. Rubble from destroyed buildings clogged the streets, and the stench of burned structures reeked in the winter air. Rats rummaged amid the debris; sickness was everywhere. People in some quarters had begun eating horse and dog meat, and were glad to get it. Citizens were dying from the shelling, the sickness, and starvation.

Jennifer lay nude on her wide double bed and listened to the distant explosions, hoping they did not come any nearer. Beside her, on his side facing away from her, lay her newest male friend, a young lieutenant in the army defending the city under General de Beauregard. Jennifer's men came and went with greater frequency now, since her grandmother, Amanda, had passed on in the fall and left Jennifer alone in the house, and since the receipt of Clayborne's letter recently.

Jennifer glanced over at the naked backside of the young soldier, with its ripe musculature, and thought that there was not as much pleasure in these affairs as there had been in the beginning. The soldier grunted and rolled onto his back, showing her the private parts of him that had so recently coupled with hers in the dim coolness of the room. His eyes were closed, and he was half-asleep.

She rose and got out of bed, her breasts bouncing as she picked up a robe and, to ward off the cold, threw it on. Nobody had enough heat in their houses nowadays. That was the way it was.

She walked to a chest of drawers, pulled a drawer open, and took out Clayborne's letter. Her hair was uncombed, she wore little make-up, and she had lost some of her good looks already. She looked tired, older than Holly, who was senior to her. She opened the letter in the light from the window—it was midafternoon—and read it for the fifth time.

> *Dear Jennifer,*
> *Since that other letter from me, I've given our marriage a lot of thought. What I've decided is that we really don't have a marriage, Jennifer, and never did. I mentioned annulment before, and it was in the heat of anger. Now, though, I am not angry anymore, and I still feel the same way, and that is what I wanted you to know. Maybe you could institute proceedings without me; I don't know the legalities of the situation. But no matter when it happens, I'll want a legal separation and dissolution of our marital bond.*
> *I'm seeing other women now, Jennifer, as I*

presume you're still seeing other men. My work,
which I cannot discuss, takes me in and out of
Union territory, and has given me a reunion with
Holly. Even though unmarried, it seems she has
been considerably more circumspect than certain
of her friends in her relationships with men. We
developed immediate and deep feelings for each
other, and I am happy to say that we have shared
an intimacy that you and I were never able to
achieve, even in the beginning.

There was more to the letter, but after the first
reading, Jennifer never read past that paragraph. She put
the letter down heavily now, and stared across the room.
Anger boiled again deeply inside her, when she thought
of Holly and Clayborne in bed together, making love,
whispering into each other's ears, pledging affection.
When she had first become unfaithful to Clayborne, he
had already gone to camp whores in Tennessee. But
Holly's sleeping with her husband, no matter what was
lost between them, was a breach of an old friendship, a
betrayal of everything that was sacred between them.
Jennifer would not have done it to Holly, and she had not
expected Holly to do anything like that to her. It was very
clear that it was over between Holly and her, and would
never be the same again.

That was both sad and irritating. She valued Holly's
friendship, had respected Holly's judgment and character. That was all changed now, gone. She was left with a
great indignation, and disgust.

The soldier's eyes fluttered open, and he looked over at
her. "Hey. I didn't know you were up. What time has it
gotten to be, my little plum pudding?"

183

"Time for you to go," Jennifer said blandly.

"You don't seem in a very good mood, considering."

"I'm not."

"I thought it was good. I thought we had a great time."

"Just get dressed, Ned."

She went from the room, the room where she and Holly had lain on their beds and talked into the small hours of the morning on so many occasions. When she got out into the corridor, she leaned up against an armoire and cried—for Holly, for Clayborne; for what could have been but never would be.

It must be the war, she thought.

You could always blame it on the war.

It was only a couple of days later, with her anger toward Holly still simmering in her, that Jennifer met Charlotte at the city market.

The farmers' market was not much now. The winter harvest was small, as it had been in the summer. But even if there had been food to buy, nobody would have had the money to pay for it. Confederate money was in bad shape already; some Charleston stores refused to accept it. They preferred barter, and a lot of that took place.

It was a cold, snowy morning when Jennifer went around the market to find something within her budget. Large flakes of snow kept falling, hitting her face and getting down her collar. She had never enjoyed shopping, even when it was easy, but now she despised it. She was in a foul mood, therefore, when Charlotte met her at a corner of two rows of stalls, where a wagon was loaded with carrots for sale.

"Well," Charlotte said to her when she saw her. "It's Charleston's gift to the lecherous male. Out drumming

184

up some business, Jennifer?"

Jennifer gave Charlotte a dark look. Charlotte was drinking more nowadays, and she looked slightly inebriated now. Jennifer did not look great, but Charlotte looked terrible. She was more gaunt than before, and looked sickly. There were many lines in her face that had not been there, when Holly had left home. The war and Uriah Quinn had taken their toll of Charlotte's physical resources.

"I think you're drunk, Charlotte. You don't know what you're saying," Jennifer said soberly. "You ought to go home and sober up, or these farmers will take advantage of you."

Charlotte laughed in her throat. Her dark hair was covered by a shawl, and she looked pinched and drawn. A large snowflake fell on her shawl, and hung there beside her face. "That's something you don't have to worry about, honey," she said sourly. "Anybody taking advantage of you."

Jennifer's anger swelled up in her chest. "I notice Uriah isn't with you, Charlotte. Do you know where he is his afternoon?"

Charlotte's face darkened, too. "Where he is? Of course I know where he is. He's down at the office trying to earn us a living through this hellish blockade. Where else would he be?" Defensively.

Now it was Jennifer's turn to laugh. "I thought you might have more guesses than me."

Charlotte scowled. She waited until another woman shopper passed, and then she moved closer to Jennifer. "Are you trying to say something, young woman? If so, let it out!"

Jennifer shrugged in her thick shawl. "It's just that

185

everybody knows that Uriah doesn't spend all of hi
afternoons at his office. Some of them are taken up by hi
friend across town."

"Friend?" Charlotte growled out.

"Yes, his mistress," Jennifer said blandly. "Do yo
mean you didn't know about the Watrous widow? H
sees her at least twice a week, I hear. Surely this comes a
no surprise to you."

Charlotte's face had gone very sober, and she no longe
felt the liquor inside her. She had suspected that Quin
was cheating on her, but wanted to believe that he wa
not. "Damn you, you evil girl!" she hissed out a
Jennifer.

Jennifer had hoped Charlotte did not know for sur
She was not satisfied with the assault, though, because c
Charlotte's hot reply, but only further aroused. "Evil
Me? You ought to look into your own family mor
closely, if you want to find evil and debauchery. Di
Uriah admit to you that he wanted to sleep with m
recently, that he openly propositioned me in a restauran
downtown? Did he mention that to you, Charlotte?"

"That's a damned lie!" Charlotte said loudly, knowin
it was not. She was breathing shallowly, and her inside
were suddenly all knotted up tight.

"If you really believe that," Jennifer told her, "I'd b
happy to discuss it with you and Uriah together."

Charlotte, dizzy with outrage but uncertain how t
respond, started to turn away. But Jennifer's voic
caught her.

"And then of course, there's your lovely daughter.

Charlotte turned back to her warily, a fierce look in he
eyes. "What? Will you even turn on Holly now, yo
damnable woman?"

186

"Turn on her? Hardly. On the contrary, it seems it's she who has turned on me, Charlotte. She's had an affair with my husband, in Baltimore."

Charlotte sucked in her breath audibly, and her jaw dropped slightly open. "An affair with—! I don't believe it!" She was white-faced. A woman passing turned to stare at her. "You're lying again, damn you, Jennifer! You're a damned liar and harlot!"

"If I'm a harlot, then so is Holly!" Jennifer said thickly. "And more. She's a betrayer of friendship and trust!"

"*You liar!*" Charlotte fairly shouted.

"I have a letter from my Randy to prove it," Jennifer said pleasantly, using the possessive pronoun to heighten dramatic effect. "Would you like to read it?"

Charlotte felt very dizzy suddenly. "*Liar, liar, liar!*" she called out as if to someone far beyond Jennifer. Then she turned and was hurrying away, down the long lane of market stalls, past the mules and wagons and winter offerings of crops.

Jennifer stood there for a long moment watching Charlotte recede into the snowfall, until she was barely visible. When she finally turned away, she was crying softly.

Her cheeks were still wet when she arrived back home, some time later.

During Holly's mission to the front lines, Preston Fayette had done some more checking on Randy Clayborne, and was becoming quite suspicious of him. He had checked with the regiment to which Clayborne had alleged attachment, and had come up empty-handed.

Then, shortly after Holly's return to Baltimore and the resumption of her job at the florist's shop, Preston had gone to Washington on a short business trip. While in the capital he went to Union Army headquarters and had more records checked, and found to his surprise that there was no record of a Randolph Clayborne in that army.

Now Preston was very excited about his sleuthing. When he reported his findings to Eugenia, she suggested they have a talk with Holly about Clayborne, and find out what she knew about him. But Preston was more clever than that. Suggesting that Holly might be part of some kind of chicanery, he insisted on going to the authorities without discussing the matter with Holly. Eugenia protested, but he stood firm.

Slightly more than a week after Holly's return, when Holly was seeing John Wilkes Booth again and had already reported her mission's success to him and Clayborne in a secret meeting with them, Preston Fayette went to the commander of the Baltimore troops, General Butler, and told that gentleman his suspicions about Clayborne. Butler was much interested, and put one of his intelligence officers on the matter, saying he would keep Preston advised.

Fortunately for Clayborne at that moment in time, events precluded his being arrested and tried as an agent of a foreign and hostile government. The Union officer assigned to investigate him had learned where Clayborne was living and was asking around about him, also about Holly, but he had not gathered anything damaging to Clayborne before Clayborne received orders to leave Baltimore.

It was on a cold evening in mid-January when Clayborne met with Holly at her place. They sat together in a parlor in the rooming house where she rented her small room, and spoke in quiet tones so that no one would overhear the conversation. Other young women moved in and out of the parlor irregularly.

"My superiors are very pleased with your trip to Virginia with the Capital Players, Holly," he told her as they sat on a long, tweedy sofa in a dim corner of the gaslit room. Through an archway to a corridor, they could see two young women standing talking in low tones. "They're going to recommend you for further work, if you want it. They think you're more valuable to them than John."

Holly arched pretty brows. "What I did was quite ordinary, Randy. Except that I did get shot at."

"You won't be getting your instructions from me anymore," he went on. "I'm being transferred in my duties, Holly."

She looked over and saw how glum his expression suddenly was. "Transferred? To another intelligence command?"

He shook his head. "No. It seems the war is going even more badly than you and I thought. They're running out of line officers, Holly, in the fighting. They're going to transfer me back to the infantry."

"Oh, no!" Holly said softly.

He grinned acidly. "I'll keep my commission. They consider that a concession, I guess. But I'll go back to the fighting. Maybe join Grant's army in Virginia."

Holly's head was spinning with the news. "Gosh, this is all so sudden, Randy—and unexpected."

"Exactly," he said. "Anyway, I did have this time in Baltimore, and we were able to renew old acquaintance. I'll always be thankful for that, Holly."

"Gosh," she said, still staring past him.

"You'll be contacted by another officer. I don't know when or how. They expect to give you more assignments."

She met his gaze, now. "I'm going to miss you, Randy. Really."

He smiled. "I'm glad to hear that." He threw an arm up over the back of the sofa. "It's really serious with you and John now, isn't it?"

Holly looked down at her hands on her lap. "Yes. It is."

"I'm happy for you, Holly. I mean that. Even though I envy John greatly."

She tried to ignore the comment. "I hope you get back to Charleston soon, Randy, to see Jennifer."

Clayborne remembered the letter to Jennifer, written some weeks ago when he was feeling angry at the world. "I have to tell you something, Holly. Get it off my chest, so to speak. It's been bothering me some."

Holly frowned. "What is it, Randy?"

He took a deep breath before he began. "I got roaring drunk one night not long after you and John started seeing each other. I sent Jennifer a letter."

Holly's frown deepened.

"I told her—about us."

Holly felt her head begin to whirl, and her ears were ringing. "Oh, God," she said dully.

"Jesus, I can't tell you how sorry I am. I hurt you, and I hurt Jennifer. The worst part is, when I did it I didn't care. I just didn't care, Holly."

"It's all right, Randy," Holly told him.

"I don't know what's the matter with me, Holly," he went on. "I get these vindictive streaks. And I don't get really close to people. I cheated on Jennifer, in Tennes-

190

see. She might have been true to me, if I'd behaved myself. But I didn't feel the obligation. I'm glad you turned me away, after that one night together. If you'd given yourself to me completely, it would have been different. I'd have been different. I wouldn't have cared so much. What the hell is the matter with me, Holly?"

She touched his face. "You're like everybody else, Randy. None of us is perfect."

"I even lied to you about Stuart. He's still very much in love with you. I tried to make it seem otherwise so you'd give yourself to me."

"Stuart isn't important to me. Only John is," she told him. "Now that's enough of apologies for one evening. When will you be leaving Baltimore?"

"I can't tell you exactly. But this is the last time you'll see me—until the war is over, that is."

Holly got a small chill inside her, and it was as if he had not needed to add the end of the sentence to his reply.

"Randy. I don't know what to say."

He rose from the sofa, and smiled his handsome smile. "You might try, good-by," he said quietly.

Holly rose, too, and came to him and placed a soft kiss on his mouth. A tear had started down her cheek, but she brushed it away. "Listen carefully to me, Randy. I want you to take care of yourself out there. You have a good knowledge of yourself, and when the war is over you'll find a way to get your life in order again—with or without Jennifer. Promise me you'll be careful."

Clayborne liked it that she still had affection for him, after all he had told her. She would always be special to him. "I promise, Holly," he said.

Then he was gone.

Chapter Eleven

They lay in hot union on the big bed, making love. His harsh breathing was labored in her ear, and sweet pleasure surged through her, inflaming her innermost places with the fire of passion.

It finished rather violently, with her nails cutting into his flesh and her cries crowding against the walls and ceiling of the darkened room.

Later they lay side by side, his hand on her stomach, her right arm lying against his side and thigh. Holly felt so good when Booth was close to her, and they gave of themselves physically to each other. She had never felt so much a part of a man, and she believed that she never would again.

The thing was, though, Booth never spoke of permanence in their relationship. He pledged his love to her over and over, but he never spoke of marriage. He kept hinting, from time to time, that there would be plenty of time for things like that when the war was over. But sometimes Holly wondered whether Booth was not more wrapped up in his plays and his acting than he was in her. And in another matter, also. He had become even more obsessive about Abraham Lincoln as the one big evil in America, as the destroyer of the South. Now that Lincoln had elevated General Grant to a three-star rank, it was clear to the world, Booth kept telling Holly, that Lincoln was willing to kill off all the youth of the country to keep the South in the Union. Grant was the ultimate executioner to Booth, and Lincoln was the power that had set him loose.

Now, as they lay on the bed in Booth's room together, Holly looked over at him and saw him staring vacantly toward the dark ceiling, in deep thought. That surprised her, since she had thought that intimacy would relax him and make them close, at least for a while.

"What is it, John?" she asked him. "Is everything all right?"

He looked over at her. It was almost two weeks since Clayborne had left the city surreptitiously and had, hopefully, crossed back into Confederate territory without incident. So far, Clayborne's superiors had not contacted either him or Holly, and that was making Booth wonder if anything was wrong.

"Oh, yes," he said, smiling rather formally for her. "It was really nice, Holly."

"But you seem—distracted," she said.

He shrugged, and removed his hand from her stomach. "That fellow you said was watching your building last week. I just wonder who he was. You haven't seen him for a couple of days now?"

"No, he hasn't been around for a while. There are a lot of women in the rooming house, John. I think eighteen in all. He could have been a shy suitor. Or at the worst, a policeman watching one of them, or a private detective."

"I wish Randy were here so I could talk to him about

this," he said. "He could probably find out whether one of Police Marshal George Kane's men is watching the building. I don't know anybody in city government."

"We could go ask Mayor Brown himself." She smiled, making a joke.

He turned to her, sober-faced. "I don't mean to make this more than it is, Holly, but we have been involved in some things that could get us into big trouble."

Holly shrugged, and her bare breasts moved. "Maybe we've seen the last of the mystery man," she said. "In any event, I don't know what I can do, or either of us."

His face became more dark-visaged. "It's all so damned frustrating, anyway. No matter what we accomplish, we backslide. The war is being lost, Holly. Even Lee is worried about the outcome now, and he was always optimistic."

"He seemed very weary, when I met him," she said.

His eyes squinted down into a scowl. "There are people in Washington who would end all this for us with honor, if that damned ape weren't in the White House. Something has to be done about him, Holly, and maybe it's going to have to be somebody like me who does it."

"Oh, John. Are you onto that again?" She felt a chill, and reached down and pulled a sheet up over both of them.

"I don't mean to bore you with the subject," he said sourly, "but I'm convinced that Lincoln can be gotten to. I know Washington well, and I have an idea how it could be done."

"How what could be done?" she said, knowing.

"How we could get him out of the capital, after taking him as a prisoner of war," he said.

"Oh, God, John."

He ignored her, and his voice changed as he continued. It became thick with repressed emotion. "If I were planning the route to take him over, I'd go across the Navy Yard Bridge at the foot of Eleventh Street, and on into Maryland, where there are a lot of southern sympathizers—through Silesia and Pomfret and Port Tobacco. That route has been used by Confederate couriers for some time, and they have friends along the way."

"But you couldn't capture the President in the nation's capital!" Holly protested. "He has men around him, John."

He ignored her. "I'd cross the Potomac by boat into Virginia, just below Fredericksburg. I've met some people down that way—an innkeeper named Chalmers, a doctor named Samuel Mudd. They might be willing to help, if they saw the situation."

She was shaking her head. "Nobody has ever kidnapped the President of the United States; stolen him out from under the noses of his personal guard, his aides, the whole damned army. It would take an army of your own, John, to even consider such a thing."

"No, I figure four or five men could accomplish it," Booth said firmly, his eyes burning now, his mouth drawn down into straight lines. "Just a few men who know how to use a gun, and would be willing to do so. After all, this is a war we're in."

"But is the President a combatant?" Holly wondered.

He looked over at her again. He started to explain further, but then hesitated. "Why don't we just forget it, Holly?"

She turned away, feeling shut out from him. There was no doubt about it, John Booth was an obsessive, multi-

195

level fellow, one she had to learn a lot more about, despite
their love for each other. There were times when she
caught him in a deeply pensive mood and could barely get
him to speak to her. Yet, when he was on stage before an
audience, and usually when they were together, he was
the most charming, affable, likable man she had ever met.

"All right," she said. "We'll forget it."

Not long after that intimacy in Booth's bed, Holly
visited Eugenia and Preston one evening, and found a
very different mood there than she had felt before her
trip to Virginia with the players. Eugenia was pleasant to
her, but with a difference. She received a strained
welcome, accompanied by a lot of forced smiles, and
Holly knew something was wrong. Preston was not even
friendly, but very reserved and stiff. She sensed a
hostility coming from him, despite his attempt to hide it
from her. She cut her evening short with them, and
returned to her room feeling a vague sense of unhappi-
ness about the visit.

Unknown to Holly, Preston had already caused her a
lot of trouble. Even though the army had let Clayborne
slip through its fingers, it had learned who his superior
was in Baltimore, a major who also operated in the
nation's capital. The man who had been watching Holly's
place was part of an investigative team who were hoping
to make some tie-in between Holly and the departed
Clayborne. They had gotten nothing yet, despite a careful
search of her room at Preston Fayette's insistence, but
they expected to arrest the major soon, and they hoped to
obtain from him a complete list of agents under his
command.

Holly knew nothing of any of this, but she wondered

196

about the abrupt change in Eugenia and Preston's attitude toward her. She thought maybe they were just showing her their disapproval of her moving out to her own place, and of the men she saw. But that did not seem to make much sense to her.

Another thing Holly knew nothing about, in that late winter of 1864, was that John Wilkes Booth was seeing other women.

Long before Holly had met Booth, he had become quite a ladies' man. From the moment he had begun his acting career he had been attractive to young women, in the acting profession and out of it, and he had sometimes kept up relationships with two or three girls at once. When Clayborne had introduced him to Holly, he had been between women, so to speak, and Holly had taken up all of his interest. But now two different females had come back into his life, one an actress and the other a businessman's daughter. Booth had already slept with the actress, since Holly's return from the front.

The fact was, Booth was not unlike Randy Clayborne in his relationships with the opposite sex. He had never expected much from them, until he had met Holly. He had been rather overawed by her, and very impressed. He had not thought of any other women, either, until they had forced themselves back into his life. But when that had happened, Booth could not bring himself to turn them away. He was too accustomed to attention from the opposite sex, from the public in general. He had come to think of himself as too important to his public, and to women in general, to restrict himself to any one member of the opposite sex, and that feeling had not been entirely dispelled by his new and sensual relationship with Holly.

Preston Fayette did not suspect that Booth was

197

involved in anything clandestine, so Booth had not yet been brought into the investigation that was being carried out. Preston was in and out of colonels' offices regularly, though, about Holly, Clayborne, and the major who had been Clayborne's superior. Finally, in the first week of March, they arrested the major, quietly and surreptitiously. He had been posing as a shopkeeper down on the basin, and that was where he had been picked up. He had been taken to an annex of General Butler's headquarters for detailed interrogation and, upon the promise of leniency, confessed to his Confederate commission on the way there in the carriage, and to being an agent of the Confederacy. Preston Fayette, because he had started the whole thing and because he was influential in Baltimore, had been invited to attend the interrogation.

It was late evening when it began, in a small room of the annex. A table sat in the center of the room, and the major, a fellow named Fiske, was seated on a chair there. A Union colonel named Phillips sat across from him, and was the interrogator. There were two aides to Phillips in the room, and Preston Fayette. They stood around the table and listened as Phillips began.

"So you admit to being a Confederate agent then, Major Fiske?" Phillips started out in a businesslike way.

Fiske, a rather heavyset, balding, bushy-eyebrowed man, nodded reluctantly. "Yes, Colonel. I was sent here almost a year ago, by our intelligence service, to collect information which might aid the Confederacy in the prosecution of the war. I make no excuses, sir, for my role in the defense of the seceded states."

Phillips asked him what kinds of information he had gathered and passed on, and Fiske gave him some examples, listing only a few items and holding back most, hoping not to tell all. That went on for about a half-hour, while Preston and the other two men present listened quietly. Preston was impatient, though, because he wanted to get to Clayborne, and to Holly.

"There must be more than that, Major, since you've been here for a year," Phillips was saying to him.

"It's difficult to recall every detail of the past months," Fiske lied. He was perspiring on his upper lip, even though he maintained the appearance of calm otherwise. "Perhaps I'll be able to remember more later."

"Who were the people you used for your nefarious purposes here in the city, Major?" was the next question. "We want a complete list of everyone you dealt with and used."

Again, Fiske had decided not to tell all. He would give a few names, of individuals who were likely to be found out, anyway, and who were now out of reach. He wiped at his upper lip with a handkerchief. "There have been only a few, Colonel Phillips: a bank clerk named Meadows, a longshoreman whom I knew only by the name of Hook. He was killed a few weeks ago in a loading accident. Then, of course, there was Lieutenant Clayborne, of the Confederate Army. He has been my liaison between myself and our agents."

"Ah!" Preston said from nearby. "I knew it!"

"Thanks to Mr. Fayette here," the colonel said, "we've been watching Clayborne. But just recently he disappeared from the city. Can you tell us where he is, Major Fiske?"

"Not exactly," Fiske said. "The young man was transferred back to the infantry, because of the need there. Quite bitter about it, too. He'll probably be in Virginia,

199

with Lee, but I don't know that for sure."

"It seems that most of the people you've mentioned as working under you as Confederate agents are either gone from Baltimore or dead," Phillips said sourly. He was a tall, severe-looking man with side whiskers and a ramrod-erect posture, and had fought in the field under McClellan, earlier in the war. "I think you're holding out on us, Major."

Fiske sweated. "I'm doing my best to recall everything for you," he said unconvincingly.

Suddenly Preston Fayette broke in, uninvited. "Are you, Major? What about Holly Ransom? You have forgotten her, haven't you?"

Fiske's face showed surprise that Preston knew her name. He hesitated a moment, then decided not to hedge on this question. Fayette seemed pretty certain of his information, anyway. Fiske would offer Holly up as a sacrificial lamb to them.

"Uh, yes, we did use Miss Ransom for a few things. She gathered information at parties and receptions and so forth—from talking with officers of the services."

"Damn!" Preston spat out angrily.

But now Phillips took over again. "Mr. Fayette has proof that Miss Ransom—who is his niece, incidentally—made a trip to the front lines recently and carried information with her to deliver to the enemy there; information which could do great harm to the Union cause, Major. Do you admit that you sent her? That it was under your orders that she went?"

Phillips and Preston were just guessing that Holly had carried intelligence to the enemy on her trip with the players, but Phillips did not want Fiske to know that.

Fiske had narrowed his eyes down on Preston. He had

not known that Preston was Holly's uncle, and was trying to understand a man who would so vigorously press action against his own niece.

Again, he hesitated for only a moment. "Yes, we sent Miss Ransom to the front." He was thinking fast, trying to save the situation. "But the information was not really all that important that she carried. Rumors about changes in command, and about sending reinforcements to the Charleston area. The mission failed," he lied, "because she was unable to negotiate the frontier between the armies."

"I don't believe him!" Preston fumed.

Phillips glanced at him balefully, then returned his gaze to Fiske. "When did this take place?"

"Over the Christmas holidays," Fiske said.

Phillips shook his head. "What a time to sneak about behind your enemy's back, Major! When his heart is open to you because of the spirit of Jesus in it! For shame, Major Fiske, for picking that moment to practice your devious tricks on us!"

"I did not choose the time, Colonel," Fiske said. "That was done by my superiors in Richmond. But I would not have hesitated to propose such a moment, myself, to aid the Confederacy to throw off the yoke of tyranny that Washington has imposed on it."

"There are ways to fight, Major, and there are unacceptable ways," Phillips told him severely. "You have employed the latter. To take an innocent young daughter of the South and use her in such pernicious activities is in itself a reprehensible action, sir. Mr. Fayette here, and his wife, were trying to give Miss Ransom a home and a future here, and you have ruined all that, Major. You've ruined Miss Ransom's life."

"She will be a heroine in Charleston and Richmond and Atlanta, Colonel," Fiske replied.

"A heroine?" Preston exclaimed. "You have not made her a soldier, sir! You have turned her into a damned sneak thief! Is this what the South calls heroism?"

"The Union uses agents in clandestine activities, Mr. Fayette," Fiske said acidly. "I'm sure you're aware that our southern cities have had to organize vigilance committees to combat espionage and sabotage by Union agents. It was the union who taught us how to be sneak thieves, Mr. Fayette. It occurred to us that if we had to do it to defend our land and property, we might as well do it well."

"Rubbish!" Fayette grumbled.

Phillips let out a long breath. His adjutants stood nearby, silent. Preston folded his arms defensively across his chest. "Was the information carried by Miss Ransom in writing?" Phillips asked Fiske.

Fiske hesitated, and Phillips noted the hesitation. "Yes, but that has been destroyed, of course."

Phillips scowled. "Can you remember further details of the information carried by Miss Ransom, Major? You've been very vague so far."

Fiske wanted time to think. He pressed a finger to his forehead. "I'm going to have to try to recall, Colonel—in a more relaxed atmosphere. Maybe on our next meeting, when we have more privacy." He glanced toward scowling Preston, and so did Phillips.

"We're going to need a more complete list of your agents, Major," Phillips said, "and of your superiors. We'll give you paper and pen, and ask you to give us the entire setup, from top command down to the lowliest hireling. Do you understand?"

Fiske nodded. He thought of John Wilkes Booth, and a couple of other men he had used, and figured he would be able to save them for further use. After all, they would send a replacement for him, Fiske, from Richmond. The war was not over.

"Yes, Colonel. I understand."

Phillips turned to the tallest of his two aides. "Lieutenant, we must arrest Holly Ransom. Will you see to it?"

"Yes, sir."

Phillips turned to Preston. "She is still here in the city, I presume?"

"Yes, I've kept a watch on her," Preston said, recalling Eugenia's protests over his doing so.

"Take the major to confinement, Lieutenant," Phillips said, rising. "And see that he is made comfortable."

"Yes, sir."

A moment later, they all filed grimly from the room.

On the following day, at noon, Holly went to a waterfront restaurant for her lunch, and received a surprise there that had nothing to do with Colonel Phillips or Major Fiske.

She arrived there at just after noon, thinking about seeing Booth that evening. He had said he was taking her to a play rehearsal to see a preview of a drama in which he had a major role, and Holly was looking forward to it, because she always liked to see him perform. When she got inside the restaurant, though, and was being taken to a table at the rear of the place, she stopped short and just stared for a moment. There sat Booth, across a small table from a very good-looking young woman. She was the actress who had insinuated herself back into Booth's life.

203

Booth's hand was holding hers across the table, and as Holly watched, stunned, Booth and the girl reached over to kiss softly.

"I'll be damned!" Holly whispered.

"Is something wrong, miss?" the waitress escorting her asked.

Holly asked the waitress to leave her, and then she walked on over to the table where Booth and the actress sat. The actress saw Holly coming, but Booth did not.

"Damn you, John!" Holly said huskily upon arrival at the table.

Booth looked up at her in quick surprise, and his face went somber. "Oh, God. Holly." He rose from his chair, awkwardly.

"Is this how you show the love you pledged to me?" she said in a low voice to him. She gestured toward the other woman. "Like this?"

"Now, just a minute!" the actress protested.

"I should have known!" Holly said angrily. "I should have understood that you and Randy were the same kind!" She was trembling with rage and frustration. "Don't bother coming around this evening, John! Don't ever bother coming around again!"

She turned and hurried away from them, toward the street door.

"Holly!" Booth called out after her.

But Holly left quickly, letting the door slam after her, her cape flying out behind her. Booth turned quickly to the actress. "I'm sorry, Beth, but I'm going to have to go after her."

"Oh, hell!" the girl said irritably.

"I'll be right back, just as soon as I can," he said. He turned then without waiting for her further comment, and rushed from the restaurant.

Outside it was a rather chilly March day, with a few snowflakes drifting down from a leaden sky. Down at the end of the street could be seen the masts of tall ships in the harbor; gulls circled above them. Booth saw Holly just a half-block away, headed back toward her place of employment. He caught her before she had gone another block, and turned her toward him.

"Holly, please," he said to her when she had locked her gaze on his. "Let me explain."

"I think I can anticipate the explanation," she said heatedly, her dark hair flying in the soft, cool breeze. "She's an old friend from the theater, and she means nothing to you."

He sighed. She had taken the very words from his mouth. "Well, yes, that's about it, as a matter of fact."

"You don't kiss old friends the way I saw you kiss her," Holly said darkly. "I might have believed you a year ago, John, when I first came here to Baltimore. Before Randy, and my involvement with both of you. Before you both used me for your own selfish purposes!"

"I can't speak for Randy," he said, "but I never intended to use you, Holly. I care for you. I didn't want Randy to take you into his group of agents, and told him so."

"You're just like him," she insisted. "You can't settle for one woman, you can't give up all those others who hang around, making themselves available. I understand very clearly now what you are, John. I could have guessed, all along. But you—caught me off guard. I fell in love with you. Not caring all that much whether my love was returned. I see now that it wasn't."

"Oh, Holly," he said lamely. He had always lied freely to women, from the very first, and he had been lying to Holly, and deceiving her. But now, for the first time in his life, he felt like being honest with a woman—because this one was different.

"Your love was returned," he began. A carriage went past, and he waited for the sound of it to pass. He had not put a hat on before leaving the restaurant, and his dark hair was blowing, too. The snow had stopped, but there was still a cold breeze from the harbor. "I can't prove that to you, Holly, but it's true. When I met you, I stopped seeing other women. But then a couple of them drifted back into my life recently. I don't know why I accepted them back in it, I don't understand why I felt the need for anything physical with them."

"There are two, for God's sake?" Holly said.

He averted his gaze. "Neither of them mean a thing to me, Holly. I mean that sincerely. You're the only woman I've ever met that I could really talk to, since my mother. It's just that I've had this weakness about women, until you came along. I guess I just had a kind of relapse into bad habits."

"Hell," Holly said.

"I'll stop seeing them, honest to God. I'll make a promise to you, that I won't see any other woman but you."

"I no longer want that promise, John," she said, her eyes moist.

He touched her, and she pulled away.

"Listen to me. I told you I love you, and I do. I know now that these other women have no substance in my life. I think less and less about them now, and more and more about what I'm doing with my life, and what I can

206

do to help save the Confederacy. I think about you, of course, but my thoughts are turning more and more toward politics and the war, and away from creature comforts and physical pleasures, and even the stage. Give me a second chance with you, Holly. I'll make good on my promise to you, you'll see."

Holly hesitated only a moment, then shook her head. "It's not a matter of a second chance for us," she told him. "It's a question of my getting straight in my head what I want out of my life. I'm very unsure about my personal life now, again, except that I know I want to help defend South Carolina and the Confederate States, just as you do. Maybe we should let that be our common bond for a while, John, instead of a more personal relationship."

Booth was genuinely distraught. "You mean you won't forgive me my transgressions?" he asked her solemnly.

"I don't want to judge you, John. I don't want to tell you how to live your life, or interfere with your own private beliefs about how to end this war. But I don't want to involve myself further in personal relationships for a while. Maybe we'll be able to talk it all over at some later time."

"And in the meantime, you don't want to see me?"

"Of course I'll see you," she said. "But that's all, John."

"Oh, damn, Holly."

She looked down for a moment, then back to him. "I must get back, John. And so must you. Good afternoon." She turned as he stared after her, and hurried on down the busy street.

She could not get much work done that afternoon,

though. She had been very much in love with Booth, and still was. Seeing him with another woman like that had been devastating to her. With Clayborne gone and Booth estranged from her, she felt once again like an outsider in Baltimore, like a gull lost at sea.

It was early, therefore, when she left the florist's shop that day. She could not keep her mind on her work, so she asked for the last hour off, and was given permission to leave. She decided to walk home, even though it was some distance, because she thought the exercise would help relax her.

When she arrived at the rooming house off Philadelphia Road, she noticed the man standing across the street from the front entrance, and wondered about him. He just stood over there in a doorway, watching her as she approached the building. She was still mulling that when she went through the parlor of the rooming house, and a couple of young women there eyed her suspiciously. She did not like any of it. She went up to her room quickly, having decided to find the landlady and ask if anything was wrong. But when she let herself in with her key, she received her second surprise of the day.

Three men stood in her room, two of them in the Union uniform.

The third was Preston Fayette.

"Uncle Preston!" she said, the door still standing open behind her. She glanced past him, around the room, and saw that drawers had been ransacked. Even the bed was unmade. "What's going on here?"

"Maybe we should be asking you that, Holly," Preston told her grimly.

Holly closed the door behind her, slowly, and looked the two soldiers over. One was the lieutenant that

Phillips had assigned the task of coming to get her, and the sergeant with him was just there as his backup.

"You—let yourselves into my room," Holly protested now. But she was already guessing what was happening.

"I'm Lieutenant Walters, Miss Holly," the lieutenant spoke up at that juncture. "I'm afraid I'm here to place you under close arrest. For treason and espionage against the United States Government."

A cold chill passed entirely through Holly's body, and left her weak and shaking.

"Treason?" she bluffed it out. "Espionage?"

"Don't bother denying the charges, Holly," Preston told her blandly. "You will only make yourself look foolish." He came up closer to her, a sarcastic smile on his long face, and in that moment Holly began to dislike him very much. "Eugenia and I have been suspicious of your activities, and the men you see, for some time. It did not require much imagination to see that your Lieutenant Clayborne was some kind of impostor. We missed him because of his leaving Baltimore. But we have his superior, a Major Fiske. He has implicated you quite clearly in espionage activities, Holly—including your journey to the front lines, under the pretense of entertaining our fine and loyal troops there."

Holly went and leaned against a table, and sighed heavily.

"Are you all right, Miss Ransom?" the lieutenant asked her.

"Yes, I'll be fine," she said.

"Do you have anything to say for yourself, Holly?" Preston went on. "Do you have any explanations or apologies to the family who took you in and befriended you, gave you a home and a future? If there is any miti-

209

gating circumstance, I'd like to hear about it. Were you threatened or intimidated in any way? Were you blackmailed?"

Holly looked over at him. He had asked the questions in a way that revealed he expected her replies to be negative.

"Of course I wasn't intimidated or blackmailed," she said evenly. "Randy Clayborne is a Charleston friend, Preston, whom I've known since school days. I undertook to carry out small tasks for the Confederacy, through Randy, because of my unwavering loyalty to the southern cause. I am surprised, Uncle, that your and Eugenia's sympathies are not the same as mine."

"Foolish girl," Preston said, clucking his tongue. "You have not helped the South in these dark enterprises. You have only helped prolong this ugly conflict and postponed the inevitable. You have been duped by unscrupulous men."

"Fighting for what you believe to be right is not a dark enterprise, or a foolish one," she said bravely. "But I think that ensnaring one's own niece in a trap perhaps is, Uncle."

He laughed a harsh laugh in his throat. "Do you think I would stand by and allow saboteurs to operate out of my own home without doing something about it?" he said. "Even if one of them happened to be a relative? I think you don't know the Fayette side of the family very well, Holly. We have always been very protective of our integrity—in wartime or peace. Enemy agents must be dealt with, even if they are found within one's own household. To us you are no more than a common criminal, deserving of punishment. That is what you will now receive, Holly."

Holly turned from him. "I suppose I may be allowed a few minutes to get some things together?" She felt very faint, as if she might pass out. She had never seriously considered the possibility of arrest. She wondered if they shot women agents, as they often did the men they caught.

"Yes, of course, Miss Ransom," the lieutenant told her.

"Then in the meantime, may I be rid of this man?" she said coldly, referring to Preston.

The lieutenant glanced at Preston, and Preston smiled a smug smile. "I'm finished here, Lieutenant. Just keep Mrs. Fayette and me advised of developments."

"Yes, sir," the lieutenant said.

When Preston was gone, Holly turned away from the two soldiers and began crying softly. The sergeant came over to her, and spoke to her over her shoulder. "It's all right, ma'am. They don't shoot women agents in this war."

Holly turned to him, brushing at her cheek. "It's not that, Sergeant. It's a lot of other things. I'm sorry to make a scene."

"You just take all the time you want, Miss Ransom," the lieutenant said from across the room.

She got some clothes together, and some toiletries, and packed them into a small suitcase. It all seemed so final, so unchangeable. She was glad to hear they were not shooting women. But even prison did not sound like something tolerable to her. To be put behind bars was a humiliation that was unthinkable. She looked around the room, realizing she probably would never see it again. More tears came, and she could not seem to stop crying. She brushed them away once more, before turning back

211

to the two men.

"Will I be allowed to write letters from confinement?" she asked them, thinking about Charlotte.

"I'm certain you will," the lieutenant told her.

"What's the procedure from here on out?" she asked him, under more control now.

"You'll be placed in confinement at military headquarters for a few days, maybe more, Miss Ransom. Then there will be a quick hearing before a military tribunal, made up of staff officers. If convicted, you'll probably be taken to the Old Hempstead Jail to serve out your sentence. It's an old city jail that houses women convicted of espionage and federal crimes."

"Oh, God," Holly murmured.

"It won't be so bad, ma'am," the sergeant told her. "Some say it's a regular sewing club there, what with teas and social events."

The lieutenant gave him a look. "Are you ready to go then, Miss Ransom?"

Holly nodded. "Yes, let's leave," she said.

The lieutenant locked the room up behind them.

Then they filed down the long flight of stairs together, toward the whispering, wide-eyed women who waited there in the parlor below.

Chapter Twelve

Handcuffed and accompanied by two military guards, Holly was marched up the short flight of steps and then into the old brick building. Inside Old Hempstead, she was taken to a desk where she was checked in; all her belongings were taken from her, except for the plain dress she wore, her shoes and her underclothing. The guards left, and Holly was taken down a corridor by a woman guard who worked at the jail. Old Hempstead was a small old jail. Downstairs it had a couple of cells and some offices; upstairs were a half-dozen cells. Holly was taken to one of the two downstairs cells, which were slightly larger. As she moved down the corridor with the beefy woman, the odors of soap and disinfectant reached her nostrils. They stopped before the other cell, and the guard pointed to another prisoner.

"That's Crazy Nellie," the guard announced. "She's in for the same thing as you. She got caught with a whole purse full of military maps she had stolen from Butler's headquarters. That was two years ago."

Holly looked into the cell. It contained a real bed, not just a cot, and a chair and small writing table. The barred window on its back wall had curtains at it, and there was a small rug on the floor. It seemed likely that those in charge had made an attempt to give these female prisoners some special consideration. A scrawny-looking woman sat on the straight chair, leaning her head onto her hands, and stared at the table top where a sheet of writing paper lay. There was no writing on the paper. The prisoner called Crazy Nellie did not look up at them, but just stared blankly at the table top.

Holly sighed, and tried not to think of how she would look if she'd spent two years here.

"Hi, Nellie!" the gruff-voiced guard called out. "How's everything going today?"

Nellie finally looked up, but not at the guard. Her narrow, dark eyes focused on Holly; they gave Holly a little chill. Then the woman looked back down.

"She don't talk much," the guard told Holly. "Just recites poems out loud sometimes, when nobody wants to hear them. That's how she got her name. Come on, Ransom."

The guard unlocked Holly's cell, next door. The entire front wall of it was made up of bars, with a barred door set in its center. The cell was very much like the other one, except that there were no curtains at the windows, and no carpet on the floor. It looked fairly clean, though, and Holly was grateful for that. There was a musty smell about it, but she figured it came from the bedding.

"O.K., this is home for a while," the guard said, gesturing for Holly to enter. She did, and the guard followed her in. "You've got a good bed, and a place to write or work. Some of the nonpoliticals upstairs like to knit and sew. All toilet facilities are down the corridor. You'll eat three times a day, and the food isn't bad. We

214

furnish writing paper, and books, if you want them. It's a regular hotel here, honey."

When the guard was gone, and Holly was locked in, she sat down on the narrow bed by the wall and cried softly. A military tribunal had quickly heard the testimony against her, and sentenced her to ten years' imprisonment. Agents working undercover were not treated like ordinary prisoners of war. If the war ended the next day, in theory Holly would serve out her term of imprisonment.

But at least she was not being lined up against a wall with other agents and shot. That was happening to some men.

"What's your name, honey?"

Holly was startled by the female voice that seemed to come from the wall behind her. She turned quickly, and realized that Crazy Nellie was speaking to her from the next cell. Holly rose, went to the front of the cell, and leaned against the iron bars.

"Is that Nellie?" she said.

"Yes, and I'm not crazy, honey. I just want the guards to think so. They treat me better that way."

"My name is Holly. Holly Ransom."

"Nice name. Are you a political?"

"I'm a Confederate agent," Holly said proudly, deliberately choosing the present tense of the verb.

"Humph," came the reaction. "Me, too. But the war will be over before we ever get out of here."

"How is it?" Holly asked her. "How do they treat you here?"

A short pause. "Do you want the truth, or a song and dance?"

"The truth," Holly told her.

215

"Well. Those three meals the guard told you about. Make it two. In the morning, you only get a crust of bread and water. The other two meals are usually so lousy you can't eat them: rancid meat, rotten vegetables. I don't even like to think about what they put in the soup."

"Oh, God," Holly said.

"I've lost ten pounds here," Nellie said. "So far."

"But the cells are clean and neat," Holly said. "Better than anything I've seen."

"You should have seen them before a recent cleanup. Some colonel came through and ordered it. We haven't seen him since."

"How is it other than the food?" Holly said.

"It's not like home," came the sour reply. "We are allowed no exercise. Even the men get that, at the big prison. They think women don't need it, I guess. They give us work to do. Those books the guard mentioned—there are a half-dozen in all, and I read them the first week here. When you take your toilet, one or more guards stand over you."

Holly was shocked. "You mean, there's no privacy?"

"That's exactly what I mean," Nellie said. "They love to stare."

"Why, that's—outrageous," Holly told her.

"Agreed. But don't complain too loudly, honey. They get on a complainer."

"In what way?" Holly wondered.

"Oh, they find ways. Verbal harassment. Deprivation of the few privileges we have here. Short rations on food. There hasn't been any physical harassment since they got rid of Big Bertha."

"A guard?" Holly said.

"Yes, a guard. She liked the girls, if you know what I

216

mean. She's gone now, but you never know who they'll hire next week or next month."

"God," Holly muttered.

"She would have taken a real liking to you, honey. Even now you'll have to be careful, because of your good looks. Guards resent good-looking inmates. You'll see."

Holly felt very low suddenly. "Well. Thanks," she said.

When she went back and lay down on her bed, Holly felt an overwhelming depression settle over her. When she had been in the temporary facility awaiting the hearing, she had felt too much uncertainty to become depressed. She was afraid, but she had been afraid before. Now that she knew her fate, it was as if a lead weight had been placed on her chest, and she could not free herself from it.

That evening she had her first meal at the small prison, and it was as bad as Nellie had predicted. All of the inmates, from both floors of the old facility, ate together, and there were some interesting women there. The food was stew, and Holly could hardly get it down. In early evening she was taken to the washroom and toilet, and every personal activity she performed was scrutinized closely. Holly was humiliated and deeply offended, but said nothing to the guard. The next day, though, she asked to speak with the male warden of the facility, and after three days of waiting, she was taken to him.

She was seated on a straight chair before his desk, and then the matron guard left. When she saw this, Holly protested.

"Can't I have a matron in here while we talk?" she said to the warden.

He turned to her, from where he stood looking through

a window behind his desk. He wore a gray suit and tie, and looked military, although he was a civilian, a part of the federal prison system. He was big, thickset, and hard-looking.

"Are you going to be a troublemaker, Ransom?"

Holly swallowed hard. "No, sir."

"But you do have complaints to make," he said.

"Yes, I do," Holly said. "A couple of things that I thought you would appreciate having brought to your attention."

He sighed heavily, and sat down at his desk. "New inmates always want to bring things to my attention, Ransom. They always want a matron present at all times, and they want to make suggestions about how to run this place. Men aren't quite so bad this way, and that's why I'd rather run a male facility. What are these suggestions you want to make?"

Holly took a deep breath. "Well. I thought you might like to know that our food is often bad. I mean, rotten or spoiled. I thought maybe you didn't know. You might want to look into it."

"No, I don't," he said flatly. "Anything else, Ransom?"

Holly was taken aback by his abruptness, but tried not to show it. "Well, yes." She did not know how to proceed. "There is no privacy here, Warden."

"Privacy?" he said with sarcasm. "You expect privacy in a prison facility?"

"In highly personal matters, yes," she said with embarrassment. "We are not creatures of the forest here, Warden. We're entitled to certain considerations, in the name of humanity."

A slow grin broke over his face. "You're a Charleston

girl, aren't you, Ransom?"

She saw the way he was looking her over now, and did not like it. "Why, yes."

"There's no doubt about it, you girls are different from our northern variety. You think a lot about privacy and such, I guess."

"We think a lot about personal dignity," Holly said.

He grunted in his throat. "Tell you what, Ransom. You mind your P's and Q's around here, and you might just earn some privacy. Don't make any trouble. Try to be friendly to the help, including me. We'll treat you right, if you treat us right."

"I'm hardly in a position to treat you wrongly, sir," she reminded him. "On the other hand, your policies here can make our life tolerable, or a living hell. We ask only that it be the former."

"We'll talk about this again, Ransom," he said. "That will be all for now, unless you have any further questions."

"No, sir," she said with disappointment in her voice.

Several weeks passed, and no improvements in the food or situation came. In the war, Grant finally marched against Lee in Virginia, crossing the Rapidan River, and there was a wild, bloody draw, with both sides losing heavily, but Grant the most. Jeb Stuart's rebel cavalry was now considered the best on both sides. But the South was having difficulty winning anywhere. The North now had too many men, too much equipment, too overpowering a Navy.

Holly heard the war news with growing sadness, but she had not given up on the South's winning the conflict, or at least gaining some concessions in a peace

219

treaty. She lamented the fact that she was not outside prison walls where she could do something about it. She wondered about Eugenia, and Booth. She had not seen either of them since her arrest. Despite Preston's hostility toward her, she wanted to tell Eugenia she was sorry if she had caused her any trouble. As for Booth, she would have liked to tell him that she forgave him, and would always love him no matter what. But she had no contact with outsiders for many weeks, and had no idea what was happening outside the prison, except for vague reports about the war.

In April, Eugenia finally showed up one day.

Holly had just been returned to her cell from a very bad lunch, of which she had eaten almost nothing. She had lost several pounds already, and her skin was looking pale and rather lifeless. She still wore the same dress she had come in with, although she was allowed to launder it as often as she wished. But she was not able to put her hair up, or fix herself in any way. She was beautiful without any of that, but she felt bad inside, at not being able to take care of herself properly. She was just thinking about all of this when a guard showed up outside her cell, and Eugenia was with her.

Holly rose slowly, staring at Eugenia. "My God," she said.

"You have a visitor, Ransom," the guard told her.

There was a quiet exchange between Holly and Eugenia, and the guard let Eugenia into the cell and locked it behind her. Then Holly and Eugenia were alone, except for Nellie in the next cell.

Holly felt as if a breath of the outside had come in with Eugenia who stood there in her lovely satin dress with the smell of perfume about her. Seeing Eugenia like that made her realize that she had already become accustomed to and somewhat hardened by the new prison world. Just a glimpse of Eugenia reminded her how beautiful it was out in the real world outside, and how grim was her own existence.

"It's so good to see you, Holly," Eugenia said, her eyes moist. She came and embraced Holly, and Holly returned it.

"The same with me, Eugenia," Holly told her, her own vision slightly blurry from quick tears.

Eugenia stood back and looked at her. "You've lost weight, my dear. Don't they feed you properly here?"

"Not as well as at your house." Holly smiled. "But I'm all right, Eugenia. I'm surviving."

"I'm—so sorry, Holly," Eugenia said. "About everything."

"And I'm sorry if I've caused you any pain," Holly told her.

"I so wish that Preston had not felt obliged to become personally involved in all of this. We had some big differences about it, I must tell you. I think it's the lawyer in him, Holly."

"Don't apologize, Aunt Eugenia," Holly told her. "Preston and I just happen to be on the opposite sides of something, that's all. Just like Lincoln and Davis, Grant and Lee. I can't hold any grudges about any of this. I moved out of your house so I wouldn't cause you any real trouble through my activities. But I know that I still gave you a bad time, Eugenia. After you had taken me into your home and treated me like a daughter."

"Oh, Holly! Why couldn't you have just left it all to

others?" Eugenia said heavily. She sat down on Holly's bed. "Why did my niece have to become so personally involved?"

"They said they needed me," Holly said. "I think they did, and still do. If I were still free, Eugenia, I'd still be trying to do my part to help the South gain an honorable peace."

Eugenia smiled tiredly at her. "I suppose I should respect you for that, and I do, dear girl. But look at you now! God, it tears my heart out to see you here! I won't sleep with Preston now. I can't forgive him for what he's done to you."

"Please don't feel that way, Eugenia," Holly said. She sat down beside her on the bed. "I did what I had to do, and Preston did what he felt he had to do. If I can forgive him for that, so can you."

Eugenia touched Holly's pale cheek, and more tears came. "I wrote to Charlotte yesterday. I thought she ought to know, Holly."

Holly nodded. "I've been meaning to send a letter, myself. But I couldn't think of anything to say to her, except the bad news. And I didn't know how to tell her that."

"Your former employer was very nice to me the other day. He said he understands perfectly, and holds nothing against you. In fact, it seems you're a celebrity downtown now. There are more in Baltimore that think you're a heroine than a criminal."

"I'm glad to hear that," Holly said.

"I wish you were back with me and that none of this had happened," Eugenia said quietly. "That we could start all over again, and it would all turn out differently."

"You might as well try to wish the war away," Holly said.

222

"Is there anything I can do, Holly? Bring you anything? Talk to anybody for you?"

Holly knew she could ask Eugenia to talk to the warden about conditions there, but that that might cause her trouble after Eugenia was gone. She wanted to ask if Eugenia had heard from Booth, but thought it best not to.

"I guess not," she said. "Don't worry about me, Aunt Eugenia. I'm a lot stronger than you might think." She thought a moment. "Well, there is one thing, though."

"What is it, honey?" Eugenia asked.

"You might send a reporter over here. They wanted to talk with me before, and I wouldn't allow them. But I'd like to talk to one of them now about women and prison."

"Well, of course, Holly. I'll mention it to the newspaper editor. I can do it today; I'm on my way down to the Corn Exchange."

"I'll appreciate that, Eugenia."

When her aunt left, a short time later, Holly found herself crying softly into her pillow.

She was in a black mood for the rest of the day.

In Charleston, just a few days later, Charlotte Ransom-Quinn sat at her kitchen table and stared blankly at the letter from Eugenia that she had just received through the mail. Her face was ashen, because of what she had just read about Holly.

"God," she kept saying to herself. "God, my Holly!"

Quinn was not there. Even though it was past the time he used to come home for dinner, he was coming home later and later, it seemed, and quite often he was drunk when he got there. He would also go back out in the evenings now, saying he had business to attend to. But Charlotte was more certain than ever that he was seeing a woman across town named Watrous, a widow with a

223

liking for other women's husbands. She had not challenged him with her suspicions, though, even after Jennifer's accusations against him that day in the market. Charlotte had been hoping that somehow it would all go away if she did not press him about it.

Charlotte had been stunned by the news about Holly. She had had the idea that everything was going along well in Baltimore, with Holly working at the florist's shop. She did not know about Clayborne, or Booth, or any of Holly's involvements with them, except for the charge against Holly made by Jennifer, that Clayborne had been in Baltimore for a while and had been intimate with Holly.

She was very low, with tears standing in her eyes, when Quinn drove up out front with his buggy, and came on into the house. She looked up dully when he came into the kitchen and stood, staring down at her from slightly bloodshot eyes. He had been drinking again.

"That bombardment this morning tore down the building just two doors down the street," he said darkly. "They're still clearing rubble out of the street. I may have to just close the business up, by Jesus."

She looked up at him, but said nothing. He glanced at the letter on the table, then went over to a cupboard and took a bottle of liquor out of it. He poured himself a glass and did not ask Charlotte if she wanted any. He swigged it, and stood there for a moment. Finally, he looked over at her. "There's a lot of looting going on. I'm taking my pistol down there tomorrow, by God."

Charlotte sat, silent.

"What the hell is the matter with you?" he asked her

She looked down at the letter from Eugenia. "It's Holly," she said,

"Holly? What about Holly?"

She finally looked over at him. "She's in a federal prison."

He narrowed his hard eyes down. "What?"

"She was arrested weeks ago," Charlotte said. "She was sentenced to ten years."

"Huh. I told you that daughter of yours would get into trouble sooner or later. What's she been doing, whoring? Like that friend of hers here?"

Charlotte's face filled up with anger. "You bastard! Don't you talk about Holly like that! She was carrying secrets into Confederate lines. A job for a man, I'd say, but there are men who don't give a damn about how the war comes out."

"Is that supposed to be a reference to me?" he growled.

"Take it the way you like," she answered him. "But don't bad-mouth my daughter, damn you. Not after what happened here in my own household."

"I thought we were past that," he said arrogantly.

"Past it?" she said. "You tried to rape her, didn't you? Just like she said? Why don't you finally admit it?"

"Think what you like; it doesn't matter to me." He poured himself a second shot of whiskey.

"If I hadn't come home that day, you'd have succeeded," Charlotte went on, knowing the truth of it in her heart now. "You'd have forced yourself on her."

"Go to hell," he said.

"You tried to seduce Jennifer, too," she said loudly, very upset by Eugenia's letter. "It wasn't enough for you to have a mistress across town, was it?"

He turned to her darkly. "Where did you hear all that?"

"Isn't it all true?" she demanded.

He set the shot glass down carefully, and came and leaned over the table, where she could smell his foul breath. "Yes, it's true," he grated out.

Charlotte caught her breath. "All of it?"

"All of it," he said slowly and deliberately. "I tried to get into that whore Jennifer's bed, yes. I've had to settle for the widow Watrous, yes, because you don't do anything for me anymore, woman. And yes, I would have given your daughter a lesson in man-woman relationships if you had not returned that day to interfere."

Charlotte's face had gone rather pale during these confessions. Now she sat staring past him, unable to speak further. The truth seemed so much more awful when it came from his own mouth. She rose from the table, stared hard at him for a moment, and then slapped him hard across the face.

Quinn was surprised by the blow, and deeply angered. In a swift moment he returned the slap, hitting Charlotte across the left side of her face. She stumbled backward, lost her balance, and hit the floor on her backside.

"Don't ever hit me, woman!" he said harshly.

Charlotte half-lay on the floor, her face inflamed, breathless and dazed. Tears sprang into her eyes.

"You bastard," she sobbed.

"Let that be a lesson in domestic relations," he said in a hard voice. "And now, since my welcome home has been less than civilized, I'll spend my evening where I'm appreciated."

He moved past her, and she turned to call after him, "Where are you going?" in a sobbing voice.

At the doorway, he turned back. "Where do you think?" He grinned with his hard grin.

When he was gone, Charlotte picked herself up and leaned against the dry sink, drying her eyes now, a hard look coming onto her face. "Damn him!" she muttered. "Damn him forever!"

It was all too much for her, knowing all of it to be true, knowing he was such a conscienceless man. She felt depressed about Holly, too, and that compounded her emotional upset. She stood there and thought of him going to the Watrous woman's house, and getting into bed with her, and making love to her. And slowly a great, deep-seated anger rose through her and overpowered her depression to become the dominant emotion in her.

Charlotte was ordinarily not a violent or vindictive woman. But she had never experienced such complete humiliation or frustration. Holly's father, Col. Ashby Ransom, had been a fine husband and father, and had treated Charlotte like a lady always. Charlotte had assumed wrongly that most men were like Ransom, and was finding out differently the hard way. Reflecting now, she realized that Holly had understood what Quinn was from the first, but Charlotte had been blinded by her need.

Now, the blinders were off.

Charlotte remembered, in that black moment of fury, Quinn's mention of the pistol he kept in their bedroom, and a dark thought wormed its way through her head. She went upstairs and into their bedroom, and rummaged through some drawers. In a bottom drawer in a big chest, she found the hard object under some clothing. She pulled it out and stared hard at it. It was a brass-and-wood, two-barreled gun, and it looked deadly. She swallowed hard, and then began looking for its ammunition. It was stashed in another drawer. She loaded the weapon the way she had seen Quinn do it, very carefully. Then she returned downstairs, put the gun in a large purse, threw on a cape, and left the house.

Quinn had their buggy, and there were no hansoms readily available. So she began walking through the dark streets of Charleston, to where she knew the Watrous woman lived. It was a cool, early-spring night, but because of her tension, she began shivering in her clothing. She passed an area close to downtown, and had to walk around some rubble from shelled buildings. The Fifty-fourth Massachusetts Infantry and Artillery had been active earlier, but now the streets were silent. Armed sentries stood on street corners, though, to keep locals from looting. General de Beauregard had warned that punishment for such crimes would be severe.

The widow lived on Elm Street, and when Charlotte turned a corner onto that dirt lane, her pulse began racing, her heart pummeling in her chest. She walked the block and a half, slowing as she approached the house where she knew the widow lived.

There was a warm, yellow glow coming from the house, from all its windows, a glow that only oil lamps can make. Charlotte stood out on the path along the street, and let the fury build in her as she imagined what was going on inside. There was a ringing in her ears now, and her face felt very hot in the cool night. It was all over with Quinn now, she knew, if there ever had been anything. The things he had done to her, and to Holly, were atrocious. Also, he felt no remorse. Quinn would never change, he was an evil man who had to be dealt with for what he had done, and was doing.

She went up onto a long, dark porch, and looked through a window. She could see no one inside, just as

228

she had thought she would not. She opened the door and let herself into a dimly lighted parlor.

That was when she heard them. There was a low sound from Quinn's throat, and then some soft whisperings of a woman's voice—from a ground-floor bedroom, just through an open doorway.

Charlotte felt the rage rise again in her. She drew the rather heavy pistol from her purse, and walked across the parlor to the doorway.

When she looked into the bedroom, where only the light from a low-turned oil lamp made a soft glow, she saw them on the bed.

They were lying side by side, completely nude—Quinn looking middle-aged and bulky, the widow frowzy. She had dishwater-blond hair and stretch marks on her hips. The sight sickened Charlotte, and she made a low sound in her throat.

The widow glanced toward her, pushing away from Quinn's passionate kiss on her throat. "Oh!" she gasped out.

In the next moment, Charlotte aimed the pistol at her and fired. The shot resounded loudly in the small room, making a yellow flash that made Quinn squint. The widow was struck by the hot lead in the right breast, and then she was falling away from Quinn, crimson staining her ripe flesh as she fell back wide-eyed and in shock.

Charlotte moved the muzzle of the gun, aiming it now at Quinn.

"My God! Charlotte, what the hell are you doing?"

"What does it look like?" she said in a low, brittle voice.

Quinn glanced at the widow. She was dying, a glaze forming over her gray eyes. Blood was on the sheets now, and there was a gurgling sound coming from the widow's mouth. Quinn turned back to Charlotte with narrowed eyes.

"You've killed her!" he exclaimed darkly.

"Yes, and now I'll deal with you," Charlotte promised him.

He held his right hand up defensively. "Wait, Charlotte!" he pleaded licking suddenly dry lips. "Don't compound what you've already done! I have some friends in this town; I can help you make up a story!"

"A story?" she said. "I already have a story for them— a story of assault, cruelty and infidelity, you bastard! A story about lying and cheating and molestation! Do you want to add to that?"

He rose off the bed, and she looked him over, seeing him as others might, and she wondered why she had ever thought him physically attractive. She leveled the gun at him, hating him even more than she had thought. He came toward her, slowly.

"You can't pull that trigger again," he said. "It was one thing to shoot her. But you've slept with me, been intimate with me. I'm your husband, Charlotte, whether you like that idea or not, right at this moment. You can't kill your husband, you're not the type. You—"

There was a second, bright explosion, and Quinn felt the fiery lead hit him just over the heart. His eyes saucered, and he stared at Charlotte for a moment as if she had just given him some very bad news, and then he collapsed onto the bed, sliding from there to the floor and leaving a red smear on the covers. His left foot kicked the floor hard; then he was gone.

As Charlotte stared down at him, the anger slowly drained out of her. She let the gun slip from her fingers and fall to the floor. It clattered there at her feet. She went and stood over Quinn, and let the emotion drain out of her. She looked over at the widow, and was sorry about her. If there had been time to consider, she might not have hurt her. But she was satisfied about Quinn. It was the kind of thing that Ashby Ransom would have wanted her to do. Holly was avenged, and she herself was avenged.

Charlotte did not much like the sight of blood, so she turned and left the room and the house.

Outside, she went into the street and took in several deep breaths of fresh night air. Then she began to calm down inside. She turned and took one last look at the house, at the warm glow from its windows, then headed back down the dark street on foot, shunning Quinn's buggy which she knew sat at the rear of the widow's house. She would walk directly to the police station and tell them everything that had happend tonight, and before.

They would have to know everything.

She would have a debt to pay, and she had always been one to pay her debts.

Chapter Thirteen

In Baltimore, the weeks passed slowly for Holly. Cut off from the outside world, she knew little about how the war was going, or even what was happening in the city around her. Other women in the small prison kept hoping for news that the war was over, and they did not care which side won. But Holly's fond hope was that the Confederacy would somehow improve its position to bargain for a respectable peace. Small news items filtered in to her, about Grant's big offensive push around Spotsylvania, and about lesser actions in the West. But she never saw a newspaper, never read a magazine account.

The food remained bad at Old Hempstead and Holly began seeing rats and bugs in the cell, but nobody in charge seemed to care about those things. Eugenia visited her every week, but Holly refused to complain to her. The warden would not listen to Eugenia, anyway, and Preston Fayette would not bring any pressure to bear, she knew. Finally, one sunny day in May, Eugenia brought the first news of Charlotte since Charlotte's nocturnal attack on Quinn and his mistress.

It was midafternoon when Eugenia arrived in Holly's

cell, and Holly knew immediately that something was wrong. Eugenia seemed tense to her, even as she delivered a small cake to Holly. Eugenia always brought Holly something: a piece of clothing, a food delicacy, a bouquet of flowers. But this time the gift was delivered with a strained manner, and Holly caught it immediately.

"Is there something wrong, Aunt Eugenia?" she asked, when they were both seated on Holly's bed, side by side, and the chocolate cake was decorating the nearby table.

Eugenia turned to her somberly. "I have news from Charlotte, Holly." There were more delicate lines in her face nowadays, and there was some more gray in her hair. But she still had a regal bearing, an elegance that came to her naturally.

Holly studied her face closely. "What is it? Is Mother ill?"

Eugenia shook her head sideways. "No, Holly, she's apparently well. But she's had some terrible trouble with Uriah Quinn."

"Oh, Jesus," Holly muttered. Her young face was slightly thinner and more pale than it had been when she had been admitted to the prison facility. "What's he done now?"

Eugenia took in a deep breath, unconsciously. "It seems he took a mistress, Holly."

"I would have expected as much," Holly said bitterly.

"Charlotte says that he even . . . proposed intimacy to your friend Jennifer Clayborne."

"Oh, no," Holly said.

There was a small silence between them. "They had a big fight about it, Holly, and then Uriah went off to his mistress. Charlotte followed him there and—"

233

Holly regarded her aunt quizzically. "And what, Eugenia?"

Eugenia caught her gaze dully. "And shot both of them with Uriah's pistol," she said in an almost inaudible voice.

Holly was suddenly staring past Eugenia, not believing her ears. "Shot them?" she heard herself saying.

"She . . . killed them both, Holly."

"My God!" Harshly.

"I didn't know my sister could have such violence in her," Eugenia went on, slowly. "But I think I understand her motivation. Men have always been faithful to women in our family."

"My God," Holly repeated.

"Unknown to us, Charlotte, too, has been behind bars for these past weeks. But there is a bright side of the story, Holly. After hearing all the facts—apparently Charlotte told authorities about the incident between you and Uriah, with full credence to your version of it— the law there is not going to prosecute, Holly. Charlotte has just been returned home. A lawyer friend convinced everybody that Charlotte had lost control of her reason for a short time, and that her reaction was justifiable."

"Oh, thank God for that much," Holly said hollowly.

There was another silence; then Eugenia spoke again. "Of course, Charlotte still has murder to live with, and her letter would seem to indicate it's bothering her— bothering her a lot, Holly."

Holly's eyes teared up. "What a thing to go through, Eugenia! I knew that Uriah would be trouble for her one day."

"I'm sure she'll be all right, when this is all farther behind her," Eugenia prophesied.

Holly nodded uncertainly. "Yes, she probably will."
But she did not see how.

The news about Charlotte sank Holly into an even lower well of depression, and she almost stopped eating entirely. Then, almost a week after Eugenia's bad news, she had another visitor. When the guard announced that fact, Holly hoped against hope that it was Booth. He had not shown his face at the prison, and Holly liked to think it was because of their tie-up in espionage activities. But she knew it could be because he had written her off completely, and despite her anger and disappointment with him, she knew that she still was in love with him, deep inside her.

The visitor, was not Booth. It was a reporter from the Baltimore newspaper, named Criswell. He was responding to Holly's request to see a reporter.

"I didn't identify myself as a newsman," he told her when the guard had gone. He stood just inside the barred door, and Holly was facing him from the far side of the small table where she had been trying to compose a letter to Charlotte. "I thought the warden might not admit me."

"I'm very glad you could come, Mr. Criswell," Holly told him.

"Your aunt said something about your having complaints about conditions here," he said, taking a pad from his jacket pocket, and poising a pencil over it. "Exactly what were you referring to, Miss Ransom?"

Holly told him about the food, about the terrible lack of privacy in the most private matters, the vermin, and the occasional mistreatment of the women inmates. Criswell took copious notes, not talking, only listening. At the end, he asked her a few questions about it all, and she went into some more detail. He had seated himself at the table, and Holly still stood near it.

"I think I see why you don't like the treatment here," he finally said.

"It isn't just here, either," Holly went on, "and I want you to make that clear in your report. I have firsthand accounts from another federal prison and from prisoner-of-war camps. The camps are much worse than this. There is no food, no medicine, no heat in the winter for those poor men who are kept in those places. The authorities must do something about this, Mr. Criswell. Mr. Lincoln himself should do something about it. It's his responsibility ultimately, isn't it?"

Criswell made a face. "I guess you're right, Miss Ransom." He made some more notes, and then looked back up at her. "You're the young lady who carried intelligence into Confederate lines, aren't you?"

"That's right," Holly said.

He smiled at her. "My sentiments have always been with the Union, Miss Ransom, and still are. But I have the greatest respect for you, ma'am. A lot of us do. I just want you to know that."

"Why, thank you, Mr. Criswell."

"I'm going to do an article on all of this, Miss Ransom, and I'm going to tell everybody just what kind of woman I think you are. Maybe it will help you in some way."

"If it helps improve conditions in federal prison facilities, I'll be very grateful, Mr. Criswell."

When the reporter had left, Holly allowed a small hope to build inside her that somehow something might come of his visit to her. She began eating again, and asking about the war. But then, at the end of May, she had another setback

It was midevening on that spring day when the guard came to her and said that the warden wanted to see her. Holly thought he had gotten wind of the reporter's visit, or that the article had come out in the newspaper, and now she was going to be punished somehow for causing trouble. The warden hated inmates who caused trouble.

But the trauma she would sustain that evening had nothing to do with the interview she had had with the reporter.

"I don't know what he wants, missy," the guard told her gruffly. "He just said to bring you in."

"But it's almost time for bed," Holly protested. "Surely this can wait until morning?"

"Get a move on, Ransom," the guard told her.

Holly was taken down a darkened corridor and into the front of the building, where the warden's private quarters were located. The guard knocked on the door to the small apartment, and a male voice replied. The guard entered, taking Holly with her.

Holly looked around. This was not the office where the warden had received her previously. She was in a parlor, one badly furnished with heavy, dark furniture and lit with wall gas fixtures. Across the room sat the warden at a wall desk, facing away from her. He was in his shirt sleeves. He turned when they came in, and grunted at them.

"Ah. Good evening, Ransom. You may leave us, Guard."

The female guard, a hefty, tough-looking woman, nodded. "O.K., Warden." Giving him a smile, she was gone from the room.

Holly stood there uncertain. He straightened some things on the desk, then turned to her, remaining seated on his straight chair.

"Well," he said, giving her a hard grin. "How have things been with you, Ransom? Are you settling in now?"

Holly shrugged. "As much as can be expected. Things are about the same as when I spoke with you before, Warden. I haven't noticed any changes."

"Improvements come slowly, Ransom. May I call you Holly, by the way?"

Holly hesitated. "Why not?" she said, warily.

"You may call me Burt," he told her. "In the privacy of these quarters, of course. Not out with the other prisoners."

Holly made no comment. She did not like being there alone with him, in the evening.

"Would you like that?" he asked her.

She shrugged again. "It doesn't matter, Warden," she said, not using his given name.

He leaned forward on the chair, clasping his hands before him. "You may recall, Holly, that on your visit to me at my office, I told you that your privileges here depend in part on how well you get along with us. Do you remember that?"

Holly hesitated. "Yes, I guess so," she said.

"How—cooperative you are with us," he added.

Holly frowned slightly. "I haven't given anybody any trouble," she said, hoping he did not know about the reporter.

"No, of course not. But to gain special treatment here you must do more than keep out of trouble. You must— shall we say, participate? The evenings alone here are lonely, Holly, as you already know." He rose and went to a cabinet on a wall, and brought out a bottle of whiskey

"Sometimes I have to drink a little bit, to make them pass more quickly."

He turned to her so she could see the bottle.

"I never drink alone, Holly."

Holly's insides began tightening up. She had feared something like this, when she had come into the room with the guard.

"I'm not seeking any special treatment, Warden," she said rather breathlessly now. "I want only what the other women receive."

"We all want to be special," he said, ignoring her objection. He uncorked the bottle, went to a table, and poured drinks into two short glasses sitting there. "I need company, Holly, for my lonely evenings here. And I prefer female company to male." He grinned at her again. He came over to her with the two drinks, and proffered one to her.

"Please. Have a drink with me, and we'll talk for a while—on the sofa over here. All I want is a little friendship tonight, Holly. I can make it well worth your while, believe me. Will you sit, please?"

It was clear to her what he had in mind. He obviously felt that the women at the prison were his property, to use as he wished. She was suddenly very frightened.

"No, Warden," she said firmly. "I'd rather not. I rarely drink, and when I do, it's not whiskey. I'm quite tired this evening, and I'd like to return to my cell, if you don't mind."

His face had sobered throughout the refusal. Now he went and set the glasses down on the table, and turned back to her. He came very close to her, and he seemed very big and dangerous in his proximity. His square face was straight-lined now, his hard eyes narrowed on her.

"I don't think you understand, Holly. It would please me very much if you stayed here for a while this evening. Refusal on your part would displease me very much."

Holly swallowed hard. It was like the episode with Uriah Quinn all over again. The stricture in her stomach seemed to grasp at her to suffocate her. "I'm sorry, Warden. But I'm not the kind of girl you seem to think I am. Please return me to my cell."

Suddenly, without warning, he reached and grabbed her. She jumped visibly, and then he was pulling her to him, grabbing at her, and his mouth was seeking hers. She tried to pull away, but he found her lips and kissed her with a hard, savage kiss. She felt his rough hands on her waist, her left breast. She finally broke loose, stumbling backward, and she was breathing raggedly.

"Damn you!" she yelled at him. *"Leave me alone! I have friends on the outside, some of them influential! You go any further with this, and I'll find a way to let them know what happened here! I'll scream my head off to them! I know a newspaper man and I've already spoken with him!"*

The warden scowled at her, also breathless. "You saw a reporter?" he growled out.

"That's right," Holly said defiantly. "With a little luck, very soon this facility will be under close scrutiny by outsiders. When that happens, Warden, I hope you don't have too much more to answer for than you do at this very moment!"

He was dark-visaged and angry. "By Jesus, Ransom!" he grated out harshly. "I knew you were going to be trouble, from the moment I laid eyes on you!"

"I asked you to look into conditions here," she reminded him. "When you didn't respond, I was forced

240

to go to somebody who might."

He turned away from her, very distraught. He picked up one of the glasses from the nearby table, and swigged all of its contents in one gulp. "Who is this reporter you spoke to?" he finally said, more under control.

"I can't tell you that," she replied.

He turned to her slowly, and now she saw the great suppressed rage in his face. He had forgotten his intentions with her now, and seemed like a different man. "You've violated prison rules in this meeting with a news person, Ransom, and violations are punished at Hempstead."

She stood there, getting her breath back, feeling dirty because he had mauled her.

"You'll go on bread-and-water rations starting tomorrow morning," he told her. "You won't leave your cell for anything—*anything*. You won't speak to anybody from the moment you are returned to your cell this evening. Any violation of this rule will result in the severest additional punishment."

"Nobody told me I couldn't speak with a reporter," Holly said to him. "I didn't know I was violating one of your rules here."

"Ignorance of the law is no excuse for breaking it," he said grimly. He strode past her angrily to the door that led to the corridor, and yanked it open. *"Guard!"*

Holly heard the footsteps outside. "Yes, Warden?"

"Miss Ransom will be returning to her cell now."

A curious look from the guard.

"You heard me, Guard. Then I want you to return here to receive special instructions about the prisoner."

"Yes, sir," the woman replied.

241

A moment later, Holly was marching back down the dim corridor toward a renewed and more ugly imprisonment.

The next week or so was bad for Holly. She was given bread and water twice per day, and very little bread. She could not leave her cell, could not write at her table, could not read. A guard heard her speak to Crazy Nellie one day, just in reply to Nellie's greeting on return from mess, and the guard came into the cell and slapped Holly around for a few minutes, leaving welts on her face.

Holly was very low, again.

In the middle of that, though, John Wilkes Booth came to visit her. He was denied admittance to see her at first, but when he complained to the warden personally, and convinced him that he was not another reporter, the warden grumblingly admitted him, not wanting trouble from the outside.

When Booth appeared at the cell door with the female guard, Holly was sitting at her table, just staring into space. She looked thin and pale; her clothing was wrinkled and slightly soiled, and her beautiful hair was unkempt-looking. She saw Booth immediately, and rose slowly from the chair she was sitting on.

"John!" she said in a small, hollow voice.

The guard unlocked the door; Booth went inside, and she locked it behind him. "I'll be back in a few minutes," she said in a surly voice.

Holly and Booth were suddenly alone. Booth was staring at her with moist eyes, shaking his head. "Oh, God, Holly!"

He came and embraced her tightly, urgently, and she felt herself responding, clutching at him. Then his lips were on hers, and it was the sweetest thing she could remember since her arrival there. He drew back then, and stared into her face. "What have they done to you, Holly?"

She shrugged her shoulders. "I'm all right, John. I'm on short rations right now, as punishment for an infraction. But I'll be all right. It's only temporary."

"I've missed you so much, darling," he said, his voice thick. "I—couldn't come." He looked around toward the corridor. "They wouldn't let me."

"Don't say any more, John. I understand."

"I haven't seen another woman since—they took you," he said, sincerely. "I haven't thought of anything but you, honest to God—you and the war."

"I believe you, John." She touched his face. He looked different, too—a bit thinner, and there were dark circles under his eyes. "Are you working?"

He shook his head. "Not much. I can't seem to keep my mind on play-acting anymore. I keep thinking about the war, and the cause, and what I can do about them. I forget my lines. I was released from a production in Washington recently, Holly. They said I wasn't concentrating on my work. I can't disagree with them."

"Oh, John," she said. "You've always taken all of this so seriously. How is the war now?"

"Terrible," he reported. "Have you heard about Cold Harbor?"

She shook her head. "No."

"They're calling it the worst half-hour of the war. Grant attacked Lee again, and Lee finally turned him back. There were much greater casualties on the Union side, but Lee can't afford even those lesser losses. Every time we lose a couple of thousand men, the war gets closer to its end for us. We were bloodied at Cold Harbor, Holly. The irresistible force met the immovable object, and Grant just kept sending them into our guns, as if there were no end to them."

Holly glanced past him. "Don't talk about it anymore, John."

"As soon as this is all over," he said, "I'm going to work on getting you out of here. It's outrageous to hold women like this. Of course, until the shooting is over, there's no chance."

"Don't worry yourself about me," she said. "I'll make it somehow, John."

"What can I do to make your life more comfortable?" he asked her, putting his arm on her waist. "What can I bring you?"

"Are you sure it's all right to come back?" she wondered. "Won't this draw attention to you?"

"I got permission from a temporary replacement of Fiske," he told her. "He says there should be no problem. Anyway, he'll be leaving Baltimore soon; they're not maintaining an operation here for a while. I'll be on my own, to do whatever I think is best."

"Whatever you think is best?" she said quizzically.

He shrugged. "About the war." But he did not expand on it.

"I don't think you should take any independent action to gather information, John," she said, almost whispering now.

"I'm not speaking of gathering information," he said quietly.

"John, please don't—"

But he put a finger to her lips. "Now it's my turn to tell you not to worry. You didn't answer me. Can I get you

244

anything to make things better for you here?"

She shook her head. "No, Eugenia has brought me soap and towels and things." Some of it had been taken from her, but she did not want him to know that. "I don't want you to come very often, either, John. No matter what they tell you that you may do."

"I miss you every hour of the day and night," he said. "Tell me you've forgiven me, Holly. Tell me you still love me. I need that, now."

Holly hesitated, then nodded. "I forgive you, John. As for my loving you, you needn't ask."

When he spoke next, his voice was uneven. "Thank God, darling. I really have reformed. You'll see, when you get out. When this damned war is over."

Holly did not know how she would feel about renewing her relationship with Booth, or about marrying him, if he were to ask and if she were free of iron bars. There was no doubt that she loved him and always would; there would never be a man she loved more. But she had to wonder whether Booth would give her happiness, over the long haul. He was a very complex individual, a difficult fellow to get to know; and she thought she would have to learn a lot more about his deeper layers of personality before she would want to commit her entire future to him.

"Let's hope we're reunited—really reunited—one day soon," she told him.

"God, I wish they'd let me stay with you here tonight," he said in a low voice. "I miss the touch of you so much, Holly; it's almost unbearable sometimes."

She looked away. It was best not to talk of such things. "I know, John."

He was just about to speak again, when the bulky female guard reappeared at the cell bars. "All right, you two. You can't stretch this out all day, we have things to do around here."

They said a quick good-by then, as the cell door was being unlocked. Then Holly was alone again, sitting on the edge of her bed, trying to keep from crying.

Three days after Booth's visit, a long article appeared in the Baltimore newspaper about prison conditions in federal facilities, and especially in the women's prison at Old Hempstead. The article named Holly and another woman, and told quite a lot about Holly's private life. The article made a big commotion in Baltimore, and was repeated just a few days later in the Washington papers.

The warden at Old Hempstead was furious about the publicity, and immediately cut off Holly's visitation privileges. Both Eugenia and Booth were turned away in that following week, with Holly not even knowing they had tried to see her. The warden came to Holly's cell, and told her that if he had anything to say about it, she would never get out of his prison. He cut her food ration down again, and Holly knew she could not survive for long on it.

But now things were happening. A citizens' group in Baltimore began making complaints to federal authorities there about Old Hempstead, and other reporters came to the prison and were turned away. There was a rumor that even Lincoln had read the newspaper accounts and was personally interested in the issue.

Then, one night after the guards had left their small cellblock, Crazy Nellie called out to Holly from her adjoining cell.

"Hey, Ransom!"

Holly had been lying on her bed, fully clothed, staring

246

at the ceiling and remembering good times in Charleston. That was how she got through the long days and nights now, by reliving better days, in her head. When she heard the voice from the next cell, she rose and got off the bed slowly, and weakly. She was thin and pale, and had little energy nowadays. She went up to the front of the cell and sat on the foot of her bed there. "Yes, Nellie?"

"That fellow Booth. He got a message through to you, by way of an inmate here. A visitor of hers passed it along from Booth. He's going off to Washington for a few weeks. He'll insist on seeing you when he gets back."

Holly sighed. "Thanks, Nellie. I appreciate your passing it along." She missed Booth more, now that he had been there once.

"There's something else, too," Nellie told her.

"Yes?" Holly said.

"There's a rumor—just a rumor—that Lincoln is coming to town to talk about transportation of war material with the B. & O. and his generals, and that he just might make a stop here."

Holly's face changed. "Here? At this facility?"

"That's what I hear, and it's from outside, not upstairs."

Holly's face brightened slowly, but then fell again into straight lines. "Oh, hell. That's ridiculous," she murmured.

"Maybe not. He's told reporters before that he doesn't like the idea of women in prison. He just might take a special interest in us."

"God, I won't even let myself think about it," Holly said.

But the very next day, there was a sudden order for

cleanup in the facility, direct from the warden, and Holly was put back on regular meals without any explanation. Then, two days later, on a Saturday morning at breakfast, the announcement was made. The President himself would be arriving at the prison in less than an hour. The warden himself made the announcement, but Holly still could not believe it. When she was returned to her cell, the warden stopped there for a moment, and convinced her.

"He'll be here very shortly," he said darkly to her, standing just outside her cell. Holly remembered that evening when he had tried to seduce her through intimidation, and she hated him for that and for his subsequent treatment of her. "He's going to inspect the facility personally, all because of that damnable article you caused to be published, here and in the capital. I hope you're satisfied, Ransom."

Holly stuck her jaw out, standing there opposite him behind the bars. "It pleases me very much, Warden," she said coolly.

"There are reporters outside, and presidential guards, and police," he told her. "We've never had anything like this at Hempstead since I've been associated with it. But then we've never had anyone quite like you here, either, Ransom."

Holly smiled a wan smile. "That's a compliment, Warden."

He scowled at her through the bars. "You've already caused more trouble here than any inmate we've ever had," he said. "I suggest you don't compound the trouble you're already in, Ransom, by opening your soul to the President about—certain things that have happened here. He'll return to Washington, and you and I will be

248

here still, Ransom. If you take my meaning."

"Yes, of course I do." Holly smiled. "You're threatening me again, Warden. But then I'm getting quite accustomed to that."

He held her gaze with a stony one. "Just remember what I said, Ransom. You've got a ten-year sentence hanging over your head. You and me are going to be here a long time after the lawyer from Illinois is gone."

Not a half-hour after the warden had left her cell, the entourage came through.

Holly could hear them, when they came into the cell-block area of the main floor of the building. There were Lincoln, two aides, a bodyguard, and a couple of reporters from Washington. The corridors and cells had been cleaned up spotless, and rugs had been thrown down in all the cells, and there were odors coming from the kitchen area that usually did not emanate from there, the smells of good food cooking for a midday meal.

"They're coming!" Nellie's voice hissed at Holly.

Holly could hear Lincoln's voice now, talking to the warden, and a guard who also accompanied the entourage. They stopped at Nellie's cell, next door, and Holly heard Lincoln speak briefly to Nellie, and Nellie's awed response. Then the group came past Holly's cell, where she sat at her table facing them, her hands folded before her. The reporters came into view first, and then the warden, who gave Holly a warning look, and then Lincoln.

He was even more impressive to her than that first time they had met, at the ball. He looked incredibly tall and straight and distinguished, and his face had even more fatigue lines in it than it had had before. His gaze met Holly's, and fixed on hers.

"And this is the Ransom girl, Mr. President," the warden was saying, acting a little nervous. "The one we allowed to speak with the reporter." He had already suggested to Lincoln that the reporting had been very biased, and that conditions were not as bad as suggested. However, he had told Lincoln, plans were already under way to upgrade the facility and to improve the quality of the food there. Lincoln had listened without comment to him. Holly now rose from her chair.

"Holly Ransom," Lincoln said pensively, still staring at Holly. "Why, I thought that name sounded familiar. We've met, haven't we, young lady?"

Holly was too excited about the President to take note of the warden's lie about "allowing" her to see a reporter. "Yes, sir, we have. When you honored the French ambassador with a visit here."

Lincoln nodded. "Yes, of course. The niece of the Fayettes." She was amazed at his memory. "I recall now."

"It's a pleasure to see you again, Mr. President," Holly told him.

"The pleasure is mutual, Miss Ransom, but it grieves me to see you here in this place. You did a little under-cover work for the Confederacy, I hear?"

"Yes, sir," Holly said unhesitatingly. "My sentiments have always been with South Carolina and the seceded states."

Lincoln nodded gravely, then turned to the warden. "Warden, I'd like a few minutes alone with Miss Ransom."

Holly, the warden, and all the others in the corridor were surprised by the announcement. The warden looked very scared, suddenly. "Why, of course, Mr. President."

250

He turned to the prison guard, a bulky woman in charge of the cellblock. "Guard, you may admit the President to the prisoner's cell."

The guard gave him a look and complied. Lincoln turned to his aides. "You may go on upstairs, gentlemen. I'll meet you at the warden's office shortly."

The guard opened the cell door, and the warden stepped up beside Lincoln, standing much shorter than him. "Mr. President, you'll want either myself or a prison guard here, surely?"

Lincoln shook his head sideways. "No, I won't. I want some privacy with Miss Ransom, sir. I'll see you in your office shortly."

The warden nodded uncertainly. "If that's the way you want it, Mr. President. I'm merely concerned for your safety."

Lincoln smiled a disarming smile that Holly liked. "I think I am probably safe with this young lady, sir. The presidency has not completely debilitated me; I believe I could still defend myself from most members of the so-called weaker sex, if the need arose."

The warden mumbled another few words, then everybody disappeared down the corridor and Lincoln was admitted to the cell by the woman guard. She locked him in as she did all visitors, and then she, too, left the area. Holly and the President were alone, except for Nellie in the next cell.

"Well," Lincoln said soberly. "Please sit down, Miss Ransom." He looked somber in his dark coat with tails, and his tight vest. He was bareheaded, and a lock of dark hair had fallen onto his forehead. He had a rawboned face that was made quite handsome by the dark beard.

Holly seated herself on the chair again, and Lincoln

went and leaned against the wall near her, across the table. She liked his informality, his easy, casual manner.

"Does the Confederacy really have to use such youth and innocence to defend itself behind the front lines?" he said to her.

"I'm afraid so, Mr. President. We've become the underdog, you know. There are fifteen-year-olds going into battle on our side. Can I refuse my duty, in the face of those conditions?"

"I suppose not," he said heavily. His gaze traveled past her, as if looking into the unseeable future, to weigh the effects of the war on the country—a war many held him responsible for. "It's just that it becomes so utterly grim, when women and children are hurt."

Holly saw the real pain in his face, and knew he was sincere. "I know, Mr. President."

"I want you to know that I deeply regret, Miss Ransom, this position I've had to take with respect to secession, that has drawn us all into this bloody confrontation. But I don't know how to adequately defend our Union any other way, a union that I believe to be absolutely necessary to the survival of the American people as a political entity."

"You talk like a lawyer, Mr. Lincoln," Holly said.

He grinned. "I am a lawyer, Miss Ransom." The grin faded. "But I'm a backwoods rail-splitter, too, and I like to think I've always been close to and had a special feeling for the common folk. I hate to see women serving time in a federal prison because they've been caught serving a cause they believe in. Are conditions really as you told the reporter who interviewed you, Miss Ransom, here at the facility?"

Holly nodded. "Yes Mr President. They are."

252

"I imagine your warden did a little cleaning up, when he heard I was coming, didn't he?"

"He surely did, Mr. Lincoln," Holly said sourly.

Lincoln sighed wearily. "And I suppose you can't depend on things remaining just the same after I leave."

"No, sir, we can't," Holly said, recalling the warden's warnings to her.

"There comes a time for most of us when we want things to be the same for just a little while," Lincoln said quietly, "and politicians are no exception. It reminds me of the story about the two Washington legislators who went out on the Potomac fishing together in a small rowboat. They found a perfectly wonderful fishing spot and pulled in fish all morning long. When it came time to leave, the younger man of the two, a congressman, suggested they come back to the same place the following week. The older fellow, a respected senator, agreed, but said they might have trouble finding the same spot, since spring was coming on and the banks of the river looked different every week. They bemoaned the fact that man could never count on a situation remaining the same, and particularly when times were good. But the congressman, in his legislative wisdom, came up with a bright idea. He suggested taking a small paint can he found in the bow of the boat, and marking an X on the side of the vehicle, to mark their spot for the next week."

Holly smiled nicely for him.

"But of course the older man, the senator, saw the error of that reasoning immediately. Remembering they had rented the boat from a livery at the nearby ferry dock, he replied sagely to the junior legislator, 'Why, you can't mark our spot on the side of the boat, lad. Things may not stay the same at the livery, either. Other fishermen may beat us out next week, and we might not get the same boat!'"

Holly laughed softly, and realized it was the first time she had done so since she had arrived at the prison. "That's a very entertaining story, Mr. President."

Lincoln smiled. "I'm afraid my back-country stories are judged by some to be the ramblings of a befuddled brain." His face slowly went sober again. "I'm going to make certain things don't change too radically for you in the next couple of weeks, Miss Ransom. I have my ways of checking."

Holly regarded him curiously. "Why, thank you, sir." She wondered why he had mentioned a time limit on the order.

"In those two weeks, there are certain things I intend to do, as the result of this visit here, and others I sent subordinates on, following the reading of your account here. I'm going to send inspectors around to military prison camps, with the hope of upgrading any that don't meet minimum standards for prisoners of war."

"Oh, thank you, Mr. Lincoln, for your interest," Holly said.

"The same goes for federal prisons," he added. "I've already made a list of improvements for this facility that I expect to be carried out. But if things go as I expect them to, they won't really concern you."

Holly frowned curiously again. "Why not, Mr. President?"

"I'm going to initiate a prisoner exchange with Jeff Davis," Lincoln told her, "and most of the exchange will deal with women held in imprisonment for just the kind of things you were sent here for, Miss Ransom. I'll see to it that your name is at the top of the exchange list."

254

Holly could not believe it. "Do you mean, sir, that I would be returned to Charleston?"

"If things go well, it should take only a week or two." He pushed off the wall, and strode over to the iron bars with his lanky stride. "Guard!"

Holly was dumbfounded. She was overawed by his raw power, and deeply moved by his concern. She followed him over to the bars. "I don't think I can accept my freedom as a gift, Mr. Lincoln. If you set me loose in Charleston, I'll still fight for the Confederacy in any way I can."

He turned to her. "I figured that, Miss Ransom. But that has nothing to do with this. I'm not doing you a personal favor; I'm also getting northern women back here in return for you and others, remember, women that may return to their husbands and families if I give them the opportunity, and let their men finish up this war for them. I hope you will do the same, but that is not a condition to your release. You will have no choice, in fact."

Holly started to protest, but the guard had returned and was unlocking the cell door. Lincoln stepped through it a moment later, and turned back to Holly for just a moment.

"Good luck to you, Miss Ransom. It was certainly a pleasure meeting you."

"The pleasure was mutual, Mr. President," Holly told him.

For the next five days, Holly did not see the warden or hear any more about what Lincoln had told her in the privacy of her cell. Crazy Nellie, for once, knew nothing more than Holly told her, so Holly just sat and waited hopefully. Her meal privileges were not revoked again, however, and there were no further threats to her by the warden. Then, one warm day in mid-June, the warden came to her cell grim-faced and somber, and it obviously nettled him to give her the news.

"Well, Ransom," he said, standing, bulky, before her cell on that end-of-spring day. "It seems we're going to lose you. You're going to be repatriated in a big prisoner exchange—you and Nellie and most of the other political prisoners held here in the city."

"My God," Holly said in a whisper, her eyes filling with tears. "When? When does it happen?"

The warden sighed a sigh of defeat. Unknown to any of them there, he had just been relieved of duty at the prison by an order coming directly from the White House. "Tomorrow," he told her. "Tomorrow is the big day. Today is your last day at Hempstead."

Chapter Fourteen

Holly was released from Old Hempstead the following morning, and turned over to a military guard. There was a brief processing period in late morning, down at the Corn Exchange, and then Holly and about twenty other southern women, most serving lesser sentences than Holly, were loaded aboard B. & O. railroad cars and sent off to Virginia and the front lines.

Holly found out very quickly that she was the celebrity of the group. Reporters crowded around her at the station before they left, ignoring the other women and wanting Holly's whole life story. She tried to avoid most of them, and was glad when the train was under way. At a couple of stops along the way, the pattern was the same. But when they had arrived at the front lines, there were no newsmen about.

Holly could not remember ever having been so excited inside. Her only regret was that she had been unable to see either Booth or Eugenia before leaving Baltimore. Booth had still been in Washington, and Holly figured that Preston Fayette had forbade Eugenia from going to the station. The whole idea of Holly's repatriation had been a blow to him. It had made his action against her look bad, he thought, and he had lost a lot of face in Baltimore. The only time Preston had ever disagreed with the President was over Lincoln's decision to repatriate Holly and the other women in trouble because of the war. Holly figured she would write to Eugenia from Charleston, and she hoped Booth would get in touch with her through Eugenia.

There was a formal processing at the front for them, too, and then they were on their way to their separate destinations, by way of the coach lines. As it turned out, Holly was the only woman returning to Charleston. After a couple of nights on the road in the custody of an emissary of General de Beauregard, Holly arrived home in Charleston.

There was a crowd at the coach station on that sunny June afternoon, and an official reception for Holly. She was incredulous when she found out that Lee had come for the reception, and De Beauregard, and the mayor of Charleston. There was a small school band, a military contingent, and a lot of banners proclaiming Holly as a heroine of the South. On a platform erected especially for that purpose, adjacent to the coach stop on Elliott Street, Holly was introduced for the second time to General Lee, and to De Beauregard. Holly looked for Charlotte, but did not see her or Jennifer in the crowd. Lee addressed the crowd informally, telling what Holly had done for the Confederacy. The crowd waved and cheered, and threw paper confetti at her. Then, in the middle of all of that, Holly spotted Charlotte, who had just arrived.

Charlotte was drunk.

"*That's my daughter up there!*" she was calling out to

those around her. *"That's my Holly, by Jesus!"*

Many present knew Charlotte by sight, because of the murder charges leveled against her, and then dropped. Holly wanted to go to her, but Lee was speaking to her at the foot of the platform, just before his leaving there.

"If you have any needs, Miss Ransom, please convey them to me through General de Beauregard here," Lee was saying to her. He looked very dapper in his gray uniform and sash, his saber at his side. "I'll see that you don't go needy."

"That's right, Miss Ransom," De Beauregard told her. He was a much younger man than Lee, and dynamic-looking in his uniform. "We won't forget your great service to the cause."

"I appreciate that, Generals," Holly told them. She was embarrassed at having arrived at such a reception in the plain and rather worn clothing she'd been wearing when released from the Baltimore prison, and was conscious of looking very unkempt generally. But nobody had seemed to notice. "I'm deeply honored by your interest."

Lee left then, with a military entourage, and there was more shouting and waving of banners. De Beauregard and his aides remained, and he turned to Holly just as Holly saw Charlotte approaching them.

"We intend to have a gala banquet for you tomorrow evening, Miss Ransom, after you've had a chance to rest. One of my subordinates will contact you at your home to arrange—"

"Holly! My baby!"

Charlotte came and threw her arms around Holly, and Holly returned the embrace, her eyes moist. She could smell the liquor on Charlotte's breath, and could see the unsavory look of her clearly now. But she did not mind. It felt good to be in Charlotte's embrace.

"I knew we'd be reunited!" Charlotte was saying in a heavy, slurred voice. "I knew you'd be back home one day soon!"

Nearby onlookers were eying Charlotte narrowly, and whispering among themselves. Holly did not care. She turned to the erect, very military De Beauregard. "General de Beauregard, this is my mother—Charlotte Ransom." She deliberately left out Quinn's name.

"I gathered as much." De Beauregard smiled. "I'm pleased to meet you, Mrs. Ransom."

"She's always been my baby," Charlotte said thickly, hugging Holly. "No matter what there was between us. You know what I mean, General?"

De Beauregard hesitated. "She's a lovely daughter, Mrs. Ransom. And a credit to the Confederacy. We're very proud of her."

De Beauregard furnished Holly and Charlotte transportation home—Charlotte had sold the buggy and horses months ago to meet her expenses for food and booze—and it was not long before they were removed from the hubbub of Holly's welcome home. All the way there, Charlotte talked loudly of how she had fixed the house up for them, and laid in a supply of food in advance, and how she had been looking forward to seeing Holly since being notified of her return, on the previous day. Holly noted that Charlotte did not mention Uriah Quinn once, or the shooting incident; nor did she speak of Jennifer Clayborne.

Holly was shocked by the appearance of Charleston. The city had been torn apart by shelling from land and sea; rubble lay heavy in the streets amidst the ruins of burned-out buildings and houses. De Beauregard and Lee had both mentioned the heroics of the citizens of Charleston throughout the siege. Charleston's head was bloodied, but unbowed. That made Holly proud of her city, her birthplace, just as it was proud of her. But she also felt guilt that she had not shared its trauma, even though she had aided the war effort from Baltimore.

The excitement and liquor were too much for Charlotte, and Holly had to put her to bed when they got back to the house Charlotte had once shared with Quinn, and in which Holly had almost been raped by him. The house, despite Charlotte's announcement to Holly, was messy and dirty. It showed the lack of interest in it—and in life—its occupant felt. There was litter in every room, and a lot of empty liquor bottles. Windows were unwashed; dishes were stacked in the kitchen.

Holly spent two hours cleaning up to make the place livable. She knew it would take much longer to really clean it, but that was a start. Then she decided to go find Jennifer and have the inevitable confrontation with her.

It was late afternoon when she walked across town to the house where Amanda had died and where Holly and Jennifer had shared a bedroom those many nights ago. It was springtime again in Charleston, almost summer, but it did not look the same. The trees and shrubs put up a good front, but behind them lay a lot of ruins of the war. The children on the street looked pale and sickly, like Charlotte, and there was a smell about the city that overpowered the fragrance of spring. It was the smell of death and destruction.

At first, when she knocked on the front door of the house, Holly thought she had missed Jennifer. But then suddenly Jennifer was there, standing behind the opened door. Her mouth fell slightly open when she saw Holly. She had not known Holly was coming home.

"My God," she muttered.

"Hi, Jennifer," Holly said with a hesitant smile. She had put a clean dress on, a gingham one that Charlotte had outgrown, and had fixed her long hair in an upswept pile on top of her head. Her dark-blue eyes and dark hair gave her pale skin a milky look that was not unbecoming.

Jennifer, though, did not look good. She was without make-up at the moment. Her light-brown hair was down and rather straggly, and her face had taken on a hard look since Holly had last seen her. She was wearing a robe with nothing on under it, and part of a thigh was exposed as she stood there taking in the significance of what she saw.

"I'll be damned," she said. "It's you."

"May I come in?" Holly asked her.

Jennifer hesitated, then shrugged. "Why not?" she said.

Holly went inside, and Jennifer asked her to sit down on a short sofa by a window where the sun came in and a breeze moved the curtains. This house was better kept than Charlotte's, but it had the look of a brothel to Holly—too much red cloth and the odor of cheap perfume. Jennifer sat on a chair removed from Holly. She had not kissed or embraced her, and her manner was very reserved.

"So, the heroine of the war returns," she said finally, looking Holly over soberly. She had heard of Holly's escapades, but not through Charlotte. "I thought you had been thrown into jail."

"Prison," Holly said. "But I was released on a prisoner exchange, just this week. President Lincoln ordered it."

Jennifer nodded. "Gosh, that's great," she said

262

without enthusiasm.

Holly watched her face, and saw the subdued hostility in it. "I haven't heard from Stuart," she finally said.

"Neither have we here," Jennifer told her.

"Randy went back to the front," Holly said.

Jennifer eyed her narrowly. "I'm aware of that."

Holly sighed audibly. "Jennifer, I'm so damned sorry."

Jennifer looked at her, holding her gaze tightly.

"It just happened. I don't even know how," Holly said. "There we were in Baltimore, two old friends away from home. We felt very—close those first weeks of reunion, Jennifer. But it was a one-time thing. I was sorry as soon as it happened. He's yours, Jennifer, no matter what there is between you; I understood that even at the time. There was never any real love between us, Jennifer—not like between you and him. It was just loneliness that drove us together there that evening."

Jennifer shrugged. "You don't have to explain to me, Holly. We all do what we have to do. None of us is an angel with wings—no matter what the press may say." Sourly. "Anyway, none of it matters anymore, does it?"

Holly frowned at her. "Doesn't matter?"

"I mean, because of Randy," Jennifer said. "Because of what happened."

Holly was still frowning, trying to understand her meaning. "What happened?" she said.

Jennifer eyed her closely. "You mean you didn't know?" she said, unbelieving. "About Randy?"

Holly felt a tension mounting inside her. "I haven't heard anything since he left Baltimore."

"Randy joined Grant in Virginia," Jennifer said in a dull monotone. "He was at the battle of Cold Harbor. He

263

was killed in action there on June 1."

Holly felt a frigid chill pass through her body, and the room began spinning around her for a moment. She was afraid she might pass out. "Oh, Jesus in heaven!" she whispered.

There was a long silence between them, as Jennifer watched her reaction to the news. After a long time, Jennifer finally spoke again. "I thought you must have known."

Holly replied through misty eyes, "No, I didn't."

"All I had in my heart for him was anger," Jennifer said. "Right up to the moment I got the news."

"God, I'm so sorry, Jennifer," Holly told her.

"I had a man in my bed when I heard," Jennifer added. "Another soldier. Ironic, isn't it?"

Holly felt devastated inside. She remembered that last visit of Clayborne had made to her place, just before he left Baltimore, and his confessions to her about himself. She had liked him, that night. "I was so happy for him, when he escaped arrest there," she heard herself saying now. She wondered if Blaisdell might be dead also, with the news merely delayed in getting to them.

"I'd lost him, anyway," Jennifer said philosophically.

"Oh, Jennifer! I hoped you two would get together again somehow. I finally found a man to love in Baltimore, and I so hoped you and Randy would find your love again. I hoped Randy could explain what happened better than I'm doing it, and that you would forgive both of us."

"Like I said, what does it matter now?" Jennifer said in her new, hard voice.

"It matters to me," Holly told her, brushing at a tear. "Maybe even more than before. Oh, God!"

Jennifer made a small face. "Hell, you're forgiven.

Who am I to judge, anyway?"

Holly tried to smile through the tears. "Do you mean it, Jennie? Will you really put it all behind us?"

"I said so, didn't I?"

Holly went over and pulled Jennifer to her feet, and embraced her tightly. Jennifer finally responded, but not with enthusiasm. "I'm so glad, Jennifer!" Holly said, brushing at her face again. "I'm so very glad!"

Jennifer let out a long, ragged breath, and felt that she really could get past all of it, now. "Why don't I get you a cup of hot tea, heroine of the war? And you can tell me all about this man in Baltimore."

Holly touched Jennifer's cheek fondly. "I'd really like that, Jennifer," she said wearily.

The war was going worse for the South with every week that passed, now. Grant gave up on taking Richmond for the moment, and by-passed it for Petersburg. There was a big siege there now, and rebel forces were complaining about running out of ammunition. In Georgia, General Sherman was laying waste to the land, and was nearing Atlanta. He was repulsed momentarily at Kennesaw Mountain, but again the rebels ran short on equipment and ammunition.

Holly heard all of this news with much sadness. She had taken on chores at the local general hospital again, more responsible ones this time, and was also helping raise funds from the locals for the war effort, as Sherman attacked Atlanta. But Holly did not feel as if she was doing enough. Other repatriated women had pretty much given up on the war, but Holly could not. She realized that even if the South lost, there was more than one way to lose. She now wanted some final successes for Lee's army so he could negotiate some kind of honorable peace for the seceded states.

Holly visited Jennifer often in those early weeks of summer, and she mentioned the possibility of doing something more in the war effort. But Jennifer was not interested. She did not care how the war came out. She thought nowadays only of herself and her private life. She told Holly that she was doing her part in the war effort by entertaining De Beauregard's siege soldiers.

Holly could not talk to her.

Charlotte was not interested in discussing the war, either—or much of anything else. She had become not only an alcoholic in the past couple of years, but sickly as well. She had a lung condition that she treated occasionally, and she spent many days in bed with it, nursing a bottle of rum or gin. She used her health condition as an excuse for her drinking, although her doctor had advised her to stop imbibing. All Charlotte talked about with Holly were the old days before Uriah Quinn, and especially the time before Ashby Ransom's untimely death. Holly always listened to these reminiscences patiently, but she worried about her mother.

The bombardment of the city continued, from the federal navy and from the Massachusetts Artillery regiment that held a small chunk of the shoreline, protected from De Beauregard by the guns of the warships. Neither Charlotte's nor Jennifer's houses were in range of the guns, but much of the rest of the city was being hit almost every day. It was unnerving to Holly, and frustrating. She thought of John Wilkes Booth all the time, and wrote him a couple of letters, hoping he was still at the same address in Baltimore, and that the letters were allowed through by military censors. She feared they were not, because of her notoriety in the press.

Reporters continued to come to see her, through those first weeks of summer, and there was a second banquet in her honor, sponsored by a vigilance committee devoted to counterespionage. That group tried to recruit Holly for work against enemy agents, but Holly judged that that problem was an almost nonexistent one at this juncture. She already had ideas of her own, and they involved the procurement of ammunition for the Confederate Army: musket balls, Minié balls, primer, percussion caps. Holly's idea was to go north for them, through the blockade, because these items could be purchased quite freely in New York and Massachusetts, even now at the height of the war. She proposed the idea to a leader of the vigilance committee, but he was an officious middle-aged man who thought the idea incredible and harebrained, and declined to be involved in it. So she was momentarily stymied. She needed one or more associates for such a mission, and she needed financial backing to purchase the ammunition when she got to her destination. She had neither. She was certain, though, that De Beauregard would find finances for her, if she could gather a few people about her in whom she had confidence.

She went to De Beauregard's city headquarters in July, while Atlanta was busy defending itself from Sherman, and put the idea to him and several of his staff. A couple of his staff took the same position as the vigilance committee chairman had, but De Beauregard himself, and two of his people, liked it because it was so bold a concept. The general got in touch with Jefferson Davis, and within days a shipment of cash came to him by courier. Holly, posing as a Canadian arms supplier, was to use it to go to Massachusetts and buy quality primer and percussion caps for Confederate guns. She expected to take a male agent along, to play the part of her business partner—a friend, someone good with a gun. De Beauregard recommended she take one of his intelligence officers, but Holly hedged in accepting, because she wanted somebody she knew, somebody she could trust implicitly. She picked out her own sloop captain for running the blockade and taking her north, and mulled the notion of going it on her own when she was landed in New England. But while she was in the midst of that, another big development occurred in her young life.

While working at the hospital one day, news came that a group of veteran soldiers, mostly wounded ones, was arriving in the city that evening, for discharge and rehabilitation. A cadre of hospital personnel was meeting the arrivals down at the train-station platform, and Holly volunteered to go along.

It was early evening when she and the others arrived at the station, and there was plenty of light in the summer sky. The funnel stack of a greasy locomotive stood belching and wheezing on the track, with its emptied-out cars looking hot and dusty behind it. Steam hissed and the boiler grunted and there was a clatter of yelling and talking along the platform. Many of the soldiers there were not ambulatory, and were waiting for medics to move them from where they lay on litters. Others stood about with bloody bandages on their heads, arms, or legs; they seemed stunned by what they had been through. Holly's eyes watered when she looked at the mass of them, over two hundred: the same young men who had gone off a couple of years ago with such high hopes and proud promises, their cheeks blazing and fire in their eyes. She supposed it was the same in Chicago and New

York. Except that their side was winning the war.

Holly walked along the platform, carrying a jug of hot coffee to give to the soldiers who wanted it. She stopped and poured a couple of cups for those on litters, and was grateful when she did not know either of them. Then she saw Blaisdell, leaning against the station wall, not thirty feet away.

He had not seen her. He had a crutch under his right arm, and a bandage on his right thigh that showed thick and bloody through his ragged and torn uniform. He looked dirty, tired, defeated. He was looking up and down the platform, as if hoping to see someone he knew among the throng that had greeted them. But Holly knew that Blaisdell's father would not be there. He was in a wheelchair now, and also probably had not known about Blaisdell's coming. Holly walked over to him, her heart pummeling her chest.

"Stuart!" she said to him.

He turned quickly to her, and she saw the change come into his face, the life returning to it. "My God. Holly. I heard you were in—"

"I feared you were dead," she said.

They hesitated for a moment, while she studied his mature, fatigue-lined face and decided she liked it much better than before. Blaisdell had become almost handsome, despite his weary look. She came and embraced him warmly, and he grabbed her to him with his free left hand.

"Oh, God, Holly. It's been so long—so damned long."

He kissed her, and she did not try to stop him. It was a firm, urgent kiss, one that had been pent up inside him for all that time. When it was over, Holly averted her eyes, blushing slightly.

"Your leg. Is it bad?" she said.

"The lead nicked the bone. They say I'll always limp, for the rest of my life. But I hope to get rid of this one day soon." He lifted the crutch to show her. It was just a stick with a piece of wood pegged across its top. Holly looked at his darkened brass buttons with the big "I" for infantry on them, and his tarnished belt buckle with its bold "SC" for South Carolina. He had looked so beautiful when he had left, and now he looked so beaten, so used.

"I'll help you with it," she promised him. "We'll get you so you can walk without any support, you'll see."

"How's my father?" he asked her.

"About as well as can be expected, Stuart. I've visited him a couple of times, and he talks of nothing but you. He never gave up hope that you would make it through all those battles. I'll take you home to him as soon as I can get clear here."

"What about your mother?" he said. "Jennifer?"

"Charlotte is not well, Stuart," Holly told him. "She's had a bad time. You heard about Uriah, I guess."

"Yes," he said quietly.

"Jennifer worries me," she went on. "She lives a very—promiscuous life. I suppose it's worse since she heard about Randy. You know about him, don't you?"

But it was obvious he did not. "Do you mean—"

"Yes, he was killed in action, Stuart."

"Oh, God."

"It was quite a shock to all of us. Randy and I had become quite close, in Baltimore." She watched his face, and it was obvious he knew nothing of her intimacy with Clayborne.

"How did you get free?" he finally asked her, his face still somber. "I heard you were carrying letters for the Confederacy."

"I was," she said, and in that moment she knew it was Blaisdell she wanted to take to the North with her. "I was imprisoned, Stuart, but freed in an exchange of prisoners—by Lincoln himself."

He managed a grin, and she was reminded of how boyish he had looked to her, at one time, before everything had happened to all of them.

"How about that?" he said.

"He said he didn't like the idea of women in prison for political reasons," she added.

He grunted in his throat. "I guess he can't be all bad."

"He isn't, Stuart. Most of the leaders aren't all bad, up there in Washington. They just have some wrong ideas—a different perspective on things."

"I suppose if we won the war, we might have trouble with our people in Richmond one day, too," he suggested. "Maybe that's the way the world is."

"But we won't win the war, will we, Stuart?" she said.

He hesitated, while a nurse walked past helping a wounded soldier walk to a wagon. "I doubt it," he finally said.

"But we can't quit fighting," Holly added quickly. "We have to negotiate a peace from a strong position, Stuart. That's very important, in this last stage of the war."

He grinned again. "Somebody else will have to do my fighting for a while, I guess. But let's not talk about the war, Holly. Let's talk about you and me." He looked down for a moment, then back into her blue eyes. "Remember what you said to me, when Randy and I left here, that thousand years ago?"

Holly recalled what he meant, but she did not want to

discuss it. "Why, we talked about a lot of things, Stuart."

"I'm not talking about a lot of things, just one conversation—when you told me you'd reconsider us, when I got back. Whether there was a chance for us, Holly. I've kept the memory of that conversation strong inside me for all this time. It helped me to survive, Holly. It gave me something to come back for, to come back to."

"I remember, Stuart," she said almost inaudibly. The locomotive chugged and grunted behind her somewhere. "But let's not talk about that now. Come on, let's get you to a wagon over here. I'll ride to the field hospital with you, and then I'll take you home from there."

He nodded. "All right, Holly. But we're going to have to talk."

"I know," she said. "I know, Stuart."

Chapter Fifteen

It was August, and the battle for Atlanta was almost lost for the Confederacy. Georgia had been laid to waste, and now its most elegant city was being burned to the ground. If Lincoln had unleashed a tiger in Grant, Grant had unleashed another in Sherman.

In Charleston, the streets were now full of rubble and soldiers; the shelling from land and sea continued. The only business booming was the liquor business; transient soldiers bought it in large quantities and slept in streets and alleyways and caused the locals concern. There were some muggings and lootings, and some of them were attributable to this welter of outsiders.

Morale was low.

Holly was glad to have Blaisdell back, but she knew she faced a problem with him. She had probably misled him when he had gone off to battle, she realized, by giving him hope for them on his return, hope that she might marry him. But she had to give him that hope, to help him survive. Now, she would have to face the situation she had created, in her earlier attempt to be kind to him.

The first thing she did, when she had a free moment,

was to go pay Jennifer a visit. Jennifer had not seen Blaisdell yet, and Holly wanted to get to her before that happened.

Jennifer was looking somewhat better than on their first visit when Holly returned from Baltimore. She was dressed in a satin dress, her hair was up, and she was made up expertly. She looked to Holly like a high-class whore, which is about what she was.

Jennifer got Holly a glass of iced tea, and they sat down beside a bay window that looked out over the street. It was late afternoon; sunlight streamed in from outside, and a warm breeze moved the airy curtains at the windows.

"Did you know that Stuart is home?" Holly asked Jennifer, after they had sat down together.

Jennifer raised her arched eyebrows. "Oh? Really? My God, I was sure something had happened to him."

Holly was surprised by Jennifer's lack of interest, her lack of feeling. They had all been close, before the war. Jennifer had once said that Blaisdell was like a brother to her.

"Something did happen to him," Holly said. "He has a leg wound, Jennifer, and is walking on a crutch."

"Well. He's damned lucky, I'd say. A lot of them aren't coming back at all."

Holly met her gaze, and they both thought about Clayborne.

"I suppose so," Holly said. "He thinks the same, I guess. He looks older, Jennifer—ten years older."

"We've all aged a bit," Jennifer said, smiling a wry smile.

"He'll be over to see you, I'm sure," Holly said, "as soon as he gets settled in."

Jennifer eyed Holly impishly. "I suppose he will. Most men seem to get over here sooner or later, don't they?"

Holly held her gaze for a sober moment, then looked away.

"I'm sorry, Holly," Jennifer finally said. "I told you I was past being angry about you and Randy, and I was. But Stuart's coming back now seemed to bring it all out in me again. I was just trying to hurt you. Forget I said it."

"It's all right," Holly said. She was grateful that Jennifer was being open and honest with her, for the first time since Holly's return to Charleston. She reached over and touched Jennifer's hand. "If you have any bitterness left in you, it's my fault."

"What's done is done," Jennifer said.

Holly sighed heavily. "Jennifer, do any of our old friends know about—Randy and me?"

"Not from me, they don't," Jennifer replied a little abruptly. "Why?"

"Well, that means you and Charlotte are probably the only ones who know," Holly said slowly. She looked down at her folded hands. "It would be nice if it stayed that way, Jennifer—for all of us. I particularly would hate for Stuart to find out. He doesn't know, and I don't want him to—for him, not me."

Jennifer looked at her balefully. "I have no interest in telling the world that my dead husband slept with my best friend," she said without emotion or recrimination.

"Oh, God," Holly whispered.

Jennifer made a small face. "There I go again. Jesus."

"I shouldn't have brought it up," Holly said. "I have no right to ask anything."

"Let's just forget it, Holly."

"All right, Jennifer."

275

                          *   *   *

That same evening, Blaisdell and Holly had a date.
They went to a music hall that was still open despite the
siege, and there were some war songs and jokes, and the
two of them had a good time. Blaisdell was dismayed at
what he saw in Charleston: the bombed-out look, the
hunger and disease, the corruption everywhere. War did
more than destroy physically, he decided. It ate out the
heart of the people, rotted their moral core. Yet, the city
was courageous. Only a tiny minority clamored for surrender of the port to the federal navy, or to the artillery
units that now squatted on the northern shore. The war
had become rather accepted as a condition of life, and
almost nobody complained about it anymore.

But it was not the same city as before the conflict.

After the music hall performance, Blaisdell took Holly
home, and they walked the distance. He was using only a
cane now, and he walked everywhere. The sooner he
could throw the cane away, the better he would feel, and
only exercise helped heal his leg.

They did not go inside at Holly's place, because Charlotte was in there, drinking as usual in her bedroom. She
coughed more and more now, and Holly realized her lung
condition was worsening, partially because of the liquor.

The two of them stood outside the small house that had
belonged to Uriah Quinn, under the shadow of an elm
tree, and neither of them spoke for a while. Blaisdell,
having been discharged from service already, had dis-
carded his torn uniform for civilian clothing. Holly wore
a light summer dress made of gingham and lace, and she
looked more lovely than she ever had, despite what she
had gone through. She, too, had matured in her face and
body. She was more womanly in appearance, with a fuller

                              276

bust line and hips, than when she had left Charleston for the North. Her face was slightly longer and more regal looking, and one of the newspapers that had covered her triumphant return had described her as the loveliest girl in Charleston.

Holly had sensed all evening that Blaisdell was slightly tense about their being together, and it did not require much imagination to deduce why. When they had stood under the shadowy elm for a short time, her suspicions were confirmed when Blaisdell finally spoke to her.

"Here on this street, in the quiet like this," he began, "it's almost like before, isn't it? Like on those dates before Randy and I went off to the war."

Holly was leaning against the tree trunk. She glanced over toward him obliquely. "Yes, Stuart. Almost."

"God, I can't get it out of my head about Randy, Holly. I wish I had been nicer to him, before he left Tennessee."

"You're always nice to people, Stuart. Don't worry about it."

"It would make it all better, Holly, if you and I—"

She had known it was coming. She turned partially away from him. "If we married," she said.

"Yes," he said, "if we married. I love you, Holly. The job at the bank is gone, but I'd find a way to support us soon enough. I have some ideas already."

"Stuart—"

"Don't you have affection for me, Holly? Don't you love me just a little?"

She turned back to him. "I have deep affection for you, Stuart. But—"

"But what?"

"But not in the way you hope," she said quietly. "You see, I met a man in Baltimore."

277

His face changed, and a darkness came into it. "So that's it."

"He's an imperfect man, Stuart. He's emotional, moody, vain. He likes women—all of them—but I fell in love with him, and I think he loves me, too."

Blaisdell stood there, scowling now. "I should have expected as much," he said, looking past her. "I should have known that women don't wait for men through a war. I had a friend who could have told me all about it."

Holly caught his dark gaze. "Please, Stuart. Don't be angry. I made you no promises when you left here. In fact, I told you that I would be going out with other men, and might find one special one."

He nodded tautly. "Why not? There are always men who will stay at home and take the pick of the women left behind. I've heard that story before, Holly. Who is this Yankee, anyway? Why isn't he in the fighting?"

"His name is John Wilkes Booth, and he has been fighting in his own way, Stuart; and he's not a Yankee," Holly said softly.

"Then it's finished between you and me," he grunted out.

"It will never be finished between us, Stuart. I want you to be my friend always. But I can't marry you—not with my heart elsewhere."

"I suppose you'll be going north again then? To marry this Booth?"

She shook her head. "I don't run after men, Stuart. If John wants to see me again, he'll know where I am. But I suspect I've seen the last of him. He was—different, when I left. I think an obsession of hatred has taken hold of him—a hatred of Lincoln. It may get him into a lot of trouble, if the war doesn't end soon. But even if it

278

doesn't, I doubt that he would come to Charleston for me. He's too wrapped up in his own life in Baltimore and Washington."

"Do you mean you don't expect to ever see him again, and yet you won't give it a chance between us?" Blaisdell said curiously, and without understanding.

"That's the way it has to be, Stuart," she said, seeing the pain in his square face. His sandy hair was longer now, giving him a more genteel look, and his blue eyes almost never smiled. He smiled with his mouth now, since his return, the mirth never spreading to his whole face. Holly was afraid that this confrontation would make him even more somber.

He turned toward her house. "I've been such a damned fool!" he hissed out into the night.

"Please, Stuart. Please try to understand."

When he turned back to her, his face was full of anger. "I presume that a worldly woman like yourself can find her way up to her front door without escort." His voice was brittle. "I'll be walking back now, Holly. Good evening."

He moved past her, limping on his cane, and Holly reached out for him and missed him. "Stuart! Don't be angry with me!"

But he was gone now, in the darkness of the night.

Holly stood under the tree for a long time, letting the emotions of the moment flow through her, wishing there could be some real happiness in her life again. Then she walked disconsolately to the house.

For the next several days, Blaisdell sulked about, drinking and feeling sorry for himself. When he had been out on the fields of war, he had imagined a hero's welcome on his return to Charleston: bands playing, citizens cheering; Holly falling into his arms, praising him, pledging herself to him. He had earned all of that, and the hard way. Wounded twice, by bayonet and by rifle, he felt that the Confederacy and Charleston owed him something. Not anything material, not even a job. But he was owed respect, gratitude, affection. It seemed to him now that he was getting very little of any of that, except from his aging father. It was Holly who had been treated royally on her return to the city, he had learned, better than returning soldiers who had placed their lives on the line over and over again, until they were broken physically or psychologically. Blaisdell found that he even resented that, now that Holly was not his. It made him feel badly to feel the resentment, but he could not help himself. He was angry with Holly, and the world.

With each evening that passed, his drinking became heavier. Finally, one night on his way home on his cane, he found himself within a block of Jennifer Clayborne's house. He hesitated there in the night, and then walked over to the place.

The lights were lit, because Jennifer had just said good night to a lieutenant of artillery, who had shared her bed through the early part of the evening. Jennifer was still up, but preparing to go to bed, this time to sleep. Blaisdell knocked loudly on her door, and she thought her lieutenant was back. When she opened the door and saw Blaisdell there, she stared in surprise for a moment.

"Stuart! I wondered if you'd stop by." She looked him over, and saw the cane, and the look of inebriation on his square face.

He grinned with his mouth. "Hi, Jennifer. It's old Stuart, all right, back from the war. Just thought I'd

280

say hello."

She asked him in. She was wearing a robe over absolutely nothing, but that did not embarrass Jennifer. Nothing much embarrassed her, nowadays. She was accustomed to being undressed and half-dressed around men. She embraced Stuart a bit awkwardly, and they stood there in her parlor for a long moment in each other's arms. Then she seated him on her sofa, and she drew up a straight chair before him. Her robe fell away when she sat down, and exposed one thigh all the way up to her hip. She saw Blaisdell studying it, and pulled the cloth together.

"You're still a good-looking girl, Jennifer," he finally said. "Better looking than before, in fact. Damned fine-looking."

"Thanks, Stuart. You're a handsome fellow, too. The war put some interesting lines in your face."

"You're a fine-looking girl, Jennifer," he said. "I told Randy you were a fine girl to come home to. I loved him, Jennifer, but he didn't treat you right. He didn't."

"That's all past now, Stuart."

"You're a free woman now," he said thickly. "You can do what you want, and nobody can criticize you for it."

She furrowed her brow slightly. "That's right."

"Don't pay any attention to any of them, Jennifer. They don't know what you've been through."

Jennifer's eyes became moist without her wanting them to. "That's fine of you to say so," she said.

"You're a fine girl, too," he said. "We're both fine."

Jennifer smiled. She was wearing her make-up, but it did not look so hard, in the soft light of the parlor. She looked very pretty, sitting across from him, very desirable. "That's right, Stuart."

"Holly won't marry me," he said abruptly, looking at his broad hands. "She won't marry me, Jennifer. Talks about some man in Baltimore, by the name of Booth. Doesn't figure on marrying him, but won't marry me, either. Damned fine mess. A fine mess for fine people."

"I'm sorry," she said.

"Fine mess," he said.

"Can I get you something, Stuart? A cup of coffee?"

He shook his head rather emphatically. "Just wanted to say hello, Jennie. For old times. For old times' sake."

"Sure, Stuart."

"We're both free now, aren't we, Jennifer?" he said. "Aren't we both free people now?"

"I guess we are, Stuart."

"Nobody can second-guess us now," he said.

Jennifer got up and went over and sat on the edge of the sofa beside him, and the robe fell open again; she did not notice. "I really am sorry," she said, touching his cheek. "Would you like me to drive you home?"

He turned to her, and saw the bared thigh, and then he was looking her over hungrily. Suddenly he reached out and grabbed her and pulled her to him. His hands were on her, and his mouth sought hers and found it. She let him kiss her for a moment, then drew away. One of his hands was on her bared thigh.

"I want you, Jennifer," he breathed harshly. "We're both free people now, aren't we?"

Jennifer hesitated. She thought of Holly with Clayborne, and bile rose momentarily in her. But this would be different. She felt nothing for Blaisdell. This would be a calculated slap in the face to Holly, a gratuitous hurt, and she did not feel vindictive at that moment in time. She took his hand from her thigh.

282

"We are, of course, Stuart. But I have a couple of beaus. I don't think I can handle another one."

His face was downcast. "Oh, hell. Nobody wants me. Nobody wants a crippled veteran."

Blaisdell had never been one to feel sorry for himself, not in the old days. She figured this was a temporary thing, like the leg. It was the war, and coming home.

"You know better than that, Stuart. We all love you. You tried to win the war for us. You're a real-life war hero."

"Tell that to the proprietor who kicked me out of his establishment tonight," Blaisdell said dully. "They don't want me around now. They don't want any of us around. It will be worse when the war is over and lost."

Suddenly he was making a lot of sense, Jennifer thought. Too much sense. The liquor was not helping him now.

"I'll drive you home," she offered.

He rose, not looking at her. "I walk nowadays." He grabbed the cane, and brandished it. "With this. Got to keep walking, keep moving. See you, Jennifer."

"Come back, Stuart."

When she went to the door, he was already limping down to the street, an awkward, hunched figure in the darkness.

On the following morning, Holly visited Blaisdell. He was hung over from his drinking, but was dressed when she arrived, although unshaved. He was embarrassed to have her see him like that, and was not cordial to her. She ignored the mild welcome, and asked to see his father. They went out in back, where his father sat on a rear porch in a wheelchair. Holly talked with him for a while, with Blaisdell sitting there rather quiet, and his father kept saying how proud he was of Blaisdell, and how the South would still win the war.

After their talk, Holly went into the kitchen with Blaisdell and he made them a cup of tea. He was in his shirt sleeves, and his hair had been awkwardly combed. He avoided Holly's eyes as they sat there together. He remembered trying to seduce Jennifer on the previous evening, and wondered if that would get back to Holly. He did not know why, but he hoped it would.

"Have you heard the news?" Holly asked him, after sipping at her hot tea.

"News?"

"Atlanta has fallen to Sherman," she said.

"Oh, Jesus."

"I didn't want to mention it in front of your father. He has such faith in our eventual victory."

"Sherman and Grant were cut from the same piece of cloth," he said. "They win at any cost. They don't give a damn how many lives it takes. Hell, maybe they're right."

"He'll head for the sea next," she said. "Savannah." She remembered Jennifer's visit to her cousin there, a visit that had started Jennifer on her route to promiscuity.

Blaisdell sat there, staring at his tea but not drinking it.

"There's no way to win the war now, is there?" she said.

"None that comes to mind," he said wryly.

"Our goals must change now," she told him. "We must fight now for an honorable peace. We must not collapse and unconditionally surrender."

"Somebody ought to tell that to Grant," he said.

She leaned forward onto the table that separated them.

"Stuart, what we need most right now are equipment and supplies. Our armies are running out of them quickly."

He looked at her. "Is that supposed to be news to me?"

"No, I understand that you know from firsthand experience. But I intend to do something about it, and I want you to help me."

"What?" he said incredulously.

"I've learned some things about intelligence work, Stuart. While you were out there getting shot at. I've talked with General de Beauregard, and he's commissioned me to go north and buy primer and percussion caps there, and bring it back here for our armies."

He frowned heavily. Then he began laughing. It was the first time he had laughed since he had come home, and she did not like the sound of it. "Buy percussion caps? From the Yanks? My God, Holly, where did you dream up an idea like that?"

She was patient with him. "It's been done already, on a small scale. Confederate agents have found it quite easy to purchase war supplies in the North. There are almost no security regulations up there restraining their sale. I'll pose as a Canadian buyer, and you'll be my partner."

He looked at her with disbelief for a moment; then he was staring past her, thinking about what she had said. Finally, he shook his head sideways. "It sounds crazy to me. You'll end up in a Yankee prison again, by Jesus. And they may not be so quick to let you out, this time."

"I know all of that, Stuart. But don't you see, this is important to the war! To the way the war ends, and what we have here afterward. Somebody should try it, and nobody else seems willing to."

He met her look. "You would be in charge of this operation?"

She shrugged. "Nobody would be in charge. We would work together, as partners."

"But you've talked with De Beauregard, you've made the plans, the whole thing was your idea. It's you De Beauregard is sending, not me."

"He expects me to handle it my way," she admitted. "But you and I would make all our decisions together; it would be between us, once we left Charleston." She paused. "There is nobody else I trust to go with me, Stuart."

He rose from the chair he was sitting on, and grimaced when he put weight on his right leg. "That's a laugh. You prefer a cripple on something like this? Can you imagine what chances of success the mission would have, with me on a cane taking orders from a woman?"

He saw the hurt come into her face, and his eyes softened. "Hey, I'm sorry. I didn't mean it that way. Well, maybe I did. But I'm still sorry."

"It's all right, Stuart."

"I guess I've still got a lot of ugliness left in me, from the war, and from—"

"From our talk recently," she said.

"Yes. From our talk."

"Can't we be friends, Stuart? Can't we keep it on that basis? Does it all have to be lost to us, like so many other things have been lost?" She had waited for a letter from Booth, but none had been forthcoming. She figured it was over between them.

"Sure. We can be friends," he said without enthusiasm. "But I'm through with the war, Holly. I'm no longer fit to serve; that should be obvious to anybody. I'm sorry, but if you're bent on going off on this crazy trip, you'll have to do it without me."

286

Holly sat there, unhappy. She would not press him. She did not want to be responsible for pressuring him into doing something that was dangerous, and which he did not want to do himself. That burden would be too big inside her, and could affect the mission.

"All right, Stuart. I'll have to make other arrangements."

"I'll warm up your tea," he said to her.

But Holly did not stay to have more tea. She wanted to leave for the North in a matter of days, and now she had to rethink her plans. She left Blaisdell still sitting in his kitchen, looking glum. When she got home, she had a bad surprise.

The doctor's carriage stood outside her house; the one that had been there a couple of times recently, when Charlotte had had bad spells. When Holly got inside, she found a neighbor woman and a nurse in the parlor, and the gray-haired doctor was just emerging down a staircase from Charlotte's room.

"What is it?" Holly asked. "What happened?" Charlotte had seemed all right when Holly had left, a couple of hours ago.

The doctor came up to her. "Not long after you left, your mother started coughing up blood, Holly. It just got worse and worse. Your neighbor friend here heard her, and called me out here."

"How bad is it?" Holly asked tersely.

He sighed. "I think she's going, Holly. She just asked for you. You'd better get up there."

When Holly got upstairs into the dimly lighted room, she saw Charlotte propped on pillows, looking ashen in color. Her eyes were closed, and it appeared she was asleep. But when Holly walked over to the bed, Charlotte opened her eyes and focused on Holly.

"Oh, you're here. Hi, honey."

Holly sat down on the edge of the bed. They had cleaned her up, but there was still the stain of fresh blood on her top pillow. Her dark hair was awry, and the flesh of her once-lovely face was sagging and gray-looking. But it was her eyes that caught Holly's attention. She had never seen death in anyone's eyes before, but she saw it now in her mother's. There was a lifelessness about them that was frightening, and upsetting.

"Hello, Mother. I hear you had a bad time while I was gone." She tried to keep her voice calm, unemotional.

"I didn't tell you, but I had a bad night. I didn't want to worry you. Now, I guess it's pretty clear. I'm dying."

"Don't say that, please," Holly said, her throat tight. "I want you to rest today. I'll stay right with you. Tomorrow you'll feel better, you wait and see."

Charlotte shook her head slowly. "No, that's all past, now, baby." She stopped, and holding a handkerchief to her mouth, coughed out several raking coughs. Although she tried to hide the handkerchief from Holly, Holly saw the blood on it. Charlotte breathed hard, trying to get her composure back.

"Just take it easy, Mother."

Charlotte licked dry lips. "There are a—couple of things I want to say to you, honey. It seems like you never get things said to those that are—closest to you."

"You don't have to say anything right now, Mother. Please, just rest. I want you to get better."

"This won't take long. First of all, I want to say—how ashamed I am about not believing you. When that damned *man* assaulted you."

Holly felt tears well up in her eyes. "It's all right,

288

Mother. Really. How could you know?"

"I should have believed my own daughter," Charlotte said. She gave another small, loose cough. "I should have—believed you, and I know I was wrong."

"Mother—"

"I want you to forgive me, Holly." In a rasping voice. "If you can find it in your heart, honey."

The tears rolled down Holly's face. "Of course I forgive you. You're my mother."

Charlotte grabbed her hand. "Thanks, honey. I appreciate that; it's important to me." She had a moisture in the lifeless eyes. "And now there's one more thing. I want you to know I'm proud of you. For what you did in—Baltimore, and for all the things you did for me and for others here in Charleston, long before that. You grew up different, and nobody understood you but Ashby. I wish to God he—were here to see you now."

"He would be proud of both of us," Holly said in a broken voice. "Now, please rest, and I'll—"

But in that moment, the hand on Holly's tightened until it hurt hers. Charlotte's lifeless eyes grew very large for a moment; there was a gurgling sound in her throat. Then her eyes glazed over quickly, and a worm of crimson appeared at the corner of her mouth; she was gone.

"Oh, God!" Holly muttered. "Mother? Mother!"

The door to the corridor opened, and the nurse came in. When she saw the scene at the bed, she hurried over, and put a hand to Charlotte's throat. She turned then to Holly.

"She's no longer with us, Holly."

Holly felt the sobs rise into her throat; there was nothing she could do to keep them back. The nurse pried

Charlotte's hand off Holly's, and helped Holly from the room.

An hour later, the body was taken from the house.

Because of the hot weather, Charlotte was buried the next day. There were two shell holes at the cemetery from the bombardment; one shell burst had hit nothing, but the other had demolished a couple of markers not far from Charlotte's open grave, and had almost disinterred a citizen at eternal rest. That unsettled Holly, who was already upset. Stuart Blaisdell was there, and Jennifer, and some friends and relatives. It was a hot afternoon, so the ceremony was short. Holly had asked a friend to tell Jennifer about Charlotte's death, but the friend had somehow missed Jennifer, and Jennifer had had to learn about it from a third person. That had made her unreasonably angry with Holly again, because she was already very sensitive about being treated like an outcast by some of their old friends. So she stood apart at the graveside ceremony, feeling anger more strongly than her sadness about Charlotte. About halfway through the short ceremony, when an aide of De Beauregard arrived out of respect for Holly, Jennifer was reminded forcefully of Holly's status in Charleston in comparison with her own, and suddenly, it was almost too much for her. Whereas Jennifer was maligned, avoided, and talked about, Holly was still being treated like an important personage, although Jennifer did not see that much difference between them. What she was beginning to feel was envy, and it was not sitting well inside her. Even though she really had fairly well gotten past the Holly-Clayborne thing, as a barrier between her and Holly, nevertheless it lay deep inside her somewhere, nurturing this other resentment that had sprung up quite unexpectedly now.

290

> *"Therefore we were buried with Him through our baptism into His death in order that, just as Christ was raised up from the dead through the glory of the Father, we also should likewise walk in a newness of life. For if we have become united with Him in the likeness of His death, we shall certainly also be united with Him in the likeness of His resurrection."*

Holly watched the minister's solemn face, at the head of the grave, and thought of all the soldiers who had had words spoken over their still bodies in the past couple of years in the same manner—and those who were still having eulogies spoken over them. Charlotte was a victim of the war, too, no less than they. But no one would ever set a flag on her grave.

> *"If anyone is in union with Christ, he is a new creation; old things will pass away, and new things come into existence. Amen."*

There was a chorus of amens in response, quiet, muffled. Then, after a concluding prayer, the gathering broke up. Some people came up to Holly and offered their condolences, but Jennifer hung back, staring darkly at the grave. When Holly saw her, over by herself, she went over to her, and Blaisdell followed her there.

"I expected you beside me at the graveside, Jennifer," Holly said, her eyes red-rimmed.

"I expected to be told that Charlotte had died," Jennifer told her in a hard voice. Holly could see that she had had a couple of drinks before she came. "But then I guess I'm an embarrassment at a public function."

Holly frowned in surprise at her. "Jennifer, I did send word to you. Didn't you get my message?"

"No, I didn't get any message," Jennifer said. "I didn't know that you and I sent envoys to each other to deliver messages. We used to do those things for ourselves. Of course, that was before you began hobnobbing with De Beauregard and Lee."

"Jennifer!" Blaisdell said, scowling. "For God's sake!"

Jennifer shot him a hard look. "Ah, the war hero. I'm sorry I couldn't accommodate you the other night, Stuart. You'll have to stop back sometime when I'm in a more affectionate mood." She turned a hard smile on Holly. "You have my sympathy, of course, Holly." Then she turned and walked away.

Holly just stood looking after her, bewildered by the confrontation. Finally, she turned and regarded Blaisdell curiously.

"She's not as bad as she'd like to sound," he said quietly. "She turned me away that night."

"You don't have to explain anything to me, Stuart," she said. "You know that."

"I just wanted you to know about Jennifer," he said. They started walking toward a carriage together. "Well, there's even less reason for me to delay my trip north any longer," Holly told him, "now that Charlotte is gone. I'll be leaving in a couple of days, Stuart."

"I figured as much," he said. He stopped, and she turned to him. "Holly, have you arranged for a confederate yet, to accompany you? With General de Beauregard?"

She cast a sideways look at him. "Why, no, Stuart. I was going to do that at the last moment."

A small grin broke across his lower face. "Good.

292

Because the doc says I can discard this cane in the next couple of days, and—I'd like to go with you."

Holly's face slowly brightened, through the red in her eyes. "Really, Stuart?"

"I can't let you go off on something like that with a stranger," he said. "Anyway, I decided that maybe I still have some fight left in me, some good I can contribute yet."

Holly managed a smile, despite the open grave behind her only fifty yards away. "I'm sure you have, Stuart," she said warmly. "I'm very sure you have."

Chapter Sixteen

The next couple of days were hectic ones. There were three meetings with De Beauregard and his staff. Blaisdell was introduced to the general, and liked him; and De Beauregard was impressed with Holly's choice.

"There is nobody I would trust more absolutely than a line officer like yourself, Lieutenant, who has served in the heat of battle under my command, and that of General Bragg," De Beauregard told Blaisdell on that early-September day when Holly and Blaisdell saw him. De Beauregard was very physical-looking in his gray, brass-buttoned uniform with its gold epaulets, very competent and martial. But he no longer had the look of a young man. The war and the long siege of his beloved Charleston had taken their toll on him. "You proved your worth in the battlefields, sir. We are glad to be having you with us on this important mission."

"I'll do my utmost to justify your trust in me, General," Blaisdell told him.

Blaisdell felt good about his decision to go with Holly. He felt of some use again, felt valuable to the cause again. As for Holly, she was scared now that her plans were

294

seeing fruition. The responsibility was an awesome one. De Beauregard was delivering over to her a large sum of money that Holly had to carry north safely and use to purchase needed supplies. If the money was lost, or the material after purchase, the Confederacy had gambled on Holly and lost. That reality was now very frightening to her.

After introducing Blaisdell to De Beauregard, Holly took Blaisdell down to a cove just off the main harbor of Charleston, and they went aboard a sloop named the *Carrie Mitchell* to meet its captain, a fellow called McNeil who had known Holly's father. He was a grizzled man in his forties who had opted for blockade-running over going into the battlefields of the war. He had taken the sloop out through the federal blockade a dozen times, and twice had had to fight his way through the warships. He had lost a crewman to federal guns, had had a mast blown away, and had been injured himself. But he was still soliciting business from the Confederate Army and private individuals. Most of his trips out had been to the Caribbean to pick up and bring back needed supplies and food for the besieged city. He had never been farther north than Baltimore, and was looking forward to the trip as a real adventure. Not thinking much of a woman's being in charge of such a mission, he treated Blaisdell with more deference than Holly. But Holly did not mind. If the mission was a success, nothing else mattered.

The evening before they were to leave, Holly went to see Jennifer. She could not bear to think she might leave Jennifer with hard feelings and possibly never see her again.

Jennifer was not at home that evening, but a neighbor told Holly that Jennifer had gone down to a store to look for some dry goods, so Holly walked down to the place to find her. She met Jennifer on her way back, and Jennifer was surprised to see her. Their meeting was rather stiff. Holly asked if she might walk back with Jennifer, and Jennifer agreed to the suggestion.

"I'm sorry about how I acted," Jennifer said quietly as they moved along the dirt walk under tall live oak trees. "At the cemetery. Stuart was right, it was disgraceful. I guess people have come to expect that of me, though. You shouldn't have been surprised."

"You know how I feel about your not being notified about Charlotte," Holly said. "There were just so many things to do, and I was so confused, Jennifer. I wrongly thought it was all right to send someone to tell you. It wasn't."

"Oh, hell," Jennifer said. "It wasn't that. It's you and me, Holly. My God, I've envied you from the time we were kids. I just seem to have more reason, nowadays." She made a face. "There I go again. What a thing to say to a girl who's just lost her mother! I don't know what's wrong with me, Holly. Randy had every right to be disgusted with me; we both know that. I've never been able to live up to other people's expectations of me, like you have. I don't have it in me, for some reason."

"You're too hard on yourself, Jennifer. You always have been. If you had thought more of yourself, maybe things would have been different somehow."

Jennifer gave her a look. "I don't mean to sound like a crybaby. But what have I had to be happy with myself about? I was never pretty, like you—or smart like you, or poised like you. I couldn't believe it when Randy wanted to marry me, instead of someone like you. Then later, of course, I realized that he had probably wanted you all the time. Now, everybody that counts here looks at me as though I have some kind of contagious disease, and they all adore you. That's partly my own doing, but then I never had any strength of character. You have."

"Oh, God, Jennifer. You're a warm, affectionate, likable girl. People love you, no matter what you think. I love you, and Stuart loves you."

"Don't pay any attention to me," Jennifer said. "That's the way I am nowadays, not very pleasant to be around. I don't know why you bothered to come. I don't deserve your pity."

Holly shook her head sideways. "Pity you? I'm sorry, Jennifer, but there are a lot of people around that really are pitiful—veterans, war-sick locals, those who can't get enough to eat. I couldn't pity you. You're young, pretty, and you have your whole life ahead of you. One day one of these suitors of yours will marry you, set you up in a big house on King Street, and you'll live happily ever after. No, you couldn't ever be the object of my pity."

Jennifer smiled slightly. "Thanks, Holly. I needed that."

They walked along. "I'm going away for a short time, Jennifer."

Jennifer regarded her curiously. "Away? Where?"

"I'm going north. Under General de Beauregard's orders. It's something I can't talk much about. But when I return, I want to see you often, Jennifer, like we used to. I want us to be real friends again."

Jennifer nodded. "All right, Holly."

They had arrived at Jennifer's place. They stopped, and Holly turned to Jennifer. "Also, I want you to start taking care of yourself, Jennifer. Start having some respect for yourself."

Jennifer hesitated. "I guess that doesn't seem much to ask."

"Will you? Will you go easy on yourself for a while just to see how it feels?"

"Why not?" Jennifer said lightly. "The other way hasn't done much for me."

"I may be gone a couple of weeks. When I get back we'll talk again. O.K.?"

Jennifer nodded soberly. "O.K."

When Holly got back home later, Blaisdell was waiting there for her. She had given him a key, and he had let himself in and had made coffee for them. They sat at her kitchen table together, and Holly was now all geared up about their departure the following evening.

"Did you see that McNeil got his fee?" she asked Blaisdell while they sipped at the hot coffee.

He nodded. "Yes, he's paid. He said he would rather have the whole thing now, but I told him neither we nor De Beauregard operate that way. He has three crewmen and they seem all right. They're all pledged to secrecy about our time of departure. And, of course, he hasn't discussed the objective of the mission with them."

"I haven't told him much either," Holly said. "Did McNeil get that sail replaced?"

"Yes, I saw it myself. He says he's ready to sail."

"I'm scared to death," Holly told him.

"Of the federal guns?"

"No, of our responsibility."

"I know what you mean. I had the same feeling in the fighting, because I was in charge of other men. It never seemed to bother Randy."

"Randy was very different from you," she said.

He studied her lovely face. "I would never have thought that Randy was your type," he said.

She looked at him in shock. "What—do you mean, Stuart?"

He shrugged, missing her reaction. "I mean, that you'd get to be good friends, there in Baltimore. You didn't seem to think all that much of him, here in Charleston."

She relaxed inwardly. She had been sure for a moment that Jennifer had told him about her and Clayborne. "Well. It was different in Baltimore. Randy represented home to me, I guess. And he was different, there—less self-oriented, I think. Having him there was like having you and Jennifer there with me."

"I think I understand that," he said. "I felt pretty much the same way, being out there in the field with him. His memory will always be dear to me, I guess."

Holly watched his face for a moment, then rose and walked to a dry sink and placed her coffee cup in it. Blaisdell got up too, and followed her over there. When she turned around, suddenly he was very close to her. Without any warning, he pulled her to him and kissed her hungrily on the mouth.

A moment later Holly broke away, breathing hard, her face flushed. She looked into his eyes accusingly, his hands still on her narrow waist. "What are you—doing, Stuart!"

"I can't stand it," he said, gasping out his passion. "Being so close to you all the time—touching you, smelling the good smell of you."

"Stuart, we had a talk, remember?" She pushed him away. "We were to keep this on a friendship basis. You agreed."

299

"I'm not asking you to marry me," he said in a low, emotional voice. "I guess maybe you never will; you've convinced me of that. But you said so yourself, you'll probably never see this Booth fellow again. It isn't like you'd be unfaithful to anyone. We're going to be physically close for some time now, Holly. Maybe sleeping in the same cabin or room with each other. Why can't we at least enjoy that physical closeness? Would that hurt anything? Since we can never have anything permanent, can't we at least find some momentary pleasure in being together, some physical pleasure?"

Holly hesitated only for a moment, then shook her pretty head. "I don't think so, Stuart."

"But why not?" he persisted.

She looked into his urgent eyes. "I'm not Jennifer, Stuart. I have to give my heart to a man before I give my body to him."

She knew that she had made an exception to that rule, with Clayborne, under very unusual circumstances. But she hoped Blaisdell never found out about that.

He turned away in utter frustration. "Damn it, Holly. You don't know how difficult this is going to be for me—being with you day and night, not being able to kiss you, to touch you, to have you. It's going to be damned difficult."

She sighed. "Maybe you would rather not go," she said quietly.

"No. I'll go." He looked back at her. "I want to be the one who watches over you out there, the one who takes care of you. That's the way it is with me. It's the way it will always be."

"I like that, Stuart. I like that very much."

He went and leaned on the table, facing away from her.

"Damn," he muttered. "Damn, damn, damn."

There was never any shelling of the city at night. That was when the Union warships sat silent out beyond the harbor; they loomed ominous in the blackness, waiting, watching—for saboteurs, for blockade-runners. There were ironclads and brigantines, steam sloops and men-of-war, imposing, dangerous. In February the Confederacy had sent a newfangled submarine boat out to sink the steam sloop *Housatonic* with a spar torpedo, and a few other small craft had been sunk with floating mines in the harbor. But mainly the federals were untouched by Confederate resistance, and the blockade was even stronger than it had been at the inception of the war.

That was what Holly and Blaisdell were up against when they went down to the dark cove that next night in the cover of darkness, and boarded the *Carrie Mitchell*. The *Mitchell* had no steam engine, no power other than sails. But with a good wind, she could outdistance most of the warships readily in a short run, and that night in September, there was a wind off the sea.

Along the waterfront, as they approached the boat in a disguised military carriage, they could see discharged soldiers standing against old buildings, and some lying in the street. There were tattered Zouave uniforms, torn jackets of dragoons, and many of the gray official uniforms, dirty, ragged, battle-scarred. When the war was over, Holly thought as they passed, it could be more this, or there could be a grand restoration and recovery—depending on how the war was lost: honorably, with dignity, or not.

Holly had been aboard only a couple of boats in her life, despite her upbringing in a great seaport. With the

301

wind up, the first thing she noticed was the movement of the craft under her feet. McNeil met them at the gunwale and a crewman took their small bags to a cabin below that they would share.

"Well, then, lass! It's a fine night you picked for the run. There's no moon, and the wind is high out of the southwest. That's luck, by Jesus!" McNeil, grinning at them through his thick red beard, looked a bit like a madman out of an asylum.

"Then let's get this sloop out of the harbor," Holly told him. "I want to be up the coast when the sun rises tomorrow."

McNeil grinned his crazy grin at Blaisdell. A square-built Irishman, he looked like a boozer to Blaisdell and Blaisdell was uncomfortable around him. But Holly had told Blaisdell that McNeil was the best blockade-runner in Charleston, and Blaisdell trusted Holly's judgment. "You hear that, Lieutenant?" McNeil said above the flutter of the sea wind. "I never heard a woman talk like that in my life! Just like she's running things, by Jesus! Ain't she just like that daddy of hers? Or did you know him, lad?"

Blaisdell did not return the grin. "I'm not a lieutenant anymore, Captain McNeil. But yes, I suspect Holly is a lot like her father, even though I never met him. And she *is* in charge here; the general put her in charge."

"Oh, hell, I know that," McNeil said good-humoredly. "You'll do just fine, too, Holly. You'll do us all proud. Bates, get that cloth up, and douse all lights! We're heading out! I want to be under way in ten shakes of a pig's tail!"

A second crewman came up, McNeil's mate, and took Holly and Blaisdell down below deck to a forward cabin.

where they would sleep. It was very small, with no head-room, and the bunks were narrow; it stank slightly of bilge water.

Holly glanced at Blaisdell, after the mate had gone. "Well. This is going to be home for a few nights, I'm afraid."

"It can't be any worse than a muddy battlefield," Blaisdell said. "I guess I can put up with it. But it's no place for a woman."

"I can take more than you might imagine." Holly smiled at him. "I've slept in a tent, myself." She looked around. "I guess we'll have to take turns in here, dressing."

"Dressing?" he said.

"Yes, when we go to bed. Our night clothes."

He made a face. "Holly. I won't be changing into night clothes, not for this short a time. And I don't think you should try to, with all of these men aboard."

Holly held his gaze for a moment. "You're not going to start acting in a proprietary way toward me, are you, Stuart?"

He averted his look. "I had no such intention."

"Don't overprotect me, Stuart. I'm a big girl now; I've taken care of myself for quite a while."

He nodded reluctantly. "Sure," he said. "I was just trying to—"

But then the boat rolled sharply, and they could feel it begin to move, under them. Holly was thrown against him, and ended in his arms. They looked into each other's eyes for a long moment.

"I guess we're under way," he finally said.

Holly removed herself gently from his grasp. "Yes," she said. "Let's go take a look."

303

When they got topside, they found the three-man crew and Captain McNeil very busy, manning the rigging, steering the sleek boat, keeping watch for the hulking shapes out in the sea beyond the harbor. McNeil asked his mate to relieve him at the helm, then walked over to Holly and Blaisdell, who were now leaning over the starboard gunwale, peering out into the night, the spray bouncing up on them.

"Yes, they're out there, all right," McNeil told them. "See that dark shape there? And there?"

"They look formidable," Holly said.

"Oh, they are." McNeil grinned. He and the crew wore black slickers now to keep the sea water off them. Holly and Blaisdell had been offered them, but had not put them on yet. "The five-pounders of those ironclads out there will cut you to pieces before you can raise a surrender flag. And if they sink you, not many of them bother about picking up survivors, either. If the shells don't get you, the sea will."

Blaisdell, seeing the fear in Holly's pretty face, gave the captain a hard look. She was wearing a cape and hood, and the cape was wet already.

"Will there be much danger tonight, Captain?" she asked him.

"There's always danger, lass," he told her genially. "They're watching for us, with their spyglasses. They may have seen us already. If they do, they'll raise an alarm, and we could come under fire from several ships and boats at once. But generally only one will give chase, one of the lighter craft, that has a chance of catching us.'

"Have you been chased?" Blaisdell wondered.

"Oh, sure, lad. Three times I've had a romp over the water with brigantines and sloops. They haven't sunk the

Carrie Mitchell yet, though. She's a hard lady to catch hold of."

"When will we be clear of them?" Holly asked.

"Well, I'm hugging the shoreline pretty good tonight. We're heading right between shore batteries and the fleet. Look over there, on shore. See those lights off there? That's the federal artillery that's part of the siege force. They can turn them guns, too, if they have a mind to. A blockade-runner was blown right out of the water a couple of months ago by shore batteries. But with a little luck, we'll run right between their army and navy and not cause any—"

But at that moment, a crewman came running up to McNeil, his face full of excitement. *"Captain! The brigantine on our starboard bow! We think she's sighted us!"*

Blaisdell's face lengthened and Holly's heart began pounding in her chest as McNeil turned quickly and peered out over the black water. Running lights had been lighted now on a brigantine not much larger than McNeil's sloop, and a sail had already been hoisted against the black sky. McNeil took a glass and studied the other craft through it for a moment, then lowered it with a dark visage.

"You're right, Hollis. She's under way, and heading on a collision course with us."

"Oh, Jesus," Blaisdell muttered.

"See to foremast rigging!" McNeil snapped suddenly. "Secure the hatches, and keep her steady as she goes!"

"Aye, Captain!"

Suddenly there was a flurry of activity aboard. The *Mitchell* was too light to carry cannon, but McNeil went below and broke out some rifled muskets he always carried aboard. Other men were running along the deck, preparing for an assault. The sloop went on cutting the black water smoothly, riding the sea with grace. Wind tore at Holly's cape, and salt spray hit her at the gunwale.

"Damn," she was saying to herself.

"It will be all right," Blaisdell told her, not believing it. He turned to McNeil as he went past. "Is there anything I can do, Captain?"

McNeil shoved a gun into his arms. "Here, you ought to be able to handle a rifle, soldier. Don't fire on the enemy unless I give the order."

Blaisdell nodded, and McNeil was gone. Holly and Blaisdell now stared toward the other boat, which was moving on a diagonal path that would cause it to intercept the *Mitchell*, if it made enough headway. Also, lights had been lighted aboard two other craft not far away, a steam sloop and a bigger man-of-war, and whistles were being sounded in the night.

"My God, I thought it was easier than this," Holly said, fear in her voice. "I thought we'd go right through."

"There will be some shooting," Blaisdell said. "Get below, Holly. I have to take a position at the bow."

She shook her head. "No, I want to know what's going on. I'm staying on deck."

Blaisdell gave her a sober look, then turned and moved along the gunwale toward the bow of the boat, gun in hand. As he went, suddenly there was a booming flash of light from the nearest of the bigger ships, and a moment later a shell splashed into the water only twenty yards off the starboard bow.

"*We're under fire!*" McNeil bellowed. He had taken the helm, his legs planted well apart, his back stiff in the wind. "*We'll begin tacking for avoidance course. Keep that cloth full!*"

There were other shouted orders by McNeil and his

mate, and a couple of more bursts of fire came from the enemy, this time from the big man-of-war. One shot plunged into the sea just aft of the sloop, and one just missed its bow. The brigantine fired, too, running along seemingly parallel to the *Carrie Mitchell*, and the shell exploded on the rear gunwale, not far from Holly, tearing a hole down to deck level, and almost knocking Holly down.

Blaisdell ran back along the deck to her, the tilting boat throwing him against a bulkhead of the cabin structure for a moment. Holly was leaning against the gunwale, shaken badly, and there was a small amount of blood on her cape, from her arm.

"Holly! Are you all right?"

She nodded dizzily. "Yes, I'm fine, Stuart."

"There's blood on your cape!"

"It's just a small scratch from shrapnel," she told him. "Really, I'm all right. Don't worry about me, go to your post. Please."

Reluctantly, Blaisdell left and made his way back to the bow. Now the brigantine was closing, but it was going to be outrun in the meeting. Another cannon shot came, and sailed over their heads, and then the sloop was pulling ahead of the brigantine, and leaving it behind. The brigantine was only thirty yards away now, and Holly could see the crew on deck, manning the big guns, and now aiming handguns toward them. There was an exchange of small-arms fire, and one of McNeil's men went down, hit in the chest, falling right beside Blaisdell. Holly saw Blaisdell fire back, and then the *Carrie Mitchell* was pulling away from the larger boat, cutting the water beautifully, sliding and bucking through the sea.

In another ten minutes it was all over, the brigantine barely in sight in the darkness behind them. The sails billowed tight in the wind, and the sloop pulled further and further beyond its pursuer, and the other craft gave up the chase.

Blaisdell came back and examined Holly's arm. She had been right; it was just a shallow wound that had hardly broken the skin.

"What about Bates?" Holly asked, looking down the deck to where McNeil bent over the crewman. "How is he?"

"He'll be all right," Blaisdell said. "I offered to help, but I think McNeil figures I'd just be in the way."

Just at that moment, McNeil rose from tending the wounded Bates, who was sitting against the gunwale, and came striding past Holly and Blaisdell. That inane grin was back on his flushed face, and he seemed happy as a lark.

"That was a good run, all right! Makes the blood course through the veins, eh? You're all right, lass?"

"Oh, yes," Holly said.

"Fine, fine. Bates caught a shot in the chest, but we'll dig it out all right. God, but that was a damned fine run! Lucky we didn't get caught with the shore batteries, too; you can get smashed in those crossfires. Well, if you need anything, just holler!"

He moved on briskly, swaggering in his walk, and they both just stared after him for a moment. Then they both turned and exchanged a look between them.

"Let's get below and bandage that arm," Blaisdell said heavily, still tight inside. "Then maybe we ought to try to get some rest, what do you think?"

Holly was still trying to calm herself, trying to get past the trauma that McNeil had savored so greatly. "I think that we've earned it," she said in a low, heavy voice.

Chapter Seventeen

It was several days up the coast, and the rest of the trip was rather uneventful. There were federal warships everywhere, but they were not interested in small sloops that looked like fishing boats, as the *Carrie Mitchell* did. They were hailed once by a patrol boat at Chesapeake Bay, but McNeil convinced the other captain that he was fishing out of Baltimore. They all had forged papers for their cover story. Holly and Blaisdell were supposedly relatives of McNeil, hitching a ride to New York. But when they arrived in that great port, with McNeil sneaking in under the cover of darkness, down by the Battery, Holly and Blaisdell switched I.D.s and went to the papers that showed them to be partners in a Montreal manufacturing firm, she a young widow and he a bachelor.

Holly was glad to get off the sloop. Blaisdell had been right, the cramped quarters were no place for a woman. They said good-by to McNeil the morning after their arrival, showing their papers to port officials without trouble. Their cash for purchase of ammunition—all in good, hard Union tender—was stashed in the fake bottom of Holly's luggage, and escaped notice. McNeil was to wait in port for their return, then take them back to Charleston. If they did not show up within seven days, he was free to return without them.

Neither Holly nor Blaisdell had ever been to New York, and they were impressed with it. The island of Manhattan was a veritable wonderland to them, with its massive buildings, paved streets, concert halls, and playhouses. Shops were bigger and richer looking than in Charleston; there was more evidence of wealth about, despite the war. The draft riots of 1863 were long past, and Holly sensed a quiet determination throughout the city. The North could smell victory.

Holly and Blaisdell had no difficulty fitting in. They took adjoining rooms at a small Forty-eighth Street hotel where they stayed two nights while making coach arrangements to Hartford. Posing as manufacturers and distributors of guns and ammunition for the Canadian Army, they hoped to do some business with an arms manufacturer in Hartford.

On their first day in the city, they were walking back toward their hotel after purchasing coach tickets to Hartford, when Holly suddenly stopped short in front of a small theater. Blaisdell stopped beside her, regarding her curiously. Then he saw the playbill she was reading: THE LOWER BERTH, A NEW PLAY BY ROSCOE ADAMS, STARRING JOHN WILKES BOOTH AS HARRY BASCOMBE.

"My God," Holly was saying to herself.

"It's him?" Blaisdell said. "It's the Baltimore fellow?"

She nodded numbly. "Yes, it's him."

Blaisdell made a face.

"The play has two more days to run. He must be here in the city."

"You don't have any time for diversions, Holly,"

310

Blaisdell said to her irritably. Then he was sorry he had done so.

She turned to him. "I know that, Stuart. But I have to see if he's free. Do you mind if I go in and inquire?"

He shrugged. "Hell, no."

"Will you come with me? I'd like for you to meet him if he's here."

"I'd rather not," he admitted. "I'll be across the street at that little restaurant over there, having a cup of coffee—when you're finished."

She hesitated, then nodded. "All right, Stuart. I won't be long."

A moment later, she went into the theater lobby alone. On a playbill inside was a drawing of Booth and his leading lady, and Holly felt a tightening inside her as she viewed it. It had been so long, it seemed, and yet it was not. She wondered what she would say to him, how she should act.

"Can I help you, ma'am?"

She turned and saw the heavyset, waddling man who had emerged from the theater auditorium. He was looking at her openly and curiously.

"Oh, yes. I'm looking for a member of the play troupe—Mr. Booth. We know each other from Baltimore."

"Oh?" the fellow said.

"Yes, my name is Holly." She could not give her real family name; it would be too dangerous, she knew. "He'll know who I am. Is he here this afternoon?"

He shook his head. "No, ma'am. He left New York a few days back. Got in trouble with the producer. They had to get somebody else to come in and play his role."

"Oh, dear," Holly murmured.

311

"Seems John couldn't keep his mind on his acting. Kept talking politics to anybody that would listen. I think he's a reb at heart. Hates Lincoln. A real funny bird."

Holly ignored the insult to Booth. "Do you know where he went?"

"I think he was working in Washington, before he came here for this. I suppose he went back there. You could check with the producer. All I know is, when he left he had a fancy woman on his arm. He always did, while he was here."

Holly felt the old anger well up inside her, quite without justification. There were no promises made between her and Booth. He was free to see whom he liked and do what he preferred, just as she was. But the anger and hurt were there, anyway.

"I see," she said. "Well, thank you very much. It appears I've missed him for this trip."

"The producer might be in his office," the heavyset man said. "You want to wait a minute, I might be able to get a Washington address for you."

"No, that won't be necessary," Holly said rather loudly. She lowered her voice. "Thanks, anyway."

Blaisdell did not even ask about Booth, when Holly joined him at the small restaurant across the street. She volunteered that Booth had left town, and then the subject was dropped. They had a cup of coffee together in almost absolute silence; then they walked on back to the hotel, Blaisdell limping along beside her on his healing leg.

Their hotel was a small Victorian place with plate-glass windows looking into the lobby, and a short row of hansom cabs, their horses anchored in place with heavy iron weights, waited at the curb for potential customers. The clerk at the desk treated them as if they were registered for the purpose of having a clandestine affair; Holly resented it. When they got up to the rooms, Blaisdell asked Holly if she wanted to come in and talk for a short while before they decided where to have dinner, and she accepted.

The room was tiny, with one double bed and one small window on the street. The wallpaper was a rose-colored, intricately patterned kind that depressed Holly. In her room it was the same, except that one wall had been painted over. Hung above the head of Blaisdell's bed was an etching of Lincoln, and Holly found herself standing and staring at it for a long moment. Blaisdell had purchased a bottle of Burgundy wine, and now offered Holly a glass. To his surprise, she accepted it. He was also surprised when she sat down on the edge of his bed, in preference to the chair across the room. He seated himself beside her, and they sipped the wine.

"Something is wrong, isn't it?" he said. "Is it disappointment over missing Booth?"

She sighed. "No, that's not it, Stuart. It's just me. I'm in a bad mood, that's all."

"I'm sorry you saw the playbill."

"So am I."

"It was pretty serious between you two, wasn't it?" he said.

She turned and looked into his eyes. "Yes. For me, it was."

"I wish he had been here," he said to her.

Holly smiled tenderly. "Oh, Stuart." She turned away, frustrated and still a little angry. "That's very kind of you. But I suspect it's just as well this way."

313

"Is there anything I can do? To make it better?"

She turned back to him, and they were very close. He closed the small distance and touched her lips with his; she did not pull away. He took her in his arms and kissed her again. Suddenly it was a passionate kiss.

When it was finished, he released her. "I'm—sorry. I know you didn't want that—especially not now."

She averted her eyes for a moment, then looked back into his. "You're wrong, Stuart."

He frowned slightly. "What?"

"I want you—to make love to me," she said.

He could not believe it. He looked searchingly into her blue eyes. "Are you sure, Holly?"

She did not hesitate. "Yes. I'm sure."

He sat there immobilized for a long moment, then he was pulling her to him and kissing her hotly again. His rough hands were on her, his mouth hungry for hers.

She did not respond at first, but then she felt the fire inside her, reacting to his nearness and his touch. She broke loose from him, and for a moment he thought it was aborted. But then she rose, walked to the window and drew the shade down, dimming the sunlight that filtered into the room. Outside she could hear the clatter of carriages and hansoms on the cobbled streets. Without turning back to him, she began undressing.

When Blaisdell saw what she was doing, he swallowed hard. This was something he had waited for for years, what he had dreamed about on those long ugly nights in the war. He began undressing too, and in a few short moments they were both finished. When she turned to him, he could only stare for a moment. She was the most beautiful thing he had ever laid eyes on. Her physical beauty took his breath away and flushed his cheeks.

"My God!" he muttered.

"Take me, Stuart," he heard her saying.

Then they were magically together on the bed, their fiery flesh intertwined, his hands seeking her, exploring and caressing. Blaisdell had had a couple of women in the war, but those incidents had been nothing like this. His emotions were raised to new heights, his passion aroused in a way he had never known possible. The pleasure was so sweet that it made him giddy with satiation. In the middle of it he wondered if he were hurting her in their physical abandon, but that concern was unfounded. Finally, when it was over, their flesh glistened with their mutual heat, and Blaisdell gasped raggedly.

When they lay side by side on the still-made bed later, no cover on their warm flesh, Blaisdell turned to her.

"It was—wonderful!" he breathed unevenly.

Holly looked over at him. He lay big and muscular beside her, looking very masculine. He had been much more sensual than Booth or Clayborne, and there was something about that that she liked, on a purely physical level. But she still felt little for Blaisdell on an emotional level. He did not excite her just by being with her, as Booth did. They did not touch, psychically, on enough places.

"You were wonderful," he added, after a moment.

Holly looked upward, toward the ceiling. "It won't happen again, Stuart."

He looked over at her, curiously.

"It was a one-time thing," she said. It had been her anger at Booth, and her wanting him, and maybe also that she felt she owed Blaisdell. It had been all of that. But she knew that those circumstances would not coincide again. Further intimacy with Blaisdell could only serve to encourage him to think there was really something between them, something more than she had given him on that bed.

"Why?" she heard him saying.

"It's too complicated, Stuart." She rose, and went and pulled on some underclothes while he watched.

"Just know that more than this would not be right," she said.

He sat up on the edge of the bed. "Can't we even talk about it?"

"No," she told him. She pulled on her floor-length skirt, and then a blouse.

"You're a hard woman to figure, Holly."

She was all dressed now. She turned to him, where he sat on the edge of the bed, still nude. "Don't forget to do your leg exercises later."

Blaisdell made a face. "Jesus. All right."

"Be satisfied, Stuart," she said seriously.

He grunted out a laugh. "That's easy to say. You make my blood boil, just looking at you. Now it will be worse."

"You'll have to be content," she said.

His face softened, and he remembered how incredible it had been. "All right," he said deliberately. "All right, Holly."

"Tomorrow we're on our way to Hartford. When we get there, we want to present the picture of two hard-nosed business people—not lovers at odds with each other."

He held her soft gaze. "You can count on me, Holly."

"I thought so," she said.

Then she went to her own room.

After an overnight trip they arrived in Hartford, on a

316

cool, leaves-changing September day. It was not a large town, but Holly was impressed with its Victorian elegance. It was old, like Charleston, and had a proud history. She thought how lucky it was for its citizens that the war had not ravaged it, as Charleston was being ravaged. Most of the war had been fought on southern soil, and it was the South that had suffered the most because of that.

The Hartford *Courant* carried vivid accounts of the progress of the war, and there was a general feeling of elation about its progress in that small city, as there had been in New York, as opposed to the absolute gloom that prevailed in Charleston.

The arms manufacturer that Holly had chosen to go to was called the Connecticut Manufactory. It made rifles, sidearms, and many kinds of ammunition. Holly intended to purchase primer and percussion caps, both of which the company sold to the United States Army.

On the very afternoon of their arrival, Blaisdell went to the offices of the company alone. Trying to hide most of his southern accent, he spoke to a secretary there and having identified himself as a junior partner in a Montreal firm that made and distributed guns and ammunition to the Canadian Army, he made an appointment the next morning with the president of the company—a fellow named Ruskin. The secretary seemed to accept the cover story, and gave Blaisdell the appointment.

The next morning, Holly and Blaisdell dressed up in fine clothes, to give the impression of moderate wealth, and went to see Ruskin.

"Yes, I'm very pleased to meet you, Mrs. Smythe," Ruskin greeted them on that sunny morning. "And Mr.

317

DuBois. Please have a seat, and tell me exactly what kind of business we can do today."

Ruskin was a short, stout fellow with hair of a sandy color, like Blaisdell's, only there was some peppering of gray in his. He dressed severely, in a dark suit and dark tie, and wore spectacles on the bridge of his nose.

Holly and Blaisdell took seats before Ruskin's carved oak desk, and then Holly began.

"Your firm was recommended to us in Montreal, Mr. Ruskin, as the most reliable arms manufacturer in Hartford," Holly told him. "That is why we came to you." Having lived in Baltimore for a while, it was not difficult for Holly to disguise her accent somewhat. Blaisdell affected a French accent that completely hid his own.

"Well, I'm delighted you thought of us, Mrs. Smythe," Ruskin said. "You apparently don't make primer and caps yourself?"

"We don't have the raw materials available," Holly told him. "Other Dominion companies attempt to keep our army and police supplied, but there is always a shortage. Since we already make arms for our services, we thought we ought to see about distributing primer and caps to them as jobbers, through American firms. I know you're busy supplying federal troops at this juncture, but our business will go on well beyond this civil strife of yours."

Ruskin nodded his understanding.

"Of course," Blaisdell said in his French accent, "we need supplies immediately, Mr. Ruskin—to make our gun deals more attractive to the army. They are more willing to buy from manufacturers who can supply primer and percussion caps and ammunition also."

"Yes, of course," Ruskin said, studying Blaisdell

318

closely. "We found that out ourselves. How much of this material would you need, and how often?"

Holly had wanted to take back a million or two caps and a couple of tons of primer, but had been limited by the size of McNeil's sloop. She told Ruskin now she would like to buy a half-million caps and several crates of primer, but that she had to get the supplies at a wholesale rate. "The whole idea is to make a profit on resale to our army," she told him.

"Yes, of course," he said. "Incidentally, you seem to have an unusual accent, Mrs. Smythe. I can't quite place it."

Holly felt herself twist up inside. If this fellow guessed that they were Confederate agents, he might just call the police in on them, or some unit of the Union Army. Blaisdell would surely be shot summarily, and she would undoubtedly spend the rest of her natural life in a prison on this second offense.

While Holly was trying to think of a reply, Blaisdell spoke up for her. "Yes, it is unusual, isn't it? I've told her that many times, *monsieur*, but she won't believe me. One cannot hear such things from one's own mouth. Mrs. Smythe was raised in a household where her father spoke a peculiar dialect of Scottish, and she picked up some of a French accent from her deceased husband. The mixture of that with the English is quite mellow, I believe, almost like that found in certain of your southern states."

Holly glanced at Blaisdell, not believing he had mentioned the South. But she did not let her face show her surprise.

Ruskin was nodding. "I suppose there is some similarity," he was saying, "but it's not really southern. It's more like that in women of ours who have lived among

319

the Indians. No offense intended, Mrs. Smythe."

Holly relaxed slightly. "None taken, Mr. Ruskin."

"I can fill your order, Mrs. Smythe, and I'm sure we can agree on price. We'll be changing over to making metal cartridges one of these days soon, and we'll want to deplete our stock of caps and primer, anyway. Will you be paying in Canadian currency?"

"Oh, no. We have dollars," Holly told him. "We stand ready to pay half now, and half on delivery of the supplies to wagons that we'll hire to carry the shipment to Mystic."

"You have a ship there?" Ruskin said.

"Yes," she lied, "a hired Yankee frigate. He'll take us north to Portland. From there we'll transport the cargo overland again to Montreal."

Ruskin nodded. "Sounds right, Mrs. Smythe."

"I hope this won't cause a shortage for your fine troops?" Blaisdell offered.

Ruskin drew his mouth down at the corners. "We're in business to turn a profit, Mr. DuBois. The Union Army has cut back on purchases of material of this kind, and we have to survive beyond this war. You can be damned well sure that General Grant can take care of himself, sir. Don't worry your mind about that."

Blaisdell nodded. "I had heard that about him," he said.

"This war will be over shortly," Ruskin went on, "as you've pointed out. When that happens, we'll need every customer we can get. Connecticut Manufactory is pleased that you came to us, an American company, to buy your needed supplies. We will try to serve your needs well, both now and in the future."

"We will be making those buying trips once or twice

320

per year," Holly said. "If we're satisfied with your products, Mr. Ruskin, we'll be dealing with your company exclusively."

"We would appreciate your patronage, Mrs. Smythe." Ruskin smiled nicely. "Shall we go draw up a contract of purchase?"

"I was just going to suggest that, Mr. Ruskin," Holly said.

The next couple of days were hectic ones. Blaisdell hired two wagons and teams for them, and the morning after their meeting with Ruskin, the crates were loaded aboard. The mule skinners were told that they were headed for Mystic, but before they got out of town that morning, Blaisdell revised their orders. He told them there had been a change of plans because of shipping in the harbor, and that they would take the wagons to New York. A new payment arrangement was made, satisfactory explanations were given—they would make up the cargo charge aboard the New York ship because it was a larger vessel and could give them lower rates for the longer voyage—and they headed back to New York. Holly and Blaisdell rode aboard the wagons, and when it rained, they all got wet. There was an overnight stay at a country inn, at which Holly was impressed with New England hospitality. The next day, they were back in New York.

The cargo was covered with tarpaulins, so no curious eyes could see what they were hauling. In early evening, the mule skinners unloaded it all on a dock about a half-mile from where the *Carrie Mitchell* was tied up. Under the cover of darkness Blaisdell stenciled TIN CUPS and HARDWARE on the sides of the crates, and, reporting their destination as Halifax, they later registered the cargo that way with port authorities. The next morning, McNeil brought the sloop up to the cargo dock so the stacks of crates could be loaded aboard it and the two trailing boats that would be pulled by the sloop. Even with that distribution of weight, though, the sloop sat so low in the water that McNeil feared it would capsize in the lightest weather.

That evening, the sloop sailed. Since no pilot boat was necessary to get her out of harbor, no one in port knew that she headed south instead of north after she cleared port.

The voyage back was very different from the one up the coast. Crates were everywhere—on deck, in the cabins, in the hold. They got in the way of everything and everyone. There was barely room to sleep, and there was constant danger that shifting of cargo would cause damage to the sloop or injury to its occupants. The trailing longboats were securely sealed with canvas against the weather and the sea, but they dragged on the sloop badly, slowing travel.

McNeil became ill-tempered, and so did the crew. Their courtesy on the voyage up was gone; McNeil snapped at Holly and Blaisdell regularly, because he felt they were in the way, they and their cargo.

"I should have asked double the price," he grumbled to Holly on the second day out. "We can't even get at the rigging. I don't know what the bloody hell we'd do in a storm."

"What do you think of your captain now?" Blaisdell asked Holly at the end of their third day out, as they stood at the gunwale at dusk, watching the white foam in their wake.

Holly's hair was blowing dark in a small wind. "I don't care how much McNeil rants at us," she said, "so long as we get this shipment to De Beauregard safely."

"If a patrol boat stops us, it will all be over," he said. "I hope McNeil continues to hug the shoreline. Any boat heading south is suspect, nowadays."

Holly looked over at him, studying his square, sober profile. Blaisdell had not attempted any further intimacy with her since their love-making in Manhattan, but he had seemed different to her. Allowing him that one episode in bed had not satisfied Blaisdell's desire for her. In fact, it had been like fanning a low fire into one of incendiary proportions. It was obviously very difficult for him now, being near her, and it showed in his behavior.

Of course, Holly had not encouraged the intimacy for Blaisdell. She had done it for herself in a very angry, selfish moment, not thinking about how it might affect him. It had given him a rich taste of something he had wanted all his life, and then cruelly snatched it away from him. She had been thoughtless, almost wanton, and once again she had cause to be ashamed of herself for the way she had behaved with a man.

"Is it all right, Stuart?"

He looked over at her, the wind blowing at his sandy hair.

"Is it all right between us now?" she asked him.

He sighed slightly. "I guess it's as all right as it can be, Holly," he told her.

"You must understand how it is," she said. "Two wrongs don't make a right. We can't complicate the error we've already made."

"The error you made," he said.

323

"All right, the error I made," she said. "I know it will be difficult, Stuart. But I want us to go back to the way we were—before Manhattan. If it's possible."

"I think the thing that surprises me," he said, "is that you could be so intimate with me—without loving me. That you could do that with any man."

It hurt her inside to hear him speak that way about her. But she deserved it. She looked out over the blackening water to the endless expanse of sea to the east. "I do love you, Stuart," she heard herself explaining unconvincingly. "But not in the way I loved John Booth." She used the past tense to describe her feelings for Booth, but she wondered if she still did not love him as deeply as ever. She hoped not, because Booth was obviously a very mixed-up individual; not the kind she would want to marry.

"You've made that quite clear," Blaisdell replied to her.

"Oh, Stuart!"

"We can't go back, Holly. Don't you see that? It can't be quite the same with us, ever again. Not after Manhattan. I'm surprised that you thought it could."

She shook her head. "I really did it, didn't I? I guess I had convinced myself I was being generous with you, but it was just the opposite."

Blaisdell turned and his face had softened. "Don't worry over it, Holly. We'll always be friends. I'll always tag after you, doing what you want me to, hoping for your affection. I can't help myself. That's the way it's always been with me, and always will be, I guess."

"You don't give yourself enough credit. You'll find yourself a Charleston girl one of these days soon; maybe when the war is over. And then you'll laugh at all of this

You'll know it was just a phase you were going through. You've been in a war."

The wind was suddenly blowing much more fiercely, tangling Holly's dark hair, blowing her cape around. There were white caps out on the dark surface of the water, and boiling clouds overhead, and some rain now began pelting them.

"Damn," Blaisdell said. "We're in for a blow, it seems. We'd better get below."

Holly cast a dour glance toward the trailing longboats and their precious cargo. "Oh, dear. The captain feared a storm."

Just at that moment, McNeil came elbowing his way down the deck toward them, between a narrow double row of crates, looking angry.

"Well, here it comes!" he said loudly. "I told you we'd be in trouble if we overloaded her, and now we have it, by Jesus! I'm not going to be responsible for what the storm does to this cargo!"

McNeil was short a crewman, because of the wounded Bates. He, still recovering from being shot, was below in the larger quarters where McNeil and the crew slept. Holly's small scratch was healing nicely. She caught McNeil's eye now. "Is there something we can do, Captain?"

"Yes! Keep out of the bloody way!" McNeil spat out at her.

Holly had to agree with Blaisdell that maybe she had chosen the wrong man for the mission, despite McNeil's having known her father. That fact was not earning her any goodwill at this moment. McNeil seemed to have soured on the mission while he waited in New York; then his disposition had become downright ugly when he saw

325

how much ammunition supplies he had to take aboard. He strode on down the deck now, shouting orders to his mate and the other crewman. Holly followed him, and when he turned to her she spoke to him again.

"What about the longboats, Captain? Will they be all right?"

"All right!" he said loudly. "Of course they won't be all right! We'll be damned lucky if they stay secure to the sloop! If they threaten the safety of the boat, I'll cut the bloody things loose!"

Holly's face drew down into straight lines. "You will cut the boats loose under no circumstances, Captain. Almost half of our supplies are on those boats—supplies needed badly by the Confederate Army."

"I don't give a damn about the Confederate Army!" McNeil said angrily to her. "The damned war is lost, anyway! What I do care about, and what is important to me, is this sloop! If we have to cut the boats loose, we'll cut them loose!"

Holly was very angry herself, suddenly. Her eyes blazed fire at him. "I am the agent in charge of this mission, Captain McNeil. If you have no respect for the spirit of my dead father, then at least remember that! General de Beauregard would not allow you to cut those boats loose, and I won't allow it. We must get that cargo to Charleston, no matter the cost in property or lives. I thought that was clear to you when we embarked on this voyage."

The wind was really blowing now. It pelted the side of McNeil's face with needles of rain and sea spray as he replied to her. "I don't care what you're in charge of, Holly Ransom. I'm the captain of this bloody sloop, and I'm seeing to her first, last, and always! If you don't like

326

that, I'll cut you loose with your bloody cargo, at the nearest cove!"

But Blaisdell had followed Holly down the deck, and he now came around her to face McNeil. He had a Smith & Wesson pocket revolver in his right hand, one of the many kinds of arms smuggled in to the Confederacy from Britain and the Caribbean. He stuck the revolver up against McNeil's left cheek, and pushed it so that McNeil's flesh bunched up there, under its muzzle.

"I don't like to hear you talk to the lady like that, Captain," he said in a low, hard voice.

McNeil eyed the gun sideways. The anger did not leave his face, but he did not retort to Blaisdell's challenge. Blaisdell held the handgun against McNeil's face. "You cut either of those longboats loose," Blaisdell went on in the low voice Holly had never heard before, "and I'll kill you, Captain."

Holly glanced toward Blaisdell and saw that he meant what he said. She had never seen the soldier side of Blaisdell, not until that moment. He had killed and been shot at for a long time in the war, and had become the kind of fellow who had no hesitation in placing lives at stake to settle an important issue. The menace in his voice and manner surprised her, but she was suddenly glad Blaisdell was with her.

McNeil backed down somewhat with the gun in his face. "Well, the bloody storm may take them, anyway, and there'll be nothing I can do about it."

"Remember this, Captain," Blaisdell said, removing the gun finally from McNeil's face. "We'll risk every life aboard this sloop to save that cargo. Don't make any mistake about it."

McNeil hesitated, then said, "You want to let me get

my bloody work done now, Lieutenant? This sloop just may capsize if we don't—"

Just then a big wave crashed over them, almost throwing them to the deck. Holly was hurled against a pile of crates, and hurt her healing arm. She yelled aloud, but her outcry was torn away by the wind and the sea. They were all drenched now, and the sloop was listing in the wind. McNeil hurried away from them, to assist his crew to secure the cargo and lower the mainsail.

Blaisdell wanted Holly to go below, but she would not. He went around checking on the ropes that secured the crates to the sloop; some of them were working loose already. He worked at tightening them, but their own flexibility, combined with the heavy weight of the crates, was allowing them to stretch. At the stern, a stack of crates suddenly broke loose, and several of them went sailing overboard, lost into the sea. Blaisdell hurried over there; he and the mate fought to restack the pile and rope them secure. Holly helped, too, despite her bruised arm.

"For God's sake, Holly, get below! This is dangerous out here!" Blaisdell said loudly to her, over the wind and spray.

But Holly was ignoring him, as she had in the sea fight on the way out of Charleston. She went to examine the line that held the smaller boats. The longboats were bobbing like corks in the sea, but were still afloat. The line that secured them to the *Carrie Mitchell*, though, was fraying on the gunwale, and was about to be severed.

"Stuart!" Holly cried out to him. *"The line!"*

Blaisdell limped over to her and stared hard at the frayed line. Dark-visaged, he turned to find McNeil, but could not see him. *"Captain!"* he yelled out. But in that moment, the line snapped.

328

It just missed slicing across Blaisdell's face, whipping in the wind. Blaisdell turned and saw the longboats receding in the storm, being bounced about by the sea.

"My God!" Holly murmured. "They've broken loose!"

Just then McNeil came swaying up to them, leaning into the wind on the slanting deck. A big wave washed aboard, and staggered him.

"*The longboats!*" Blaisdell told him. "*They're gone! Turn the sloop around, we have to recover them!*"

McNeil stared at him as if he must be insane. "*Turn around, you say? In this? Do you know what you're saying, for God's sake?*"

Blaisdell drew the Smith & Wesson again. "*Turn it around, Captain!*"

McNeil looked as if he might have some kind of fit right there. But then he turned and shouted orders to his two-man crew, telling them to make the turn. The sloop slowly turned, her mate at the helm. At one point it appeared as if the sea would capsize her, then she was heading back toward the longboats. They came into view almost immediately, and before Holly knew what was happening, Blaisdell was stripping his cape and shoes off.

"*What are you doing?*" she yelled at him.

"*Saving our cargo,*" he told her. He turned to McNeil. "*When I get out there, throw me a good line.*"

In the next moment, before Holly could protest, Blaisdell climbed onto the gunwale and dived into the boiling sea. Holly made a little cry in her throat as he disappeared into the dark water, and in that moment she wondered just how important the cargo really was.

Moments passed, and she could not see Blaisdell anywhere.

"Bloody fool!" McNeil muttered, near her.

"Oh, God, where are you?" Holly whimpered in her throat, urgently.

Then his head bobbed out of the water, not three feet from the nearest escaped boat. Holly's heart lurched inside her, as she saw him washed over by a big wave. But then his head reappeared, closer to the boats than before. He grabbed at the line in the sea, and caught it. He was only fifty feet from the port side of the sloop, but the sloop was moving past the smaller boats now. McNeil grudgingly picked up a coiled line not far away, secured it to the gunwale, and then threw the line out toward Blaisdell.

Blaisdell did not catch it, but he swam toward it and grabbed it. In just a moment, he was busy tying the two lines together, although waves washed over him, blinding him with their spray. Then his work was done, and the longboats began following after the sloop again, bouncing about in the water.

"Now head her south again!" Blaisdell called out.

The captain grumbled an obscenity, then shouted out his orders to turn the sloop. Blaisdell inched his way along the line until he was back at the stern, and the mate helped him aboard. When he finally stood beside Holly again, looking like a drowned rat, the sloop had made its second hundred-eighty-degree turn without incident, and was heading back toward Charleston, the boats in tow.

"Thank God you're back!" Holly said emotionally. The wind was dying down now, and it was clear that the storm was abating. They were going to make it, and with just a few crates lost.

"I was always a strong swimmer." He grinned at her. "And that's something that this leg can't hamper much."

330

"You saved the cargo, Stuart. Thanks."

"Like I said," he told her, "I'll always be around, Holly—when you need me."

She held his sober gaze. "Let's go down and change into dry clothes."

He nodded. "A good notion," he said, water still dripping off him.

The storm abated in the next hour, and there was no more trouble all the way to Charleston. The next night, the *Carrie Mitchell* slipped into Charleston harbor without attracting any attention from the federals, her longboats still strung out behind her.

The most successful blockade run of the war was completed, and it had been an unqualified success.

The South now had enough materiel for its guns to hold out against Sherman and Grant just a little longer.

Chapter Eighteen

Only two days after their arrival back, General de
Beauregard arranged a welcome-home banquet for Holly
and Blaisdell. There were a lot of military officers
present, and the mayor and other dignitaries. The press
was there, too, and the reporters crowded around Holly,
who was already a celebrity, and rather ignored Blaisdell.
Blaisdell, somewhat bitter beforehand because of the way
veterans were being treated in Charleston, resented that
he was not sharing much of the limelight, but he said
nothing. After all, it had nothing to do with Holly. She
did not even like the publicity; that was obvious. She had
tried to avoid the reporters all through the evening. Holly
and Blaisdell were each obligated to say a few words at the
banquet table about the success of their mission, and
then De Beauregard announced that some of the supplies
they had brought back with them were already on their
way to Confederate troops at Savannah and in Virginia.

In Holly's short address to the small assemblage, she
stressed her personal belief in the importance of the
South's fighting for time now, in the war. Every week
that passed would make citizens of the North clamor

more loudly for peace, and that peace might be an honorable one for the South, if the South still had some military clout.

De Beauregard agreed, and advised Holly that Lee had expressed the same sentiment. Even though continued fighting by the South would mean a further loss of life, it was important to what the South would be like after the war.

There was dancing after the meal, and drinks. While several officers danced with Holly, Blaisdell stood to one side listening to a captain discourse on military tactics, but jealous of the men who whirled Holly around the floor. Later, De Beauregard got Holly and Blaisdell alone in an anteroom, and thanked them both privately for what they had done for the Confederacy, on their mission and before.

"It's southerners like yourselves that have given us a fair chance of establishing our position with the North," he told them as they stood together in the privacy of the small room. "I hear you were wounded, Miss Ransom. But I gather you're all right."

"It was nothing," Holly said. "Just a scratch on the arm, General."

"How is your leg healing, Lieutenant Blaisdell? I see you're not on a cane now."

"It's much better sir," Blaisdell said. "But I can't do much dancing yet."

De Beauregard smiled. "I'm requesting a citation for each of you, from President Davis. If anyone deserves one, it's you two. I ought to be hearing on the matter within a couple of weeks."

But Blaisdell was shaking his head. "Please, General. Not for me. Nothing I've done is out of the ordinary. For

Holly it's different; she's a remarkable woman. But my soldiering was very commonplace, I'm afraid. I couldn't accept a citation."

De Beauregard rested a hand on Blaisdell's shoulder. "We'll talk about that after I've heard from Davis. Now, you two. Is there anything special I can do for you? To try to make your lives more comfortable in the coming weeks and months?"

Holly shook her head. "We don't want any special consideration, General. If there's some further way we can aid the Confederate cause, we stand ready to help."

"Well, I'm afraid it might be difficult to duplicate the mission you just accomplished." De Beauregard smiled tiredly. "It was one of those one-time attempts, I'm afraid. Anyway, what we need now is something neither of you can give us. We need courage. With wheat flour at a thousand Confederate dollars a barrel, and locals eating rats in some sections, the war, for Charleston, had better end soon."

"How is it going now?" Blaisdell asked him.

"Well, General Early advanced well into Maryland, but he's now being driven back into Virginia," De Beauregard said. "I wish we could have marched out of here to support him, but it wasn't possible. Admiral Farragut is getting ready to take Mobile, I hear. And in Atlanta, General Sherman is mad as a hornet because Lee won't surrender our army to him. He says he's going to Savannah shortly, and that the South will suffer in that march if we force him to fight for every inch of ground."

"I don't like that man," Holly said soberly. "It's the likes of him that we have to control, if we're to win a peace."

Blaisdell caught De Beauregard's eye. "We've lost the

war already, haven't we, General?"

"Oh, yes. I think we probably lost it at Chattanooga, Lieutenant. Chickamauga gave us some last hope, but then it was dashed rather quickly by Thomas at Missionary Ridge. Most of us haven't believed in victory from that moment on. But as Miss Ransom points out, we must not give up on winning an honorable peace."

"It's difficult to imagine men like Grant giving us an honorable peace, no matter how hard we fight," Blaisdell offered, "when they have not fought an honorable war."

Holly glanced over at him. That was the first time she had had any indication of the deep frustration inside Blaisdell, because he was not able to go on fighting in the war.

"Grant will offer it because we'll force the offer," she said to Blaisdell. "And because Lincoln will want to preserve some dignity for the South."

"Oh, it's Lincoln again," Blaisdell said acidly, "the friend of the southern belle."

De Beauregard smiled at the remark, noting Holly's discomfort. "I'm sure Miss Ransom had no intention of defending Lincoln's political policies," he said easily.

"No, of course not, Stuart," Holly assured him. "Only his basic belief in human dignity."

De Beauregard changed the subject. "Now that that's settled, would you mind, Lieutenant, if I danced with your lady once before the evening is finished?"

"We would both be delighted, I'm sure," Blaisdell said soberly.

Holly was still embarrassed by Blaisdell. He seemed such a simple young man on the surface, but was very complex to understand. Maybe the war had made him

335

complex. At any rate, she was glad to leave him, at that moment.

"Yes, General," she said. "We would be."

Holly had invited Jennifer to the banquet sponsored by General de Beauregard, but Jennifer would not go. She was now going out with a couple of different soldiers every week, and taking most of them to her bed, and there seemed to be nothing anyone could do to stop her. She had slowed down some for a short time, while Holly was gone, but she had revived her promiscuity with men in a shameless way. She and Holly had another long talk, and Jennifer made half-hearted promises about her behavior, but Holly now understood that they were not promises that Jennifer intended to keep. Jennifer just could not seem to take herself seriously, or even to like herself, despite resolutions to the contrary.

In mid-October, during General Sherman's delay in Atlanta, Jennifer finally received some of Clayborne's personal things; they had gone to Virginia by mistake before coming to her.

She was excited about the package at first. There were a couple of books, his wedding ring, a wallet containing some Confederate money, and a second ring Jennifer had never seen before, an ornate gold one. A note came with the belongings, from a company commander, and he said that Clayborne had wanted the second ring to be given to one Holly Ransom.

Upon reading the note, Jennifer rose from the chair she had been sitting on at her house, in the parlor, picked up an expensive vase handed down through Amanda's side of the family, and hurled it against a wall. It broke into a hundred pieces there. Jennifer then went and knocked an oil lamp off an end table, spilling its contents

336

onto a good carpet. Lastly, she went into her kitchen and turned the kitchen table over, together with all four of its chairs; then kicked the nearest chair several times, bruising her right foot.

It would not have occurred to Jennifer to keep from Holly the fact that Clayborne, her deceased husband, had wanted Holly to have the beautiful ring, a ring much more expensive than Jennifer's wedding ring, and one that Clayborne had apparently purchased in Baltimore. Jennifer did not play by those kinds of rules. Also, if she had kept the informal bequest a secret, she could not have been righteously indignant, which she violently was.

She intended to find Holly alone and give her the ring without comment, letting Holly's guilt about it blossom behind her, Jennifer's, back. But when she went to give the ring to Holly, she did not find Holly at home.

She did find her, however, outside a local bank one October day. Holly was with Blaisdell, in one of their infrequent meetings nowadays. Blaisdell was becoming more and more bitter about Holly, and had made the comment to her that there seemed little point in seeing her. But they had met inside the bank, and Blaisdell had just offered to buy Holly lunch at a nearby restaurant. Holly was glad that he seemed to be in a more relaxed mood toward her. Seeing Jennifer out on the street took them both by surprise.

"Oh, Jennifer!" Holly said with a wide smile. "How nice to run into you downtown!"

Blaisdell nodded to Jennifer, and she acknowledged the greeting with a dark countenance. "Hello, Holly. I see you're never without a man on your arm. Of course, you don't enjoy the variety that I do."

Holly frowned slightly at her. "Stuart and I just met in

the bank, Jennifer. We were just going to have something to eat. Maybe you'd like to join us."

"Sure, it's on me," Blaisdell told Jennifer. He looked rather bucolic in his too-tight civilian suit, but he was limping very little now. He had tried and failed to find a job in Charleston. "What do you say, Jennifer?"

"Oh, I'm too busy at the moment," Jennifer said breezily. She was dressed well, like Holly, but her clothing was a little loud, a little garish in color, and she wore too much make-up. She reached for a purse on her arm. "I do have something for you, though, Holly. It's a gold ring."

"A gold ring?" Holly said, curious. "I don't understand, Jennifer."

Jennifer had it out now, and it shone radiantly in the sunlight. "It's from Randy," she said with a sober look. "He wanted you to have it."

She handed it rather forcefully to Holly, and Holly took it, uncertain. "From Randy?"

"Yes, it was one of his last requests," Jennifer said bitterly. "I guess it was the best thing he owned, at his death. Ironic, isn't it? That he would leave it to you, instead of me?"

Holly found herself blushing from embarrassment. "My God, Jennifer, I don't know what to say! The ring wouldn't mean nearly as much to me as to you, I'm sure. Why don't you take it?"

"No, it's your ring," Jennifer said stubbornly. "It was given to you, and it's yours. Perhaps Randy looked upon it as a kind of payment to you."

Blaisdell was very embarrassed for Holly, but also very curious. "A payment? Surely Randy didn't owe Holly any money, Jennifer," he said in a way that seemed patronizing to Jennifer.

It was then that Jennifer went too far. "I wasn't talking about a loan," she said bitterly. "I was referring to services rendered."

Holly stared hard at Jennifer, then glanced quickly toward Blaisdell. "Oh, God," she said quietly.

Blaisdell was frowning now. "Services rendered? What the hell are you saying, Jennifer?"

"Maybe we ought to forget it," Jennifer said.

Holly turned to her. "No, go ahead," she said levelly. "You might as well tell him now, Jennifer."

Jennifer did not feel remorse, though—not yet. Her eyes blazed at them. "All right! I'm referring to your affair with my husband, damn it! Your Baltimore interlude that made you closer to Randy than I had ever been!"

Blaisdell's jaw fell slightly open, and he stared at Jennifer as if she had struck him across the face. "What?" he whispered. "Randy and Holly were—"

Holly saw the deep hurt in Blaisdell's open face, and something constricted inside her. He looked over at her with the most accusing look she had ever seen, and it tore her up inside.

"Stuart, let me explain it," she said.

"Explain it?" he said hollowly. "*Explain* it?" His expression had changed to one of hot anger. He glanced darkly toward Jennifer, then back to Holly, and finally turned on his heel and strode quickly away down the street.

"*Wait, Stuart!*" Holly called after him.

But he was on his way, stiff-backed and unyielding.

Holly turned back to Jennifer, and there were already tears in Jennifer's eyes. "Oh, hell," she said.

Holly went to her and put an arm around her. "Don't cry, Jennifer. Please."

"Hell, I promised you!" Jennifer said, sobbing now. "It was the ring. God, why did he have to do that? Why did he have to give you the ring?"

Holly looked at the gold ring, still in her hand. Clayborne had been somewhat like John Booth in his cavalier attitude toward women. Now he had found a way to hurt not only herself and Jennifer in one stroke from beyond the grave, but also his best friend, Blaisdell.

"That's the way Randy was," she said. "He should have thought of you first, but he didn't."

"Oh God, Holly!"

"I'm going to give the ring away, Jennifer. I couldn't keep it."

"You don't have to do that."

"I wouldn't feel right, keeping it," Holly said.

Jennifer held Holly's gaze. "If you could really do that," she said, "I think we could be friends again— really friends, like it used to be."

Holly nodded, understanding. "I can," she said, "and will."

"Oh, Holly," Jennifer cried, leaning against her in the cool October sun.

Holly saw Jennifer home that day, and then she went to find Blaisdell. Jennifer wanted to go, too, to apologize to him. But Holly decided she had better confront Blaisdell alone.

Blaisdell had gone directly home, so there was no trouble in finding him. His father had been taken out by friends, so Blaisdell was alone in the house when Holly arrived. When he saw her at the door, he did not invite her in.

"What is it, Holly?" he said darkly.

"I want to talk with you, Stuart."

340

"I don't believe we have anything to talk about," he said.

"Yes, we do," she insisted. "Even those accused before the courts are allowed to speak in their defense."

He hesitated, then stepped aside for her to enter the house. "All right, but keep it short, please."

Holly went in, but he did not ask her to sit down. They stood together in the center of a large parlor with dark oak furniture and hooked rugs and tintypes on a small table. Holly hesitated before beginning, while he waited impatiently.

"I'm sorry you had to learn about Randy and me in that way," she finally said, very quietly.

He stood there, grim-faced.

"I would have liked to tell you myself. But there seemed no point in it. It could only hurt you."

He made no comment.

"It was a one-time thing, Stuart; one mistake made on one lonely night away from home. Randy wanted it to be more than that, but I wouldn't let it."

He turned partially away. "This Booth thing was understandable," he said. "You said you were in love. You should have told me, but it was understandable. But to take Randy to your bed—for Randy to seduce you, knowing how I felt . . . that I thought about you every day, dreamed about you in the night, carried your letters over my heart into battle . . . you both knew all of that. How can I even believe there was anything serious between you and Booth, now? All I see, Holly, is a licentiousness in Baltimore that is inexcusable. I must have been a very big joke to the two of you."

"My God, Stuart, that's not true!"

"If you didn't care about me, what about Jennifer?" he said. "How could you make love to the husband of your

341

best friend? What the hell has happened to you, Holly?"

She sighed. "I guess the war happened to me, Stuart. Estrangement and loneliness happened to me. Maybe those aren't excuses, but they may allow you some understanding, if you'll keep your mind open."

He was shaking his head. "I couldn't understand why you came to my bed in New York, when you didn't really love me. But now I see that wasn't a first, for you. My God, I've been so critical of Jennifer, in my head, and all the time you were just as bad! You're worse, Holly! Jennifer doesn't try to hide what she is! But you have all these people here in Charleston thinking you're something special! Well, you're not, Holly! You're not special at all!"

Holly's lower lip trembled slightly, but she fought back the tears. "I never said I was," she said in a low voice.

He was breathing unevenly, trying to get his emotions under control. He walked across the room, away from her, and stared out through a bay window.

"Christ," he said dully.

She stood there, hoping it was over.

"Just forget that I said all of that," he said from across the room. "I'm so goddamned mad I can't think straight."

"I know," she said.

There was a long silence between them, as he quieted down inside. "I had no right to judge you," he finally added. "You're not my woman, and I'm not your keeper."

"Everything you said is true," she said.

He took a deep breath in, and let it all out raggedly. "As long as you're here, I might as well tell you, I've made a decision today, Holly. I'm joining up again."

She furrowed her pretty brow. "What?"

342

"A captain of infantry was talking to me the other day," he said. "He said my leg is healed enough now so that they'd take me back. And I'd get my commission back, too. They need men in Georgia and Virginia."

"Oh, Stuart! You've done your part in the war! You're not fit to fight, with that leg! Don't even think about going back!"

He turned to face her again; his anger had drained away, leaving him pale-looking. "My mind is made up, Holly. There's nothing to keep me here. I'll at least feel that I have some value again, back in the fighting. You said yourself that the longer we hold out, the harder we fight, the better peace we'll be able to bargain for. Maybe I can help make a difference in the way it turns out. I'm going to try to, anyway."

Holly went over to him, her eyes tearing up. She felt responsible for this decision of his, and she realized there was nothing she could do about it now. But she had to try. "Stuart, Sherman will soon be in Savannah. When that happens, it will be only a matter of weeks until the war is over. Maybe you and I could find another way to help out undercover. That would be as important, at this stage, as your going into the front lines again."

"There isn't any contribution quite as important as defending our land on the battlefield," he said. "No, I want to show the Yankees that we're not beaten yet, Holly—not in spirit, anyway."

"Then I can't dissuade you?"

"No. You can't."

The way he said it, she felt he meant that she, especially, could not.

"What will your father say?" she wondered.

"He won't object," Blaisdell said. "He's a very patriotic gentleman of the South."

343

She knew that Blaisdell's father needed him there, that he had come to expect he would have Blaisdell with him now, to the end of his life. But she could not say that to Blaisdell. He knew it.

"Where will you be sent?" she asked him.

He shrugged. "Probably into Virginia; there are some South Carolina Volunteers there. Early needs help badly, it seems. Sheridan is raising hell in that whole area now."

"Will you be leaving—soon?"

"Quite soon, I'm sure," he said.

She turned away, forcing back the tears. "Oh, God. It seems as if it's starting all over again, like a recurrent nightmare. It's just too difficult, Stuart. All of it is just too damned hard."

He laughed a little bitter laugh. "You can take it, Holly. You've proven that you can take it." He started to tell her to go out and find herself a man, but he thought better of it. The rancor was not as strong in him, now.

"Would you mind if I saw you off?" she said.

He hesitated for a long moment. "I'd rather that you wouldn't," he told her finally.

"All right."

"I just don't think it would be appropriate," he added.

She looked at him. The anger was still there, somewhere underneath the surface. He was still punishing her.

"I understand," she said. She sighed heavily. "Well, I suppose I ought to get back. Please take care of yourself, Stuart. Despite what you think at this moment, you're very dear to me, very important to me."

"Right," he said tightly.

After an awkward farewell at the door, she was gone into the autumn afternoon.

344

Chapter Nineteen

When Blaisdell left to return to the fighting, Holly was very depressed for a while. Morale in Charleston was low, anyway, but Holly's was at rock bottom. She went to one of De Beauregard's aides and asked where Blaisdell would be sent, but the fellow did not know. He said it depended on the need in the field.

There was almost nowhere where the rebels were winning. Sheridan was laying waste to the Shenandoah Valley, and Sherman was ravaging the state of Georgia now, in mid-November. Sherman was angry that Jefferson Davis would not surrender all Confederate forces to the Union, and he warned the South that his advance to the sea would be an all-holds-barred one. Already there were reports of unnecessary arson, rape, and plunder.

The end of the war was getting ugly.

In Charleston, almost everybody had given up any hope of winning a decent peace with the North. The siege continued, and shelling was intermittent but steady. Slowly, the Charleston that Holly had known as a child was being destroyed, building by building, street by street. That, too, was having its effect on her, and she could not seem to keep her spirits up. She visited Jennifer regularly, and even those visits contributed to Holly's depression. Jennifer was seeing all kinds of men, not just soldiers. She was getting quite a reputation in the city, and the bigger it got, the more men showed up at her door. She turned few of them away. They gave her things, and that helped her get through the hard times. Every once in a while, one would give her money, and Jennifer would not refuse it. She was a prostitute and knew it. She never walked the streets, and she never solicited from a man. But she took what they gave her without exception, and they all knew she did.

Holly talked to Jennifer, but the talking did not seem to do any good. She began taking Jennifer cooked dishes, because Jennifer hardly ever cooked for herself nowadays. Jennifer accepted the food, but not Holly's advice.

Reporters came to visit Holly occasionally, because she was still news to them. They asked what her present activities were, in regard to the war, as if she had something in progress at every moment. A vigilance committee tried to recruit her, but she declined. She believed that the best way she could help the Confederacy at this juncture lay in political action, rather than further undercover work. De Beauregard invited Holly to a couple of dinners, one at his own home. Holly accepted the one at his place and declined the other. She did not like being the focus of attention. She pinned a war map to her bedroom wall, where she could see it from her bed, and she lay for hours at a time staring at it—wondering where Blaisdell was, conjecturing what might be done to slow the vise that was closing on the Confederacy, day by day, so that negotiations might occur, so that a dialogue could begin between Lincoln and Davis.

One cool November evening Holly took her horse and buggy out for a drive, to get some fresh air and to try to clear from her head all the tangled thoughts and fears that had settled inside her, like fog on a muddy river bottom. It was quite brisk out, but there had been no snow yet, and most Charlestonians were thankful for that. Many had no blankets or firewood to ward off the winter cold. Holly drove along slowly, toward the devastated waterfront where there were many saloons open all night. She had been asked to return to the hospital to help out again, and was mulling that idea. She wanted to help, but in the most effective way possible. If she somehow became involved in some further special effort which she now thought was likely, she could be of no use at the hospital.

She drove along the waterfront finally, seeing the drunken sailors and soldiers there, standing in shadow or moving awkwardly along. It was all very sad to her, and further depressed her. She had just decided to turn the buggy around and go home, when she saw the girl stagger out of a saloon not fifty feet away.

She thought the girl looked familiar, even at that distance in the dark, so she took a second look. To her surprise, it was Jennifer. Jennifer was obviously inebriated, hardly able to walk straight. A young sailor came out after her, and they seemed to be having a disagreement about something.

"No, I don't want to!" Holly now heard Jennifer saying in a slurred voice. Holly reined up on the mare she drove, and stared hard at Jennifer, only twenty feet away now. "I take my men one at a time! I don't want any party!"

"Oh, come on, Jennie," the sailor urged in a likewise slurred manner. "My friends have heard how great you are. You won't have to do anything you don't want to do, honest to God. Just come with us, and we'll take real good care of you."

Jennifer pulled away from his grasp, and fell against the building wall. "I want to go home," she said thickly.

But the sailor was persistent. He put a hand around Jennifer's waist now, and started moving her back toward the saloon entrance. The place was one of the few establishments in the city that would allow a woman inside, escorted or unescorted. The sailor had Jennifer almost to the door when Holly stepped off the buggy with her light whip still in hand.

"Unhand her, damn you!" she heard herself say harshly.

The sailor focused on her. "Huh?"

"I said, release her, you bastard, or I'll cut you!" Holly grated out in a low voice.

The sailor scowled, and Jennifer now saw Holly. "Holly, what the devil are you doing down here? Come to slum, darling?"

The sailor steppd in front of Jennifer. "I don't know who you are, but you ain't her mother, that's for sure. So just light out of here, lady, and leave us be."

Holly was incensed. She flung the whip forward, and it cracked loudly on the sailor's neck, and he yelled in pain. He released Jennifer and stumbled back against the wall, holding a bleeding cut at the side of his neck.

"Damn!" he muttered.

Jennifer was suddenly wide-eyed. "Hey! Take it easy, honey! I'm all right!"

"Now get out of here," Holly told the sailor, ignoring

Jennifer, "before I use this again."

The sailor gave her a hard look, then moved off and back into the saloon. Holly went over to Jennifer. "Come on, Jennifer. Get in the buggy. I'm taking you home with me tonight."

Jennifer was still wide-eyed. "Wait, you don't have to spoil my fun!"

"Please, Jennifer, Don't give me any trouble," Holly told her.

Jennifer eyed her narrowly, and then went over to the buggy and awkwardly climbed aboard it. The mare reared slightly. Holly climbed back aboard and touched the mare's flanks with the whip; the buggy moved off.

By the time they reached Holly's place, Jennifer had almost passed out. Holly could not help but wonder what the sailor and his friends could have thought of to amuse themselves with her, in that condition. She parked the buggy in the rear, unharnessed and bedded the mare down for the night, and went inside where Jennifer was already sitting dully at the kitchen table. Holly made them some coffee, and they sat and drank for a while without saying much. Slowly, Jennifer sobered some.

"Do you know what you almost got into tonight?" Holly finally asked her.

Jennifer looked over at her. "The sailor? He wasn't so bad, Holly."

"He was going to give you over to his friends," Holly reminded her. "God knows how many of them there might have been."

"Oh," Jennifer said. "Yes, I remember now."

"And you were in no condition to defend yourself."

Jennifer nodded her agreement. "Thanks, Holly. I really am glad you came along."

Holly leaned forward toward her. "What are you trying to do to yourself, Jennifer? And why?"

Jennifer stared into her full cup of coffee, steaming on the table before her. "I don't know. I just don't know, Holly. I think it all began by feeling deprived, as an adolescent. You and girls like you got most of the dates, most of the men. When I landed Randy, I thought I was satisfied. But I wasn't. I needed to show the world—or maybe myself—that I was desirable to men, like you and the others. I guess that's it—or most of it. You're right; I've never thought a lot of myself, I guess."

"Oh, Jennifer!"

"I don't know if there's anything to be done about it," Jennifer added. "I mean, like you think there is. Too much has happened, Holly. I've come too far along a certain road. The war helped some to send me in this direction, I suppose. But you can't go back from this. Just give up on me, Holly. Give it all up."

Holly touched her hand. "I can't, Jennie. You're my friend, no matter what you may think of me."

"I'm glad you asked me over tonight," Jennifer told her.

Holly stirred a spoon in her coffee. "Jennifer, what would you think of moving in with me for a while?"

Jennifer frowned. "Moving in?"

"Yes, bag and baggage. We're both living alone, and for no good reason. I'd love your company. We could share household duties and cut our work in half; also, our expenses. You could rent your house across town, and that would help us financially, too. We could try it just until the war is over, and then we could both re-evaluate the situation. What do you think?"

Jennifer was already thinking. She arched her eye-

350

brows, and stared into her cup. "Gosh, I don't know, Holly. That would be a big step for me."

"I'm well aware of that," Holly said. "There would be rules here, Jennifer, to protect our privacy. Men could be entertained in the parlor, but not in a bedroom."

Jennifer gave her a sober look.

"There would be alcohol in the house, so that neither of us would have to drink out in public," Holly went on.

Jennifer sighed heavily.

"We would sleep in our beds here every night," Holly finally added, "and make an attempt to keep regular hours."

Jennifer began shaking her head sideways. "It wouldn't work, Holly. I know what you're trying to do—save me. But it's too damned late, I told you."

"It's never too late," Holly said insistently. "Please, Jennifer. Give it some serious thought. You're lonely over there; I know it. We could have fun here together, just like the old days. Before—everything. We could take care of each other."

"You could take care of me," Jennifer said sourly.

"I didn't mean that. It would be a two-way thing, Jennifer. Really. I need you here to brighten up the house, to give your touch to it. Just say you'll try it, that's all I ask. If we don't get along, you can move back to your place. We'll hold it open for a while."

Jennifer thought for a long moment. At last, a small, uncertain smile came across her made-up face. "Hell. All right, Holly. But I'm not promising I'll stay."

"You don't have to."

Jennifer nodded slowly. "Then it's a deal."

Jennifer moved in with Holly over the next several

days. She came hesitantly, tentatively, like a bird into a strange nest. But she brought everything. She even brought rugs, lamps, some furniture. She made the house look even more homey than it had before.

Holly was happy again.

The girls got along well, too, in those settling-in days. Jennifer made a real attempt to live up to Holly's rules. Some men came to see her at her new residence, and she turned most of them away. She laughingly told Holly that Charleston would assume that Holly's place was a new house of prostitution. But the men callers tapered off quickly because Jennifer quit going to bars and saloons with them; she began looking and acting better. Color came back into her face, and she quit using so much make-up. She ate better and rested better, and she did her share of the work around the house.

December came, and snow. Sherman was almost to Savannah, and was wreaking havoc as he went. The Union was winning everywhere in Virginia and the Carolinas, and the vise was closing on Charleston and Richmond.

One afternoon when Holly was in the house alone, thinking deeply on the subject of Sherman and how he would probably swing north toward Charleston after he had taken Savannah, she had a visitor at her door. It was Captain McNeil, of the sloop *Carrie Mitchell*.

Holly was not delighted to see McNeil, because of the way he had abandoned his responsibility toward their cargo in the storm on their way home. She had acknowledged to herself that she had chosen wrongly in him, and was glad to have gotten back with their valuable cargo intact, supplies that were now in the hands of Confederate troops, helping them to defend themselves from humiliation. But she was polite enough to ask him in, anyway. When he had seated himself on her sofa, without her invitation, he smiled a hard smile.

"Well. It seems I made you a celebrity for a second time, eh, lass? Rubbing elbows with De Beauregard, and all that. Newspaper men after you all the time."

"Is that what you came here to talk about?" Holly said pointedly.

He stroked his red beard and regarded her narrowly with his rheumy, washed-out-blue eyes. "I hear you've got that Clayborne girl in with you now. Bringing in some extra cash from the boys now, is she?"

Holly stood angrily before him, her blue eyes flashing fire. "I don't know what you're talking about, Captain. But nobody maligns my friend in my own house. If you have nothing else to say, I wish you'd take your leave!"

He held up his weathered hands defensively. "Easy, girl. You have to allow a man his occasional joke, you know." His face went straight-lined. "I came here to make you a business proposition."

Holly frowned at him. "Business? What kind of business?"

He crossed one leg over the other. "There's a small group of men in the city who are trying to think of a way to survive financially to the end of this bloody war. Merchants, most of them. They've come to me to make a trip to the Caribbean for them. But they don't have the fee I'd require. You seem to be a woman of property; I thought you might want to help finance the voyage."

"For what?" she said. "What would you bring back?"

He grinned. "Men. Black men."

"Slaves?" she said.

"That's right. Most of them have run off since the war.

A lot of good families are without servants at all. They're selling for next to nothing in the Bahamas nowadays."

"The market is dropping fast here," Holly said.

"I know. But there are a few families who are willing to pay top dollar for good strong bucks. Families who think Lincoln's infamous proclamation will never be honored in the South, no matter how the war ends." He grinned. "There's a quick profit to be made, for you. We could triple your investment in a week."

Holly thought about all of that for a long moment. She had not had to consider her position on slavery, since the war had begun. She had always considered the issue rather closed in Charleston, had always accepted Charlotte's Cleo as part of the family rather than an owned chattel. She had never considered what it was like to bring a black man into the country for the express purpose of selling him at public market, as a side of beef was sold. When Lincoln had issued his proclamation to free all slaves everywhere in the boundaries of the United States as those boundaries had stood before secession, Holly had resented the usurpation of power on his part, but still had not addressed herself to the underlying moral issue. Now, McNeil was forcing her to do so.

"Well, what do you say?" he was saying to her now. "Shall we talk business? If you need quick cash for the investment, you could always mortgage this house. I'm sure General de Beauregard would make you a loan, he thinks so highly of you." The last was said in an acid tone.

Holly glowered at him. "After due consideration, Captain, I've decided I don't want to be a part of a renewal of the slave trade. Here in Charleston, or elsewhere."

McNeil frowned.

"I think Mr. Lincoln is right in his position that even the Negro is deserving of some measure of human dignity however wrong the Yankee President may be in his other political positions."

"Well, I'll be damned!" McNeil said softly. "I never thought I'd hear a daughter of Ashby Ransom defend that comic buffoon in the White House!"

Holly's face reddened. "My father was much more liberal than a man like you could ever imagine," she said in a slow, level voice. "And whatever Lincoln may be, he is not a buffoon. He put Grant and Sherman in charge of this war, Captain, and they've managed to beat our armies at almost every confrontation."

McNeil rose. "You don't sound like no rebel to me, Holly Ransom! I wonder what your fine general would think of you, if he heard such talk from your sweet lips!"

"I think our business is finished here, Captain," she said coldly.

"Then you're against slavery," he said accusingly. "Is that what I shall tell my associates?"

Holly hesitated only a moment. "Yes," she said, "I believe I am."

"I'll be damned."

"Now, if you'll just leave, Captain. I have some work unfinished."

"What about the profit?" he said, incredulous at her reaction to his proposition.

"Do you think I would turn a profit at an enterprise that my conscience will not approve?" she said easily. "I know that you and others in Charleston consider that a small factor, Captain. But I still have some moral fiber left, despite what the war has done to me. Good day, sir!"

Grumbling something about crazy women, McNeil left then, a black figure ambling down her walk with white

355

snowflakes alighting on him tentatively, as if they did not wish to disturb his dark mood.

The next day, two things happened. News was received that Sherman had taken Savannah, and Holly heard from Blaisdell.

On the way in to Savannah, Sherman's troops had torn up all railroad lines, burned crops that were left in the fields, razed private homes and farmhouses, and herded refugees into barbed-wire enclosures resembling the field prisons adjacent to the battlefields. Fort McAllister defended the city, and Sherman's soldiers were harassed in their approach also by remnant Confederate units and by irregulars. But only just over nine thousand men stood in Sherman's way, and the fighting was minimal. Sherman referred to the defenders as a "mongrel mass." They had been strung out from the Savannah River to Rose Dhu on the Ogeechee River, but were not much more than a thin skirmish line. Sherman gave his subordinate, Hazen, the job of attacking the fort manned by less than two hundred men, under the command of a Major Anderson, who took his orders from General Hardee in the city. The fort fell in fifteen minutes. Most of the defenders in the city then escaped capture by crossing the Savannah River at night, and Sherman made no attempt to stop them. He had promised Lincoln the city as a Christmas present, and he did not want this climax of his deadly march to be a bloody one.

All through the shooting during the brief siege, the Confederate soldiers had remained in high spirits. At one point, just before the fall of Fort McAllister, the Union troops heard them singing.

Jeff Davis rides a very fine horse

> *And Lincoln rides a mule;*
> *Jeff Davis is a gentleman*
> *And Lincoln is a fool!*

But it was the Yankees who had the last laugh. Mayor Richard Arnold formally surrendered to General Geary, another subordinate of Sherman, on December 21. That finished, William Tecumseh Sherman moved into the fashionable and elegant home of one Charles Green that very evening, and made it his headquarters. Green was a British subject who had welcomed the Yankees with open arms.

Charleston was moody when the news came. Holly and Jennifer were at home together when a neighbor came past to spread the bad news, and they both felt very low. Now Sherman would bring his war machine north, and it would not take him very long at all to reach Charleston, everyone knew.

It was only an hour after that news, that Holly received the letter from Stuart Blaisdell.

As soon as she saw the military designation on the envelope, her face brightened and she felt a great lift from her dark mood. She opened it on the way to the kitchen, and by the time she arrived there, where Jennifer sat with a cup of hot tea, she was already reading it.

"Jennifer! It's a letter from Stuart!"

Jennifer's face brightened too. "Oh, God, that's wonderful, Holly! We needed that today."

"He's been in the fighting again, but he's all right," Holly said excitedly. "Here, I'll read it aloud to you."

"That isn't necessary," Jennifer protested.

"I want to," Holly said. She held the letter up to the sunlight.

Dearest Holly,

It didn't take long to get back into the thick of things. Sheridan is doing a good job on us here in the Shenandoah Valley. We fight hard, Holly, but we just don't have the men now, or the supplies. Some of that stuff you and I brought back showed up here, though, and it was much appreciated, believe me. With every skirmish now we're being pushed backward. Toward the east, and the coast, and—Charleston. Grant is moving south in Virginia, and now soon Sherman will be marching north to meet up with him and Sheridan. But we're making them earn every foot of ground, Holly.

I want you to know that I'm all right, and that my leg is doing just fine. It just breaks my heart, though, to see these brave kids putting their lives on the line every day, when they know the war is lost to them. You wouldn't be able to take it, Holly; it would tear your heart right out. Nobody wants to surrender; they all seem to know without being told that it's important to keep going as long as possible.

Holly, I want to apologize for the way I acted before I left. Out here, you get perspective on things very quickly again. What you and Randy did between you was your business, or at least yours and Jennifer's.

Holly stopped reading, and looked up at Jennifer, and Jennifer gave her a reassuring smile.

I have no anger left in my heart for you, Holly, only love. I hope you have just a little for me,

358

*despite the way I've treated you, and I hope
Jennifer can find it in her to forgive you, and
Randy too.*

There was another short paragraph of small talk, and
then the letter was finished. When she was through
reading, Holly just sat there silent for a long moment, her
eyes moist. Maybe now it would be possible to keep Blaisdell as a good friend, always.

"That was a nice letter, Holly," Jennifer finally said.
"And I do forgive you. Really, I mean it this time."

"I'm glad, Jennifer," Holly said.

"When Stuart gets back from Virginia," Jennifer said,
"why don't you marry him?"

Holly regarded her soberly. "God, I hope he gets
back," she said. "It would kill me, if he didn't get back. I
don't even like to think about it."

"He'll come back," Jennifer said. "I feel it inside me.
But you didn't answer my question."

"About marrying Stuart?"

"Yes," Jennifer said.

Standing beside the table where Jennifer sat, Holly
looked across the kitchen. "That would make it all easy, I
admit. Marry Stuart, let him give me a home and family.
But I can't, Jennifer; I'm not in love with him."

"Does that matter?" Jennifer asked seriously.

"With me, it does," Holly said.

"It's that Booth fellow, isn't it?" Jennifer suggested.

Holly smiled. "I guess it is. But not in the way you
think. I'm not waiting to hear from John, hoping it will all
start up again between us, hoping it will end in wedding
bells. I wouldn't marry John, either, Jennifer. Beneath
all the charm, I don't think there's enough substance for
me, enough stability."

359

"Then what does he have to do with it?" Jennifer wondered.

"John showed me what it's like to be really excited by a man, to be really in love the way a woman should be in love. I was in love with him that way, and I still feel most of that toward him. I can't settle now, Jennifer, for less than that, for less than it can be. Maybe I'll never find that kind of excitement in a man of substance, a man of emotional stability. I don't know. Maybe I'll never get married. But I can't accept a lesser relationship now. I can't wed myself to a man who won't make life a real adventure for me."

There was a short silence between them; then Jennifer finally spoke again. "Would you mind if I took an interest in him?"

Holly regarded her quizzically. "Stuart?"

Jennifer nodded tentatively to her.

"Why, of course I wouldn't mind, Jennifer! I had no idea that you and Stuart—well, that you liked him, in that way."

"It's a one-way attraction, I'm afraid," Jennifer admitted. "When you're around, Stuart can only see you. But, yes, I find Stuart attractive in many ways. He's virile; he's stable, you said you like stability; he's considerate. Of course, I know what he thinks of me, and why shouldn't he? But maybe if I change, Holly, I'll look different to him. I don't know; I'm probably just dreaming. But I thought I ought to tell you about the dream."

"My God, I think it's a wonderful one." Holly smiled. "And I think Stuart thinks better of you than you imagine." The smile faded. "Would it bother you to know that Stuart and I were—"

Jennifer laughed. "Are you joking? I figured as much.

360

No, Stuart has been yours to do with as you pleased, whether you figured so or not. That wouldn't bother me. God, listen how we're talking! As if Stuart were a book you're giving me out of your library!"

"I hope that if you decide it's Stuart who will make you happy, Jennifer, you find that he feels the same way."

"Thanks, Holly," Jennifer said. "Maybe when the war is over, you ought to take a trip to Baltimore—to find out if John Booth is the same man you left. Maybe you'll be pleasantly surprised. People do change, as they mature."

"It's no farther from Baltimore to Charleston than from here to there," Holly said. "I would rather that John made such a trip, if he still has any interest." She folded Blaisdell's letter, and tucked it into her dress at the neckline. "Jennifer, I suppose you can get along alone here in the house for a few days or a week, can't you?"

Jennifer regarded her curiously. "Sure, but where are you going?"

"Maybe nowhere, but maybe to Savannah. I'll tell you more about it after I've spoken with General de Beauregard. I have an appointment to see him later today."

"More secret-agent stuff?" Jennifer wondered.

"Not exactly," Holly said, "but it pertains to the war."

"Is it something I can help with?"

Holly appreciated that. It was the first time Jennifer had ever evidenced any real interest in the war. "No, I don't think so, Jennie. But thanks for asking."

"Like you said, we're friends," Jennifer told her.

The appointment with De Beauregard was in late afternoon that day, and Holly was at his headquarters punctually, wearing a dark dress and hat and a cape over her shoulders. Around the headquarters building were many armed guards, carrying long muskets and rifles, bayonets affixed to them. On her way, all along Tradd

361

Street and Church and Broad Streets, there had been soldiers and military wagons and even some cannons. Charleston, after lasting through one of the longest military sieges in history, was now gearing up for an even greater assault by land, as Union forces closed in. Heavy artillery had been moved into the Ansonborough area, and out to the east beyond Legare Street. Fort Sumter was in a shambles, but it was still held by Confederate forces, and nobody was clamoring for a quick surrender. Not yet.

Holly was escorted into the big gray building by a guard, and taken directly to De Beauregard's offices on the second floor of the building. A male aide-secretary met them there, and took Holly into De Beauregard's private office. De Beauregard had just returned from Savannah himself, just before its surrender to Union forces, and had conferred with General Hardee about the nocturnal withdrawal of most of Savannah's defenders before they could be captured.

"Ah, Miss Ransom," he greeted Holly warmly now, in the spacious office that was command headquarters for the city. "What a pleasure to see you on this blustery winter day. Won't you please have a seat here near the fire?"

He seated Holly before a wide fireplace where a crackling fire warmed the room; then he joined her there, facing her in a broad armchair. "Now, my aides tell me you want to discuss the war." He smiled. "Do you have any ideas about saving Richmond? We can use them."

Holly returned the smile. "No, I wouldn't presume, General." She liked sitting across from him, bathing in his strength and warmth. She liked the gray uniform with its gold braid and sash, and everything that was Confederate. Unlike the Union uniform and equipment, all of

362

this would be gone, when the war was over—thrown into trash bins, burned, disposed of as if it had never mattered. The Yankees would make sure of that. It all seemed irredeemably tragic to her.

"I've had an idea, General, and I'd like your opinion of it," she went on after a moment. "An idea involving General Sherman."

"Oh?" De Beauregard said. His handsome face looked more lined than ever, now. "What about Sherman?"

"He'll be heading north now, through the Carolinas," Holly said. "And it will be Georgia all over again, if some overture isn't made at this juncture."

"I'm well aware, Miss Ransom," he said.

"We've shown them what it will be like if they have to fight for every inch of ground," she said. "Now, if we don't make some offer to them, that will all be lost. It won't make any difference. We've shown them they have something to gain by accepting a reasonable peace treaty. But now we have to offer it to them before the war is over, General."

He nodded. "All of us are aware of that, of course. Even Lee, who has been so reluctant to admit the war is lost, is. If some offer were made right at this moment, we might salvage something from this. But the trouble is Davis. He can't admit to himself that it's irreversible, now."

"If there were a delay at this juncture," Holly suggested, "maybe President Davis would have time to listen to his advisors. There is a lull at this moment in Virginia. It's Sherman who will fan the war to a blazing inferno again, shortly. What if he were to delay his march north, by three or four weeks even? Wouldn't that give the Confederacy time to catch its breath, and formulate an offer of peace?"

"It very well might," De Beauregard said.

"Then let me go to Savannah, General. Let me talk with Sherman personally. Not as your emissary, but as a private citizen who has had enough of war and wants peace. Maybe Sherman will listen to a woman. He allowed a withdrawal from Savannah, without interference. Maybe he will see the wisdom of delaying his army in that city for a short time, in the hope that Jefferson Davis and Lincoln can find a way to have a dialogue."

De Beauregard was somber. "I would feel badly, Miss Ransom, sending a lady into the thick of the federal lines—to speak with an ugly man like William Sherman."

"I'd be safe, General. I'd ask for a letter of introduction from our mayor, keeping your name out of it. But I won't go without your private approval."

The general sat there pensive for a moment; then he nodded slowly. "All right, Miss Ransom. Have your talk with Sherman, if he'll see you. It might do us some good. Do you need funds?"

"No, I can finance the trip, General. I would appreciate a guard, until I get to the Union lines."

"I'll arrange it," De Beauregard told her. He rose from his chair. "You're an exceptional woman, Miss Ransom. Incidentally, I've heard that both you and Lieutenant Blaisdell will receive citations for your work in the supplies mission. I'm very pleased."

"So am I, General, and thank you."

"Do me a big favor," he said as she rose from her chair, too. "Be careful out there. You're going into enemy territory."

Holly smiled a lovely smile at him. "I've been there before, General."

Chapter Twenty

The very next day, with a quick farewell to Jennifer, Holly was on her way to Savannah. She had a letter from her mayor in hand, and she left in a military carriage with a driver and a bodyguard.

It was a cold December day, and Holly remembered a similar one when she had left for Baltimore and said good-by tearfully to her mother. That seemed like a hundred years ago, in a different life. So many things had happened to her in the interim that it had all been a whirl, with John Wilkes Booth and Blaisdell at the vortex of it.

In places, the road was jammed with refugees, fleeing north. Farmers came up to the carriage and begged for food, but Holly had none to give them. Entire families were on the move—in wagons, on carts and horseback. It was a terrible sight, one Holly would never forget.

They expected that Holly would reach Savannah that very evening, because of hard driving. When they got to within five miles of the Union lines, and not much farther from Savannah, the guards stopped the carriage at a closed-down roadside inn, and Holly left them there. She boarded a chestnut gelding that had been roped behind the carriage, and went on alone. The guards would wait for her until her return to that rendezvous site, no matter how long she took.

Holly found it frightening to be on her own in that country. She rode sidesaddle on the gelding for a half-hour and was looking for the Union pickets ahead, when she came upon a group of men sitting beside a fire alongside the road. They saw her approach, and two of the five came out to bar her path.

Holly reined up and looked them over. They were grubby-looking renegades from some Confederate outfit, she figured, men who had either deserted the cause or never been a real part of it. The biggest of them came up and took her mount's reins in hand.

"Hey, there, missy! Where you think you're headed on that pretty animal?"

"I'm going to the Union lines," she said. "Are they far from here?"

The big man, a brawny, greasy-looking fellow, turned and grinned at the other one who had come over to her, a stringy-haired, gaunt fellow with a tooth missing. "You hear that, Tom? The lady is going off to consort with the Yanks. You ever hear the like?"

"I never did," the gaunt fellow remarked. In the background, the other men at the fire laughed softly among themselves.

"Them Yanks ain't far from here, honey. But you don't want to go down there, do you? When you can stay a while with us Johnny Rebs? We got a nice fire for you over here."

"We can heat you up good," the gaunt man grinned showing the black hole in his teeth.

Holly gave him a look. "I have business with the Union

Army," she said. "Now let me pass."

The big fellow held on to her reins. "Now don't be in such a hurry, missy. What's a pretty little thing like you doing sneaking off to the Union lines? You some kind of traitor or something?"

Holly's face flushed. She tried to pull the reins free of his grasp, but was unsuccessful. "Let go, damn you!"

"Bring her over here, boys!" one of those at the fire called out. *"Don't keep her all to yourself!"*

"Why don't you just get off of that chestnut, miss?" the gaunt man with the missing-tooth grin said. "Them Yankees don't need you down there. We got use for a horse and a woman right here."

The big fellow came up and put a thick hand on Holly's thigh. "You heard Tom, honey. You better stay here with us a while. I'll just help you down off of there, and we'll—"

Holly was desperate now. With a wild slap on the gelding's haunches, she kicked her heel into its flanks. *"Go!"* she yelled at the animal.

The horse reared first, tearing loose from the big man's grip. Then it bolted ahead, starting into a gallop, Holly barely hanging on. The big man made another grab at it and missed, and the gaunt fellow jumped onto the horse's haunches, holding onto its tail as he was dragged along behind it. Holly saw him there and gasped, but the horse kept moving under her. The gaunt man made a reach for her from behind, missed, and fell to the ground, raising a cloud of red dust when he hit and rolled. The mount broke clear and raced away down the trail; Holly held on desperately.

The horse had hardly slowed when she reached the first Union pickets. Two soldiers raised their rifles toward her simultaneously, challenging her progress, and she reined in sharply, managing to halt the mount just as she reached them.

"Are you crazy, lady? Riding into our guns like that? Where are you from?"

One picket held her reins while the other fellow helped her dismount. Then Holly was showing them her safe-passage papers, and the letter from Charleston's mayor. "I'm on my way to see your General Sherman," she told them, "on official business."

"General Sherman!" the thin one of them laughed. "You might as well try to see God, ma'am!"

Holly was tired of masculine effrontery for this day. She replied hostilely, "Soldier, if you want to avoid a court-martial, you'll take me to your commanding officer immediately!"

Their faces went sober. "Hell, take her on in, Bill," the other picket said. "The major deserves a laugh; it's been a hard day."

When their commander read Holly's letter, though, he did not laugh. He put Holly on a buggy with an aide, and told the fellow to drive Holly on into Savannah, to Sherman's headquarters. Subordinates of Sherman could handle the situation there, and Holly would not be his, the major's, responsibility.

It was dark when Holly arrived in the city with her driver, and it was just as well. There was devastation everywhere; in some areas the damage was worse than in Charleston. Holly had visited Savannah as a child, and she did not even recognize it now. Factors Walk was in rubble; there were shell craters in Forsythe Park, and at Chippewa Square. Many of the city's famous row houses were burned to the ground.

368

However, the Green House where Sherman was quartered, and most of the mansions around it, were intact. As Holly arrived at the big house on the tree-lined street, she saw the soldiers in knots on the grounds, the cannons on the lawn. The American flag flew from a pole out in front, in place of the Confederate one that had fluttered there. There were several carriages parked on the gravel drive, and a supply wagon with no team. Holly's driver took her right up to the front entrance to the place, where they both disembarked. The driver showed his papers and Holly's to a guard. After a few moments of discussion, they were allowed to climb the steps of the place and enter the mansion.

She did not get to see Sherman, though. She was taken to an aide-de-camp, a captain whose duty it was to shield Sherman from crank visitors. He met with Holly in a first-floor anteroom, while the driver returned outside to wait for her.

"Oh, no, Miss Ransom. General Sherman does not see anyone from the town, except on very official business. Maybe I can help you."

"I'm not from the town, and I am here on official business," she said stiffly. "Please read the letter, Captain."

He did, very slowly, and then he looked back up at her. "This is very unusual, Miss Ransom. Very much out of the ordinary."

"I know that, Captain. But please take the letter to the general, and ask him if I may have a private word with him. If another time would be more convenient, I'll come back. But I'm not leaving Savannah until I've spoken with him personally."

He studied her pretty but serious face for a long

moment. Finally, he sighed heavily. "All right, Miss Ransom. If you'll return here tomorrow morning early, I'll see that you get to speak with the general—if only for a few minutes."

Holly hesitated. "Very well. I'll be back. What about my letter?"

He smiled. "I'll keep that, if you don't mind."

Holly's driver took her to a downtown hotel, and she checked in there. On the way, she saw Union soldiers everywhere, and military wagons, and cannons. Soldiers drank openly on the streets, and some had hard-looking local women on their arms. Holly realized that this was the way it would be in Charleston, when it fell.

There were a few Union officers billeted in the hotel, and Holly worried all night that someone would come into her room and attack her. A woman alone was fair game in Savannah now. She got almost no sleep. But finally morning came, and when she got ready and went outside on the street, her driver was miraculously there waiting for her, although looking somewhat hung over. In another twenty minutes, Holly was back at Sherman's headquarters.

She was admitted again, but the aide of the night before was nowhere in sight. She was told to wait under guard in the corridor. An hour passed and she became concerned that she had been forgotten. Then the aide finally came and took her upstairs to another corridor, where she waited outside Sherman's office. In another forty-five minutes, some officers emerged from the office, the aide with them, and the aide said that Sherman would now see Holly.

Holly went in past two more guards, into a room that had been a bedroom of the mansion, but where Sherman now held court. Sherman was studying a wall map when she and the aide came in, and the aide waited until Sherman turned to them.

"General, this is the Charleston girl I was telling you about."

Sherman and Holly exchanged stares. He was in uniform, but wore no tie at his shirt collar, and his hair looked uncombed. He had the hard-looking face of a drinker, and Holly thought she had seen better looking specimens coming out of the lowliest saloons in Charleston. He had a scrawny beard, and his face wore many lines, even though he was a relatively young man. He looked like the kind of man who would break into your house at night and rape your daughter. If Holly had met him in a dark alley of her city, she would have been scared to death of him.

"Oh, yes," he said after a moment, in a deep, growling voice.

The aide left them alone then, and Sherman went and sat on the corner of a walnut desk where a big revolver lay heavily on top of a pile of papers, as a weight to keep them in order. Sherman did not ask Holly to sit down, and offered no amenities, as a southern general would have done. He lighted a cigar without looking at her.

"You represent a political segment of Charleston?" he said without looking up at her.

"Yes, General," she said rather stiffly. "A segment that would like to keep the end of this struggle as bloodless as possible."

Now he looked up at her, narrowly. "They sent a damned fine-looking woman, Miss Ransom. Do you know De Beauregard?"

"Yes, sir. I know him well."

371

"Did he send you down here?"

"No, General. It was my idea to come," she said honestly.

"I'll bet if Lee were in charge at Charleston, you wouldn't be here," he offered.

"I've met General Lee," she said diffidently, "and he seems to me to be the kind of man who would welcome any honorable disposition of this conflict, through any honorable means."

Sherman studied her face with more interest. "You met Lee?"

"That's right. When I carried information into Confederate lines, General," she said proudly, "from Baltimore."

His eyes lighted up. "Damn, I remember your name now! You're one of those Confederate lady agents!"

"I was, for a while," she admitted, wondering if he would throw her behind bars after the confession. "I was imprisoned in Baltimore, but then released after a personal visit by President Lincoln."

"You spoke with Lincoln, too?" Sherman said.

"Yes, sir, I did. I rather like him, despite his politics."

He was shaking his head sideways. "You've had a remarkable life so far, Miss Ransom. I think I see why it's you who's here, now, instead of one of your men."

"Our men are fighters, General," she said flatly, "not talkers—as you've undoubtedly found out. Most of them want to fight to the last Confederate soldier."

"I found that out, yes," Sherman acknowledged. "The South should have surrendered after Atlanta, Miss Ransom. Notes were sent to Davis, and Lee. Mr. Lincoln wants peace badly. But we had no response, Miss Ransom. You can see that I had no choice but to march to Savannah,

372

showing Davis what a continuation of this struggle means to him and to the people of the South."

Holly held his tough gaze. "You had a choice, General."

He narrowed his hard eyes further. "You disagree with the way I'm prosecuting the war, Miss Ransom?"

"A good officer does not allow the men under him to run rampant, General Sherman. There are rules, even in warfare."

"My troops were righteously indignant because they had to continue fighting, Miss Ransom, keep on laying their lives on the line. I felt they had earned the right to vent some frustration, and I still feel so."

She shrugged. "I'm not here to judge you, General. Posterity will do that."

He grunted in his throat. "Exactly why are you here, Miss Ransom?"

She let out a small sigh. "I'm here to ask you to give us some time, General Sherman. Despite what I think of your march to the sea, I believe you acted wisely in allowing a withdrawal of Confederate troops from this city. I think down somewhere inside you, you regret what happened between Atlanta and here, and that regret expressed itself in your humane strategy here at Savannah."

Sherman allowed himself a smile for the first time since she had entered the room. "Are you a dabbler into men's minds, too, Miss Ransom?"

"I'm just hoping to understand you a little, General," she told him. "I'm hoping that at this point, you want a winding down of the shooting war almost as much as we do."

He nodded. "I probably do, young lady. Mr. Lincoln

wants it, General Grant wants it, and I want it. There's no point in further killing. But your President doesn't see it that way."

Holly came over closer to him. "Give him a chance to think, General! Give him the opportunity to retain some dignity! If you force the war now, sir, the Confederacy will fight to its dying breath. But if you allow an interlude for an exchange of thought between Washington and Richmond, some sane end to this may yet be achieved."

"Are you asking that I stop my prosecution of the war?" he said sardonically.

"Only temporarily, General. Give us three or four weeks of breathing room, sir. Suggest to General Grant that he do the same. I see that some of Savannah was saved. It would be nice if some of Charleston were, too. These will still be American cities, General, after this is all over. The men on both sides who would die in a death struggle are all Americans, some related by blood."

Sherman sat there, thinking. "President Lincoln's own brother-in-law was killed in Tennessee," he said; "by our own troops. He was fighting for the South."

Holly had not known that. "I'm sorry for the Lincolns," she said.

He rose off the desk, and walked over to a window, his hands folded behind his back. "You realize that your Jefferson Davis might use a lull in the fighting to build a last desperate defensive position against us?"

Holly nodded. "That is a possibility, General, but isn't the possible gain to all of us, on both sides, worth that risk?"

He turned back to her. "You could be an agent sent by Davis to lull us while he does just what I've suggested."

"I'm not, General," she said simply.

374

He looked into her open, blue eyes and believed her. "Tell you what, Miss Ransom. I'll give your idea some thought."

"That's all?" Holly said, disappointed.

"That's all I'll promise," he said, "to a Confederate emissary."

She finally nodded. "All right, General. But please think very seriously about it."

"I will, Miss Ransom."

That same evening in Charleston, Jennifer was very lonely in Holly's absence. She thought of contacting a young lieutenant whom she had known intimately a couple of times, but then she thought of Stuart Blaisdell, and of Holly. If she really intended to mount a campaign to win Blaisdell on his return, she had to reform in the interim. She had to be a different woman when he came back. So she decided to stay at home and be lonely.

At midevening, though, something happened to alter the expected course of the evening. Jennifer was sewing on a needlepoint pattern, sitting alone in the parlor, when two men came up on the porch and banged loudly on the door.

She went to answer it curiously, opening the door onto the cold night. There were two burly men standing there, wearing remnants of Confederate uniforms. One still wore a gun on his hip, so Jennifer presumed he was still in the army.

"There she is, I told you she'd be here!" the heaviest of the two said in a slurred voice. "You are Jennifer, ain't you?"

Jennifer squinted to see them better. "Do I know you two?"

375

"Hell, a friend sent us," the shorter, less burly fellow said. "Sergeant Wilkins, you remember him."

"I'm afraid not," Jennifer told them. "What do you want?"

"Want?" the smaller fellow said. He held a liquor bottle loosely in his right hand. "Hell, we want some fun, honey! A few drinks together, a couple of kisses. You know."

Jennifer's face hardened somewhat. She had had this before, but not since moving in with Holly. "You got your information wrong," she said. "I'm not the fun type anymore. Go on downtown and do your drinking, fellows."

"Hey, now wait," the bigger one complained dully. "We didn't come all the way over here for nothing. The least you can do is have a couple of drinks with us!" He was the one with the revolver on his hip, and he was more inebriated than the other fellow.

"I'm sorry," Jennifer said firmly. But she did eye the bottle with interest. She had no liquor in the house at the moment. "But I'm afraid you boys are going to have to leave."

She started to close the door, but the smaller one came up to the screen and opened it. "Come on, honey. Don't be so damned tough."

"We ain't leaving till you have a drink with us," the bigger one said loudly. "We'll sit out here all night, by Jesus. That right, Wade?"

The shorter fellow nodded vigorously. "All night, by Jesus! That's the truth of it, Jennifer my dear! Big Jim and me, we don't give up easy! The Yanks found that out, eh, Jim?"

Big Jim grabbed the bottle from Wade, nodded his

agreement, and swigged a drink of gin. Jennifer licked suddenly dry lips. "Oh, God," she said. "O.K., you can come in for one drink, all right? But then you have to leave, no funny business."

"Sure, one drink," Wade told her. "Just one long one, honey."

Jennifer let them into the parlor. So far she had not violated any of Holly's rules, and she did not intend to. She would let them stay for a few minutes, and then usher them out.

"Here, honey. Taste this; you ain't never had any better," the fellow called Big Jim told her, when they were all standing together in the center of the room.

Jennifer took the bottle and carried it to a cabinet on a wall nearby, and took a small glass out. She poured a generous amount of gin into the glass, and came and handed the bottle back to Big Jim.

"Here's to the quick end of the war," she said.

"I'll drink to that!" Big Jim said loudly. He swigged from the bottle, and Jennifer drank from the glass. When he was done, Wade grabbed the bottle rather rudely, and also swigged some gin. Jim scowled toward him as he drank.

"You've drunk two-thirds of that bottle, by Jesus," Jim said.

"You got your share," Wade said off-handedly. He went over to Jennifer, and threw an arm over her shoulder. "Now, honey. You sure you don't want a little loving tonight? You look like you could use some; I can see it in them pretty eyes of yours."

Jennifer shook her head firmly, taking another drink of the gin from her glass. It went down warmly, and made her feel good all through her insides. "I take my men one

377

at a time, boys. It's too bad you got the wrong impression from your friend."

Big Jim jerked the bottle away from Wade, and Wade gave him a hard look. "Maybe that gin might make you change your mind, honey," Big Jim suggested, swigging more gin while Wade looked on.

Wade had forgotten Jennifer momentarily. When Big Jim took the bottle from his mouth, Wade focused on its contents, and found that the gin was getting low.

"Don't tell me you ain't getting your share of that swill!" he said angrily. "You been sucking on that bottle like a baby on its mother's breast, by God! You always did want more than was coming to you!"

Big Jim glowered at him. "What the hell does that mean?"

"You know, by Jesus. You was always the first in mess line, or for supplies. You even stole that raisin cake that my sister sent out to Mechanicsville."

"Now, fellows," Jennifer said, a little concerned suddenly. "I think you both had better go. Take your argument downtown." She drank the last of the gin in her glass.

But they did not even know she was there, now. "I told you once," Big Jim was saying, in a low, more sober voice. "I never laid a hand on that damned cake of yours."

"It takes a certain kind of man to take another soldier's raisin cake," Wade said harshly.

"Are you calling me a goddamned thief?" Big Jim said.

"What else?" Wade said in a loud voice, and grabbed the gin bottle out of Big Jim's hand.

Big Jim's face went slightly crimson, and suddenly he drew the heavy revolver from its holster on his hip.

378

Jennifer gasped loudly as he aimed the gun at Wade.

"I'll blast your crazy head right off your shoulders, by God, if you call me a thief!"

"I'm calling it!" Wade defied him. "A thief you are, and a goddamned coward! You ain't got the nerve to pull that trigger and kill a man that knows what you are!"

Jennifer saw the deadly intent in Big Jim's eyes. "No, wait!" she said loudly. "Here, give him the gin back, and the two of you—"

She had gone to Wade to take the bottle from him, when the gun went off, almost without Jim's planning it. Jennifer felt the violent blow to her back, and the hot, searing pain inside her, and then she was thrown hard against Wade. She knocked him off-balance, and they both fell to the floor, side by side.

Jennifer lay on her face there, groaning, and now both men were staring at her wide-eyed. Jim looked down at the revolver as if he had never seen one before.

"What the hell!" he muttered.

"Jesus Christ, you shot her!" Wade hissed out, getting his feet under him. He bent over Jennifer, who was barely conscious. "You maybe killed her!"

Big Jim waved the gun helplessly. "It just—went off. I don't know. It just went off, and there she was."

"I can't hear her breathing."

Jim holstered the revolver as if returning a poisonous snake to a bag. "We—got to get out of here."

Wade rose from the floor. "She might need a doctor. Maybe a doctor might save her."

"You want to go get one?" Jim said. "And try to explain what happened here? You'd be in it too, you know. Just like it was you that pulled the trigger."

Wade eyed him darkly.

"We better leave," Jim repeated. "Somebody will find her. She's either dead or she ain't. Our getting out ain't going to make no big difference."

Wade rubbed a hand across his beard-stubbled chin. "O.K., let's make tracks."

In another moment, the house was quiet again.

Jennifer lay on the parlor floor, bleeding from her back and chest—lifeless.

When Holly left Sherman's conquered Savannah the next day, the general sent one of his own aides with her and the driver from the front, with instructions to see her safely into enemy territory.

They left at midmorning, and when Holly arrived at the front, the mount she had ridden there earlier was tethered to the rear of the buggy she was riding in, and then her two Union escorts drove her on toward the closed-down inn where her Confederate guards awaited her. The Union soldiers were to deliver Holly over to the two Confederates personally. A white truce flag was secured to the buggy, and the soldiers carried no arms but sidearms. The delivery was supposed to be completely peaceful.

But things did not work out that way.

The buggy had covered only two miles of the five-mile distance to the coach inn, when suddenly a small band of Confederate cavalry appeared out of nowhere and attacked the buggy.

The first shot from the rebels struck the driver in the left arm, and the second one snapped the foot-long staff supporting the truce flag and threw the flag to the ground. Then the five riders were upon the buggy, firing wildly and whooping loudly. The Union driver kept the buggy moving, despite his wound, and Sherman's aide, a captain of infantry, yelled to the attackers that they were under a truce flag. But, among the assailants, nobody heard him. The aide drew his sidearm and returned fire, and then the driver was smacked in the back with a chunk of hot lead, and went plummeting off the buggy. He was dragged along beside it by one foot for fifty yards, while the captain fired and hit a Confederate rider, knocking him off his mount. Holly, mumbling protests, huddled low in her position behind the driver's seat; the aide, back there also, now tried in vain to grab the reins of the galloping horse. The trailing horse was forced to gallop along, too, to keep pace with the buggy horse. Holly looked up and saw pursuers all around them; she shouted at them at the top volume of her voice. *"No, stop it! Stop shooting!"*

In the next instant, the aide was struck in the neck with a musket ball. His head whiplashed violently, then he fell slowly off the buggy, as if it was all in slow motion. Holly screamed, and screamed again. Finally a rider came up and grabbed the reins; the buggy slowed to a stop.

Dust settled around the buggy and riders. Holly sat there dazed and in shock, as three riders gathered around her. The fourth one rode back to find out if their comrade was dead. Holly finally looked over at the lieutenant in the gray uniform who came up beside her.

"Who are you, ma'am?" he asked curtly.

Holly's lip was quivering. She looked back and saw the crumpled body of the aide, in the dust. The other Union soldier was too far back for her to see. She turned back to the lieutenant.

"We were under a truce flag, damn you! Are you insane?"

The young lieutenant narrowed his eyes on her. "You're a southern girl, aren't you? What were you doing on a Union buggy, out here in the middle of nowhere?"

Holly tried to keep her voice under control. "I am an agent of the city of Charleston," she said slowly and acridly. "I have been in Savannah to talk peace to General Sherman. I was returning to my Confederate bodyguards under a truce flag, escorted by these men you have just wantonly murdered!"

The lieutenant's face darkened. "We didn't see any truce flag, ma'am," he said defensively. "All we saw was those Union-blue uniforms."

Holly felt suddenly physically sick. "Sherman will be sure I came here with some kind of chicanery in mind! You've undone everything I came here to accomplish!"

"Is something wrong?" one of the officer's subordinates asked.

"Look, ma'am," the lieutenant told her. "I've never apologized for shooting a Yankee, and I'm not going to start now. Especially not any people of that devil Sherman! Now if you'll lead the way, ma'am, we'll escort you to your transportation."

Holly felt like turning around and going back to explain what had happened, to assure Sherman she had had nothing to do with it; but that would probably accomplish nothing.

She nodded dully, as a soldier climbed onto the driver's seat. "This damnable war," she murmured to herself.

Then the buggy started off toward the north.

Chapter Twenty-One

Holly arrived back in Charleston late that evening, and had another trauma awaiting her.

Jennifer had so far survived the accidental shooting in their parlor, but she was in critical condition at the hospital. A neighbor had come past that same evening, found Jennifer, and gone for help. Jennifer was still fighting for her life. The bullet had been taken from her chest, but she was still in shock, her body trying to come back from the violent attack on it.

Holly could not believe what had happened, when she was told that evening. But the evidence was there in her own parlor. A spilled bottle of gin on the floor, an over-turned chair, the dark stains on a carpet from Jennifer's bleeding onto it. Holly imagined a drunken party given by Jennifer for some old flames, and an argument in which Jennifer was involved. She immediately drove their buggy to the hospital, and found Jennifer in a small ward there. There were no private rooms in hospitals now, and there was very little special care. Jennifer was just one of many.

When Holly walked into the six-bed ward, she saw

Jennifer at once, lying motionless on a stark-white bed, eyes closed, looking very pale and lifeless. Holly felt a hollow feeling in her chest. "Oh, Jennifer!" she whispered.

"She won't be able to talk much," a nurse told her. "She's having a difficult time."

"Are her temperature and pulse rate being monitored regularly?" Holly asked tautly. "How often is a doctor seeing her?"

"We're doing the very best we can with her, Miss Ransom," the nurse said with restrained impatience, "under the circumstances."

The nurse left, and Holly went over and seated herself on a straight chair beside the bed. She took Jennifer's hand in hers, and Jennifer's eyelids fluttered open. She turned and looked at Holly, and her brow furrowed.

"Oh, Holly!" she said thickly. "Thank God—you're back!"

Holly felt a heavy tightness in her throat. "Yes, Jennie. I'm back."

"I got—myself shot, Holly." She looked terrible. Her face was all drawn and pallid, her hair uncombed, her lips dry and cracked.

"I know," Holly said.

"I never saw them before. I had to promise to have—a drink with them, to get them to leave. They argued and—I got in the way."

"Oh, God," Holly whispered. She had presumed the worst of Jennifer, and been very wrong.

"It wasn't my—fault, Holly. But I did want—that drink."

Holly put a hand on her face, tenderly. "Don't explain it, honey. Just lie quietly. You have to get well—for both of us."

"I'm glad you're back," Jennifer said in a harsh whisper.

"I'll take care of you, Jennifer. Just rest quietly."

A few minutes later, Holly went out into the corridor, leaned against a white wall, and cried. As she stood there, a doctor walked up to her, a young, serious-looking man.

"Are you Miss Ransom?" he said to her.

She nodded. "Yes."

"I'm sorry you have to see her this way," he said.

"She's dying, isn't she?" Holly said.

"We don't know that, Miss Ransom. She's having a bad time, but she hasn't given up yet."

"I want to tend her," Holly said.

His brow furrowed. "You, personally?"

"I have practical nursing experience, I've worked here in various capacities. I want to be with her until we know, one way or the other. I won't get in the way of you or the nurses."

He hesitated. "All right. I'll clear it at the front office."

"It might help her to know I'm here," Holly added.

"There should be no problem, Miss Ransom."

In the next few days, Holly was at the hospital day and night. She did not even bother to go to De Beauregard to advise him of the results of her journey to Savannah. On the third day, De Beauregard came to her, with a couple of aides. They found Holly sitting at Jennifer's bedside, checking her pulse. They all went out into a waiting room, and the aides were dismissed momentarily. Holly and De Beauregard were alone.

"It all went wrong," Holly told him. "Sherman's personal aide was killed in escorting me past the front lines—by a Confederate raiding party. I'm sure Sherman thinks I planned it that way, for some obscure reason." She sighed. "My mission was a failure, General."

But De Beauregard, sitting facing her in his gold braid, shook his head with a soft smile. "No, Miss Ransom. It was not a failure; that's what I've come to tell you."

Holly regarded him quizzically.

"We've just gotten the news from Savannah. Sherman has announced his intention to remain in that city for a few weeks, to rest his troops."

Holly was stunned. "Really?"

De Beauregard nodded. "Old William Tecumseh must have guessed what happened to you out there. He is a battlefield general, after all. We have the time you sought. Grant seems to have laid back some in Virginia, too. Of course, it's a natural time to have a cease-fire, at the holidays."

"Thank God for Sherman's insight into the ways of war," Holly said.

"I'm already in touch with President Davis, through couriers. I'm asking that no further devastation of southern cities be allowed to occur, that he consider drafting a truce paper in this lull. If the war moves ahead despite such an effort, I'm asking permission to withdraw Confederate forces from Charleston in advance of a Yankee incursion, to save what's left of the city—as was done in Savannah."

"I hope Davis listens to your suggestions, General," she said.

"We all have to gear toward trying to save lives and our cities now," he told her. "How is your friend, Miss Ransom? Is she getting any better?"

"Yes, she appears to be, General. The doctor says now

that things look better for her. She's begun eating just a little."

"That's good news, Miss Ransom." His face went serious. "I'm glad you've had some, from me and from the doctor. Because there is a small bit of bad news, I'm afraid."

Holly looked up at him.

"The Yankees took a rather large number of prisoners recently, in the Shenandoah Valley—under General Sheridan. I'm afraid your Lieutenant Blaisdell was one of those captured."

Holly's insides clutched up. "Oh, Stuart! Is he all right? Is he wounded?"

"I asked about that. It seems he did sustain a further wound, but it's not a serious one. Our information is that it's the same leg that was involved before."

Holly's face was flushed, hot. "Where was he taken?" she asked dismally.

"We think he went to Camp Douglas near Chicago," he said.

"What's it like there?" Holly asked him.

De Beauregard sighed. "Well, I won't lie to you. It's an overcrowded, undermanned tent camp, just like many of ours. In the wintertime, it might not be so nice. They won't get much food or medicine. The best thing for them is if the war ends very soon."

Holly was churning inside. "But he might not make it through the winter, General!" she said. "If he has a wound!"

"I'm sorry, Miss Ransom. If there were anything at all I could do, I would."

"Could I go there?" Holly asked him. "If my friend here gets better?"

"I don't think they would allow that," De Beauregard told her. "There are special prisoner exchanges, of course, arranged in Washington and Richmond. You might try to get Blaisdell exchanged in one of these repatriations. The trouble is, there might not be much interest in them, now. You could talk to some generals in Richmond or Washington. I guess if it were me, I'd prefer to try those in Washington. Their subordinates are holding Blaisdell, after all."

"Could I get to Washington?" Holly wondered. "With all the fighting betwen here and there?"

"You did it once." De Beauregard smiled. "But they didn't know your name then. You hadn't been convicted in a federal court as a Confederate agent."

"I'd use an alias," Holly said, telling herself, "like I did when Stuart and I went to Hartford."

"It might work," he said.

"I can't just leave him there," she said, "through this long winter coming. I just can't."

In the meantime, in Washington, John Wilkes Booth was laying very serious plans. The last couple of plays he had acted in were in the nation's capital, but they were small parts. Booth was not really interested in acting anymore. He had caught a fever, and the fever was an almost uncontrolled hatred of Abraham Lincoln.

Booth was no longer a ladies' man. The woman he had been with in New York had been only a casual acquaintance with whom he had not been intimate. He had no time nowadays to think of women. He knew now that he loved Holly, that he always would love her. But his fever kept him, even, from thinking of her often. He had written two letters to her, over the past six months, but had torn both of them up without trying to get them across the fighting front.

Booth had made some new friends, too, since Holly had been repatriated to Charleston. Most of the friends were Washington residents. When Lincoln was reelected quietly in November of that year of 1864, about the time that Sherman had left Atlanta on his infamous march to the sea, Booth was living in a boardinghouse where he met a fellow named John Surratt, who had been a Confederate courier as Holly had been for a while. Surratt and Booth, after the reelection, began talking seriously about capturing Lincoln and forcing an honorable peace out of the Union. Booth suggested it could be done during one of Lincoln's many evening visits to the Ford's Theater with his first lady. Surratt liked the notion. The two of them recruited several other dissidents, a couple of them Confederate Army veterans living secretly in Washington. They actually went to the theater one dark night with a rough plan for execution, but the President did not show. That had been in January, while Holly was still tending Jennifer, but making plans to come to Washington. In the war, Wilmington had just fallen to Union troops.

After the failure of Lincoln to show up at the theater, a couple of conspirators dropped out of the group, and another joined. The group was now composed of four persons, including Booth. There was a fellow named George Atzerodt, a carriage maker from Port Tobacco who was an older man than Booth, and there was David Herold, a withdrawn, quiet drugstore clerk who had not fought in the war. The new man was Lewis Paine. Paine, a Confederate veteran of Antietam and Chancellorsville, was built like an ox. He very impressed with the intense, charismatic Booth, and made an excellent follower of Booth's plans.

It was on a dark January night in Booth's rented room at the Surratt House—John Surratt had moved away and wanted nothing more to do with this frightening enterprise—that the four conspirators met and discussed their plan.

"Maybe it wasn't meant to be," Herold said to the group as they sat around the small room with its print wallpaper and framed needlepoint florals. Herold was rather small and thin, and pale-looking. "Maybe Lincoln just has the fates on his side."

"Maybe they know something is afoot," Atzerodt suggested. "It's odd he would cancel out at the last moment like that."

"Hell, it was just luck," the thickset, burly Paine grunted out. "Blind luck."

"I think you're saying the same thing as me," Herold said.

"Now, wait," Booth told them. Everybody looked toward him. He was the acknowledged leader of the group, the idea man and the strongest of them. "Lincoln doesn't have any goddamned good fairy sitting on his shoulder. He changes his plans all the time. That's the way it is, in that office he holds. He never knows from one minute to the next whether he'll be able to keep a date. Things come up, things he can't anticipate. We can't let that deter us. The next time, he'll probably be there. If we're patient, we'll succeed."

"Getting to him will be one thing," Atzerodt said. "Getting him out of the city will be another." Booth still had the same plan for escape he had mentioned to Holly: across the Navy Yard Bridge and into Maryland, through

Silesia and Pomfret, then across the Potomac by rowboat into Virginia. "I wish I could convince myself it will work." He was a mature-looking fellow with a square face and the look of a back-country farmer.

"I know that route in every detail," Booth said. He was more pale than he had been before, and there were lines in his face that had not been there when Holly had known him. "I know every tree, every bend in the road. It's the best way there is."

Paine grunted again. "We wouldn't have to do it at the theater. When he goes out in that fancy carriage, he don't have much of a guard. We could ambush it along its route somewhere—or outside the gate at the goddamned White House."

"Oh, no, not me," Herold said. "Not at the White House."

Paine gave him a hard look.

"I agree with David," Atzerodt said to Paine. "There might be too much military around. The theater is better."

Paine flexed his biceps under his frayed suit coat. "If you really want to reduce risk, just forget the last part of the plan."

They all frowned toward him. "Forget it?" Herold said.

Paine looked at Booth. "It would be a whole lot easier if we didn't bother taking him prisoner. If we just ended his damnable life, once and for all."

A heavy silence filled the room like a black fog.

"End his life?" Herold said. "You mean, murder him?"

Paine shrugged. "Who said anything about murder? Lincoln is an enemy of the Confederacy, isn't he? The

391

biggest enemy of them all? I'm talking assassination of a political enemy, execution of a rapist of the South. Stepping on a goddamned snake!"

Another silence. Finally, Herold rose from his chair. "I didn't get into this for no killing," he said hollowly. "I'm not a killer, Paine."

"What would be the point?" Atzerodt wanted to know of Paine. "John's idea is to use Lincoln to extort a treaty with honor from the Yankees. If Lincoln were dead—a martyr, I might add—there would be little interest in Washington for negotiation."

But Booth was sitting there thinking quietly about what Paine had said. "Maybe not, George," he said slowly now. "But maybe saner heads than Lincoln's would then take charge in the capital, and the same end would be accomplished—without his arrogant presence."

They were all staring at Booth again, now. Booth also had had thoughts about an assassination instead of a mere hostage taking. But he had shied away from the thought of actually killing—until this very moment. Now, with Paine voicing the possibility, it sounded right for the first time.

"You'd actually kill the President?" Herold said now to Booth. "Shoot him down in cold blood?"

Booth looked at Herold soberly, but things were happening to him inside that were making subtle changes in his face. "Does anybody here in this room doubt that an assassination would be justified?" he said deliberately.

Herold sat back down, numb.

"Maybe we ought to think of the penalty for failure," Atzerodt said solemnly. "By some miracle we might not be shot, if we were caught trying to take the President hostage. If we were apprehended in an attempt to assassi-

392

nate him, successful or not, there would be little doubt about the death sentence."

"Are you afraid to die, George?" Paine said, grinning.

Atzerodt scowled at him. "Only a crazy man courts death," he said evenly.

Herold took in a deep breath. "I don't know if I could be a part of it. That isn't what we were talking about, a half-hour ago. That isn't what I came into this group to do."

Booth made a face. "This is all talk, David. None of us even owns a gun. But I think we should hold the idea in the back of our heads, as an alternate plan of action. Our escape route might become unsafe for a sizable party to move on. Lincoln may stop attending the theater, so that we can't get close to him to grab him away from his guards. But barring anything of that nature, we'll proceed as planned, watching for the best opportunity to grab Lincoln and run. All right?"

Atzerodt finally nodded. "Sounds reasonable, John."

David Herold averted his gaze to the floor. "I guess so."

Booth turned to Lewis Paine the muscleman. Paine met his gaze, and shrugged his thickset shoulders. "Whatever you say, John."

Over the holidays that year, Holly had nursed Jennifer back to health. Jennifer had rallied nicely under Holly's special care, and shortly after the new year of 1865, she came home.

Holly had to tell her about Blaisdell. Jennifer took it well, though, and urged Holly to go try to do something for him. So, after Jennifer had been home for a couple of weeks, and was sitting up in a chair and eating well, Holly arranged for a neighbor to come in to cook for Jennifer for a while, and tend her. Then Holly prepared to leave for Washington under papers issued by De Beauregard himself.

"I'll be back soon, Jennifer. Both Stuart and I will be back," Holly told her that cold January day she left.

"I'll be here waiting." Jennifer smiled at her.

"Try not to get into any more trouble this time," Holly joked.

"You know me, Holly. I can't promise anything."

Holly was sorry to leave Jennifer before she was up and on her feet, but time was of the essence. Blaisdell had already had to suffer through several weeks of cold weather, deprivation, and exposure to disease. She could wait no longer.

The trip north was more involved with red tape this time, and Holly was traveling under an alias because of her previous notoriety in Baltimore and Washington. She called herself Carolyn Blaisdell, a fictitious cousin of Stuart Blaisdell, but otherwise admitted her purpose in traveling to the nation's capital. There were no real problems. She was passed through the lines without difficulty, and arrived in Washington on a cold, snowy day.

Washington was even more hectic than Baltimore had been when she had previously been in the North. There were Union Army uniforms everywhere she looked and traffic on the streets was heavy. Warships sat on the Potomac, braving the winter with naked masts. But the city had a vibrant, almost fresh look. The new capitol building had been completed a year before, and was very impressive with its white dome and long wings. But Holly could only think of how southern cities looked, by comparison. Southern cities had suffered terribly in the war, but most northern ones had been untouched. It did not seem right. But those were the facts of life.

Holly was not even thinking of John Wilkes Booth when she arrived in the capital. She thought Booth was in Baltimore or New York, following his career as an actor. She had no intention of going to Baltimore to look him up, even though the trip was a short one. She figured she would never see Booth again.

She could not have been more wrong.

Holly found herself a small hotel room not far from the gray buildings of military headquarters where the war department did business under Secretary of War Stanton, and his chiefs of staff. That was where Holly had to make her plea for Blaisdell. She had thought of going directly to Lincoln—of admitting her real identity and taking the chance of being arrested again. But it might take weeks to see the President, if he would see her, and then he might be angry that she had returned to the northland after his intervention to set her free.

The safest thing, and probably the most expedient, she decided, was to go to the military people responsible for the detention and welfare of prisoners of war.

The very day after her arrival, Holly began her campaign. She was seen by dozens of people on that day and the following ones, but nobody seemed to want to take responsibility for the prisoners at Camp Douglas in Chicago. After she was there over a week, she finally was allowed to speak with a general who admitted having certain responsibilities regarding prisoners of war. But after talking with her for a half-hour, he stated that he had nothing to do with the repatriation of prisoners. There was another general who took care of that, and a colonel under him did the real work. He did not know if any special repatriations were planned now, until the end of the war. When Holly asked when she might see the colonel, she was told that he was out of the city for a couple of weeks, but that she might see him on his return.

She had the same problem with finding out whether Blaisdell was all right. The general found a list of prisoners from Camp Douglas that showed Blaisdell to be alive as of Christmas, but nothing beyond that. Blaisdell was on a wounded list, and the general admitted quite callously to Holly that, in a prison camp, that was bad luck for him. Many wounded, he told her, would not survive the winter. He said that conditions were much worse at Confederate camps like Andersonville, however, and that the North made every effort to keep its prisoners alive.

Holly was more scared after talking with him than she had been on coming to Washington. Blaisdell was obviously in more trouble than she had realized. He could even be dead already, due to the lack of proper medical care, food, and shelter from the cold. Suddenly Holly could not sleep at night, and she almost stopped eating. She went to a different staff officer in order to ask permission to go see Blaisdell. But no such permits were being issued at that time, she was told. Even if she were to travel to Chicago, she would not be allowed near the camp.

The general in charge of prisoners of war told her that, while she waited for the colonel to return to the city, he would attempt to get an update on Blaisdell's condition. But that, too, would take several weeks.

Holly did not know what more she could do. She seemed to be stymied until Colonel Masters returned from his errand in Baltimore. Finally she gave up for the moment; she stayed in her room, and worried.

*   *   *

As it had turned out, Holly's concern for Blaisdell was
not unwarranted. In an open, windswept camp in Illinois,
poorly clothed and fed and suffering from a leg wound
that would not heal properly, Blaisdell had caught a fever
and was in bad shape.

Camp Douglas was not far different from the ugly
Andersonville of the South, despite the general's assur-
ances to Holly that it was superior. It consisted of a few
log-and-wood buildings for the officers and guards in
charge of the prisoners, a double fence around a large
enclosure, and rows upon rows of tents, shanties, and
lean-tos where the prisoners were forced to find shelter
from the winter.

The Union Army had supplied the small sleeping tents,
when the camp had been created. But very soon the
prisoner population had exceeded the facilities provided
to care for them. Newcomers then were required to go
out on foraging trips for materials to make shanties and
lean-tos, to keep the weather off them. Now there were
two and three men sleeping in one tent or small shanty.
Food was scarce—even for the guards, sometimes—and
medical care was almost nonexistent. A chunk of lead had
been extracted from Blaisdell's lower leg when he'd
arrived. and his wound had been bandaged. But little had
been done beyond that. He had not even had enough
nourishment to sustain him if his wound had not been
healing. Now, the cold was bad at night. Since Blaisdell's
arrival, many prisoners had died from lack of medical
attention, the cold, and disease.

Then, a morning finally came, in the first week of
February, when Blaisdell found that he could not get out
of his ragged blanket for roll call. His fever was worse, his

leg had begun to smell slightly, and he had chills running through him most of the time.

He slept with another man, a lanky Tennessean named Tate, who when he saw that Blaisdell had not gotten up, came back into the tent and squatted beside him, blowing on his bony hands to warm them up.

"Hey. You all right, Charleston boy?"

Blaisdell looked up at the fellow, and a shiver rippled through him. "I tried to get up, Tate, but I can't. I don't have any strength this morning. I can't even lift my arms."

"Man, you got to get up," Tate said earnestly. "If they think you ain't making it, they'll stop feeding you."

"I'm not making it," Blaisdell said in his weak voice. He looked terrible. He had lost weight, and his robust appearance was gone. His cheeks were sunken, his eyes dark around them. It had been particularly distressing to him that, after healing the leg so he could walk on it again, he had been hit a second time in it. Now, gangrene had set in. "My leg is dragging me down, now. I'm not getting over this fever."

Tate sighed. "That leg ain't never going to be any good to you no more, Blais. Maybe we can get them to bring a doctor in to do some surgery on it."

Blaisdell looked at him. "And then return me to this tent? No, thanks. I'll just go along like this." He stared past Tate. "I just wish I could see Holly one last time—or even Jennifer."

"Holly?" Tate said. "Jennifer?"

"They're friends," Blaisdell told him. "Good friends."

"I guess there ain't no use in wishing," Tate said. He came up close to Blaisdell, and hauled him up into sitting position. "Come on, old boy. You're going to make

398

roll call."

"I can't," Blaisdell protested. "Honest to God, Tate."

"You're going to, anyway," Tate said. "If you have to ride on my shoulders."

It was difficult, but Tate got him up. They went out into the wind then, Blaisdell's cheeks afire, and Blaisdell leaned on Tate while a Union sergeant came along and took roll. Blaisdell felt faint through it, and thought he might pass out, but he made it. When Tate got him back inside, Blaisdell fell heavily onto his ground mat, breathing hard.

"Now," Tate said. "You got through one more roll call."

"I don't know, Tate," Blaisdell said. "I think I might as well—have stumbled out against the dead line and let some guard shoot me."

"Don't talk like that," Tate said. "I got a gut feeling that you're going to make it, Blais. I don't know how, but I got this feeling."

"I wish to hell I had it," Blaisdell told him.

Then he closed his eyes and tried to forget the cold, and the empty feeling in the pit of his stomach, and the fever that was burning him up with every minute that passed.

In Washington, Holly waited. Emotionally caught up in the matter of repatriating Blaisdell, she had no idea that soon she would be involved in a much more emotional incident, a world-shaking one. Day followed day, and she was very restless. She checked with the office of Colonel Masters, but he had not yet returned.

She waited some more.

One afternoon as she came back into the lobby of her

small hotel, the clerk greeted her excitedly. "Miss Blais-dell, did you hear the news?" He knew she was from Charleston.

Holly frowned. "What news?"

"I'm sorry to tell you, ma'am, but Charleston has fallen."

Holly felt the blood race into her head. "Oh, damn," she whispered.

"It fell to black troops," the clerk added. "I reckon you'd have to call that ironic. I mean, most of them were ex-slaves, I hear."

"General Sherman didn't take the city?" Holly said.

"No, ma'am. I hear it was the Fifty-fifth Massachu-setts Infantry Regiment. But Charleston is surrounded on all sides by different armies, of course."

Holly worried suddenly about Jennifer, wishing she had not left her there with just a neighbor. There might be looting, rape. There was no telling, she thought, what black troops would do. She had hoped that, with Sher-man's delay in Savannah, Jefferson Davis might offer a surrender with terms, but he had not.

"Was the city fought for?" she asked the clerk.

"I don't think so, ma'am. I hear General de Beauregard got his troops out of there ahead of the assault, and the Massachusetts Infantry had orders to allow the with-drawal."

Well, Holly thought, something had been accom-plished. Maybe her talk with Sherman had helped. Maybe it had accomplished something, even if Davis continued in his stubbornness.

"It won't be long now, though," the clerk added, "for De Beauregard or any of them. Grant, Sheridan, and Sherman are now closing in on your General Lee at

Petersburg. The war will be over soon, thank the Lord.''

Holly met his open look. "Yes, thank God,'' she said.

After hearing that news, Holly wanted only to get her business over with in Washington so she could get back to Jennifer and Charleston. She checked with Colonel Masters' office again, and found he was delayed in his return to the capital. She fretted and worried, about both Blaisdell and Jennifer. Some letters would be getting through now to Charleston, she figured, so she wrote Jennifer a long letter, telling her everything that had happened to her, and promising Jennifer she would be back in Charleston just as soon as she could get some action on Blaisdell.

The same evening of the day she sent the letter off by a federal courier, Holly received a surprise that shook her completely. She was walking down Pennsylvania Avenue, along a row of shops, when she looked up and saw Booth walking toward her.

They both recognized each other at the same moment. They stopped twenty yards apart, and just stared for a moment; then Booth was calling her name.

"Holly! Is it really you! My God, Holly!''

He came almost running to her, and before she could even say his name, he had embraced her tightly. Holly, all aflutter inside, returned the embrace, her old feeling for him alive again, just as if it had never left her.

"John! I can't believe it! I thought you were in Baltimore—or New York.'' She remembered being told he was with a girl in Manhattan; she recalled that he had never sent a letter, and her smile weakened.

"I've been here in Washington for some time,'' he said, "on a special project.'' His tone became conspiratorial for a moment. "But what are you doing here?''

"I'm here incognito," she told him. "You heard me talk about Stuart Blaisdell, a friend to me and Randy. I'm trying to get him freed from a prison camp in Chicago."

"Oh, God, those Union camps are absolute hellholes!" he said. But then his face brightened. "God, it's good to see you again, Holly! I thought I never would. I appreciated your letters, though."

She studied his pale face, and his hollow eyes. "John, are you all right? You look as if you need sleep."

He shrugged. "I've had trouble sleeping lately. I've been planning something, Holly—something big. But I can't talk about it here. How long are you going to be here?"

"I don't know," Holly said. "I hope not long; I have to get back to Charleston. But an officer I have to see is out of town."

"I want to talk with you," he said earnestly. "I want to *be* with you, Holly. I've thought about you so often. It was damned bad luck that I was out of town when you were repatriated from Baltimore. I couldn't believe I'd missed you."

"You could have written, John," she told him.

"I didn't know what to say," he told her. "I didn't know for sure you'd want to hear about me, once you'd returned home."

"I couldn't think about anything else for a while," she admitted. "I expected to hear from you. When I didn't, I figured you had written me off."

He took her chin in his slender hand. "I love you, Holly Ransom. I always will." He touched his lips to hers, and she felt the old fire flame up through her.

"Where are you staying?" he asked her,

"At the Jefferson Hotel—not far from army headquarters."

"I'd be happy to have you stay with me."

Holly dropped her gaze to the street. "I'm not sure that would be advisable for me, John."

"May I see you this evening?" he asked her. "We can eat out at a nice little café I know, and you can stop at the Ford's Theater with me; it will take your mind off the problem of Blaisdell for a while. I'm going to have a part in the forthcoming production of *The Apostate*—a very serious play."

"Oh, congratulations, John. Yes, I'd like to see you this evening very much, and the theater stop sounds nice."

"We can go up to my room later, and have a cup of coffee together," he said to her, watching her face.

Holly hesitated. "We'll see," she said.

The two of them had a fine meal out that evening, the best meal Holly had had in a long time. She was reminded of how bad things were in Charleston, with the extreme food rationing, and felt very guilty. When they stopped at the theater for Booth to have a brief talk with a director there, Holly was very impressed by the place. It was one of the finest theaters in the country, including New York.

"Lincoln comes here regularly, doesn't he?" she asked Booth.

When he replied, his handsome, pale face was grave. "Yes. He does," was all he would say.

Holly recalled Booth's earlier habit of talking about taking Lincoln captive, and wondered if Booth's big plans involved that. She put that idea out of her head. She had enough troubles. Booth asked her again to stop up at his room at the Surratt Boardinghouse, and she acquiesced. She could not help herself, she was still in love with Booth, despite his seeming lack of interest during their long separation. Just his physical proximity to her made her all quivery inside, made her ache for him as she had never ached for any other man. She wondered if her acceptance of his invitation was an urgent demand from her deep subconscious, a crying out for physical satisfaction. It certainly was a signal to Booth that she might be in a mood for seduction, she knew.

Booth's room, where he and his co-conspirators had sat not so long ago and talked of assassination, was surprisingly small to Holly. When Booth was taking his acting more seriously, he had always had fine quarters. But now something else was occupying his mind, something else was driving him.

They had only had a short cup of coffee, Holly having been seated on a straight chair near Booth's bed, before Booth came, pulled her to her feet, and kissed her urgently. The kiss was almost desperate, she thought, as if he had been waiting for it for a long time. That both gratified her and scared her. Everything he did nowadays seemed to have a desperate hue to it.

"Please, Holly," he whispered to her. "Don't deny me. Not after all this time. Make it like it was—if just for now, for this moment in time."

Holly knew that it was not wise of her to submit to her longing for him. But she needed Booth that night, as much as she had ever needed him, wanted him as much as she had ever wanted him. She went and turned an oil lamp down low.

"All right, John," she said quietly.

404

By the time they had undressed, they were both tight inside with anticipation; that made their first moments awkward. But Booth's bed was big and soft and they lay under a thick cover to ward off the cold; that helped. With Booth's hands on her, and his flesh pressing against hers, Holly had to admit that it was like before, inside her. She reacted almost without control to his touch, a dormant passion for him thrusting itself into her body without restraint. They spent a long time exchanging caresses, and then they were one again; it was as if time had melted away, and it was Baltimore, and they were new lovers with the hopes of the Confederacy riding high in their breasts.

Afterward, Holly lay very close beside him; she tried to retain the feeling that it was the same, for them and for the world—but she knew it was not. The Confederacy had almost lost the war; now, it was a matter of a few weeks. And they were both different. Holly expected more of life, and of men. She had matured. Booth had become—Holly did not know what. Even now, lying beside her after their love-making, he seemed tense. It was as if nothing could satisfy him, nothing could relax him.

"What are you thinking about, John?"

Booth turned to her. "A lot of things, I guess."

"Earlier, you said you still love me; that you always will."

He smiled and touched her face with his hand. "It's the truth."

She regarded him soberly. "You don't seem happy here, John. When this play has run its course, why don't you join me in Charleston? You could help us rebuild, become a substantial member of the community. You don't belong in the capital of the North; you're a rebel. You could even leave with me when I go. We could get you through with no problem; Charleston is occupied now by federal troops."

He shook his head. "I can't go anywhere right now."

"Do you mean, because of the play?"

He looked over at her. "There are several reasons, Holly."

"Can't you tell me what they are?"

He hesitated. He wanted very much to tell her what he and the others were planning, but he did not want her involved. He loved her too much. "No, I can't," he finally said.

She was hurt. "All right. If that's the way it is."

He reached over and kissed her, gently. "Let's not talk about it now," he said. "Let's just enjoy what we have: tonight, here and now."

She sighed heavily. "If you say so, John."

He pulled her to him with that urgency she had come to expect, and kissed her hungrily on the mouth.

Reluctantly, Holly let it start all over again.

Chapter Twenty-Two

Two days after her night with Booth, Holly finally got to see Colonel Masters, who had just returned from Baltimore.

The first thing he did was apologize to her.

"I understand you've been waiting to see me for a while, Miss Blaisdell. I'm sorry to have kept you coming back here all those times. My business in Baltimore, however, was quite urgent."

They were sitting in his whitewashed office in the war-department complex of buildings. Holly sat across his desk from him, looking very tense. "I understand, Colonel."

Masters was rather young, with a face that held empathy for her, and a manner that was courteous and pleasant. Holly figured he had been worth waiting for. He was a trim, erect fellow with a strong jaw and deep blue eyes and a long mustache on his upper lip. He was in charge of arranging prisoner exchanges, which had tapered off in recent months, because of expectations of the war's termination.

Masters glanced at a thin file before him. "Now, Miss

Blaisdell. You're interested in your cousin, a Lieut. Stuart Blaisdell, who is incarcerated at Camp Douglas."

Holly nodded. "That's right."

"You're both from Charleston?"

"Yes, Colonel."

"Please accept my condolences for the fall of your great city recently," he said to her.

Holly was surprised by that. "Why, thank you, sir. Your sentiment is greatly appreciated. Charleston is a fine town that has been through hell in the past few years."

"It's defense by General de Beauregard is one of the heroic epics of the war, Miss Blaisdell," Masters said seriously.

Holly was put very much at ease by this understanding Yankee. "It is General de Beauregard who recommended I come to Washington to see about Stuart," she told him.

"Indeed?" Masters said. "Although I've never met De Beauregard, I have the greatest respect for him. Of course, you understand that there must be special circumstances in a repatriation such as you desire. Do you know of any?"

Holly nodded. "Stuart is wounded, Colonel, in a leg where he was wounded previously, earlier in the war. I'm afraid he may be having trouble with it. I'd like to get him back to Charleston for medical attention. He won't be fighting against the Union again; I don't see what possible harm can come of his release."

Masters pursed thin lips. "There are occasional exchanges of wounded prisoners. Do you feel that the wound might be a present danger to the lieutenant's life?"

Holly realized that the expected reply was an

affirmative one. "Yes, Colonel. In this winter weather, and under the circumstances of life in prison camps."

Masters rose from his desk, and walked to a file cabinet. He pulled a drawer open, took out a paper, and studied it. When he came back to his desk, he had the paper with him. His brow was furrowed, and that worried Holly.

"I think we can do it," he said, standing there.

She felt a sudden flush in her cheeks.

"There's to be a special exchange shortly, by the end of this month, probably. I see no reason why I can't add Lieutenant Blaisdell's name to the short list. That would save him from the latter part of the winter."

"Why, that would be wonderful, Colonel!" Holly exclaimed, her eyes damp now.

He smiled at her. "I'm glad to be able to do it, Miss Blaisdell. You'll have to give my secretary some additional information, so we'll have it for our file here, but there shouldn't be any further difficulty for you."

Holly beamed, but felt guilty inside because she was obligated to lie to this nice man about her identity. "I don't know how to thank you, Colonel. My cousin's father will be particularly pleased to have him back."

"In the meantime, I'll send a message to have his wound tended to, in preparation for his repatriation," the colonel told her. "We want him to last until he gets home. If there's any serious surgery involved, we'll let that wait until he's in Charleston, probably."

"That sounds good," she said.

"How long will you be in Washington?" Masters asked her.

Holly hesitated, thinking of Booth. "Why, I hadn't thought. I did want to get back to my friend in Charleston;

409

she is also in recuperation at the present."

"Well, I might be able to tell you how Blaisdell is, before you leave, if you'll be here a week or more," he told her.

Holly hesitated only a moment. "All right. I'll stay that long," she said.

"Check in with me in about a week, and we'll see if there's word from Chicago."

Holly was very pleased. "You're a good man, Colonel."

"Nonsense, it's nothing. I know you'd do the same for me."

At Camp Douglas, Blaisdell was in very bad shape. His tent mate from Tennessee, the fellow called Tate, had finally given up on trying to get him to roll call. Consequently, the guards had cut Blaisdell's ration, having given up on him, too. His fever was worse, and he had almost no strength now.

But Tate had not quit on Blaisdell. He now spent much of his time feeding his tentmate from his own rations, and trying to keep Blaisdell warm with his own body. "I got this gut feeling, buddy. You're going to make it, by God. I'm never wrong." Tate just would not give up.

"O.K., Blais. Time to eat your mush," Tate said upon his return to the tiny tent, where he had to crouch over Blaisdell. Tate had just been given his morning ration. He had asked for one for Blaisdell, and the guard had said they were out. So Tate was about to feed Blaisdell his own breakfast.

"It isn't my mush," Blaisdell said weakly. "It's yours."

"It's yours, goddamn it!" Tate told him.

Outside the tent, it was a relatively good day, for

February. It had warmed up some, and there was no wind. They were having a small thaw. The sun was out, and there were only small patches of snow at the perimeters of the camp. But the ground was still damp in the tents and shanties. It was always damp.

"I can't eat, Tate. I just can't. I don't have it anymore; you might as well give up on me. My leg stinks to high heaven and I've got the fever deep. Let me go, for Christ's sake. Let me go!"

"I ain't give up on getting a doctor for that leg," Tate said. "Now will you eat, or do I have to cram it down your throat? I'm a goddamned bulldog, Lieutenant!"

"Oh, hell," Blaisdell moaned.

"Come on. Just a little, for strength."

Blaisdell took a spoonful of the stuff, and chewed numbly. It had no taste to him. His taste buds were not operating. Some of it came out of the corner of his mouth. He kept chewing, for Tate. He swallowed, and most of it went down. "God," he said thickly.

"Now, you see? What the hell is so bad about that?"

"Please, Tate. Eat your own food, for God's sake. You have a chance to survive until spring. Don't cheat yourself."

"You talk too damned much for a sick man," Tate said firmly. "Now let's see if you can get down another spoonful of this—"

But at that moment, the flap of the tent was pushed open, and an officer of the guard stood there. "Is Blaisdell in this tent?"

Tate and Blaisdell both regarded him soberly. "This is him, Captain. You didn't happen to bring a doctor to see him, did you?" he said sarcastically.

The officer came in. He was a thickset fellow with a

411

tattered uniform and a hard face. He had a ledger-type book in hand, and he opened it now as he squatted beside Tate. "In bad shape, is he?" he said to Tate, ignoring Blaisdell.

"You're damned right he is, Captain," Tate said. "He needs some medical help, damn it. Where is it?"

The captain looked over at Blaisdell finally. "How are you feeling, Lieutenant?" he said.

"He feels terrible!" Tate said.

"Sergeant, if you don't mind," the captain said.

"I feel terrible," Blaisdell said.

"You look terrible," the captain said, making some notes in his black book. He wrinkled his nose. "How long has that leg wound been infected like that?"

"Awhile," Blaisdell told him.

The captain put the book down, and began unwrapping the bandage on Blaisdell's leg. When he got a look at it, he frowned. The stink was greater.

"That's a bad leg," he said.

"No kidding," Tate said.

The captain gave him a look, then turned back to Blaisdell. "I think we're in time, though, to save your life."

Blaisdell frowned. "You're going to do something about the leg?"

The captain nodded. "Open your mouth."

Blaisdell did. The captain stuck a thermometer into it. "We have to do it all ourselves out here," he said. He waited, then took the thermometer out. "Yeah. You'll have to be treated for the fever first. We may have to delay on the leg. I expect you'll lose it."

Blaisdell took the news rather calmly. Tate cast a dark look at the captain. "Are you really going to help him?

Bring a doctor in?"

The captain picked up the book again. "You're going to an army hospital near here, Lieutenant."

Blaisdell frowned in bewilderment. "You're taking a Camp Douglas prisoner to a Union Army hospital?"

"We've had special orders on you, along with several other men. You're going to be repatriated."

Blaisdell stared hard at the captain, as if he were eying an insane man. "Repatriated?"

"Repatriated!" Tate said, his long face full of hope for Blaisdell.

The captain nodded. "It's an order straight from Washington, Blaisdell. You're going back home, by way of our hospital here."

Blaisdell's ears were suddenly ringing, and his pulse was pounding in his ears. Tate was grinning at him laconically.

"You're going home, buddy! Didn't I tell you? You're going home, by God!"

"Home," Blaisdell said thickly, in his throat. "Charleston."

"Frankly, I had no idea you were so bad off," the captain said. "I would guess that this order saved your life, Lieutenant. That, and your friend here."

Blaisdell's eyes watered up so that he could not see their faces clearly. He could not believe it. It did not seem possible.

"You'll be moved out of here later this morning," the captain went on. "We'll take you directly to the hospital. Washington expects you to be on that exchange, and we don't want to disappoint the big brass. Get your belongings together, and be ready to leave here by eleven."

Blaisdell nodded emphatically. "I'll be ready," he said.

Holly saw John Booth a few more times in that week of further waiting for her news about Blaisdell. They were intimate on one more occasion, but it was different from the first reunion. Booth could not seem to keep his mind on their love-making. He had begun performing in *The Apostate*, and had a good review that mentioned his skill in acting. But to Holly he did not seem pleased by that. He did not seem pleased by anything.

No word came from Chicago. While Holly waited, things were happening with Booth that she knew nothing about. One of the conspirators had suggested they attempt to grab Lincoln at an appearance he would be making at the Soldier's Home. Booth demurred, preferring his selection of Ford's Theater, but he was outvoted. They actually went to the Soldier's Home and waited for the President, armed and serious. But for the second time, Lincoln canceled out.

Booth was worried that somebody in the White House knew about them, that maybe information was leaking out of their group. They had picked up a few more cohorts in the past couple of weeks; Booth was not sure about them, but they dropped back out. Now it was only Booth, Atzerodt, Paine, and Herold again. Booth did not think he could count on Herold.

Booth was very tense now, and in a brief meeting between him and Holly, one cold evening, she was very aware of it. She almost asked him about it, but decided not to. That same evening, Booth called the other three men together at his room and said he wanted to reduce the complexity of the operation. He said he no longer believed it was feasible to capture Lincoln as an enemy

414

prisoner. He wanted to assassinate him.

This came as quite a surprise to all but the strongman Paine, who had suggested the idea in the first place. Petersburg, Virginia had just fallen to federal troops, and Richmond's fall was imminent.

"John, the war is almost over!" David Herold said in frustration. "I was going to suggest we give up this whole notion about Lincoln. It's too late. We're too late. Taking the President prisoner is impractical, as you say, but killing him is absurd. What's to be gained?"

Booth's face was tight-lined. "Satisfaction," he said tautly, "a last satisfaction in the face of defeat on the battlefield, a last small victory, a punishment—a retribution, if you will."

"Oh, hell, John!" Herold said.

Paine grunted. "I think you're right as rain, John. Why should the biggest villain of this goddamned war get off unscathed? The man responsible for thousands of deaths on both sides. I think it would be a great gesture, a demonstration of southern backbone, by God!"

Booth turned to Atzerodt. "What do you think, George?"

In the close air of the small room, there was a crackling excitement that was almost palpable. Atzerodt's stomach had knotted itself up beyond his control, and his upper lip was sweating.

"Well, I've never thought of myself as a killer. But then neither have a lot of other men who had to participate in this war. I guess it would depend in part on whether I had to personally pull the trigger. You did expect to use a gun, didn't you?"

Booth nodded. "Yes, a gun. I've already purchased a revolver that should do the job nicely." He took a deep breath. "I'd do the actual shooting myself. The rest of you would back me up in various ways."

"Just tell me where and when," Paine said in a hard voice.

"Jesus," Herold muttered, his face flushed with sudden frustration.

"I still favor Ford's Theater," Booth said. "I went up to the presidential box yesterday, when nobody was about. I broke the lock on the door."

Paine grinned.

"It will take them awhile to fix it, even after they discover it," Booth said. "Security is pretty loose at the theater. Some evening when Lincoln is at the theater for a special event, I could go up there, enter the box before his guards knew what was happening, and kill him with one shot to the head. I know I could do it, I've already run every detail of it over in my head fifty times."

"If there were a guard outside the box, I'd be happy to handle him," Paine said gruffly.

"There sometimes isn't," Booth said. "Well, gentlemen? I know it's a big idea. But it's not too big for us to manage, is it? It's not so far different from what we've been talking about for months, from what we've geared ourselves to do twice already—except that if we make it the next time, our own escape should be easier."

"I'm not sure," Herold said. "We won't have Lincoln as a hostage, as a shield."

Booth suddenly turned on him, face dark with anger. "For God's sake, David! Can't you think of anything positive to say, ever?"

A silence fell over them. Finally, Herold spoke. "Hell, I'm sorry, John. I'm just speaking my mind."

"We don't need irresponsible outbursts about what

might happen if things go wrong!" Booth said, more in control. "We need to start thinking that everything will go right, this next time."

"Agreed," Paine said.

Booth looked around at the three faces. "I know you're with me, Lewis. How about it, George? Do you have the stomach for a presidential assassination?"

Atzerodt hesitated for a long moment, then said, "Count me in."

Booth smiled harshly, and turned to Herold. "I'll give you something easy to do, David, like keeping a buggy ready in the alley. You probably won't even hear the gun go off."

Herold regarded Booth soberly. "You're sure I won't have to shoot anybody?"

Booth sighed. "Yes, I'm sure."

Herold nodded. Maybe he could do it, not having to actually squeeze any triggers. He would have the glory of it, the incredible notoriety, without actually being a killer. "All right. I'm with you."

Booth grinned darkly. "Good," he said with satisfaction. "Then we're committed. We'll iron out the details in the next few days."

On the following day, Holly heard that Richmond had fallen.

The rebel capital was burned, because its defenders would not surrender it unconditionally.

Now there were only Lee and his ragtag army, retreating into the hinterland of Virginia, surrounded by the armies of Grant and Sherman and Sheridan. And even now, Jefferson Davis would not give the word to Lee to surrender.

It was a black time for the South.

Holly was even more impatient to get back to Charleston, but she had to know about Blaisdell. March was almost over, and she had had no word. Then one day a courier came from Colonel Masters. Holly returned to his office. He wore a big smile when she entered. Blaisdell was being treated in a hospital outside Chicago. He might lose part of his leg, but he would otherwise survive. He would be back in Charleston within a week.

Holly broke down and cried, embarrassed greatly by her show of emotion. The colonel was very understanding. He suggested she arrange for immediate transportation south, so that she would get to Charleston at about the same time as Blaisdell.

Holly felt, upon leaving the colonel's office, that she had accomplished something worthwhile in these past weeks, despite her qualified success with Sherman and Davis. She had helped Jennifer survive, and she had helped Blaisdell survive. And with Jennifer's new interest in Blaisdell, their survival took on new meaning.

She agreed with Masters, too; now was the time to leave Washington and get back home. But she had to see Booth again. She had to make another effort to break through his recent distraction, in the hope he would see that he was changing, becoming a different man. She still did not think there was real hope for their ever having anything like a marriage together. But at least he could regain his old verve, his old love of life, if he could just pull himself out of the stark well into which he had fallen.

When Holly went to find Booth at his rented room on the evening after she had spoken with Masters, she got a surprise. Booth was there, all right, but so were his three co-conspirators.

Also, as Holly came up to the door of the room, out in the corridor, she heard the men talking inside, and she heard three words distinctly: "Lincoln," "theater," and "gun." Her head in a whirl, she knocked on the door and Booth answered it.

"Why, Holly!" he said when he saw her. He seemed embarrassed. "What a nice surprise!"

Holly glanced past him, and saw the three solemn faces of Paine, Atzerodt, and Herold. They each rose slowly from chairs they had been sitting on.

"Hello, John. I thought I'd stop past and share my good news with you. Stuart Blaisdell is being repatriated."

"Oh, that's great, Holly." He looked particularly pale tonight, Holly thought, and harried. So did the thin man behind him with the scared look. "Hey, come on in and meet some friends of mine."

Holly hesitated, remembering what she had heard from the corridor. Then she went on into the room. Booth closed the door behind her, and turned to the somber-faced threesome.

"Gentlemen, this is Holly Ransom," he said lightly, "a Charleston girl and an old friend of mine."

Paine grunted, and made no comment. Atzerodt extended his thick hand awkwardly. "Miss Ransom." Herold eyed her with a worried look. "Pleased to meet you, ma'am."

"These are theater men, Holly," Booth lied. "We get together once a week to talk shop. We were just discussing a new play at a theater across town."

"You were discussing Abraham Lincoln," Holly said slowly to Booth.

Paine scowled toward Booth. "Jesus Christ, John!"

Holly looked at him, and at Atzerodt, and then at

419

Herold. "What's going on here?" she said.

"Oh, God," Herold said.

Booth sighed wearily, and put a hand on Holly's arm. "It's nothing, Holly. Really."

"Isn't it?" she said. "I also heard mention of guns."

Paine glowered at her. "Did you have your ear to the door, lady?"

Holly turned and held his dark gaze defiantly, then turned to Booth. "What's happening here, John? What have you gotten yourself involved in?"

George Atzerodt shuffled his feet. "It might be better if you didn't ask, ma'am."

"A hell of a lot better," Paine said harshly.

"No, wait, fellows," Booth said to them. "Holly is just like us. She worked with me in running information to the Confederate lines. She's all right, believe me."

Paine grumbled something, and sat back down. Herold turned away, his face full of new concern.

"These men aren't friends from the theater. Are they, John?" Holly said to him.

He shook his head slowly. "No."

"Are you back on that Lincoln thing of yours, John?" Holly said deliberately. "Are you still thinking of trying to capture Lincoln like a Yankee soldier, even at this late stage of things?"

Atzerodt and Paine exchanged glances. Booth went and sat down on the edge of his bed. He hesitated for a long moment, and when he looked up at her, his face was straight-lined. "It's gone beyond that, Holly."

Holly's face went ashen as she remembered the use of the word "gun." "What—do you mean?" she said.

"John—" It was Paine, ominously.

Booth met his hard look. "I told you, Lewis. She's all

right." He looked up at Holly again. "We're going to assassinate Lincoln, Holly."

Holly could not believe her ears. She found herself short of breath, and light-headed. She went and let herself down onto the chair that Herold had vacated, slowly.

"My God," she said.

"I don't like this, John," Paine told him.

Booth ignored him. "Can you think of anyone who deserves more to die?" he said to Holly.

Holly met his gaze numbly. The man she loved was talking about murdering Abraham Lincoln, the President who had taken a special interest in Holly, had freed her to return to Charleston, who had joked with her in prison. The man who, although wrong in many of his political positions in Holly's view, was nevertheless a humanitarian man, a compassionate one that it was difficult not to like.

"My God, John," she said.

Booth rose from the bed, and took hold of her arms. "We have it all planned out. It's just a matter of waiting for the right moment. It will work, Holly!"

Booth had changed much more than she had imagined, she knew now. He had never been one to speak of killing casually. "John," she said, "you're talking about taking a man's life. You're talking about killing the President of the United States."

He frowned at her. "Do you see something morally wrong with ending the life of a mass murderer? Of a man who mutilated and destroyed the South? Including your beloved Charleston?"

"The man I met at Old Hempstead was no monster," Holly said to him. "Anything but, John. Do you have any

421

authority from any Confederate agency for this proposed action?"

Booth turned away from her. "You're being difficult, Holly. We're not in touch with what's left of the Confederacy, now. The war is almost over."

Herold had been staring out through a black window. Now he turned to take a renewed interest in this dialogue.

"Exactly," Holly replied to Booth. "In a couple of weeks or so it will be over, John. The North and South will be trying to heal old wounds, set things right again. Do you think the murder of Lincoln is the way to begin a restoration period?"

Booth turned back angrily. "I think it is something that has to be done," he grated out almost psychotically.

Atzerodt studied Booth's emotional face, and wondered if he had been right in agreeing to go along with Booth. All of it seemed so pointless to him, now.

Holly saw she could not talk with Booth. She rose from the chair, trying to organize her thoughts. She almost wished she had not gone there tonight. She had been ready to return to Charleston, to have a wonderful reunion with Blaisdell and Jennifer, to begin thinking of how to help the city rebuild from the war. But now she did not know what to do. She had been given a terrible knowledge; and the man she had loved for so long was involved in an ugly enterprise.

Booth came to Holly. The anger drained from his face as he turned her toward him, gently. "It's right, Holly. It will be a small payment for what they've done to us. I want you to join us, to be in this with us. With your experience as a Confederate agent, you could be of great value to our mission."

Holly looked into his dark eyes and tried to see the man

422

there she had known back in Baltimore, and could not. She wondered why, when they had been intimate recently, she had not seen the enormous difference. She wished she had not allowed the intimacies.

"I can't, John," she said.

"Christ," Paine grumbled. "Now what, John?"

"Yes, now what?" Herold wondered, hoping this would end it.

"Hell, let her go," Atzerodt said to Paine. "She won't say anything. Will you, Holly Ransom?"

Holly turned to Atzerodt, but said nothing.

"Holly, are you sure?" Booth said to her. "As soon as it's over, we'll all go south. You and I will go to Charleston, Holly. We'll be together there. But we'll have something to remember that will last the rest of our lives!"

Holly saw the glittery look in his eyes, and was afraid for him. He had allowed a hatred to take hold of him so completely that he might never get free of it.

"I wouldn't want to remember that the rest of my life, John," she finally told him. "But you're right, I would. It would tear me up inside. Please, John. Don't do it. It isn't necessary. It isn't reasonable. It isn't right!"

His face changed again, and darkened. "I see we've finally come at odds on something, Holly. I'm sorry, but you can't dissuade me. I feel as if I've been chosen for a kind of holy mission. I can't explain it to you, but I have this feeling inside me that it's all inevitable somehow, and that I'm the agent who must carry it out. I'm committed, Holly. *We're* committed." He waved a hand at his dubious partners.

"Oh, God," Holly said.

"You going to give us any trouble, ma'am?" Paine said

to her pointedly.

Holly looked over at him, and then back to Booth.

"*Are* you going to give us any trouble, Holly?" Booth said.

"What would you do to me if I did?" Holly said to him.

Booth shrugged. "Nothing, I guess."

Holly sighed. "I'm leaving for Charleston just as soon as I can make arrangements for transportation," she told him. "I won't be around long to give you any trouble."

"I—suppose I won't see you again, then," he said.

She knew he referred not only to her stay in Washington, but for the rest of their lives. She hesitated. "I suppose not, John." Her lower lip trembled slightly, but she held back the emotion.

"I'd like to take you out to the street," he said quietly.

"That won't be necessary," she told him.

She hurried out of the room then, and down the stairs and into the blackness of the night.

Chapter Twenty-Three

The Union Army was so successful in treating Blaisdell's pneumonia, at the Chicago hospital, that they went ahead and amputated his right leg just above the knee. He recuperated there for a couple of weeks, and then was sent south on a train with several other Confederate soldiers to a replacement depot in Maryland. From there he went on alone to Charleston.

It was a chilly day in the first week of April when Blaisdell arrived back home, back from the war a second time. This time he bore two crutches, and his trouser leg hung loose below the amputated limb. He was thin now, and rather pale-looking, but he was healthy inside, and glad to be alive.

Blaisdell had heard that a cousin of his had helped with his release, at Washington. Not having any female cousins, he realized it had to be Holly. He expected her to be back in Charleston, and was surprised when she was not at the station to greet him.

In fact, there was nobody there to welcome him back. His father did not know of his return; nor did Jennifer. Thinking he would find Holly at her home, Blaisdell took a hansom cab there after being processed at the station.

Charleston looked even worse than it had when he'd left. There was more rubble in the streets, and Union troops were everywhere, most of them black. It seemed an outrage to Blaisdell that the North had seen fit to occupy Charleston with black troops. It was the final insult added to the years of injury. As his cab bumped along the pockmarked streets, he saw women and children out begging from the black troops. It made him sick inside to watch it.

It was going to be up to him now, and Holly and Jennifer and all of them, to come back from this humiliation and build their city up again, build its pride and its courage. Blaisdell now wanted to get strong again if just for that purpose. He would get along with one leg, others had had to do so. At least he had survived the war. There were many who had not.

When he knocked on Holly's door and Jennifer came to open it, he just stared at her for a moment in surprise. Then a big grin broke over his face. "Hi, Jennie."

"Oh, God!" Jennifer said tearfully. She had been up on her feet for over two weeks, and was feeling much stronger now, thanks to Holly. She came and hugged herself tightly against Blaisdell, and he found that he liked the embrace very much.

"You're back!" she finally said. "Holly said she'd help you get back here, and she did!"

"Where is she?" he said, looking past Jennifer.

"Why, I guess she's still in Washington," Jennifer told him, "or maybe in Baltimore. She might have looked up John Booth."

Blaisdell's face went sober. "Oh, yes. That's a possibility."

They went inside, and Jennifer could hardly contain her excitement. Blaisdell liked it. He liked it that somebody cared so much about his return. Jennifer looked good to him. She had stopped using make-up, and she looked pretty again. She reminded him of the way she used to look when they were all in school. They sat down together on the parlor sofa, and Blaisdell smiled at her. "You look—different, Jennifer."

She returned the smile. "I guess I am different. I was shot, too, Stuart, right here in this room. A couple of drunks I couldn't get rid of got into an argument. It was an accident. Holly nursed me, and I got well. I feel good now."

"God, Jennifer. I guess we've both been through something."

She had not mentioned his leg. She looked down at the stump now. "You lost part of your leg this time, didn't you?"

He nodded. "I'm lucky to be alive, Jennifer. We both are, I guess."

"Your father will be so glad to see you," Jennifer said. "He's not good, Stuart."

"I figured," he said. "I'll be here to take care of him now. I'm going home just as soon as I leave you." He paused. "I miss seeing Holly here."

"I'll bet," she said. "I'll be glad when she gets back here. We both owe her something, Stuart."

"I know," he said. "I love her, Jennifer. I love both of you."

She met his gaze. "I've thought a lot about you, in the last few months. I told Holly so."

He studied her face. "That's funny, because I've thought about you, too, Jennifer. In Camp Douglas I found myself thinking about—that night I came to you, when I was drunk."

Jennifer smiled. "I think of that a lot. There were a lot of times when I wished I'd not made you leave that night."

He laughed softly. "I wish so, too."

"Do you really, Stuart?" she asked him seriously. "Despite what I am?"

"What you are?" he said. "What you are is a strong, pretty girl, a warm girl who gives her affection freely. Anyway, I think you're different from what you were then."

She nodded. "I am, I guess. I feel more—vital. I feel as if I could love somebody again." She lowered her eyes.

"When I get settled in," he said after a moment, "I'd like to see you once in a while, Jennifer. I don't mean just with Holly. I mean you and me, alone. That's if you don't mind."

Jennifer felt a feeling inside her that she had not felt since those happy early days with Clayborne. "I wouldn't mind a bit, Stuart," she said. "I was kind of hoping you would say something like that."

He grinned the boyish grin that both she and Holly had come to like so much. "Maybe we could get together some in the next few days, and plan a coming-home party for Holly. To show our appreciation for what she's done for us."

"I think that's a wonderful idea, Stuart," she said.

Two days after Blaisdell's return home, Lee and his remnant army were finally cornered in the back country of Virginia, and Lee reluctantly surrendered his force at a small place called Appomattox. Grant received Lee's sword personally, and the war was over. All of the South's military machine had now surrendered, except for some bands of irregulars in the backwoods. It was only left for a saddened Jefferson Davis to sign a formal peace treaty with Washington.

In Washington, Holly's arrangements were all made to return to Charleston. She told herself that what Booth was planning was not her business, that it was between the conspirators and Lincoln. She intended to go home and turn her back on it.

Then two things happened that changed her mind, and radically influenced the rest of her life. On a blustery April morning she heard about Lee's surrender of Confederate forces to Grant. And that same afternoon, she got a glimpse of Abraham Lincoln, riding in a carriage along Pennsylvania Avenue. There were two other carriages attending his, full of aides and guards. Inside his carriage, Lincoln could be seen smiling and talking with his wife and another woman. He was obviously very relieved that the long struggle was over. Some of the terrible weight on his shoulders had been removed.

As the carriage moved on past, Holly realized that very soon, he might be dead.

The very idea of it suddenly outraged Holly. The war was over now, lost to the South. Assassination of the American President seemed even more absurd to her—and more immoral—than ever.

She did not sleep at all that night. She paced the floor of her small hotel room, wrestling with the knowledge that she held a secret inside her. She wanted to flee, to make her trip back to Charleston and put it all out of her head. But now, more than ever, she felt responsible for the President's life. He had befriended her, had shown his humanity to her. She could not turn her back on him now. Also, she could not turn her back on Booth, no matter what he had become. It was just not possible to go blithely home just as if things were all right. They were very much not all right. One man's life was in danger, and another's future was. The first man was important to the world, the second one to her—because of what they had had between them once, and the love Holly still felt for him.

There was no way around it. Holly had to cancel her trip home for the moment. She had to return to Booth, try to reason with him, try to keep him from heading into disaster and infamy—attempt to save Lincoln from deadly violence.

It would be the biggest decision of Holly's life.

The very next morning, Holly took a hansom to the Surratt Boardinghouse. But Booth was not there. He had moved out, it seemed.

"Moved out?" Holly said in disbelief to the woman who identified herself as Mrs. Surratt. She was the mother of a previous member of Booth's group, but knew nothing of the plot. "But I just met with him here very recently. Is he gone for good?"

"I expect so, miss," Mrs. Surratt told her. "He didn't give any reason for leaving, either. But then John was always crazy-acting, like my son—also named John."

"He gave you no forwarding address then?" Holly said.

"No, none at all. He was acting very secretive lately, if you ask me. Meeting with them other fellows up there, whispering and talking in low tones all the time, staying up until all hours of the night. It's not natural, I say."

"What about the others?" Holly said. "Did you know

430

any of them?"

"Oh, that Herold boy was here quite a bit, when my John was in the city; used to clerk in a pharmacy, I think."

"Do you know where I could reach him?" Holly asked.

Mrs. Surratt shook her head sideways with emphasis. "No, I never asked where he lived or worked. It's none of my business, miss. Say, aren't you a southern girl?"

Holly nodded. "Yes, I am, from Charleston."

"Ah, yes. I hear you had a bad time down there. There's a lot of us, you know, that supported the southern cause—like your John Booth. But I suppose you know that."

"Yes, Mrs. Surratt," Holly said. "Well, thank you for your help. I'll ask elsewhere about John."

"Try the Ford's Theater," Mrs. Surratt told her.

Holly had already determined to do just that. Booth was no longer acting at the theater, but he had many ties there, and someone there might have seen him. She took another cab there.

"Yes, ma'am, I seen him," a stagehand told her, when she went backstage in the beautiful theater building. "He come past here on horseback just yesterday. I never seen him riding a horse before. Told him he looked like a Maryland farmer."

"Did he mention where he's staying now?" Holly asked.

"He mentioned he had moved across town. Didn't say where. Say, can I get you a couple of tickets to the play next week? General Grant will be in town, and they say him and Lincoln might be here together on the President's night out."

"Grant is coming to Washington?" Holly said.

431

"Yes, ma'am."

"And Lincoln is expected to be here at the theater next week?"

"That's what I just told you, ma'am," he said sourly.

"Oh, God," Holly said to herself.

"Something wrong, ma'am?"

But Holly was already on her way out. She felt a terrible urgency now to get to Booth, felt that his plan would culminate in violent action in a few days, when Lincoln attended the theater, with or without General Grant.

But finding an individual in Washington, without some clue, was similar to searching for a pin dropped in a haystack. In the next few days, Holly went to almost a dozen boardinghouses around the city, and none had even heard of Booth, except as an actor. The weekend came and went, and Holly was desperate. She thought of going to the White House, telling the whole story, and exposing her own identity. But she did not want to do that without giving Booth a chance to withdraw from the scheme. It was two days to the night when Lincoln usually attended the theater. Grant arrived in Washington, and the city gave him a big welcome. He visited Lincoln in the White House, and there was a gala banquet. Holly remembered those banquets and balls in Baltimore. She remembered the evening she had met Lincoln.

Suddenly it was the day before Lincoln's theater date, and Holly checked at Ford's Theater and confirmed that, although Grant would probably not attend, Lincoln would be there tomorrow evening.

Holly was in a small panic.

She stayed up most of that night, worrying and

wondering what to do. The next morning she walked the streets, trying to decide whether to tell anyone what she knew. In early afternoon, she went back to the neighborhood where the boardinghouse was located, and looked for drugstores. She found three. At the first two, nobody had ever heard of David Herold. At the third one, Holly struck paydirt.

"Oh, sure. David used to work here. A fine boy," the proprietor told her.

"Would you happen to know where he lives?" Holly asked the elderly man. "I must get in touch with him."

"Yes, I have the address right here somewhere," he said easily.

Holly held her breath while he looked in an old ledger book. "Yes, here it is." He wrote it down for her on a slip of paper. She took it, and let out a long breath. "Say hello to David for me, will you, miss?"

"I will, and thank you very much," Holly told him.

It was just a short walk to the address on the paper. When she arrived there, at a back street just outside the embassy district, she found a big brown building containing many flats. It was late afternoon, and the sun was going down on a cool, windy day. Up on the third floor of the building, she found the room number she had been given. When she knocked on the door, it opened quite suddenly and David Herold stood there, in his shirt sleeves. She heard men talking behind him, out of sight.

"Good God," Herold muttered when he recognized her.

"Is John here?" she asked him, looking past him into the room.

Then she heard Booth's voice. "Who is it, David?"

Herold had been going to lie, but now it was too late.

He stepped aside reluctantly, and Holly entered the room.

It was even smaller than Booth's room had been at the Surratt House, and there was a general untidiness to it. The bed was unmade. Newspapers were littered about, and a couple of liquor bottles stood open. Booth sat on the edge of Herold's bed. Atzerodt was on a straight chair, and Paine was leaning against a wall. When they saw Holly, their faces went hard, including Booth's. Booth rose slowly from the bed.

"Holly! For God's sake, I thought you had left the city!"

Herold closed and locked the door behind her. At the sound of the latch, Holly turned back to Herold for a moment, and then went across the small room to Booth.

"I notice you're all on horseback now," Holly said. "Those are your mounts outside, aren't they?"

"Holly," Booth said, "what are you doing still in Washington?"

"I saw Lincoln passing in a carriage the other day, just about the time I was to leave the city. I thought of you, John, and these men. I couldn't go."

"Oh, Christ," Paine said. "I knew she was trouble."

"Damn," Herold said. They had made detailed plans now, and broadened them considerably, and Herold had finally become excited about being a part of this momentous and historic event. Atzerodt, on the other hand, was tightening up with every moment that passed. He did not rise from the chair or speak, but just sat glumly watching Holly.

Holly ignored Booth's cohorts. "It's tonight, isn't it?" she said breathlessly. "When Lincoln attends Ford's Theater to see *Our American Cousin*. That's when you're

434

making your attempt, isn't it?"

Booth hesitated, then replied. "That's right," he said tightly.

"Goddamn it, John!" Paine said.

Booth glanced at him. "She knows," he said.

Atzerodt took a pocket watch out, and saw that it was almost six o'clock. The President would leave for the theater at about eight, for an eight-thirty performance. She had blundered on them at the very last moment.

"You can't possibly get away with it," Holly was saying to Booth. She thought of the four mounts outside. "What are you going to do, try to create a diversion of some kind?"

Booth grinned harshly. She could smell alcohol on his breath. He hardly seemed like the same man to her that she had known before. "The grandest kind of diversion," he said.

Holly frowned. "My God, what else have you planned?"

Herold stepped forward. "That's enough, John."

"No, it doesn't matter," Booth said. "It doesn't matter what she knows now. She can't leave this room until it's done."

Holly regarded Booth darkly.

"John's right." Atzerodt finally spoke up. "It doesn't matter now, she's in it."

"You're going to imprison me here?" Holly said to Booth.

Booth sighed. "I have to, Holly. I know you care for me, but you also have very strong convictions about this. You're unpredictable. You might even do or say something inadvertently to someone in the next couple of hours that could hurt us. You have to try to see it from our point of view."

Holly regarded him darkly. "I beg you, John—for all
we've ever meant to each other, for the love that was so
fiery inside us—don't do this. You'll be a lesser person
when it's finished, even if you fail."

"I'll be the most famous individual of the war," Booth
said a little breathlessly. "All four of us will be heroes to
most southerners, can't you see that?"

"Heroes?" Holly said. "If you're successful in this
thing, you'll be placing anti-South Johnson in the White
House!"

Booth grinned that new, harsh grin. "No, we won't."

Holly studied his face, and it came to her what he
meant. "Oh, no," she said slowly.

"The diversion you mentioned," he said. "It will be
Johnson—and Seward."

Her jaw dropped slightly open. "The secretary of state,
too?"

"All three," Booth said, his eyes sparkling brightly.
"They won't know which way to run after us. What do
you think now about our plan?"

Holly was stunned even more than she had been on
their last encounter. "My God, you've gone mad!" she
whispered.

Booth's face became straight-lined. "I'm sorry you
don't understand, Holly."

"Understand?" Holly said, her voice uneven. "Understand? You speak of killing two men for a diversion, and
you ask me to *understand?*"

"Hell, why do you bother?" Paine growled at Booth.

"Lewis is right; it's getting late, John," Herold said.

"I don't know you anymore," Holly was saying to
Booth. "I don't know you at all!"

"I've grown beyond the man you knew in Baltimore," Booth told her. "I'm a man of destiny now, Holly. All of us here are."

"You're mad!" Holly repeated. "You're all mad!"

"Tie her up," Paine said. "Our time is getting short."

"Yes, you'd better tie me!" Holly said heatedly, "because if I were loose, I'd betray you, John! I'd use every breath in me to abort this madness!"

"I'm sorry, Holly," he said, soberly. "I really am."

Booth and Atzerodt tied her up. Atzerodt got a length of rope and they bound her to a straight chair in the middle of the room. Paine would have killed her, but he knew Booth would not go along with that. He wondered if he could slip back later and do it himself, without Booth's knowledge. He thought he might try.

Holly was tied tightly, with her hands behind her, to the chair. When they were through binding her, Herold came up and looked the ropes over. "Maybe she should be gagged, too," he said.

Booth hesitated. "All right. Do it."

Herold found a necktie and gagged Holly with it. She hated the taste of the cloth in her mouth, and the ropes dug into the flesh of her wrists. Booth bent over her as the others prepared to leave and she gave him an angry, hurt look.

"You'll be all right. An associate of David's will come here in the morning. By then it will be over. Good-by, Holly."

A few minutes later they were all gone from the room, and the door was locked behind them.

Holly sat there on the chair. It was almost seven, she knew; dark outside already. In an hour and a half, Lincoln would be at the theater. She had no idea where

the vice president would be that evening, or Seward. But
none of the three had any inkling, probably, that four
desperate men were about to attempt to end their lives.

Sitting there thinking about it, Holly realized that she
was the only person in the capital who had a remote
chance of aborting the ugly plot. Circumstances had
placed her in a position where her action or inaction at
this time could change or not change the course of
history. She had to free herself somehow, to warn
Lincoln and the others. It was more important than going
home, than seeing Blaisdell and Jennifer, than helping
rebuild her beloved Charleston. More important than
anything she had done for the Confederacy, more than
her trip north or her meeting with Sherman. The South
needed Lincoln now, she suddenly realized, more than
even the North did.

She struggled against the ropes, and seemed to get
nowhere. She looked around the room, hoping to see
something she could use as a tool to loosen the ropes or
cut them. There apparently was nothing. As time slipped
past, a tension rose inside her that was almost unbearable. Booth had left a gaslight burning low for her, on a
wall. She gazed at it and it reminded her that it was
evening now, a time for festivities and relaxation, a time
for concerts and balls and—plays; a time for diversion.

A time, tonight, for death.

The evening passed quickly. The foursome split up
almost as soon as they left Herold's room. Booth went to
the theater by himself, because he had decided he needed
no help in killing Lincoln. Atzerodt went and hung
around outside the Kirkwood House where Johnson was
in residence. It was he who was to admit himself to the

438

building at 10:30, go to Johnson's quarters and kill him. Paine and Herold went to a bar near the Old Clubhouse, where Secretary of State Seward resided, and waited tensely there. At 10:30, at the exact time Booth was to be entering Lincoln's box at the theater, they were to go to Seward's place. Herold was to stand guard outside—he was the only man who did not actually have to kill—while Paine bluffed his way into the house, found Seward, and killed him. They were then all to gallop off to the Navy Yard Bridge, meet there, and flee into Maryland together. Because all of the assassinations would take place at the same moment in different sections of the city, the authorities would be confused and not know where to look for them in their flight.

Booth was at the theater before Lincoln. He showed himself openly, because everybody there knew him. He chatted amiably with a couple of stagehands, to relax himself. Then he left and went to a bar and had a drink.

Lincoln left the White House with his wife just after eight o'clock, so they would be on time for the 8:30 performance. Grant had definitely backed out of the invitation from Lincoln; he had left earlier in the day to go see his children out of the city. The Lincolns arrived at Ford's Theater just before 8:30, with a bodyguard named Parker. There were also two military guards stationed in the corridor outside the state box, upstairs. A Major Rathbone and a Miss Harris joined the Lincolns in their box, and the play began.

Booth was getting tense now, despite the liquor. He had decided against a revolver as his weapon, and given that to Atzerodt. He had brought instead a small brass Derringer, a one-shot weapon that now fit snugly and unobtrusively into a pocket of his coat. He also carried

439

with him, under the coat, a sheathed dagger.

Finally, the time arrived. Booth left the bar and returned to the alley behind the theater, picketing his mount there. In a dark corner, he donned a thick wig, a false mustache, and a fake beard. Then he wandered into the theater, where the audience was enjoying a fine comedy called *Our American Cousin*.

Holly lay on the floor, gasping, still bound to the chair. She had tried to inch the chair forward toward a table where there was an ashtray with a rather sharp metal edge, but had fallen onto her side in the process, almost knocking herself out as she took the chair down with her.

She looked up toward the table. It was too far away. She pulled and strained against the ropes for the hundredth time, and something happened.

The knot gave slightly; the ropes loosened.

Hope surged into Holly's chest. She now doubled her effort, making the rope dig into her flesh at her wrists. There was a small further giving way, and suddenly Holly had some room. As she pulled and twisted with her right hand, the rope came up onto it. She worked and strained, perspiring from her exertion. Quite suddenly, and without warning, her right hand pulled free.

She could not believe it. She used that hand to untie the rope behind her, and in just a few minutes she was unbound. She kicked the chair away, and climbed awkwardly to her feet.

Her wrists were swollen and red, her face was bruised from hitting the floor, and her hair was hanging into her face. She quickly untied the gag, and took it from her mouth. She took in a deep breath. She was free. She was really free.

She went and looked at a small clock on the table beside Herold's bed. It was ten o'clock.

"My God, it may already have happened!" she muttered to herself.

In moments she was out of the room and the building, standing out on the dark street. There was no cab in sight, no one she could hail. She started walking.

She thought of going to the White House, but it was too late for that. She remembered Johnson and Seward, but had no idea where the attempts on them would take place. There was only one place where she might be able to do something: Ford's Theater.

Remembering that it was a long walk there, she ran much of the way. It was a cool night, and she was glad for that as she kept pushing herself on toward the theater, only a few blocks away now.

"Please, God! Let me be on time!" she murmured as she hurried feverishly along. "Let me get there before it happens!"

At the theater, Booth walked casually along the upper corridor behind the boxes. He passed the two military guards, nodded to them. They nodded back and did not try to stop him. When he reached the door to the row of boxes, the white chair that Parker occupied was empty; Parker was away for the moment.

Booth could not believe how easy it was going to be. He opened the door, stepped through it, and barred it from inside. Then he went to the smaller door to Lincoln's personal box. Through a tiny hole in the door, he could see the President sitting there with Mrs. Lincoln and the major and the major's young woman, enjoying the end of the play.

441

Booth was only moments from success.

Across town at the Old Clubhouse, Paine went to its front entrance; down the street a short distance, Herold waited with their mounts. A black servant met Paine at the door. Paine said he had some medicine for Seward and had to deliver it personally. The servant objected, but Paine pushed past him and went upstairs to where Seward was sleeping in his bedroom. An assistant stopped him again; this time Paine knocked the fellow unconscious. He broke into the bedroom and, in the dark, found the sick Seward on the bed. But there was another aide in the room, and just as Paine attacked the man on the bed, he himself was attacked. Paine was involved in a terrific struggle, stabbing at Seward and his adversary with a Bowie-type knife. After a violent few moments, thinking he had fatally wounded Seward, Paine broke away and fled the room. Out in the corridor a servant accosted him and he killed the fellow with a single plunge of the knife into the man's chest. But in the bedroom, Seward was only wounded.

Herold had heard the commotion inside, had panicked, and fled on his own mount. Paine, realizing he had been deserted, was angry. But he rode off quickly. Never thinking much of the Navy Yard Bridge as an escape route, he shunned his meeting with Booth and the others and made his own escape plans as he rode away.

Atzerodt had delayed his entry into Kirkwood House, and before he could act, a rider came up, entered, and delivered the news that Seward had been attacked in his home. Atzerodt, seeing the house in a turmoil and on the alert now, abandoned his responsibility in the plot and fled into the city. He became lost there, did not reach the bridge, and gave up on doing so.

Holly had arrived at the theater. At its front entrance, she was telling an assistant that she had to be admitted immediately.

"I'm telling you, there is a plot against the President's life!" she repeated to the fellow. "His life is in danger at this very moment! I must go inside and warn his party!"

The fellow eyed her suspiciously, noting her unkempt appearance and her southern accent. "Lady, if you don't have a ticket, you can't go in there, tonight or any other night. Who told you the President's life is in danger?"

Holly was furious, and violently frustrated. *"The assassins told me, damn it!"*

"Oh, then you know these assassins."

"Yes, I know them! One of them is John Wilkes Booth!"

The fellow stared hard at her, and then he broke into a laugh. "John Booth? What is this, some kind of joke? Did John put you up to this?"

Holly could not believe it. She turned and ran down the steps of the entrance, and then down the street. There had to be a rear entrance to the place. Maybe she could get in that way, or maybe a stage hand would have more brains than the fellow out front. She hurried down a side street, into an alleyway. Suddenly she found herself at the rear door of the theater building. The first thing she saw there was Booth's picketed horse.

"Oh, God," she moaned. She started to the door, when she heard the muffled shot from inside the theater building.

She stopped short, a short distance from the door. "No," she whispered dully. "Oh, no."

Now there were sounds of shouting from inside, and then she heard Booth's loud stage voice very clearly.

"Revenge for the South!"

Just a couple of moments later, the door banged open and Booth came limping out through it on a leg he had broken in his jump to the stage after he had shot Lincoln behind the ear. When he saw Holly, he stopped for a moment and they just stared at each other.

"It's done," he said finally. "The President is dead. Long live the rebellion."

Holly felt very sick inside. "You maniac," she said hollowly. "You damned madman!"

He moved past her, limping badly, and mounted his horse in the darkness. Inside, there was more shouting. Holly, suddenly mobilized into action, ran to Booth and caught hold of his leg.

"*Help!*" she called out hoarsely. "*Somebody help me!*"

Booth sighed heavily. He was just about to push her away, when a man leaned out of a second-story window above the stage, and aimed a gun at him. "*Stop, you damned murderer!*"

In the next moment he fired. But Booth, the horse, and Holly were all moving, and Booth was a bad target. The slug hit Holly in the back, just left of center, very much as Jennifer had been shot.

She cried out when she was hit, and Booth stared down at her in sudden concern. "Holly!" he exclaimed.

The man was gone from the window now. Booth felt the blood on Holly's back, and a dryness came into his mouth that spoiled his big moment. "My God!" he said. In a swift moment, he pulled her aboard the mount in back of him. Then he galloped away, holding her on.

It was an unimpeded ride. Booth was ahead of his pursuers. He rode right down Pennsylvania Avenue, and past the capitol; then he was on his way to the Navy Yard Bridge. He would take Holly across with him, and find a doctor for both of them. There was that Dr. Mudd he had met in Maryland. Maybe he could convince him to fix them both up.

But a few blocks short of the bridge, Holly began slumping badly on the horse. Booth looked at her, and saw that she could not go further. On a side street only a few blocks from the river, he reined up, dismounted, and pulled Holly gently off the horse.

He carried her over to an elm tree and laid her on the ground under it, propped slightly against the tree. When he brought his hand away from her, it was crimson-smeared. Her eyes fluttered open, and she looked at him.

"Oh, Holly. Why couldn't you keep out of it?" His voice was broken, uneven.

She licked her full lips, the lips he had so hungered for, in saner moments. "I thought—you were like Randy Clayborne," she said thickly, her voice slurred. "But I was wrong. Randy was a whole—human being."

"Lie quietly," he said. "I'll get you a doctor. I can always cross the river tomorrow morning."

"I don't need—a doctor," she told him.

He understood her meaning, and knew she was right. Her lovely face had gone a gray color, the color of death.

"I wanted to take you with me," he said; "to the Carolinas, maybe."

"You won't find any friends—in that direction," she told him. She coughed, and some blood came up. She saw Jennifer's face before her, and Blaisdell's beside it, and her eyes teared up.

"God, how I'll miss Charleston," she said in a hoarse, low voice.

Then she was lifeless at Booth's knee.

Booth rose and stood over her for a long moment. He

had thought this aftermath would be a time of great elation, a time to celebrate the death of a tyrant. But the fragile, still figure at his feet, and the words she had uttered to him, had changed all of that. Now it had all gone sour on him, and left a bad taste in his mouth.

He did not like leaving her there. But he could not get across the river with her. She would be found in a few hours, and her identity learned. Then she would be returned home, in all probability, to be put to final rest there.

She would like that, this Carolina girl.

Booth went and mounted his horse, took one look back at the dark figure under the elm, and rode off into the night—to Maryland, a conscience-agonized flight from the law, and his brief and violent final destiny.

Under the dark elm, Holly Ransom waited: for the shocked discovery, for the coroner, for a pine box to be loaded aboard the next train south.

For the return to her beloved Charleston.

SUCCUMB TO THE TERROR AND PASSION OF THESE ZEBRA GOTHICS!

THE MISTRESS OF HARROWGATE   (772, $2.25)
by Jessica Laurie

Margaret could not avoid the intense stare of Elizabeth Ashcroft's portrait—for the elegant bejeweled woman could have been her identical twin! When Margaret heard and saw impossible things, she feared that Elizabeth was trying to send her a dangerous and terrifying message from beyond the grave . . .

THE LORDS OF CASTLE WEIRWYCK   (668, $1.95)
by Elaine F. Wells

It didn't take long for hired companion Victoria Alcott to discover there were dreadful secrets in the old lady's past. As Victoria slowly became enmeshed in a web of evil, she realized she could not escape a terrible plot to avenge a murder that had been committed many years ago . . .

THE LADY OF STANTONWYCK   (752, $2.50)
by Maye Barrett

Despite her better judgment, Olivia took the job at Stantonwyck and fell in love with broodingly handsome Mark Stanton. Only when it was too late did she learn that once she lost her heart, she was destined to lose her life!

THE VANDERLEIGH LEGACY   (813, $2.75)
by Betty Caldwell

When Maggie discovered a Buddhist shrine hidden deep in the woods of Jonathan Vanderleigh's New Jersey estate, her curiosity was aroused. And the more she found out about it—that it was related to her father's death—the more her own life was endangered!

Available wherever paperbacks are sold, or order direct from the Publisher. Send cover price plus 50¢ per copy for mailing and handling to Zebra Books, 475 Park Avenue South, New York, N.Y. 10016. DO NOT SEND CASH.

BE CAPTIVATED BY THESE HISTORICAL ROMANCES

CAPTIVE ECSTASY   (738, $2.75)
by Elaine Barbieri
From the moment Amanda saw the savage Indian imprisoned in
the fort she felt compassion for him. But she never dreamed that
someday she'd become his captive—or that a captive is what she'd
want to be!

PASSION'S PARADISE   (765, $3.25)
by Sonya T. Pelton
Kidnapped by a cruel and rugged pirate, a young beauty's future is
suddenly in the balance. Yet she is strangely warmed by her
captor's touch. And that warmth ignites a fire that no pirate's seas
can put out!

AMBER FIRE   (848, $3.50)
by Elaine Barbieri
Ever since she met the dark and sensual Stephen, Melanie's senses
throbbed with a longing that seared her veins. Stephen was the one
man who could fulfill such desire—and the one man she vowed
never to see again!

TIDES OF ECSTASY   (769, $3.25)
by Luanne Walden
Meghan's dream of marrying Lord Thomas Beauchamp was coming true—until the handsome but heartless Derek entered her life
and forcibly changed her plans. . . .

TEXAS FLAME   (797, $2.75)
by Catherine Creel
Amanda's journey west through a haven of outlaws and Indians
leads her to handsome Luke Cameron, was wild and untamed as
the land itself, whose burning passion would consume her own!

*Available wherever paperbacks are sold, or order direct from the
Publisher. Send cover price plus 50¢ per copy for mailing and
handling to Zebra Books, 475 Park Avenue South, New York,
N Y 10016. DO NOT SEND CASH.*